Praise for *Lemon Reef*

"With *Lemon Reef*, Robin Silverman makes an imaginative, poetic, and compelling contribution to an increasingly important oeuvre. Fiction by and about queer women normalizes lesbian life as no theoretical screed can, and Lemon Reef is a worthy and valuable example of the genre."—Meredith Maran, author of *A Theory of Small Earthquakes*

"Robin Silverman writes in lushly evocative prose about the power and joyful sensuality of first love between two adolescent girls—and then about the devastation of betrayal and heartbreak. In *Lemon Reef*, what begins as a quest for justice becomes, finally, a triumph of love, a reminder that it is the best of us, and what remains." —Karen Bjorneby, author of *Hurricane Season*

Visit us at www.boldstrokesbooks.com

Lemon Reef

by

Robin Silverman

A Division of Bold Strokes Books

2012

LEMON REEF

ISBN 13: 978-1-60282-676-2

This Trade Paperback Original Is Published By
Bold Strokes Books, Inc.
P.O. Box 249
Valley Falls, NY 12185

First Edition: July 2012

Credits
Editor: Ruth Sternglantz
Production Design: Stacia Seaman
Cover Design by Sheri (graphicartist2020@hotmail.com)

Acknowledgments

Thanks to Mera Granberg, Thaai Walker, David Lenoe, Brian Crawford, Kat Meltzer, Jim Wood, Linda Lucero, and Cheryl Ossola for patiently reading and commenting on many chapter revisions. Wendy Brown, Crosby McCloy, Hillary Read, and Carol Hirth read full drafts and provided generous and thoughtful suggestions. I can't thank my editor Ruth Sternglantz enough for her dedication to this story, as well as her editorial guidance. Thanks to Radclyffe for finding a chapter of *Lemon Reef* among a pile of contest submissions and encouraging me to send the manuscript to Bold Strokes Books. My parents, Stan and Marilyn Silverman, are supportive and loving and bear no resemblance to the parents in this story. My friends Todd Jailer, Sarah Shannon, and Celia Jailer-Shannon have been a second home for us and an extended family. The same is true of Wendy Brown, Judy Butler, and Isaac Butler-Brown. I'm not sure what I or my family would have done without them these past years. *Lemon Reef* would not have been written without the support of Karen Bjorneby, the facilitator of our dynamic San Francisco writer's group and a Bay Area treasure. Noah Silverman-St. John, my sixteen-year-old son, truly is, in the words of Zora Neale Hurston, "Drenched in light." He is the most loving and courageous soul I've ever known, and I thank him with all of my heart for his unwavering encouragement while I wrote *Lemon Reef* and for his beautiful presence in my life every day. Finally, I owe the greatest debt of gratitude to Maria St. John, who was my life partner and dearest friend for twenty-one years. Maria, your fingerprints are on every page. Thank you for helping me tell this story.

For Maria and Noah, toward moonlight.

CHAPTER ONE

Monday

As Del was dying, I was going about my morning. As the ocean's surface closed in over her, erasing any remains of a last stand, I buttoned my blouse and tamed errant curls, mindful to be quiet so as not to wake Madison. As Del began feeling air starved and disoriented, I drove north on South Van Ness Avenue toward the San Francisco courthouse, noticing bright fissures in an otherwise gray sky and thinking about the cases I would hear that day and what directions they would take. As Del grappled with the invisible monster standing between her and her last breath, I sat in traffic, trying to breathe through fumes emitting from the SUV in front of me. And as I entered the secured underground parking lot reserved for judicial officers, Del left her body thirty feet under the sea, tethered to a metal chain pulled taut against a fitful and unforgiving gravitational tide.

❖

The call about Del came that afternoon from our mutual friend, Gail Samuels, who still lived in Miami. I was in chambers during a fifteen-minute recess, recovering from the last family-court case I had heard. The mother alleged the father had submitted someone else's urine to show a negative result on a drug test so he could see his kids unsupervised. The father insisted the urine was his, despite my exhaustive attempts to explain to him that the depositor—as the test incidentally revealed—was pregnant.

I sat at my desk and stared at my bookshelves, still empty but for the few books I had brought with me on my first day: A read and reread *Gender Trouble* stood shoulder to shoulder with an equally worn hardcover copy of Kafka's short stories, which Del had given me in high school. Beside them, *The Interpretation of Dreams*, *Men in Dark Times*, and *Bastard Out of Carolina* lay horizontal in a pile.

On the shelf below was a recent photo of Madison and me at a party for the seventh anniversary of our commitment ceremony. Madison was looking at me and grinning. I was looking down and away, my impish smile suggesting the intensity of her blue-lit gaze made me feel happy but shy. The rest of my office was bare except for boxes yet to be opened, a stack of framed pictures waiting to be hung, and a couple of chairs. I was considering where the couch would go when the phone rang.

Gail, my oldest childhood friend, had visited Madison and me in San Francisco two weekends before. On the plane coming, she'd noticed a mole on the back of her leg. Convinced it was getting larger by the minute, Gail could think of little else for the rest of the trip. So when I heard her voice now, I fully expected to get the results of the biopsy she had raced back to Miami to have done. But what I heard her say instead was that my high school love Del Soto—her real name was Adeline—was dead. Her death had occurred while she was scuba diving with her husband Talon on a dive site sardonically referred to by Miami locals as Lemon Reef. Unofficial word from the medical examiner's office was Del had died of a heart attack.

I was stunned speechless by the news, numbness drawing down like molasses.

"Thirty-one seems young for a heart attack," Gail said, the phone now taking on the effects of a wind tunnel, Gail's voice having to fight to be heard. Then, in response to my silence, Gail did what many people do when delivering news like this—rushed to provide more detail. "Del's husband Talon told the police they were diving and the next thing he knew, Del was trying to get to the surface and then went unconscious."

❖

Talon. Del had shown up at my parents' house after she'd started dating him. She'd walked casually past my mother, who'd hyperventilated at the sight of her, and into what had been my childhood bedroom. We were nineteen, and this was the first time she'd set foot in this room since we were outed in the tenth grade, the first time she'd initiated contact in almost as long.

"I see Norma hasn't mellowed." Del was referring to my mother, who was still sucking air in the living room.

"Uh, Del"—my back pressed against the just-closed bedroom door—"what are you doing here?" She was standing closer to me than a friend usually would, wearing jeans that displayed her jutting hipbones. Her copper hair hung long and loose. Her button-down blouse pulled tight at her breasts.

Del's gold eyes fluttered and then fixed on me. She'd wanted to tell me about him.

"Talon?" I laughed, until I realized she was serious.

He'd decided on the name himself when he'd turned eighteen. Del shrugged to say it made no sense to her either, explained further it was the finishing touch in a larger effort to reinvent himself with steroids, Sun-In, and a tattoo of a falcon's claw over his left eye. She allowed herself to look around in fleeting glances as she spoke, as if titrating how much she absorbed of this room we'd made love in as teenagers and from which my parents had banished her overnight.

Del had been with a lot of guys since we'd been together, and she'd never felt the need to tell me about any of them. I soon realized why this time was different. "Please tell me you're *not* pregnant." No response. "Del," I pleaded, "what about school?"

That was enough to make her vanish again.

❖

The receiver grew heavy in my hand, my throat tightened, sadness and confusion welled. I began to grasp what Gail was saying: Del had died on Lemon Reef. I remembered the summer before our tenth grade year. We dove on Lemon Reef every day. Then at night we hung our suits to dry in the window above her bed like flags from our own private country. And with the rest of the house asleep, Del and I, two fifteen-year-old girls, popped the elastic corners of the fitted sheet up over the edges of her mattress one by one, our naked bodies folding into breaths and winces and whispers and giggles that stifled on the edge of being caught.

"Jenna?" Gail's tone was reaching.

"Yeah."

"If you decide to come for the funeral, I'll take a few days off."

A brief silence followed. Gail had never been very close to Del, so I was curious about how affected she seemed. Then she said, "They have a daughter. She's ten. Del wanted to leave Talon, but he threatened to take the kid away from her if she did."

Gail's tone went from informative to entreating, and I knew this was the real reason for the call.

"Now Talon's moving to Texas and he's taking Khila with him. That's her name," Gail said.

I'd met Khila once. The night before I was leaving for San Francisco I ran into Del at a gas station on Miami Beach. Khila was two months old. She was sleeping in the backseat of Del's car, snuggled tightly in a soft blanket, secured in her car seat. She had light, wispy hair, long eyelashes, flushed cheeks, and pale naturally puckered lips. Her head rested against the car seat, and she had her tiny hand tucked under her soft chin like a little *Thinker*.

"I just think it can't be good for her," Gail said, "to be raised by that man. Well, and"—she paused, took a breath—"Del's family is wilder than ever. There's no way they can fight for Khila on their own."

I hung up and leaned forward in my chair, resting my face in my hands. Phones rang in the distance, officious voices crowded and dispersed, and a clock ticked a rhythmic blur. My afternoon calendar was only half over, and I was telling myself not to focus on this news now. I had to finish my day. At the same time, I found myself crying, the tears strangely disconnected from any thoughts or feelings I'd had about Del in recent years, as though a remote pipe, long thought to be inoperative, had suddenly sprung a leak.

Bea McVee, the presiding judge of the family court, appeared in my doorway. She filled the frame, standing her full five feet eleven, with gray dreads falling around her soft brown face and past her narrow shoulders.

"Jenna." She was already laughing about something, had apparently dropped in to tell me what it was. "Jenna?"

I lifted my face from my hands, watched her smile shrink and her dark-brown eyes narrow with bewilderment. "My friend died." Swatting at the tears as one would an intrusive fly, I added, "My first love. She was my…" My throat closed.

Bea entered farther and took a seat across from me at my desk. I noticed the freckles that spotted her cheeks, a youthful detail on this near seventy-year-old face.

"Died how?"

"They think she had a heart attack. She was scuba diving."

"I see." Then Bea said, "Well, how old was she?"

"Thirty-one." I shrugged, as if to say I had no idea how to explain it. "I'm thinking about going to the funeral."

It wasn't easy asking for time off without any notice and being brand new, but Bea nodded expectantly, indicating that my newness wasn't a factor, emergencies happen. She was the reason I was in this position. I had clerked for Bea when I was in law school. I was twenty-two, queer, rageful, irrepressible. I fought with anyone who disagreed with me; dismissed out of hand people far more important than I; argued relentlessly for everyone to act as though things worked the way they ought to.

After the first week, Bea sat me down. "Jenna, you have considerable legal talent, but your demeanor leaves *much* to be desired. You have all the strengths of a young person who's done it on her own." As Bea knew I had. "And," she added, "all the blind spots." In the end, my strengths won out. After I graduated, Bea lobbied to get me hired half-time as the staff attorney for the family court. "Wait until you see the salary before you thank me," she had said. She wasn't kidding.

But there was nobody I would have rather worked for and nothing I would have rather done. I filled the other half of my time working as an attorney representing indigent families at a nonprofit in Oakland. When, seven years after I was first hired, the commissioner position came open, Bea McVee, along with several other judicial officers, encouraged me to apply. I was hesitant at first because I was young and inexperienced as commissioners go. A main concern of the hiring committee, which I shared, was whether I would be able to manage the attorneys over whose cases I presided. Now, three weeks into the position, we waited to see.

Bea said, "Just let me know if you decide to go to the funeral, so

I can arrange for coverage for you." I may have been staring off, or perhaps she was responding to something else about me, but she pressed her lips together, sat quietly, and watched me. When I finally met her gaze, she said, "Why do I get the feeling there's more to this?"

"More? No, I don't think so. It's just a funeral."

"Mm, hmm." She waited.

"Well, there's a little more to it." I thought for a moment about how much to say. I was already late for my afternoon calendar. "She has a kid." The thick glass and sinuate light mired my view of the Federal Building across the street. "A daughter." As I said it, I noticed an ache, as if anesthesia was beginning to wear off, and I could feel the edges of a pain I knew to be much greater.

"How old?"

"Ten. She's ten now."

"She's with her father?"

I pushed my lips out in a pucker and nodded. "He may not be the best person to raise her," was what I said. *He's a fucking creep*, was what I thought.

Her quietness told me she was connecting the dots and drawing her own conclusions. "So, you're going to Miami to attend the funeral, right?" The question caught me by surprise. "What I mean is, do I need to worry about you?" When I didn't respond, she said, "Nobody makes commissioner by thirty, Jenna. You'll be a judge for sure, someday, if you keep your head about you."

My clerk was at my door urging me to get started. I stood up, flattened my robe, and wiped my face.

"I should go. I'm keeping Alex Sanders waiting," I said, referring to an attorney I often clashed with.

Bea scrunched her face in a way that was both curious and challenging.

"I'm too new to get a complaint."

"By him? It would be a feather in your cap, as far as I'm concerned."

As I was passing her to leave, Bea grabbed my hand, and I turned back to face her. "I'm serious, Jenna. Before you go taking on anyone in Florida, remember, you have a lot to lose." Her eyes went to the photo of Madison and me.

CHAPTER TWO

Remain seated," the clerk announced. "The Superior Court of San Francisco, Department Ten, is called to order, August 9, 1999. Commissioner Jenna Ross presiding."

I deliberately put the news of Del's death on hold and groped for the present. The tangible feeling of my chair as I trusted my weight to it grounded me, providing a softer landing than I expected. I looked out at the rows of faces watching me, waiting for me, my every movement feeling stilted and amplified, my every thought tilting me further and further into the present moment until I had it fully in focus.

I glanced at my computer screen for the next case. "Flint and Baxter," I said in the direction of those in attendance.

"Alex Sanders representing the petitioner, Your Honor."

From the other end of the courtroom, a woman, busy with two things at once, called out from her distractedness, "Margaret Todd for the respondent."

❖

Her too-large black suit showed her recent weight loss. A magenta blouse and black pumps finished off the classic attorney uniform. But her clothing was where Margaret Todd and anything like convention began and ended. She was in her mid-fifties now and had been an advocate against domestic violence for close to twenty-five years. I had read articles by her in law school and did briefly join her on the domestic-violence-death autopsy team, when I interned at the family court in my third year of law school. Our purpose then was to review the cases in which someone had died from domestic violence and to try to understand the psychological and social factors contributing to the death. The cases were so horrific; I barely stood it for the one year I'd signed up for. Margaret was a founding member of the team and in her tenth year as a participant.

What Catharine MacKinnon and Andrea Dworkin had done to raise consciousness around rape and pornography, Margaret and others like her had done in the area of domestic violence. Many believe it was the verdict in the O.J. Simpson trial that ushered in sweeping legislative changes in domestic violence law. But those changes would never have occurred without the groundwork laid by women's advocates for over two decades before the Simpson trial.

Among the more significant changes were things like what evidence was considered admissible. For example, in many states, tape-recording a person without consent was not only inadmissible, it was a crime. But new laws allowed for such tapes to be admissible if they were evidence of domestic violence. In the family court, domestic violence against a spouse in front of a child now constituted child abuse. And if a parent was found to have committed an act of domestic violence, there was a presumption against that parent having custody of a child.

As these new domestic violence laws were taking hold, many states were trying to encourage joint custody, and legislation made timeshare a factor in calculating child support. In other words, if a father spends more time with his child, then he pays less child support to the mother.

As a newly appointed commissioner, I could see how the two legislative intentions were colliding. On the one hand, parents who had never had anything to do with their kids were suddenly demanding custody in order to pay *less* support. On the other hand, it didn't take long for people to realize allegations of domestic violence were easy to assert, hard to disprove, and the fastest way to sole custody and *more* child support. With money and sole custody as possible motivations, claims of domestic violence were often met with skepticism.

Margaret Todd had been forged professionally in a time when protective laws—flawed as they may be—did not exist, and she had the battle scars and the undeniable horror stories to show for it. I had only known times since such laws were being drafted or had gone into effect, and I was far more aware of the ways in which those laws were vulnerable to corruption than I was of their origin and genuine purpose.

Margaret and I sometimes ended up on different sides of this issue. Just a year before, I had represented a father who was at risk of losing custody of his children after being accused and acquitted of drowning his stepson. Margaret represented the mother, who petitioned the family court for sole legal and physical custody of their children. If her husband hadn't killed her son, she argued, then he was unfit for allowing the boy to be close to the water without supervision. The family court denied the mother's petition, and it seemed Margaret hadn't trusted me since.

To Margaret, what I considered my objectivity represented all things wrong with the direction in which feminism was going. I—thirty years old, educated, white—at once benefited shamelessly and distanced myself from the backs that had been my bridge.

❖

I turned to Mr. Sanders, who appeared to have more to say. He balanced his briefcase on the waist-high partition separating the audience from the participants and set his hands atop it. The case supported his considerable weight as he leaned in.

"Your Honor, we've been unable to come to an agreement." His pink, fleshy jowls rippled as he spoke. "We have absolutely no faith in this mother's word that she will follow a court order."

The attorneys entered the inner circle of the courtroom with their clients in tow.

"Ms. Todd," I prompted matter-of-factly, inviting her to begin.

"Your Honor, my client has obtained a temporary restraining order and is now in a battered-women's shelter at an undisclosed location, where she is living in fear for her life. Since we've filed, her tires were cut, and she's received threatening phone messages from unidentified callers—"

"Your Honor," Mr. Sanders said, cutting her off. "Evidence. What does any of this have to do with *my* client?"

My hand went up traffic-cop fashion. "Let her finish, please."

Todd looked to Ms. Flint, the mother, who was sitting to her left. “We’re requesting sole legal and physical custody of Angie, and for Mr. Baxter to have supervised visitation.”

Ms. Flint nodded in agreement. She was pallid in complexion, her black hair gathered in a bun at the back of her head.

Sanders came out of his chair. “This is unbelievable!”

Mr. Baxter, the father, sat to Sanders’s right. His bald, dark-brown head caught the light and his brown eyes set on me.

I ignored the outburst. Sanders rolled his eyes and flung himself back into his seat.

Todd continued over him. “There is a long history of abuse in this case, and we feel Angie should not be with Mr. Baxter unsupervised. Not only is he a danger to Ms. Flint, he doesn’t know the child. He hasn’t spent any time with her.”

“Because she’s not letting him.” Mr. Sanders began waving at me. “You’re just going to let her go on this way?”

“Stop interrupting,” I said.

“I knew we should have asked for *a judge* to hear this case.” Under his breath, but loud enough for the room to hear him. And then with condescension thinly disguised as deference he added, “No offense, Your Honor.”

I ignored the remark, aware Alex Sanders had applied for the position which I now held. Any other day, Sanders’s provocation might have worked to throw me off balance, pull me into a fight. I might have felt ashamed to be so easily dismissed by him, exposed as a fraud in this black robe, reminded that in the eyes of my colleagues it had been politics and brownnosing—or, perhaps, muff diving—that had gotten me here by the unheard of age of thirty.

I had overheard him saying it. “In San Francisco, gay judges promote gay lawyers. Being a fag these days is like being a member in an exclusive club, only anyone can join.” He had laughed at his own joke.

Not today. Today, I thought of Del’s death, so far away from this place of my actually very hard-won and always-dubious power. Today, I violently rejected the futility of her strivings, and of my own, and railed against the ease with which the likes of Alex Sanders had always denied our achievements. Never mind having gone from dropping out of high school at the age of sixteen to graduating from law school at the age of twenty-three. Never mind the absurd salaries and benefits I had turned down to work sixty-plus hours a week over the past seven years for nominal wages in order to expand access to family court for families who couldn't afford an attorney. Never mind the half dozen articles I had published about improving and expanding legal representation for children living in poverty. Hard work and true devotion held no sway against the entitlements assumed every day by Alex Sanders and others like him.

I focused on Ms. Todd. "You were saying."

"My client wants to work with her baby's father, but Mr. Baxter is verbally abusive and physically intimidating. It is not possible to cooperate with him."

Wrestling with his wide body, twisting it to situate more comfortably in the chair, Sanders asked, "My turn now?" His tone was juvenile. I nodded. "Nine months. That's how long my client has been trying to see his daughter. Mr. Baxter has never been arrested. There were no police reports made during the marriage. He's been in his current job for ten years without incident. And *he* left *her*. The mother, Ms. Flint I mean, has made repeated false allegations. She has sought a restraining order three times in the last four months alone. Two were denied, one was dropped. We had an agreement for visitation after the baby was born. Mother never showed. This is our fourth time in court, because Ms. Flint there"—he pointed in her direction—"says she'll cooperate, and then she doesn't. She was ordered by Judge McVee six months ago to go to therapy, but she hasn't done that. Now she has relocated to an undisclosed location, and she is alleging that my client is following her at the exact time he can prove he's at work. This is about retaliation and child support."

Todd said, "We're not asking for child support."

Sanders laughed-blurted, "They *will* be."

My court reporter's tape ran out. While she took a few minutes to change it, the lawyers huddled with their clients, and I thought about what I would say next. I already knew coming into this hearing how it was likely to turn out based on the pleadings. Unless Ms. Flint could offer some information to support her most recent claim of domestic violence, she was continuing to interfere with this baby's right to see her father and to form a relationship with him. Since less drastic measures had been exhausted, the remedy was to place the child with the parent most likely to support a relationship with the other parent—in this case, the father.

❖

What I was about to rule would fly in the face of convention, surprise this father, and leave this mother indignant. When it comes to parenting, especially of babies, a lot of people think fathers are less competent than mothers. But what I valued most about the law was the opportunity it provided for calling basic beliefs, like that women are inherently better parents, into question, turning ideas inside out, exposing the underlying prejudices and flaws in logic that prevent us from seeing individuals for who they are and looking at each situation as unique. I went to law school because of what it had been like for me and my friends as adolescents at the mercy of unreasonable, sometimes quite cruel, parents. Striving for fairness was the way I felt safe and sane in the world.

I figured this out in my last year of college. Until than, I'd stayed the course I'd set upon with Del in middle school. Del had wanted me to be a writer. We first noticed each other in English class in eighth grade. The class had been divided into small groups, and we were going around in a circle reading poems we had written. Mine was about seeing my father hit my older brother, the experience as ordinary as if I were describing a family dinner conversation.

After I finished reading it, I noticed Del staring at me. We had been in school together since elementary school, but I was an athlete and a book nerd. Del was popular and seemed inaccessible to me as a friend. She ran with older crowds and always had a boyfriend. When I finished reading my poem was the first time I really saw Del's face. It—she—was the most beautiful thing I had ever seen. Her raised brows, solemn eyes, and softened cheeks expressed a mixture of awe and confusion and utter sadness. When I realized her reaction was in response to my words, I brimmed with pride and potency and purpose. My idea of myself as someone who could have an effect on others was born in that moment, in the light cast from Del's recognition of me.

During lunch period, I was sitting on the ground in the courtyard, book open on my lap, waiting for my group of friends to gather. A shadow fell upon the page I was reading, and I looked up expecting it to be Gail or Katie. Del was standing there, hugging her books, hips tilted from casually leaning more on one leg, soft hair falling forward around her face. Her plump, freshly glossed lips caught the sunlight.

"Hi, Jenna."

"Oh," my heart held a beat, "hi."

"I just wanted to tell you I liked your poem."

I thought how serious Del seemed, which surprised me, because she was one of the beautiful girls for whom things appear to come easily, and seriousness implied effort. Well, that, and Katie and Gail, my two best friends, hated her and were always talking about what a superficial slut Del was. She stood searching around me for a moment as I waited to see what she would say next. I felt shy and confused—on the one hand glad for her attention, on the other hand made acutely uncomfortable by it. Then she asked the oddest question. "Does your father really hit you?"

My brows pinched and my face twisted a little. "Sometimes. If I talk back." Del was quiet, her expression pensive. "Does yours?" I asked.

Del slid her weight to her other leg, swung her hair around, and adjusted her books against her body. "No. My father doesn't hit us." Her head turned. She had noticed her boyfriend, Joel Bishop, enter the courtyard. Joel was already at Miami Shores Senior High School, and he was coming to have lunch with Del. "My mother hits us." Now preoccupied with Joel, she concluded the conversation by saying, "I'm *never* gonna hit my kids." As Joel approached, Del straightened, fixed her smile, and pushed her chest out. "Bye, Jenna." Without waiting for me to respond, she walked away.

We didn't become friends until Del joined the soccer team that summer, but I had already begun to write short stories and poems. All I wanted was for Del to look at me again the way she had in English that day. I created stories the whole time we were together, writing first toward her, then to her—and then about us. Stacks of stories scribbled in pen or pencil on pages or in the margins of class notes, reading aloud to her at night stories of a heroine named Khila, basking in Del's delight and encouragement. I realized now, with Del dead, that the only remnant of those long-ago-destroyed writings was Del's living daughter. Khila.

❖

The court reporter indicated she was ready to resume.

"Back on record," I said and faced the parties. "I've read the paperwork that both of you have submitted. It does confirm much of what you're saying, Mr. Sanders."

Sanders seemed surprised. He had expected me to retaliate, twist this, make it come out a certain way for one party because I didn't like the other party's attorney or because I was a white gay woman and his client was a black heterosexual man.

"It sounds like the only new information is the allegations of abuse." Both attorneys nodded. I looked to Margaret Todd, her glasses perched on her head, a pen in hand and poised for writing. "I'm denying the request for a restraining order." Catching Todd's glare, I said, "Too speculative." Now I turned to Ms. Flint, a woman small in stature, with severe eyes and stern posture. My tone was matter-of-fact and straightforward. "I'm granting the petitioner's request for physical custody of Angie, *temporarily*."

Flint's face hardened and then wrinkled in pain. "What does that mean?" She grabbed Todd's arm. "What does that mean?" Ms. Todd leaned in and began to whisper. "You can't do that," Flint said to me. "I'm breast-feeding."

Ms. Todd's head pivoted in my direction. "Your Honor, Angie is still breast-feeding. And," she continued, "I fail to see how a change in custody is in this baby's best interest. You're removing her from the parent she has been with since birth and placing her with someone she doesn't know at all."

"I understand. Hopefully," I said, "Ms. Flint can and will provide Mr. Baxter with breast milk."

Todd said, "Your Honor, you're disrupting a well-established mother-infant bond, which is a known recipe for later psychopathology in the child."

Sanders intercepted. "Keeping the child away from her other parent is also known to throw a wrench in healthy development. Ms. Flint has made it impossible for Angie to have a relationship with anybody else. How can that be good for the child? My client"—Sanders put his hand on Mr. Baxter's shoulder—"will make sure Angie sees her mother all the time."

"Well," I said, "what *is* your plan for visitation?"

"Mr. Baxter works during the day, and Angie is going to be with her paternal grandmother. Ms. Flint can be there while he's working, and she doesn't have to see Mr. Baxter."

I jotted down what Sanders was saying. "I'm ordering a minimum of thirty hours of weekly contact to mother, with details to be worked out between her and paternal grandmother. I'm also appointing minor's counsel," I said toward Sanders. For the record, I added, "To ensure that Angie is safe and to enforce visitation."

"Your Honor," Todd said in barbed tones, "my client is not going to visit at paternal grandmother's house."

"Neither of these parents can afford professional supervised visitation. I've got a family member willing to help Ms. Todd. I'm going to take advantage of that."

"This is a domestic violence matter. Need I remind you, intimate partner violence is the leading cause of death for pregnant women in the United States"—she spat out the talking points over Sanders's loud objections and my attempts to stop her—"and that's *proven* murders. For women in general, it's number one after car accidents. There were a reported five million physical assaults and rapes last year. A women is killed—"

I interrupted more forcefully. "This is an argument more appropriately addressed to the legislature, Ms. Todd."

"It's not a legislative argument at all, Your Honor. This case brings these statistics right to our doorstep. You are making an order to turn a nine-month-old baby over to an alleged abuser. Are you sure you want to do that?"

It was a warning. Margaret Todd's program, the Family Violence Center, had just led a successful campaign to oust a long-seated judge in favor of a new judge who was, in their estimation, more sensitive to issues of domestic violence. She was letting me know that if something happened to this mother or this baby, I would have hell to pay.

Flint was standing with tears flooding down her cheeks, glowering at me.

I met her glare. "This is a temporary order, and I'm setting a one-month review date. Get yourself situated in stable housing, cooperate with the visitation, start counseling, and we'll revisit this"—I looked to my clerk for a time—"September thirteenth, nine a.m. That gives you four weeks."

"Four weeks?" Flint fell forward a little and then steadied herself by placing her hands on the table. "Who is going to take care of my baby? How do we know she'll be safe?"

I thought about Khila. "It can't be good for her," Gail had said, "to be raised by that man." Gail had called me because she knew Del's family wouldn't stand a chance representing themselves in a custody dispute. I closed my eyes for a moment, trying to regain my focus. "I've made my orders," I said, ignoring Sanders's grin.

Before moving on to the next case, I turned to my clerk and said, "Let Judge McVee know I'll be out the rest of the week."

CHAPTER THREE

My workday over, I sat on my bedroom floor tussling through the clean laundry pile seeking clothes I wanted to take with me to Miami. Madison came into the room, my favorite sweats in hand. She presented them to me, a show of conquest over the current state of our laundry.

"So, what did Norma have to say about Del's death?" Madison asked.

"'So what? She was trash anyway.'"

A slight shake of her head followed, as if she wasn't sure she'd heard me correctly. *"Okay."* Madison held up socks to see if they matched. She put one down and reached for another.

I patted Puck, our seven-month-old black Dane-pit mix—a miniature Dane on steroids. He raised his lazy eyes at me and wagged his tail. I reached over him and grabbed a shirt to fold. Suddenly remembering, I said, "I have to charge my cell phone."

"It's already charging." Madison's dark hair fell softly from a part off to the side. Her blue eyes were trained on me, and she grinned at her successful performance of wifedom. Her grin drew me in, and I was taken aback by my shyness in remembering the sex we'd had the night before. I studied her, my tenderness toward her palpable, the sudden reminder of her a pleasure and a relief.

My eyes drifted to the window, and I noticed the thinning daylight.

"We ended so badly," I said. "I don't even know what I'm doing going to this funeral." I decided to leave out the part about how I was fifteen when Del's mother met me on the porch with a shotgun, her eyes bloodshot, her breath beer-drenched, her accent a mix of Canadian French and Cuban Spanish. "If you come here again," she said, "I'll kill you."

The phone rang and Madison left to answer it. I continued to fold, remembering the years after Del and I broke up, and how every time I ran into her it was like putting my finger in an electric socket—except for on the night before I left for California. As I thought about that night when we did finally talk, the gnawing ache in my chest sharpened around my heart, causing my head to dip forward and my eyes to close.

❖

The night before I left for California, I ran into Del at a gas station on Miami Beach. It was 1989, we were both twenty, and Del was about to marry Talon. She was driving a run-down blood-orange Chevy with then two-month-old Khila tucked away in the backseat. I looked past Talon's name brandished in capital gold letters on the Chevy plate and approached, the surprise of Del making me feel hopeful. The feeling shattered against the impermeability of her grudge. It had been like this since our breakup five years earlier. Whenever we ran into each other, she would be icy and I would retreat. On this night I refused to retreat. I stood there remembering us at fourteen and fifteen, her hips sliding over mine, my tongue skirting her nipple, her finger etching my ribs, my cheek resting against her moist inner thigh after she came.

"I'm moving away tomorrow."

That did get her attention, did momentarily melt her enough for her expression to change slightly in the direction of something I thought might be sadness. But it was only momentary. Del continued to look past me when we spoke, showed no interest in introducing me to her current life or to her new baby.

That our paths crossed on that night in particular seemed poignant. I was moving to San Francisco the next morning. I had not laid eyes on Del in nearly a year. She was standing right there, further away than ever, eating-disordered thin (despite having just had a baby), with soft gold hair falling casually past her shoulders, tight blue jeans, a sheer black shirt hanging open over a fitted black silk-and-lace camisole. Feeling betrayed by my own senses, I helplessly traced the shape of her slender arms against her narrow torso, the slope and peak of her breasts.

The warm night air mixed with gasoline and Del's musky perfume. I tried to conceal my attraction to her. I felt compromised, revealed in my loneliness and desperation, but the sight and smell of her lulled me. But even the re-surprise of her gorgeousness and my easy recall of my closeness to her did not weaken my resolve. For the first time in five years, I was not hoping for her to be wherever it was I intended to arrive. I realized my leaving her was real.

My dog was barking. I turned toward him and told him to be quiet. When I looked back, Del was staring at me with a strange expression.

"Did you just call that animal Gregor?"

"Yeah. Why? That's his name."

"As in," with mild sarcasm, "*Metamorphosis*?"

Shrugging, I asked, "What's wrong with that? I like that story."

"You *like* that story? You stopped talking to anyone who didn't vote for it after you nominated it for the high school Christmas play."

Irritated, I countered, "It was the only gay adolescent coming-out story I could find."

She playfully pleaded me to reason, giggled while scolding. "You're the only one who ever read it that way."

I drank her laugh, trying to sip and guzzle it at the same time. It reassured me that Del recognized me, knew who I was, was glad to see me in spite of herself. Then, as if caught, she shifted her attention, the talking ceased, and my heart was flailing about like a decked mackerel. The moment had been like an eye of lucidity in a storm of dementia. Now she was gone, and I missed her terribly and all over again.

Del watched the meter on the gas pump, her waiting palpable. I stood behind her, invisible and foolish. "Why are you so mad at me?" I asked finally.

"You know exactly why," she said, without removing her gaze from the machine. While I shook my head, she offered both a question and an answer: "Why did you tell Gail about us?"

"What?" I laughed. "That's it? That's the reason you haven't talked to me in five years, because I told Gail Samuels that we sucked each other? You fucked anything with a dick, and that's why, because you were afraid people would think you were *gay*?" I realized the strength of my protest was the measure of my guilt, and I felt sorry for going off. "Del, Gail never told anyone."

Del unhooked the pump from her car, put her gas cap back on, and started walking away. "Wait! Del." *Again* we were fighting, *again*. I was surprised when she stopped, hoped she was agreeing by turning around to have the conversation she'd been refusing to have for years. I blew out one breath attempting to regroup. "That can't be the reason you hate me so much," I said. "You can't care about the gay thing, not really. And anyway, our friends knew about us."

"They didn't know anything, Jenna, until you told them." All I could think about was how long it had been since I'd heard her say my name. A most familiar gesture: she ran her hand along the side of her neck to lift her hair off her face, her glance cast downward in reverie. "I did care. You need me to admit it, fine. It was embarrassing. I was embarrassed by how I felt about you. But even if I wasn't"—her face hardened and her inflection turned disdainful—"what we did together was private. You had no right to tell anyone."

I groped for an explanation that would make my indefensible act seem less significant when, honestly, I knew I had broken her heart. "Del, it was just sex."

"Is that what it was?"

Now I was angry. "You would know, all that real sex you've had to compare us to."

"*Real sex?* Wait, you mean"—she laughed benignly and even fondly—"you mean because it was with boys? Jenna, I didn't mean it that way. It wasn't like that." I realized what she had meant and started to apologize. She hated apologies. She continued forcefully. "I meant…" She hesitated, and then with a hint of sadness she confessed, "It wasn't just sex to me."

Arms out, palms up, I pleaded. "Del, I was fifteen years old. *I was fifteen years old!*"

Her coolness resurrected, she folded her arms over her chest, a gesture of superiority. "So was I, but I didn't betray you." She leaned back and glanced at her sleeping baby, her tone a reminder that she was in a new life now. "You acted like you were the victim."

"You went hetero with a vengeance…"

"Are you fifteen now? What's your excuse for saying that to me now?"

"It's just, you can't call it loyalty."

"Why not?" Half laughing, she said, "What I did hurt me, not you."

"We were not that separate. And"—my heart ached as I pushed it out—"I was in love with you."

Del looked at Khila, and this time I looked with her. We stood side by side staring into the car window. Light hair and a teardrop-shaped nose peeked out from the blanket Khila was wrapped in; her tiny hand was nestled under her chin.

Del's arm brushed against mine and our fingers linked fleetingly, as if our bodies remembered something we had forgotten. I surprised and slightly embarrassed myself with what I said then. "Rounded edges and hollow spaces in which small things—small treasures—could safely, easily be concealed." I turned from Khila to Del, the pain in my heart gone from muted to stabbing. Del looked at me too, her green-gold eyes open and still, her cheeks shallow.

"What does that mean?"

I stared at her, hoping she'd remember. My neck and jaw tightened, and a wave swelled behind my eyes. I shook my head and said, "Nothing." I cleared my throat, stifled tears, smiled at her. "It's nothing."

She wrapped one hand around the other, twisted her fingers, shifted her eyes nervously. There was a long silence. Then Del said sadly, wearily, as if she was thinking it clearly for the first time, "As twisted as it sounds, I think I was trying to protect us."

I knew it was true. I had felt so betrayed by her apparently easy recourse to boys, but now seemingly disconnected, even contradictory pieces of history snapped into place. "A ruse?" I offered softly, and more to myself.

She paused and looked down. "I think so. At first, maybe. Then I don't know what." She leaned back against her car and turned her head reflexively, checking Khila again. When she brought her face back, her brows were clenched. She fixed her gaze on me, her expression impassive. "It got a lot more involved." I knew she was referring to where things had ended up, before she met Talon. Her sustaining myth about Talon was he had saved her from Ben Reed.

Ben Reed, a guy we knew from high school, owned a little fleet of flower carts. He had taken Del in when she couldn't stand to live with her mother anymore. When we were seventeen, I would drive by Del on Biscayne Boulevard, where she stood selling flowers from one of Ben's carts. The business was rumored to be a front for a prostitution gig. At the same time I'd learned this, I'd also learned Ben referred to Del as the "cream of his crap." Del's endeavors as a prostitute were well-worn grist for jokes among the kids we went to school with. The boys who had tried to sleep with Del in high school and felt indignant at her rebuffs now took loud revenge. That night at the gas station, however, I had the impression Del believed I didn't know that she had "tooted"—as we called it—for a while. I let her think that. Anyway, I was having admission problems of my own, not confessing that there had been no one else since her—knowledge I'm certain was just as common and that lent itself just as readily to sadistic jokes at neighborhood parties.

"What about you?" she asked, but I could tell it was a closing rather than an opening.

"I'm driving to San Francisco tomorrow. Berkeley, actually." My throat constricted with the knowledge that the content of our exchange from here on out was subordinate to the structure; we were saying good-bye. "Law school." But Del confused me by waiting for more. "I mean…" I scrambled, grabbing at the chance to say something more. "I am going to law school there, but I'm also going because I'm gay." I cast my gaze about seeking a safe landing, gave up, and lit on her face. "Maybe it'll be easier there, you know?"

"You've had that idea for a long time," she said sweetly. Then, "Law school? You dropped out when I did." I recounted how I had beelined through: high school equivalency test, junior college, scholarship to University of Miami. She shook her head in disbelief, smiled in a way that conveyed she was proud of me. "You always were really smart."

You are. "Del, don't marry this guy."

She ignored me, asked playfully, "Any girls?"

I was delighted at being invited into the interlude of playful banter. "I'm thinking about sleeping with someone," I lied.

"Oh, I should try that," she said, her tone gently self-mocking.

"What?"

"Thinking about it first."

❖

Madison came into the room and found me staring at nothing. She sat down on the floor facing me. “What is it?”

“I lost track of her. Once I left Miami, I never looked back.”

“What were you supposed to do? She wasn’t exactly up for staying in touch.”

“I promised her…” I stopped. The rest of the sentence, *I would never let go of her*, seemed too ridiculous to say after so many years. “Truthfully, I don’t think anything can be done to stop Talon from taking Khila now. Grandparents have limited rights. And there’s also the fact that we’re talking about *this* grandmother—I mean, what judge in her right mind would give Del’s mother custody of any kid?”

“Maybe you can’t do anything about Khila, but you should still go to Del’s funeral.” Madison’s thick, dark brows enhanced the blueness of her eyes. “You loved her and she’s dead.”

The comment, although sincere and perfectly reasonable, struck me as naïve. This, I realized, must be how a starving person feels when receiving a referral for psychotherapy. In the environment in which I grew up, how I felt about Del had never mattered at all. Madison had grown up in Berkeley. She’d had her first out relationship in high school, came out in a more defined way in her second year at Yale. She was a gay-identified writer—had published her first collection of short stories about being gay by the time she’d finished graduate school. Her first novel, recently published, recounted her last year in college and the breakup of her first major relationship. For her, coming of age as a gay woman had been empowering, sexy, exciting. For me, it had been life-threatening.

In fact, Madison’s comfort with herself was part of what had attracted me to her to begin with. The first time I saw her was at a party after the pride parade. She was dressed in tight jeans, and she was topless but for chain mail, which hung from her bony shoulders to her midriff like a medieval chest guard. She was by herself, barefoot, lost in the music on a nearly empty dance floor. I thought she was beautiful: tall and slender, with thick, dark hair to her shoulders and sapphire eyes. I was sitting at the end of the bar, tucked in the shadows, outside the reach of the lights. My friends had gone home, and I had been about to. Madison noticed me and smiled. I pushed beyond my comfort zone and joined her—me in my jeans, law-school-logo'd T-shirt, and tennis sneakers, feeling shy and out of place. There had been other girlfriends in law school, but no one I had really fallen for.

In the morning I woke up to her studying me. "I love your mouth," she said, her finger etching my bottom lip.

I was barely awake, still getting oriented to her room. I fell back on the pillow. "Not really much to it," I said of my mouth, which felt particularly dry and unattractive right then.

She hovered over me, smiled. "There is *so much* to it." I was twenty-three, and my stomach fluttered under her gaze in a way it hadn't in so many years, the feeling at first was unrecognizable.

❖

Now in our Bernal Heights cottage, simmering orange haze seeped in through our weathered-white window, which framed an incidental snapshot of the San Francisco Bay Bridge. A soft breeze rippled the frayed edges of the burlap curtain, ushering in a mixture of scents from the garden—English lavender, mint, rosemary, lemon blossoms. The day that had thrown me such a curve was drawing down. I traced its effects, afraid of how I might be different for having lived through it. Puck rolled over on his back and nuzzled me to pet him. His jutting chest, a splash of white against his otherwise blue-black body, eagerly sought to be scratched. Growing more insistent, he whacked me with his large, gawky paw. His persistence pulled me back to the present, to the here and now, to this incandescent orange room and sun-warmed bed, to Madison, to the sweetness in my current life.

I rolled my eyes at Puck with playful annoyance. He whacked me again, this time slightly harder. Capitulating, "Okay, okay," I rubbed his chest. He wagged his tail, spun around on his back in hopes then of catching it, and bounced to his still-precarious legs.

Madison stood up, glad, I thought, to be distracted by needs other than mine. "I want to take Puck out before it gets much darker. Do you want to come?" She was already heading for the door.

❖

We walked the narrow, winding path that spiraled up Bernal Hill to its peak. The bay lay out before us, the water the color of polished nickel, the sky a sweep of melting oranges and reds. The old red brick of San Francisco General Hospital stood out from the mass of buildings and streets that made up the Mission District. Beyond lay the Bay Bridge, a parking lot at this hour. It was cool enough that we needed layers, which even after ten years seemed strange to me in August. In fact, with the exception of maybe five days out of the year, I was always cold in San Francisco, always searching for thicker socks or a warmer jacket. It was something I didn't give much thought to anymore. I just dressed for cooler weather and used the heat or made fires more often than made sense to anyone else. The hardest part for me was the ocean. It was maddening to live in a place with such a beautiful landscape and ocean access and not be able to go in the water without a wetsuit, which I simply refused to wear.

As we walked, Madison took my hand. I sensed she was worried about me. Puck loped along ahead of us on his gangly legs, looking back every few feet to see if we were behind him.

"How old were you and Del?"

"When we got together? Fourteen."

"Wow, I didn't realize you were that young. How long were you together?"

I had to think about it, but certain markers helped me recall.

"First kiss, November, 1982." I knew when it was because I had just turned fourteen, and it was my first real kiss. "It was an amazing kiss."

Madison laughed.

"We were together after that for a little over a year." The last night we were together I knew without having to think about it. "Christmas Eve, 1983."

As I said it, I felt a rush of sadness mixed with nausea, and I swallowed hard and tried to breathe through it. Puck pranced in fits and starts, as if his brain and legs disagreed. It was a little like if all three Stooges had been put into one body.

"I guess there are things that one feels sad about forever," I said.

The way our relationship ended had been like being drawn and quartered. The parts of me that were pried away went without the parts of me that wouldn't let go of her. Fifteen years later, I still could feel the frayed edges of my own torn flesh. And hear bones popping. And see the bits and pieces of me that lay exposed in the space between when she was my life and when she wasn't anymore.

"Del had this bruise on her face that night," I said. "It started just under her eye and spread out onto her cheekbone." I was using my own face as a reference point. "I asked her about it, even though I knew where it had come from."

"Her mother?"

"Yeah. Del had tried to stop her from going out and leaving them on Christmas Eve." I stuck my hands in my jacket pockets, pulled my elbows in close to my body for warmth. "Del just dismissed the bruise."

Against the horizon beyond Hunters Point were ship-loading cranes. Lined up as they were, with their industrious, long necks and pulleys, they looked like a herd of robotic brontosauruses out for a sunset stroll, at once futuristic and prehistoric. As I stared at them, I thought about how everything that has ever happened in our lives is always still happening.

"I told Del I was worried about her. She said not to be, that people either make it or they don't. She was so sad when she said it, Madison. I don't think I've ever seen anyone that sad."

"That's horrible. It's like knowing you're in a coma."

Puck chased a golden retriever puppy, much smaller and younger than he. When he caught her, he went down on his front legs, as if he were trying to make himself the same height as her, and then he turned and ran, expecting her now to chase him. The puppy wagged her tail, followed him a few steps, and then ran back to her person. The puppy's owner, a skinny woman whose face was dominated by bright red lipstick, was interested in what kind of dog Puck was. Madison patiently engaged in conversation with the woman. It's one of those dog-park etiquette things—abandoning a private conversation in order to exchange niceties and inquire about others' dogs.

I stood a few feet away, my eyes drifting back to the cranes. Suddenly, a peripheral blur was followed by bloodcurdling cries. The air filled with vicious snarls and growls mixed with deafeningly high-pitched squeals. A large German shepherd had come from nowhere and was attacking the puppy Puck had just been playing with. The dogs' bodies tangled into a ball and rolled in the dust like tumbleweed. The shrieking puppy twisted to get away as her owner slapped and kicked at the shepherd, screaming for help. Madison was trying to grab the large dog by his collar.

I reached into the snarls and cries and scrambling and dust, grabbed the shepherd by his back legs, and yanked them out from under him. The next thing I knew, the shepherd lay sprawled in the dirt, jerking and twisting to get away. I held his legs apart and down as if they were the handles of a wheelbarrow. The woman grabbed her puppy and jumped back. When the puppy was safe, I released the shepherd and he ran off.

"That was so scary," the woman said to me. "Thank you so much. I'm going to report that dog to the police."

"It's okay." I petted the puppy, felt her trembling. "How is she?"

"A little scared and a few tooth marks," Madison said, fingering through the puppy's fur. "He mostly got her collar." She shook her head and smiled at me. "Where'd you learn that trick?"

I stared at her blankly. I couldn't remember, and combined with this unnerving incident on this most unreal-seeming day, it frightened me. Because having an answer felt better than not, I shrugged and said, "TV or something." My body felt strangely disconnected from my words in that way only a lie can effect.

With Puck between us, we began back down the hill toward our cottage on Elsie Street. As we made our way, I glanced again at the cranes and suddenly recalled once having seen Del's mother, Pascale, break up a dogfight between their dog Brute and a neighbor's dog the same way.

CHAPTER FOUR

The red-eye departed San Francisco at midnight with scheduled arrival into Miami International just before nine a.m. Miami time the following morning. My return flight was scheduled for Sunday afternoon, allowing five full days in my hometown. I was taking Gail up on her offer to stay with her. She seemed happy about it—although with Gail, it's hard to tell. I sipped a Bloody Mary and stared out the window, absorbing the vodka and steeling myself against the anxiety I felt whenever I thought about the onslaught of work I would be returning to.

I had received good news in a voicemail I retrieved before boarding. Carlos Robles was appointed minor's counsel for Angie in the *Flint v. Baxter* case. I knew Carlos was thorough, and I trusted he would keep Angie safe. Still, after seven years of never missing a beat professionally, it was not easy to just let my obligations fall to the wayside to attend to something I thought was so firmly behind me.

I reached into my travel bag and took out a yellowed envelope, folded over in the middle. From it I removed the only photograph I had of Del and me. Katie Dunn had taken it when we were in New Mexico for a soccer tournament. "July, 1982" was scribbled on the back. I was thirteen and Del (who was ten months older than me) was fourteen. In the photo, we were sitting side by side on a tree stump eating sandwiches. I was skinny, with coils and springs for hair (the shorter it was, the curlier), olive skin, and a round face. I was looking away from the camera and laughing, and you could see the dimples parenthesizing my smile. Del's hair, the color of honey in sunlight, fell lazily around her face. She was looking at me with a wry expression, lips slightly twisted, head at a slant, as if she was trying to figure me out.

Del had surprised everyone by deciding to join the traveling soccer team the summer before our ninth grade year. She said it was for the exercise, but she did later admit my poems in eighth grade English had gotten to her, and she joined because she had a crush on me. She and I were randomly assigned to stay with the same family in New Mexico. I offended her the first night. She was sitting on her bed reading *The Bell Jar* by Sylvia Plath, and she was unwilling to put it down.

In an awkward attempt to get her attention, I said, "I didn't take you for someone who read a lot."

Del looked up from the page and said challengingly, "Why, because I'm blond?"

"Blind?" I had misheard her. "Did you say I thought you were blind? I didn't think you were blind. I just didn't think you read a lot."

She twisted her face curiously, nodded deliberately. *"Right."* She paused, and then she said, "I'm not blind." Her attention turning back to the page, "Are you deaf?"

I laughed, joined her in making fun of me, which moved me beyond my shyness with her. Riding the laughter like a wave, I walked over and playfully wrestled the book from her hands.

"What are you reading this for anyway? It's so deep."

"I don't know." Del lifted her shoulders, glanced at a place on the wall behind me. "It's like a car accident. It's horrible, but you can't stop watching."

I felt the weightiness of her tone and it scared me a little. "Come on," I said, putting the book down with one hand and offering up a deck of cards with the other. "Spit?"

Del begrudgingly agreed, but did eventually get into it. We stayed up late talking, snuck out to share a cigarette we found in the room. A good feeling took hold between us, and we began to look for each other even when we were with the rest of the group.

After the trip, Del and I spent more and more time together. In those remaining summer days before our ninth-grade year began, when we did hang out it was either at the beach or at my house; Del never invited me over. I thought this incidental, until one day when I showed up at Del's unexpectedly. Hardly off my bike, Del met me at the fishing-pole-lined porch and ushered me away from the house, suggesting we go see a matinee at a nearby theater. I needed to use the bathroom first. Del insisted there was a bathroom at the theater. At some point I realized Del was trying to keep me from going in and meeting her family. I sensed it was because she felt ashamed. In my best thirteen-year-old self's attempt to prove to her I cared about her no matter what, I faked around her and headed in the direction of her living room door, checking back with her as I did. Del shook her head with annoyance or dread (I wasn't sure). Then she took a deep breath and followed me inside.

From the front door I could see the back door, which was wide open. The scent of stewing tomatoes and onions crept out from behind the wall separating the narrow galley kitchen from the living room. The small box-shaped living room looked as if it were about to bust apart from the heavy furniture and extensive clutter. A large greenish couch of some scratchy, woven synthetic material filled one wall. A worn wooden coffee table had to be navigated to get to the back where the kitchen was located. On the wall opposite the couch, a bulky television with wrinkled antennae rested upon a piece of brown furniture, which appeared at one time to have had doors and drawers in the places that were now gaping holes.

I hesitated before entering farther, taken aback by the sheer disorder. It was quite a contrast from my own house, which was spacious and chic and spotless. Del scrambled to clean up. I was thinking of ways to reassure her as I quickly side-stepped a large barking dog of indeterminate breed in order to keep from being knocked over. He had run in the open back door chasing two frantically squawking chickens, racing haphazardly through and around the fighting younger siblings. Water and food spilled out from overturned cat bowls, and feathers were flying everywhere.

"Chickens?" I said lightly, smiling and nodding cheerfully in Del's direction.

She heaved a palpable, miserable sigh. "My mother likes fresh eggs."

With her arms full of stuff from the floor, Del tried to subdue the frantic dog without stepping on any of the chickens—or children. Ida and Nicole, Del's little sisters, were in the middle of the living room screaming at each other over the head of the wailing eighteen-month-old Sid, while Pascale remained poised throughout a rather tense phone conversation with the person who seemed to be her boss.

On my way from the bathroom, as Del steered me toward the front door, I stopped to say hello to Pascale. She was tall, skinny, and muscular. Her face was narrow, and she had a small mouth and brown gerbil eyes. Her short chestnut hair was plowed back off her face, as if being taught a lesson for harassing her, and was held stiffly in place by sweat.

Now off the phone, Pascale stood by the stove stirring a huge pot. The kitchen was a small rectangle, with barely enough room, it seemed, for the refrigerator door to open. On the refrigerator door was a picture one of the girls had drawn and a copy of Del's last report card—all A's. A lit cigarette hung from Pascale's mouth, the smoke tracing the conversation like an echo. Can of Budweiser in her other hand, she looked up, noticed me, and said hello. In a thick, not readily identifiable accent, Pascale asked me if I liked chili. That I did made her grin hugely, revealing the slight space between her front teeth. She immediately invited me to stay for dinner. I, much to Del's chagrin, enthusiastically accepted.

My experiences with Pascale from that day on would take some radical twists and turns, and I'd come to know her at her absolute worst. Still, I was from the very beginning committed to her. I was seduced by the confusing and often entertaining way in which Pascale occupied her maternal role—at once entirely given over to and bitterly oppressed by it.

❖

Having finally gotten the stewardess's attention, I requested my second drink. I felt the effects of my first, combined with the sense of overwhelming sorrow and dread that had been constant now for nearly ten hours. I put the photo of our thirteen- and fourteen-year-old selves back in my bag and stared out the window. The sorrow I understood well enough. When you're as close to someone as I had once been to Del and you lose her, you never get over it—not really. And her death made her loss immediate in a way it hadn't been in a long time and final in a way it had never been.

The dread, however, was harder to make sense of. The recirculated air felt heavy in my lungs, the thin felt-like blanket and paper pillow only muted the chill and hardness of the sterile tube. I felt as I always felt in planes: suspended and minimally sustained. The blackness of the night drew me out. I turned my overhead light off so I could feel myself a part of that darkness. I thought then of how in my adult life I've hated flying—this prefabricated, one-size-fits-all space—and having to rely on a pilot who could be contending with who knew what personal preoccupations.

It's not unlike how it felt to be a child in my family, why the clutter and calamity in Del's home had been so appealing to me, so freeing at first, before things began to deteriorate for them. Suspended tensely somewhere between San Francisco and Miami—my present life and my past—I heard Del's words, *some people make it and some people don't*, and recalled vividly the night her family's deterioration became more evident to us both.

❖

It was Christmas Eve, 1983. The day had begun with my parents telling me our neighbor had seen Del and me making out, felt it was his duty to inform them. Mortified, horrified, terrified by the news, my parents forbade me to leave the house until, as they put it, they could "find a way to help" me. This made Del's and my plans for the night—that I would sleep over as I often did—more complicated. I was thinking of ways to get to her house when she called.

"It's me." Her voice was strained. "Are you still coming over?"

"Yeah." I leaned back and felt the pillow fold around my head. I'd already told Del in a quick phone call earlier in the day that my parents knew we were more than friends. What she didn't know yet—what I was somehow going to tell her when I saw her—was that I had been forbidden from having any contact with her outside of school.

"I was scared you wouldn't be allowed," she said.

"I'm coming."

I looked at the clock, which said six p.m. I was waiting for my parents to leave. They were doing their usual Christmas Eve thing—going out for Chinese food and to the movies with other Jewish friends.

"Are you all right?" she asked. Then, in response to my quietness, she said, "I mean, could you just get here, please. They're at it again."

I could hear her mother and father screaming in the background in Spanish.

As soon as my parents left, I stuffed my blanket to create the effect of a sleeping body, and then hopped on my bike and headed to Del's. Miami Shores, the neighborhood in which we grew up, had radically richer and poorer areas. My family lived closer to the waterway, although not on it, like the really rich kids at our school did. Del lived farther inland, on the west border of our school district. Second Avenue, which I crossed to get to Del's house, was a dividing line, a proverbial railroad track. Home and property sizes and values diminished block by block, with Del's mother's house skirting the lower end.

A year and a half since that first visit, when I had stood outside not being invited in, Del greeted me now by throwing open the door and expecting me to enter. The usual chili was not cooking on the stove on that night, just the scents of crowding and resentment folded into spindling cracks in the pasty plaster and the musky, dull air generating from a small wall-mounted metal heater.

Del's conversation with me on the phone picked up as if there had been no interruption.

"It's crazy here," she said. "I can't believe it's Christmas Eve. My father left, so my mother said she's going out, too." Arms up, palms out. "She's just gonna leave us—on Christmas Eve." Del shook her head with disgust and looked at me wearily. "She promised she wouldn't drink tonight." Another headshake. "She's *so* drunk. I feel bad for my sisters and brother, I mean, you know, they still look forward to this fucking holiday."

We were stepping over…things.

"I think she got fired again," Del said, once we had managed to navigate the shared living space and find refuge in her small but always immaculate bedroom. "She has to stop drinking, you know, it just doesn't work with a nine-to-five." A car door slammed and an engine started, followed by a shrieking reverse and a peeling into forward. "Maybe she'll get killed," Del said casually.

She turned to reveal her profile and hitched her middle finger to the edge of her tooth to gnaw at what little nail remained.

There was a red spot under her right eye that was already turning into a vague bruise. Bringing my hand to her cheek, I asked, "What is that?"

Del pushed my hand down and moved her head away. "What do you think? I don't want to talk about it."

"Del," I said, my breath momentarily skidding to a halt, "you tried to stop her from going out, didn't you?" I hooked her hair behind her ear to get a better look at the bruise. "You promised you wouldn't…"

"Will you stop?" She pushed my hand away firmly. "I have to think about what to do."

I wanted to help. "We could see what's on TV."

"*It's a Wonderful Life*," we said at the same time, then laughed.

The door flew open and eleven-year-old Ida swung in. "Sid's up. He's hungry."

Ida's fiery hair fell flamboyantly against her olive skin and dark eyes. Four years our junior, Ida loved to be included in our shenanigans. She had been the audience for our bad poetry readings, the fall guy for our practical jokes, the reluctant post for our soccer net.

"Hi, Jenna," she said when she noticed me.

"Hi." I stood up. "We're just trying to figure out what to do tonight."

Next, ten-year-old Nicole fell with full forward momentum into the room.

"Del, you should see the tire marks Mom left in the driveway."

Nicole was skinny and knobby kneed, with straggly blond hair and delicate facial features. She was either on the edge of erupting emotionally or over it, and it was never clear what made the difference.

"Jenna," Nicole said, "you're here!"

I began walking toward the door. "Del and me are gonna—"

Del interrupted, "I."

"What?"

"Del and *I*."

I twisted my face and glared at her. "I hate when you do that! Now I forgot what I was going to say."

Del shook her head. "Can we get out of my room, please?" She was ushering us toward the door. "Can we just figure this out somewhere else?"

Three-year-old Sid was standing near the refrigerator in a diaper.

He had located a pan of leftover oatmeal and was making his way through it by handfuls.

Del shrugged her shoulders. "That works."

She poured some milk in a cup and handed it to him. Then she patted his head and dutifully turned her attention to the others. "Do you girls want leftover chili and rice?"

Mimicking Del's parentified tone, Nicole began, "Do you girls—"

"Shut up, Nicole," Del said. "Quit teasing me."

"Quit teasing me," Nicole taunted. "Who died and left you boss?"

Nicole's green eyes narrowed as she picked up the milk carton, held it up to Del daringly, and began to tilt it, threatening to pour the milk onto the floor.

Ida crossed her arms and fought tears. "Nicole, just stop."

"Shut up. You fucking orphan. Go back where you came from."

Ida was actually Pascale's niece. She had come to live with Pascale a few years before, after her mother died in a car accident.

"Nicole!" Del said. "Don't say that. We're her family."

I noticed a bag of marshmallows on top of the refrigerator. "Hey, Nicole," I said lightly and in the interest of distracting everyone, "let's roast these."

"Where?" Del asked. "There's no fire."

Nicole, who had put the milk carton down upon mention of the marshmallows, clamped her palm to her forehead in frustration. "How do you stand her?"

It took me a moment to realize the comment was directed at me. When I did, I felt thrilled but also worried at the implicit acknowledgment of Del and me as a couple. "Huh?" I was stalling, trying to figure out how to answer her.

Del recognized my evasive maneuver and giggled as if at a private joke.

I persisted in my task of distraction. "We could make a fire in the yard."

"Oh yeah," Del said sarcastically. "And let's just burn the house down while we're at it."

"We won't," Ida said, pleading. "They'll never know."

"It's easy," I said. To Del, "Remember, my brothers made one in the sand at the beach party the other night. They just dug a hole, put some rocks at the bottom, and then, you know, paper, wood, and matches."

Del reluctantly conceded and grabbed Sid. The girls cheered, and the group of us stampeded into the small yard on a new adventure. The fire going, Sid perched on Del's lap, sticks in hand, marshmallows distributed, we competed for who could roast and eat a marshmallow the fastest, guessed at their shapes shifting under the flames, ate two and three at a time, made our teeth black, our lips sticky, and our throats dry.

Del shared her marshmallows with Sid. He sat in her lap, watching her face, the palm of his hand pressed firmly against her cheek. Nicole poked Ida with her stick. Ida cried. I bopped Nicole on the head with my stick. She threw dirt at me then got up and ran. I chased and caught her. Brute, the dog, circled us and barked with excitement, as we rolled in the mostly dirt lawn under the few scraggly fruit trees, laughing.

When the bag was finished, Del and I went to the corner store to buy more.

"Hurry, Jenna," Del said, "the kids are alone with a fire." Also, we had left Nicole in charge.

The storeowner, a burly russet-skinned man with a patchy beard and one thick eyebrow, was staring at the outline of Del's breasts etched through her fitted V-neck sweater—so much so, he seemed not to notice the six-pack of beer she put down in front of him. He just rang it up and pushed it over. I tossed the bag of marshmallows down on the counter, noticed the beer, and then I noticed the man behind the counter ogling Del. Del ignored him. She packed the beer into a brown bag, pressed up against me, and said softly in my ear, "It's for us, for later."

My cheeks flushed and my stomach fluttered as I tried to count out the change to pay. We had combined what little money we had, hers from babysitting, mine from allowance. Del's demonstrative gesture toward me made the middle-aged man visibly uncomfortable. He averted his gaze, looked at the sprawling change and then lost interest in it altogether, shoved the bag at us, and urged us out of the store.

"Get out," he said, pushing at the air in the direction of the door with both hands. As we walked back, her arm inadvertently brushing against mine, Del said, "I'm not sure we should let Nicole have any more sugar tonight."

"Why?" The comment had irritated me. Del sounded like fifteen going on forty, and she was trying to take me there with her.

"The doctor said she has attention deficit disorder."

"More like deficit of attention disorder," I said. "You can stop her from having more marshmallows if you want to, but I'm not doing it!"

Del laughed. "I love you." She pressed my fingers, which were now loosely hooked with hers. Then, quietly and more to herself, she said, "I don't know what I would do without you."

I didn't respond. I hadn't told her yet that my parents were not going to let me come over anymore. She was no longer welcome at my house. We couldn't do sleepovers on weekends, or spend vacation days together, or fall asleep talking on the phone, as we tended to do on the nights when we didn't sleep in the same place.

Later that night, all five of us sprawled out on the living room floor with pillows and blankets and watched television together. I fell asleep, my head in Del's lap, Jimmy Stewart on the bridge. Del tickled my nose with a loose chicken feather. I woke up to her quietly smiling down at me, her shiny hair falling around my face, her affection for me amplified by the deep crinkles near her eyes. She gestured with a slight lean of her head for me to follow her. We stepped over the small, skinny, sleeping bodies washed in the television light and made our way down the hallway into Del's bedroom.

Once inside, Del locked her bedroom door, the sound of tectonic plates shifting. We left the lights off and made our way around gracefully, guided by shadows and familiar communicative gestures. A stream of moonlight bent through the window above the bed, ricocheted off a mirror, and splashed unevenly over the off-white walls we had recently finished painting. A soft beige-and-maroon bedcover drew remaining refractions of light down into itself, absorbing them as sand does the heat from the sun. I traced the light with my eyes, imposed a pattern upon it, subjected it to order, attributed intention to it. At fifteen, I still believed it could make sense.

"Merry Christmas, Jen." Del kissed me, her eyes already leading toward a wrapped present. "I got you something."

I opened it to find a collection of short stories by Franz Kafka.

"This is a joke, right? You're just giving me this to make fun of me." I was angry all over again that *The Metamorphosis*, which I had nominated for that year's Christmas play, lost to an acid-influenced rendition of *How the Grinch Stole Christmas*. "Oh yeah," I said now, "and I'm the cynical one."

Del laughed lovingly, pressed her forehead to mine, and said, "No conspiracy theories tonight." She was telling me, as she must have sensed, there was not much time left.

I took her present out of my backpack and gave it to her. The gold crinkly paper it was wrapped in drifted to the floor, and she held a painted wooden carving in each hand. One was a blue-skinned character clad in bright yellow-and-purple silk, wearing a golden headdress and wielding a flaming sword. The figure accompanying him was his proud white horse.

She studied the figures closely. "Where did you get these? They're beautiful."

"At the Hindu market in Coconut Grove."

Dubiously, she asked, "Your mother took you?"

"No." I shrugged. "I rode my bike."

"Jenna, that's like fifteen miles."

"It's okay. I made Gail go with me. I didn't tell her where we were going. She bitched at first, but by mile ten her competitiveness kicked in."

Del was smiling and shaking her head disbelievingly. She placed the gifts on her dresser next to about a dozen other carvings of, as I had come to understand, the Hindu God Vishnu. Del had explained to me that Vishnu visits the earth in different forms called Avatars, marking and advancing its evolution. The Vaishnavas, his believers, await Vishnu's arrival in the form of Kalki, a man on a white horse. Kalki will bring about an end to evil in the world.

Del had learned about these myths from her neighbor Omri, who had moved in next door when Del was twelve. Del was tending to two baby marijuana plants she was growing in her backyard when Omri raised her head over the fence and asked about Del's interest in gardening. Gardening led to afternoon teas, during which Omri would tell Del stories about the wooden carvings. Pascale, eager for Del to do her chores, could only spit and swear at the old woman under her breath. Omri gave Del three signed, hand-carved figures. When I met her, Del was trying to complete the collection and had found several reproductions of the statues in local stores.

"I have all but one of the ten incarnations now." Del plopped down on the bed beside me. "I still need Kurma." She was excited about this.

"Which one is Kurma?" I asked.

"The turtle. It carries the world on its back." She ran her fingers along her neck to sweep her hair back from her face and gave me her green-gold eyes. "Well, actually, she carries a mountain, but it might as well be the world."

I noticed the bruise on Del's cheek again and touched it gently.

"It's nothing, don't worry about it." She shrugged nonchalantly. I sensed she felt ashamed. Del paused, glanced away thoughtfully, changed the subject back to me. "So," she said matter-of-factly, "are they flipping?"

"My parents?" She nodded. "Yeah, they're going on and on about 'nipping this in the bud' or something like that. Mostly they're talking to each other about it, but when that's not possible they walk around the house talking to themselves."

She laughed once. "I nipped your bud eight months ago."

We exchanged a mischievous grin.

I said, "They don't know that."

She asked softly, "What do they know?"

"My neighbor told them he saw us fooling around when we were babysitting for him the other night." My tone rote, I numbly recounted for her. "Came home early, didn't have a key, knocked, went around the back when we didn't answer, saw us through the window. Something like that. I didn't wait around for the details."

"He couldn't have seen much," she said. "We didn't take our clothes off." Suddenly a little shy, Del looked at me sideways. "What were we doing?"

"He said we were making out."

Del put her hand on mine. She watched my eyes and moved my hand to under her sweater. I lightly touched her nipple, buried my face in her hair, breathing in the scent of the Paris cologne I'd given her for Chanukah. I kissed her once on her neck.

"What happens now?" she asked sadly.

I could tell by her breath and her firming nipple she was getting stirred. I let my palm fall to the soft inside of her upper thigh and come to rest there.

"I don't know." I paused, wishing I didn't have to say what was coming next. I said it lightly while my heart pulsed with pain. "They've got these bizarre new rules, like I can't see you outside of school anymore."

No response. She just looked at the floor.

"And," I was embarrassed to say it, "I can't be out with girls at all, unless I'm with at least two people. Well, except for Gail."

"Wait, you mean…?" With her sweet smile and crinkly eyes she said, "You have to be with at least two girls because…" She paused, shook her head in amazement. "You're kidding."

"Yes," I said, with a straight face. "I can't be trusted to be alone with another girl—except Gail. Oh, and I can be with Katie, because, well, you know her reputation."

The exchange was playful, but the gravity of the content and the imminent separation were weighing on us—that and knowing we were at the mercy of such fools.

"Leave it to Norma." Del smiled at me, then looked the other way. Her words were slightly strained, her movements more mechanical than usual. I could tell she was trying to seem relaxed, but she felt frightened and small. Del slid onto the bed on her side and patted the space next to her. I folded in beside her.

"You better not be alone with Katie." She was playing at being jealous, but it was also true that Del and Katie Dunn were competitive over their looks, and they tended to be interested in a lot of the same guys.

Del's head was resting on her open hand propped by her elbow, her copper hair spilling over, her eyes, the color of straw, cradling mine. I watched her silver earring dangle, another trap for light. She played distractedly with my necklace—a gift from her neck to mine prompted by a compliment.

"I love you more than anything," I said. I was stroking her hair. "I will always love you."

"Jenna, don't…We both knew this could happen." Her tone was both pleading and angry.

"Del." My voice was softer than usual, imploring her to look at me. “I promise you I won’t let go of you. I promise. No matter what happens, I will *never* let go of you.”

“You’re the only thing I care about.” Her inflection was accusatory. “How I feel about you is the only thing that matters to me, it’s the only thing keeping me here.”

She kissed me, her confidence returning. I heard her submit to what was taking hold between us, her now-familiar sounds launching my stomach in fits and starts.

I stopped, took hold of her face, and whispered, “I’ve never been able to handle that.”

She was mildly annoyed by the interruption. “What?”

“Your sounds.”

She bent her face away. “You’re embarrassing me, Jen.”

“Why would you be embarrassed?” I kidded. “I’m the one it makes quick-cum like a boy.”

She laughed.

I touched her bruised skin.

She smiled and wrapped her hand around mine, holding it tightly against her face.

“I’m worried about you,” I said.

“Don’t be.” She was staring at me intently, almost transfixed. Then, in a resigned tone, she said, “Some people make it and some people don’t.”

I started to fight with her, but she looked so sad. I was afraid anything I said would make her sadder still. Without moving her gaze from mine, she played with the button on my jeans until it came undone and then pulled clumsily on my zipper.

I stopped her hand. “I don’t think we should do this now.”

“Please,” her lips pressed against mine, “I need to.” The “to” fell off at the end, nearly indiscernible.

I spread my legs for her and kissed her back.

❖

A jolt in the plane left my stomach hanging a few rows behind me. The stewardess, approaching with my second drink, performed that trick of her trade of turning momentarily to rubber rather than clutch a passenger or even a seatback. My Bloody Mary lifted and fell slightly in her hand as though she was offering a silent toast, and then she delivered it to me with notice of ceremony, collecting my four dollars as part of the same efficient gesture.

I thought about a nine-year-old boy I had represented right out of law school. While visiting with him at his foster home, I watched in disbelief as he stepped to the edge of a tall slide, called out to me, and then took an elaborate swan dive, landing headfirst in hard sand. I leaped from the bench to the ground beside him, taking hold of his arm.

"Are you okay?"

Working to bring me into focus, he said of the sand, "I thought it was water."

He was mildly embarrassed, but mostly confused, and even a little amused. Glad that he was not physically injured, I brushed the sand from his forehead and hair and helped him to his feet.

The professionals around me wondered why I was not more concerned about this "hallucination"—why I did not feel the need to rush this boy to the nearest psychiatric hospital and insist that he get some kind of medication. I couldn't explain it to them because I didn't understand my reaction myself. I didn't feel casual about what he had done, exactly. It's just that I had recognized this moment, and I saw his confusion more as a right to be protected than as a symptom to be eradicated. Now, seven years later, I understood. I could see how on that night with Del in her room, I had swallowed many mouthfuls of water before realizing that it was sand. And I would not trade all of the horror of that realization and the pain of what followed for those few moments when I believed we could survive.

Seat-belt indicators went on overhead, simultaneous with the universal single chime that sounded in anticipation of the pilot's announcement. "Remain seated, fasten seat belts, and prepare for more turbulence." I downed my second drink and fell asleep. The next thing I knew, we were landing.

CHAPTER FIVE

Tuesday

The plane landed. Tombstone gray whizzed past the oval window, matching the color of the dream from which I'd just awoken. In the dream, Del and I were at a park. I was a mime dressed in a sari, and I was gesturing to her, communicating something. Now I couldn't remember what I was trying to say. The low-grade hum of the plane's engine, a sudden rush of air, and the rough-and-tumble of the wheels on the runway added to my disorientation and stirred in me momentarily the belief that I was shooting through a portal. Carts piled with luggage zipped by, driven by dark-skinned people in beige uniforms with drenched armpits.

As I exited the terminal and started toward the baggage claim, I saw Katherine Dunn among the many anonymous faces awaiting arrivals. She raised her brows and smiled, surprised, it seemed, that I remembered her. I wasn't. I would recognize Katie forever. And anyway, she looked the same. Like yesterday—the bleached-blond, sun-bronzed, I've-been-at-the-beach-all-day look that had worked so well for us once still clung to her (or her to it). Threadbare Levi's hung off her slim hips. A snug-fitting tank top emphasized her full breasts, slight midriff, and wiry arms. By the time I got to the worn-in flip-flops, I half expected she was wearing a bikini under her clothes and wondered if she still got carded at bars.

I took a breath, steadied myself, felt confused by how nervous just seeing Katie made me feel. Strange, really—the reaches of these early friendships and what insecurities they can stir. I was no longer an adult, married, considering having a child of my own. I was no longer a commissioner responsible for life-altering decisions. I was twelve, and beautiful, blond Katie Dunn was my hero, my sense of myself rising and falling on the whimsy of her approval. One important difference between the then and the now, however, was that I had learned how not to let such vulnerability show. It was even easier once I remembered how angry I had been at her and why.

Moving with intentional casualness, I slung my backpack over my shoulder, walked to a few feet away, and lifted my chin in her direction. "Hey."

"Hey. How are you?" She smiled slightly. She wasn't at all surprised to find me there, and I realized in that moment that she had been waiting for me.

"What are you doing here?"

She nodded, as if she were asking herself the same question.

Friends since the third grade, Katie Dunn, Gail Samuels, and I had attended the same elementary, middle, and high schools. We played soccer together and traveled to tournaments every summer with the team. We knew each other's families, slept over at each other's houses, and did our homework together over the phone on weeknights. I was Katie's best friend and she trusted me, counted on me more than she did anyone else. Still, in high school, when Katie found out that Del and I were lovers, she got mad at me over it and made things worse by talking about it with other people. High school hadn't been easy for either one of us. She was giving guys blow jobs to get rides home from the beach and waking up at the bottom of empty pools without a clue how she'd gotten there. I was expected to show unqualified support and keep her confidences as if I'd sworn in blood. But my being in love with Del was something Katie did not feel the least bit obliged to try to understand. She didn't take the relationship seriously, and she neither protected me from nor helped me with the judgments of others or my pain around the loss. I had never forgiven her for that.

"Norma called me. She said you were coming home to go to Del's funeral." Katie laughed a little, shrugged sheepishly. "What can I say? She's worried about you. She didn't say it directly, but I think she's hoping Gail and I will look out for you around Del's family." Katie's face fixed curiously as she mumbled, "Not sure who's gonna look after me and Gail."

In the background fresh coffee was brewing. The expanding aroma pushed aside the otherwise sterile smell of recirculated air and synthetic carpet. Magazines and newspapers lining the coffee-stand shelves hurled headlines of Bush's lead in the primaries as the Republican nominee. On the other side of the dense glass walls, nimbus clouds gathered, and the August Miami air was thick with moisture. The atmosphere was daunting—a huge, invisible, saturated sponge. I began walking to the baggage claim, signs in both English and Spanish pointing the way.

Katie fell in gracefully beside me. She held her wallet and keys in her hand, and her sunglasses were propped strategically on her head, serving simultaneously as an adornment and an incidental hair band. "You look great. You've lost weight?" She was referring to the thirty pounds I'd gained after Del and I broke up. "I don't think I've seen you this thin since tenth grade."

"I lost it a long time ago."

"Well, we haven't hung out since high school. I hear about you from Gail, but I should have called you or something."

"I haven't been back much."

"No, I know. Norma tells us your visits to Miami are basically layovers on your way to other places."

I laughed appreciatively at my mother's pithiness. I hadn't thought of it quite that way, but it was true. My body was stiff from the flight, and my backpack felt heavier than usual. As I rotated it to my other shoulder, I caught a glimpse of my reflection in the glass wall. My light hair fell in crescents to my shoulders. My face was thinner, my cheeks more hollow. Seeing us side by side, I was surprised to realize at five foot six, I was almost as tall as Katie. She'd always been a lot taller than me. My jeans were bundled loosely at my waist and straight at my ankles, and I was wearing a fitted T-shirt with a long-sleeve button-down open over it. Although I characteristically looked younger than I felt, in that moment, it seemed unusually so. I looked as young, I thought, as Katie did.

"Seems like you talk to my mother more than I do."

"She comes into the deli where we work. And she knows I'm

always glad for news about you." She said this lovingly, and with a tinge of sadness.

When I heard her regret, I stopped and waited.

Katie pressed her lips together and stared at the ground, as if thinking about what to say next. "I've missed you, Jen Jen." Both she and Gail called me that sometimes, and hearing her say it reminded me of how close I had been to her once. "I know you've been mad at me for a long time. I'm sorry I wasn't more there for you." Her blue eyes fixed on me from under long lashes, the earnestness of her apology making it seem as if we'd had the fight yesterday, as if nothing more important had happened in the last fifteen years. "Truth is, I didn't know how to help you. I didn't understand how deep it was between you and Del. I didn't get the problem until it was too late. You always knew how to be there for me. But I didn't know how to be there for you."

Appreciating her now, I felt foolish for my grudge. For some reason, Katie had always been someone I loved for her effort more than for any result. No matter how disappointing she was, I had the sense she was doing her best, and I just forgave her. Except over what happened with Del; her disregard for my feelings about Del, the way she gossiped about us along with everyone else, was a deal breaker. Del had felt betrayed by me; I had felt betrayed by Katie. Del had cut me off; I had cut Katie off. Was this all not just adolescent-girl drama? Could I have expected us at fifteen to have behaved any differently than we did, to have known any better? I stared at her now, having missed her more than I realized, and felt as if I'd been too hard on her.

"Maybe I wasn't so easy to help."

"Well, that's true!" We were turning to walk again. "You could read rejection into anything." And as if citing the definitive authority on the matter, Katie said, "Del was just saying that about you."

"Del?" I balked. "Del made rejection her art form." Then: "What do you mean, Del was *just* saying that? When did you last see her?"

"Oh," she said. Silence. Katie strained to sound nonchalant. "We hung out sometimes."

The air left my lungs, my chest caved in, and I felt my most basic assumptions shatter. Synchronously, like a once-practiced dance the moves of which you're surprised to find you still remember, Katie took hold of my elbow to steady me. My inability to hide my sense of betrayal and anguish compelled Katie to abandon the casual tone and begin explaining.

"She started waitressing at the deli right after Gail did. We got to know each other again. It was no big deal, Jen, really. We only saw her a little. I swear. It was no big deal."

I knew Gail, who was a teller at a bank, had taken a weekend job at the deli to make some extra money to help pay off her new car.

"Gail didn't tell me Del worked there," I said, my chest feeling as if a demolition ball had just dealt it a first major blow. We arrived at the baggage conveyor belt and stood side by side, waiting for my suitcase to appear.

She focused her attention on the bags going by. "Nobody wanted to tell you."

Second blow. This one made my legs a little wobbly. I was beginning to realize this trip would test my hard-earned steel infrastructure in ways I could never have anticipated. The crushing feeling was accompanied by the thought of Del seeming so far away all these years—gone from our lives. No news of her, no idea where to find her, no sense she would want to be found. Now I was being told she'd been right next door, and I was the only one who didn't know it.

"What you're saying is my two best friends were hanging out with Del and didn't tell me."

I saw the slight twist in Katie's face, as I said "best friends." Saying it had surprised me as well. But strangely, I knew it was true. In my current life, I had Madison, and I had many close colleagues, and I had people I hung out with—but friends? Like this? Like Del, Katie, Gail? I was embarrassed to admit it, but no. When Gail had visited me in California a few weeks before, she had said growing up we were like the kids in the *Peanuts* comic strip, raising ourselves and each other. The adults in our lives had been nothing but whiny EKG lines for voices, coming at us from offstage. It was true. We had been responsible for each other. I was there now, with Katie, on our way to Gail's, concerned that Del's daughter needed help, because we still felt responsible for each other.

She squeezed my elbow reassuringly. "You were doing so well, Jenna. You were with somebody else—*finally*. You were happy."

I knew Katie was trying to be supportive. Still, I felt alone and embarrassed at the idea of people handling me and devastated in realizing yet again, yet again the decision to see Del or not had been made for me. I fought my rage, trying to hang in there, forcing myself to notice how hard Katie was trying, telling myself she and Gail didn't know Del would die, that I would never have another chance to…To what? There were things I wanted to say to Del, but I didn't know what they were or why I hadn't tried to find her before now if what I'd wanted to tell her was so important.

"We thought if we told you we were back in touch with Del, you'd want to get back in touch with her, too."

"So what if I did?" I spotted my bag and grabbed it off the belt, then turned and began walking away without concern for whether Katie was following me. Over my shoulder I said, "It was not your decision to make."

"She wasn't in such good shape, Jenna." Katie caught up to me, and we walked without speaking for a while. "Del asked us not to tell you."

"Why?"

"I don't know why. Maybe she was embarrassed about how things had turned out for her."

❖

Heading outdoors to the airport curb was like entering a steam room filled with car-exhaust fumes. Bags disappeared into a slammed trunk, car doors closed, and we were moving forward, but were we really? Katie followed signs for I-95 North—I-95 North, the signifier that for the first twenty years of my life had marked my way home. The tires turned on the car next to us. They seemed to be getting somewhere, but were we? Should I trust this? Was there any traction left to be had on this highway home? It was like a freak attack of claustrophobia, my impulse to bust open the car window and climb out of it, to take some control over the feeling of backward motion or no motion at all. I was desperate for something to happen, some way to counter the static: the static of Miami gray; the static of idling planes and cars; the static of thick windows and recirculated air; the static of time loops, ash-colored corpses, and tires that only appeared to be turning.

I watched the golf-ball-sized soccer ball hanging in a net from the rearview mirror. I hadn't seen one since high school when we all had them. It was one of those identity objects like a keychain or a charm for a bracelet, an item one displays to mark a hobby or a favorite sport, or, for Katie, a period in time. A newspaper article about Del lay on the seat next to me, noticeable only because her picture was included. The article itself was short and buried in articles about the Republican primaries, which had begun to heat up in Florida. Del's hair was full to her shoulders, her eyes were still, with pupils dark and round like the heads of iron nails. What once were subtle laugh lines now were herringboned wrinkles in sprawls around her pronounced eye sockets, cradled by shadowed crescents. She looked at the camera, but her familiar aversion to posing for pictures came through in her expression of capitulation and her typical sarcastic smile.

The headline: "Local woman dies on Lemon Reef." I held the paper in my hand and stared at her image. The article about Del was based on Talon's report to the police. He said that while diving on Lemon Reef, Del suddenly started scrambling to get to the surface. Then she went limp. Del was reportedly too heavy for Talon to pull onto the boat, so he left her body on the swimming ramp extending off the back of the boat and swam to the shore for help. Her body, he said, must have slipped back into the water. She was found seven hours later, a quarter mile southeast of the Sand Dollar Motel on Collins Avenue. Her drifting body apparently had gotten caught on a metal chain attached to debris thirty feet below the surface.

The Sand Dollar Motel referred to in the article was the same motel that my parents had owned and run throughout my childhood. Del and I spent the summer before tenth grade going there to sunbathe and swim. Lemon Reef was located a hundred yards from the shore of the Sand Dollar, and we dove on it every day that summer.

I put the paper down and watched the signs overhead, the veinal interstate and everything around it a wash of gray. The radio station Katie was listening to was called Golden Oldies. The song playing on the radio was "Dust in the Wind" by Kansas. I had landed in a circuitry of both familiar and unfamiliar currents, vaguely and aversively recognizable to me. I twisted through them, my vision corrupted by the glare reflecting from the tinted car window. I eyed the flat, dreary landscape and remembered how all I had wanted from the time I was fourteen years old was to leave this place.

❖

"Where would you go?" Del had asked.

It was the middle of the night. I was sleeping over, as I often did on weekends. We lay on her bed atop the covers, the rest of the house dark and quiet. The window above us was open, amplifying the sound of a car engine revving and people across the street arguing in Spanish.

"California," I said. "San Francisco, probably."

"Why?"

I pulled a pillow over my head to hide.

She giggled, followed me under. "Why are you embarrassed?" Bringing her face closer to mine, "Tell me," she said. "I tell you *everything*."

"They do sex-change operations there."

Del was surprised. "Why would you want one?"

"I don't know."

She just waited, resting her head on the pillow, her lifted brows and slight smile conveying a benign, thoughtful interest. I felt her light breathing on my ear, smelled her toothpaste-tinged breath and freshly shampooed hair. Suddenly risking it was easier than not.

"Then I could marry you."

She hesitated, as if not sure she'd heard me correctly. Then she said, "I'm never getting married," the implications of my confession falling to the wayside.

I just nodded, eager to have the subject change if she so preferred. A few moments passed during which I wasn't quite sure what to do. I certainly wasn't going to repeat myself.

Then Del got up, walked over to her bedroom door, and locked it. I watched disbelievingly, my heart beating staccato, as Del climbed back onto the bed and straddled my body.

"I kinda thought you felt that way about me," she said. "But I wasn't sure."

I lay there looking up at her, my hands in surrender position, my stomach getting whiplash. "Is that weird?"

"I don't know." Her eyes were set firmly on me, her fingers folded in with mine. "I'm a really good kisser. Do you want to see?"

It was all I had wanted for months, and at the same time had not for one moment allowed myself to consider a real possibility. I simply couldn't believe it was happening. It was November of our ninth-grade year. I had just turned fourteen, and I had never been kissed before. My stomach in plummets and halts, I managed to push out of my throat a sound something like uh-huh.

Del pulled her near-dry hair to one side and pressed her lips against my lips—one soft, dry kiss. Then she waited a moment to check my reaction, seemed pleased by my apparently stunned expression. She kissed me again. This time her tongue skirted mine. I came undone, my hands tightening around hers, my breath quickening, my belly lifting, my panties dampening to soaked. More soft, slow kisses, more of her tongue to mine. Then our lips were tenderly opening and closing, tips to full tongues engaging, disengaging, reengaging. She spread her legs out behind her, pressed her full body against mine, and amped up the intensity.

We continued this way more and less intently, intermittently exchanging commentary. Advice from her about how much tongue to use—with examples, homework that was due, recent school gossip, angst over an approaching school performance, recent dreams and what they might mean. My head was propped up by a pillow against the headboard; Del was on her side next to me.

"What's the furthest you've gone with someone?" I asked.

Del hesitated, glanced upward and to the side as if she were thinking about it. Then she said, "I feel funny talking about what I did with somebody else."

I thought her hesitance was because what she had done had been a big deal and she didn't want to admit it. I felt jealous.

"That's fine," I said and tried to mean it. My eyes moved from hers to the dresser, and I studied the wooden statues she had lined there. I noticed a new one, Matsya, the fish, and was just about to ask her about it.

"Joel felt me up once," she said trustingly.

"Shirt on or off?"

"On."

I was surprised.

Del studied my face momentarily. "You thought I'd done more

than that." I couldn't tell if she was angry or hurt. "People say shit about me all the time that isn't true. I don't know why." She propped her head on her elbow. "What about you? What's the furthest you've gone?" She was already starting to giggle because she knew the answer.

"Me?"

Del surprised me then by moving her hand up my T-shirt and touching my breast. Gripping my nipple, she said, "Now we're even."

I felt the zing of her pinch down my center to my groin.

"Not quite."

I began lifting her T-shirt. I wanted not just to touch her but to see her. It was the seeing her that she felt insecure about. She stopped my hand. Her lips folded in and disappeared and her forehead wrinkled with confusion and something like worry.

"Let me." I pushed against her hand on mine.

Del met my words with steely eyes, which warned how vulnerable she felt, and then she let go my hand. I'd seen her naked by way of sneaky glances when we had changed in the same room, but now I stared at her breasts, mildly sloped from her chest to her nipple, rounder underneath. I was love struck. I ran the tip of my finger around her pinkish-brown areola, brushed over her nipple, gently pinched and twisted it. I felt it stiffen and watched it grow erect.

Del moved her abdomen restlessly, made a throaty sound, her breath quickening. She laughed sweetly and said, "I can't believe how good that feels."

Her sounds and movements caused me to shiver with pleasure and sent my stomach whirling. We kissed. She rolled onto me, cupped my breast, and furtively rubbed against my thigh. I rubbed against her enough for an orgasm to trickle out. I don't know whether or not Del came or noticed that I did. We didn't talk about that part.

It was near morning when we were finally too tired to keep going; we just lay there quietly, the full weight of Del's body on mine, the side of her face pressing against my chest.

"Are you sleeping?"

"A little," she mumbled.

"Is it okay, what we did just now, is it okay?"

"Yeah," she said sleepily. "I liked it."

"You're not gonna avoid me tomorrow?"

"No," she said. "I might wanna do it again."

Lazily stroking my cheek with her thumb, her breathing fell constant and smooth.

Trying not to move too much, I used my toes to reach, then my hands to grab a blanket at the foot of the bed. I lifted it over us, held her tighter, and slept, too.

❖

"What did you mean," I asked Katie, "when you said Del wasn't doing well?"

"She just wasn't."

Katie lowered the air-conditioning, cracked her window, and lit a cigarette. Her white-blond hair hung loose around the soft angles of her face and brushed against her shoulders lightly. I watched her put the cigarette between her lips and draw from it. She still made smoking look so good. I hadn't smoked a cigarette since I was seventeen, but I had to consciously resist the temptation to ask for one now, resist the powerful adolescent fantasy this image of her stirred, that mirroring her would magically transform me into being her.

"Del was weird lately, Jenna." Considering further, Katie said, "You know how she always looked amazing?"

Her comment took me by surprise. Katie would never have admitted Del looked good when we were in high school. She was too jealous of her. Del and Katie and, to a lesser extent, Gail were part of a world I, the lesbian-to-be, was oblivious to growing up. It was a world of sundry hair products, shiny jewelry, enthralling perfumes, and tight-fitting sundresses. The objective for most of the girls was to get the boys to look at them—something I couldn't pretend to care about. Sometimes I felt left out, but most of the time I felt relieved to be outside the competition and contempt ricocheting from girl to girl like infinite images in the angled mirrors in department-store dressing rooms.

I smiled and nodded. Del did like it when guys were attracted to her, but dressing up meant more to her than that. She came from a poor family, attended a high school full of rich, spoiled kids, yet managed to set the fashion bar the other girls aspired to. It was just what was understood to be true about Del—boys desired her, girls imitated her. She didn't have a lot of money to spend on clothes, but the clothes she wore, she wore well—class drag. Del was thin, blond, and beautiful, and she could make faded jeans and a threadbare T-shirt look like they came out of a Neiman Marcus window display.

"Not lately." Katie looked at me, her lips drawn tighter. Smoke seeped from the edge of her mouth and disappeared through the crack in the window. "I don't know how to explain it, Jenna. It was really strange. The last few months…I don't know how to explain it."

"Try," I said and then felt embarrassed by the force of my interest.

"Like a nun." Katie couldn't help laughing a little. "I mean"—fighting a creeping smile and offering her bewilderment by a slight upward gesture of an open hand—"Adeline Soto wearing shirts buttoned to her neck." She paused to let it sink in. "Loafers. Her hair was greasy." Katie shrugged, pushed smoke out through her nose this time. "Not a stitch of makeup. No perfume, no nail polish, no jewelry—nothing. It was like she had joined a religious cult or something. In fact, that's what everyone was saying. The only person she saw outside of work was Talon…well and her kid, she was allowed to be with her kid."

"Allowed?"

Katie's attention seemed to shift, and she dropped her hand to her thigh. I looked at it and thought about the amount of time we had spent mocking Katie's spindly fingers, Gail's short neck, my bird's-nest hair, and Del's stubby toes.

"She didn't do anything without Talon's permission." Katie shook her head slightly, slid her blue eyes in my direction. "There is something seriously wrong with that guy," she said. "Two weeks ago Del worked a shift, didn't take her sunglasses off." My stomach tightened, and I lowered my window for air. "These guys, man." She blew out smoke. "They take what they want."

I startled, realizing immediately we were no longer talking about Del. I watched Katie for a minute, almost asked her about an incident in high school I knew had changed her life and about which we had never spoken. I decided not to bring it up.

"Was it unusual for her to be bruised like that?"

"Like that, yes. It was getting worse the last few months. They were splitting up—at least that's what Del wanted. She said she was leaving him. She stayed with him through"—Katie stammered as she spoke—"a lot. You know how it is. They have a kid together. I think that was a big part of it for Del, why she stayed as long as she did."

I nodded. "I'm sure it was the main reason she stayed."

"That's why it's so sad. Del's dead, and he gets the kid, just like that. It doesn't seem right, Jenna. We've been thinking maybe there's something we can do to stop him from taking her. Since you're a judge, maybe you could talk to the police and explain why he wouldn't be the best person for her to be with."

"Commissioner," I said. Then feeling too tired to explain, I added, "I'm not a judge."

"Norma tells everyone you're a judge."

"Yeah, well, Norma's not one for grappling with the nuances."

"We're worried about Khila," Katie said. "That's her name."

"I know."

"She's only ten. If he was capable of beating Del like that, what's to say he won't do the same to Khila?"

I stared out the window, noticed the miles of rooftops. "He's her father. He's allowed to take her."

I heard myself sounding dispassionate, and wondered when feelings had become so irrelevant for me. I looked at the photo of Del next to me on the seat, and the radio began to play "Fooling Yourself (The Angry Young Man)" by Styx. Of all the songs…

Katie turned it up, saying, "I haven't heard this song in a really long time."

Katie'd actually given me this song in high school. It was after we hadn't spoken in a while, and I had been feeling so angry at her, and alone. That she had given me this song meant more to me than she could know. I'd never told her this, but it made a difference to me, pushed me to try harder when I really didn't feel like I could. Katie always seemed self-absorbed, perpetually distracted, like she didn't care about anything. Then, out of the blue, she would say something or do something, like leave a copy of this song in my locker, which would make it clear she'd been paying attention all along. I realized now, looking at her, that her mind skittered because she cared too much—she had a low threshold for painful things. If Katie didn't like what she was seeing or hearing or feeling, she just, metaphorically speaking, changed channels until she landed somewhere else, somewhere easier.

Avoidance had worked for her when we were younger, but her apology to me in the airport, her cryptic comment about men taking what they want, and her concern about Del and Khila made me wonder if it was still working for her.

She blew smoke and said over the music, “I know for a fact Del would not have wanted Khila to go with Talon.” Then she leaned forward and turned up the volume. “This song has always reminded me of you.”

“I remember.”

The clothing, the bruises, Del’s hygiene, the custody threats mixed together in my mind with the lyrics blaring from the speakers. I closed my eyes and leaned my head against the window. If what I was beginning to realize had happened to Del didn’t push me over some emotional edge, I thought, the seventies music just might.

“You should call your mother.” She waited for me to respond.

I nodded absently. “I will,” I said, knowing full well I probably wouldn’t.

CHAPTER SIX

We exited the freeway at Seventy-Ninth Street and headed east through the old neighborhood. I noticed Del's block as we passed it. The old movie theater on the corner was now a Blockbuster Video, and the family-owned convenience store she and I had frequented was a Taco Bell. Small prefab houses with minor variations streamed by, connected like dots by dead lawns, creating the effect of a flip-book. As we continued in the direction of Biscayne Bay, the houses expanded and the distance between them increased. We turned left onto the street I grew up on and drove past sprawling ranch-style homes with long driveways and sculpted landscapes.

For a moment I thought we were going to my parents' house, but before we reached it, we turned again onto a cul-de-sac at the end of which was a small complex of modern town homes with brown wood siding and atypically shaped roofs. The structures reminded me of futuristic gingerbread houses with their sleek architectural design combined with details of cuteness, such as faux window shutters and colorful gates and rain gutters. It was exactly where I would expect Gail to live.

We knocked on Gail's door, waited, knocked again. There was no answer. There were lights on, so I assumed she'd run out for a moment. I called her cell phone. No answer. I called her home phone. No answer. Twenty minutes went by while we speculated as to where Gail might be and continued to try to reach her.

"She knew we were coming?" Katie asked.

"I called her when I landed." I knocked again. No answer. "Just take me to Pascale's," I said, finally.

Katie's expression was equal parts surprise, fear, and recognition that of course I would want that. She blew her cheeks out, nodded, and said, "Let's just hang until Gail gets back. I don't want to go without her. I'm sure she's just held up somewhere. Probably doesn't have her cell phone."

We went back to the car and waited in the speckled shade cast by reaching live oaks. Katie noticed Gail's car in the parking lot, which did confuse her.

"If she's home," Katie said, "why isn't she answering?"

I shrugged, sick of trying to figure it out and preoccupied with the heat. We were in an outdoor oven, and I swear each hour someone notched it up another degree. The air proved resistant to movement. My jeans stuck to my legs. The armpits on my red cotton T-shirt were dark. Sweat gathered at my hairline and rose between my shoulder blades. I felt a bead of perspiration trickle down my spine and then another and another. My intolerance of the heat and wetness that had once been the norm for me served as another reminder of the distance I had put between my childhood and my current life. At the same time, the heat was undeniably enlivening, and I did have an image of myself, as the sweat dribbled down my back, as literally thawing.

Katie stretched her lean, long body out across the hood of her Celica and closed her eyes. Her dark eyelashes drew a stark contrast to her bronze complexion and white-blond hair. I was struck by how familiar she was, even after all this time. I remembered that she slept the same way that she lay now, with one arm slung over her head and her face tucked into the crook of her bent elbow.

My eyes went to the soccer ball hanging from the rearview mirror. I'd been away a long time, but a lot was the same. Katie's father had left when she was not quite two. Her mother supported Katie and herself by working as a waitress at the same deli at which Katie worked now. Katie had started working there after high school. It was supposed to be a temporary thing while she figured out what came next. Nothing had come next.

❖

My phone rang. It was Bea McVee. As I answered, I checked my watch—eleven thirty a.m., which made it eight thirty in California.

Bea said, "So much for being too new to get a complaint. I just walked in to a message machine full of them. Between yesterday and this morning, you managed to piss off the Early Childhood Intervention Program, Women Against Violence, and the Leche lunatics, and then you left town."

"Baxter and Flint," I said. "I switched custody, gave the father temporary sole legal and physical of the nine-month-old girl."

"That explains Early Intervention and WAV."

"She was nursing."

"The mother?"

"The *baby*."

Bea's voice was raspy with impatience. "Those Leches would have me still nursing if they could."

"I guess Margaret Todd is organizing," I said. "We go back a long way. I worked with her on the domestic-violence-death autopsy team for as long as I could stand it. And then we really bumped heads on a case last year. It got a little personal."

I told Bea about the case in which the father had been accused in criminal court of drowning his eight-year-old stepson. "Todd," I said, "represented the mother, and I represented the father. Todd really believed the father had killed this boy. She felt I used the findings of the criminal court expert in our case in order to win, knowing the method he used to determine where the boy's body had entered the water was sketchy at best. It is a new science"—I conceded the point—"but I wouldn't say it's sketchy, and the expert, Jake Mansfield, is internationally reputed."

"I see," Bea said. "Well, she's challenging your finding."

"I would expect as much. I respect Margaret, Bea. If you think I acted rashly, reverse it."

"My only concern right now is if you might have been a little intimidated by Alex Sanders."

"Oh no," I said. "I find Margaret far more intimidating than Sanders."

Bea chuckled. "Good point. Okay, I'll review the record and let you know what I decide."

We hung up just as another call was coming in.

"Where are you?" Gail demanded.

"We're in your parking lot. Where are *you*?"

"I'm here." She was clearly irritated. "In my apartment." There was a brief pause as she realized, "Oh, uh, I've been in the bathroom. I guess I lost track of the time."

"You were in the bathroom all this time?" Katie's eyes popped open. "We're coming in." Classic, I thought. She thinks *we're* keeping *her* waiting.

I hung up the phone and looked at my watch. "Over an hour." To Katie, "What the fuck was she doing in there?"

Our sudden outburst of laughter was disproportionate to the instance at hand. We were laughing about a lifetime of situations similar to this one. Gail behaved like an infant when it came to the demands of time or to necessary frustrations—that is, she just ignored them. Saturday morning soccer games were when we felt it most. Eight a.m. at the regular meeting place, all present and accounted for, except for Gail. The next leg of the journey invariably involved climbing into the van and driving to Gail's house to find her still asleep, or in the middle of breakfast and unwilling to hurry, or in the bathroom. As we waited, eyes rolled and sarcastic remarks flew in rapid succession, swiping every topic from how much she was eating to her preoccupation with masturbation.

Del and I would sit next to each other, playing some word game or delighting in some inside joke, surfers slipped casually under the seat, bare feet furtively touching, the contact either making up for the feeling of having been separated all night or acknowledging having been together all night. The coach, usually in a huff, stormed the front door, and Gail emerged in various stages of dress, dropping a sock here and a cleat there, exaggerating her oohing and aahing as she stepped lightly to protect the overly tender undersides of her bare feet from small, smooth pebbles and overnight-cooled cement.

❖

Gail opened the door. My eyes rested easily and appreciatively upon her mousey brown hair and squat figure.

"Glad to see you still have both legs," I said, referring to the mole. I entered the house as if it were my own, tossed my stuff down on the floor in the living room, and went to get a glass of water. She followed me with a deliberate gaze, more welcoming than not.

The kitchen was small but well appointed, with granite countertops and new appliances. On the refrigerator was a photo of Gail, Katie, and me. We must have been twelve or thirteen. We were on the pool deck at my parents' motel. We were sitting on lounge chairs like ladies, a soccer ball nestled into the space between us, our skin reddish-brown from the sun. Our pubescent bodies were angular and taut, with our bikinis and flat chests, our feathered hair and smirks for smiles. I left the photo and went in search of a water glass. Gail entered the kitchen and found me one.

Filling the cup, I asked, "What took you so long?"

With an impish grin, she said, "When?"

"Before, in the bathroom?"

Katie was standing by the kitchen pass-through. She ran her hand through her hair, her facial expression and body language strongly conveying she didn't want to hear the answer to that question.

"It's my condition," Gail said.

"What condition?"

"Dry tip."

I stared at her in disbelief.

"I'm serious," Gail said. "Milk makes the tips of my shit dry."

Katie and I exchanged looks, simultaneously abandoned all attempts at holding back, and laughed until we cried. When the laughter subsided, I became concerned with being held hostage to Gail's bodily preoccupations all week and demanded, "I want a key!" Katie, in sympathy with me, laughed harder. This was us at fourteen all over again—finding the harshest things about each other the most hilarious. Then the laughter subsided, as if we all suddenly remembered why I was there, and the room filled with an awkward silence that drew us to attention.

Katie helped herself to a Diet Coke from Gail's fridge and tried to get us to focus. "What do we do now? I feel like we should do something."

We moved to the living room, a rectangular space decorated in shades of mauve and gray with a sloped ceiling. The room was furnished with a matching leather couch and chair, a chrome-and-glass coffee table, and a big-screen television with a bookshelf built around it. One wall was sliding glass doors that led out to a patio.

I looked first at Katie and then at Gail. "If you guys are really worried about Khila, I should go see Del's family."

Gail had taken a seat at the dining room table. She nodded agreeably, and then, as if suddenly realizing I'd said something different than what she thought I'd said, stared blankly at me. "Their house? Are you kid…?" She paused, thought about it. Plainly, she said, "You can't go to *their house*."

I met her eyes challengingly, lifted my hands, palms up, to say there weren't a lot of options.

Gail insisted, "Jenna, you can't just go talk to them. You can't go to that house."

"Why not?" Without giving her a chance to answer, I said, "What were you expecting would happen when you called me about Khila? I need to talk to Del's family." I said this emphatically, while privately recalling the shotgun Pascale had greeted me with in our last encounter. I pushed the image from my mind. "If you want me to go to the police or Child Protective Services and make some kind of case for them to investigate whether Talon's a suitable parent, then I need more information."

"You can't go to Pascale's house," Gail said, she and Katie exchanging a look I didn't understand. "You're not welcome there." Gail was sitting in a straight-back chair, leaning her broad shoulders and large breasts forward. "I'm serious, Jenna. They'll hurt you." Her hands pushed down on the air for emphasis.

"I've never understood why," Katie said more calmly, "but Pascale always blamed you for Del's problems."

My head jolted in her direction. "What?" I was nodding slowly and trying not to spiral into a fury. "So was I the problem before or after Pascale's daily binges and beatings?"

❖

The first time I was present for one of these binge-and-beat episodes, the fight had started over then nine-year-old Nicole not liking her dinner. It was enough—aided by several beers—to tilt the already-leaning Pascale over some invisible edge and send her into an injured rage. Ida and Nicole disappeared into their room, while Del, only fourteen years old, placed herself between her mother and the fleeing girls and tried to tell Pascale there wasn't anything to get so angry about. When reason failed, Del resorted to provocation to ignite

Pascale to get whatever this was over with. Stepping in this way was not exactly a conscious thing on Del's part—no more so than the use of one's blinker while driving, or the placement of one's fingers on the piano keys while playing a well-practiced piece.

"Mom, you're drunk." Del moved her body sideways to prevent Pascale from entering the hallway in the direction of Ida and Nicole's room. Twenty-two-month-old Sid was screaming from his high chair. Del glanced in my direction and said, "Can you get him?"

As I lifted Sid from his chair, I heard Pascale, her tone one of thinning restraint, her accent accentuated from rage. "Move. Get out of my way, Del. Get out of my fucking way." Pascale's thin, muscular figure angled to get past, her focus set on Nicole's bedroom door. "No matter what I do for you kids, it's not enough."

I held Sid and rocked him, and he quieted some.

Del nodded her head and steadied her eyes. Her expression impassive, she said, "Why do you have to drink? This is why my father left you—and us." I backed up from where I was standing, tripping over one of Sid's toys as I butted up against the television set. Sid was watching Del and his mother, his black eyes still and frightened.

Silence, as if Pascale was translating for herself what Del had just said to her, then an explosion: "That son of a bitch didn't leave me. I threw *him* out." Pascale lunged, seized hold of a fistful of Del's hair, and yanked. Del's head seemed momentarily detached and flying through space, arching up and over, the rest of her body dangling like the string from an accidentally let-loose helium balloon. I was stunned and then repulsed by the sickeningly comical nature of the image. Sid started screaming again.

Pascale slammed Del into the wall, yelling threats in Spanish, French, and English—whichever language came quickest to her. She punched and slapped at Del's head and face repeatedly. Del yelled for her to stop and tried pushing Pascale away, resorting finally to crouching down to the floor and folding over in order to protect her face and body from the salvo of flying fists and clawing nails. Pascale came to an abrupt halt, as if she'd forgotten what she was doing. She had a disoriented look and she was breathing hard; she was trying to catch her breath.

Del was curled up against the wall with her arms covering her head. The sudden stillness drew Del out; she peeked up to see if it was over. Pascale said something in French under her breath. Del covered her face again as Pascal cranked back her leg, the image of the cranking leg mimicked—caricatured—by its shadow, cast against the near wall. I could see coming what Del could not, yelled, "No," as Pascale uncoiled, ramming the pointed toe of her shoe into Del's side. Del folded in on herself and howled. Sid screamed.

Pascale looked around, as if to see where the noise was coming from. When she saw my face and Sid's her own sobered momentarily, as if she'd forgotten we were there. I couldn't tell if it was regret or maybe shame at having behaved this way in front of a guest or at all, or just exhaustion, but Pascale suddenly turned and said, "Fuck it. I don't need any of you." She stumbled about for her keys, her departure underscored by the sound of a slamming door. The cold December air rushed in and then evaporated.

I was standing there, stunned as much by the rapidity of the scene as the violence. Del lay doubled over on the floor, back to the wall, hair in tangles, nose running, face soaked with tears and snot and spit—and blood. She was sobbing, holding her side and making these small noises that struck me as similar to the noises she made when I fondled her. As I told myself this was one of those times when you're supposed to comfort someone, I was struck by the disgust I felt toward Del in that moment. Holding Sid tighter, I inched closer to where she lay. Del stood up, ignored us, threw her frazzled hair back, and disappeared into the hallway. Sid reached after her, still crying. The bathroom door closed emphatically behind her, the light emanating from the bathroom shrinking to black behind the sound as it shut.

Some moments later, Del's silhouette reemerged with her composure restored. She opened the door to the younger kids' room and, without looking in, announced lightly, "She's gone."

Del came out to the living room. I could tell by her uneasy expression and downcast eyes she was dreading having to face me. But when she saw me she recognized *me*, and I sensed she regained hope and felt relieved to have me there with her.

Rather than comfort or reassure Del, I yelled. "Why did you provoke her like that?"

Del's face fell. She backed away into the hallway and said, "Just go home." She disappeared into her room and closed the door.

I tried to go in behind her, but the door was locked. I put Sid down and knocked. "Del," I said, "open it. Open the door." I knocked more.

Sid had his hand on my leg and was peeking at Del's door from behind me. Ida and Nicole came out of their room. Nicole disappeared toward the kitchen and reappeared with a paper clip she had untwisted into a piece of straight metal. She pushed me out of the way and slipped the metal into a little hole at the center of the doorknob. A quick click sounded and the door opened. Del lay on her back on her bed, a tissue inside her nose red from new blood. Sid ran to the bed to see her. Ida ran behind him, scooped him up and took him out.

Del sat up, wincing at the pain in her side. "Get out." I stared at her. "Get out of here." She began pounding her feet on her bed and crying harder, the blood gushing more. She looked at me and screamed, "I don't want you to see me like this."

The gouges in her face, the blood running onto her lips, the swelling already noticeable under her eye, all I could think to do was what she asked me to do. I backed up and closed her door.

The plan had been for me to sleep over as I usually did on weekends. We spent our nights at Del's house, because her father was gone more and more and Pascale was either working at a night job or so plastered by midnight that the house could've burned down and she wouldn't know it. Del was reluctant to sleep out; she didn't want to leave her sisters and brother alone. Having no intention of leaving Del alone, I joined Ida, Nicole, and Sid in the living room. The girls and I played cards for a long time. Sid played with his trucks, moving them around and making *rrr, rrr* sounds. At some point, the four of us fell asleep on the living room floor watching an Elvis movie that was mostly static and snow because the reception was poor. Sometime around one or two, I woke up and went to Del's room. She was in bed reading. She didn't say anything to me, but she did move closer to the wall to make room for me beside her.

I was lying on my side staring at her pinup of Robert Plant when Del finally started talking to me.

"It wasn't always like this," she said softly. "My mother has a kind of amazing history. Did you know that Pascale is part Canadian Indian? Her tribe was Cree. Crazy Horse is her great-grandfather."

"What?" I turned over and looked at her. "Was she drinking when she told you that?"

Del laughed. "She didn't tell me. *Abuela* did." She was referring to her grandmother on her father's side. Del seemed relieved to be looking at me, as if she'd missed me. Her tone was soft and intimate and comfortable. "My dad said it's true. Crazy Horse went into Canada for a while, and he met up with the Cree tribe. My aunt told my dad their great-grandmother had this affair with him when she was sixteen years old and got pregnant with their grandmother. So my mother and her siblings are his great-grandchildren." Del paused, reconsidered the generational math, laughed a little at how confusing it was. "Things changed for them when my grandmother married this man who turned out to be really brutal with her and with his kids. He broke my grandmother's spirit and, you know, then she couldn't protect her kids."

Del was talking about Pascale's history of having been beaten when she was a girl, several of her bones broken, some of which had never healed properly. Del thought Pascale couldn't help herself when she got so out of control, she needed the release. Getting moral about it, Del said, didn't help. In her mind, they were all doing the best they could to stay together as a family.

The anger was gone. Del's attention was adoringly honed on me. Her gold eyes shimmied, then fixed on my face. She swallowed as if working toward a courageous next step and admitted, "I didn't really want you to leave before. I never want to be away from you. I need you, Jen." She had never been so candid or so clear in expressing feelings for me before. Del raised her finger to her lip and felt the place where I could see a wide crack that was crusting with dried blood. The skin under her eye was bluish and swelling. Some skin on her nose and her forehead had been scraped, leaving deep gouges that were pink and raw. She went on. "I didn't know what it meant to be close to someone until now." Del watched for my reaction, her words now flowing easily and confidently. "Please don't be mad at me, Jenna. I can't handle the feeling that I let you down." Del smiled sadly, leaned her forehead against mine. She touched my hair, wrapped her finger in a ringlet, kissed me, forgetting and then sharply remembering her cut lip. I tasted blood.

I'd like to say that I matched Del in dignity and depth, that I met her where she deserved to be received in that moment. I wish I had apologized for abandoning her earlier that evening when she looked for me. I wish I had held her, stroked her hair, told her I needed her, too. I didn't do any of those things. All I could think about as she spoke, her heart obviously broken, was the scant T-shirt and panties between her skin and mine. By that time in December, we'd made out, touched each other, mostly over our panties. I wanted more but felt too shy to do anything about it.

It was with Del in this wounded and vulnerable state that I rolled on top of her, stripped her T-shirt up and off, bit at her nipples until she winced and withdrew. I yanked her panties down, felt her insides for the first time, pushed my fingers into her without concern for her comfort, her privacy, or her pride. Del neither participated nor resisted but made of herself a line to be crossed. I began pushing her legs apart and bringing my mouth to her. I guess that was the line.

Del sat upright and yell-whispered, "I don't want you to do that."

I was staring at her clit, my tongue in reach. "Why not?"

"Just don't! Get off me." She closed her legs and slid out from under me. Her anger surprised me, and I sat up to find her eyes. She was out of bed and pulling her clothes on, still favoring her side where she had been kicked. "I think I've hit my exposure limit for one day."

My hand smelled strong, and I noticed her shit under my fingernail. I felt momentarily confused, and then I realized how it had gotten there. I started to sob. I was deeply ashamed. "Del, I'm sorry," was all I could say.

"You're *sorry*?" Del was more perplexed by that, it seemed, than anything else that had just happened. "I just want to forget about it." She left to take a shower.

I cried and at some point fell asleep. When I woke up the next morning, Del was spooning me. I heard her breathing in my ear, could feel her pressed against my back, her arm and leg wrapped around me, holding me protectively. I was relieved then, told myself I was good again, stole her forgiveness, and ran.

❖

I said, "It was not my fault things went so wrong for her."

Gail sighed loudly. "I can't believe we're still trying to understand why Adeline Soto did the things she did, or whose fault it was. Who cares why, anyway? It wasn't easy for any of us, and we're not taking our fucked-up childhoods out on the rest of the world."

"In the same ways," I said.

Gail responded sharply, "Yeah, well, that matters."

Does it? I thought of Mr. Baxter and Ms. Flint and Angie and how my decision had turned their lives upside down. For the better? I would never know.

Katie chimed in. "It's not what you think, Jenna. You've been gone for a long time. You don't know what all's gone down with that family. They're out of control."

I laughed. "They've always been out of control."

"No, not like this," Katie said. "Not like they are now."

I took a deep breath. "Look, you don't have to protect me. I'm gonna need to know what Del was involved in if I'm gonna try to do something about Khila going off to Texas with her father. That's gonna happen unless you can come up with a damn good reason why it shouldn't." I looked at Gail and said, "You called me."

"Oh, right," she scoffed. "As if you ever would have forgiven me if I hadn't."

I could hear the blood coursing through my ears and feel heat starting at my center and emanating to my limbs. So typical, I thought. She entreats me to leave on the next plane, offers her home, tells me that I'm Khila's only hope, and then she experiences my being here as a burden and as evidence that I'm still stuck and miserable.

To Gail, "Why didn't you tell me you were back in touch with Del?"

"You really want to know? Because she was unhappy. She was leaving her husband, and I didn't want you anywhere near that."

"But *that* I could have helped her with. I don't know that we can do anything for Khila now, or even that Khila would want us to. For all we know, she's a daddy's girl, glad to have him all to herself."

"Del asked us not to talk to you about her."

"Do you have any idea why?"

"I assume because she didn't want to be back in touch with you."

"So why should I help, then?"

"Because no matter what, she would not have wanted Khila to go to Texas with this man."

Katie interrupted us. "Del and Talon were involved in some kind of drug thing, and they brought her little brother Sid into it. Do you remember this kid, Tom?" Katie asked. "He was younger than us, and he lived down the block from you. We used to see him around. He had brain damage, I think—totally uncoordinated. And he had a killer crush on Del."

"Of course I remember him." I pictured the skinny, wobbly boy with arms turned out and legs turned in. "He was sweet. He used to help my mom bring in groceries. What about him?"

"He's dead," Katie said, without a hint of sentiment. Her eyes were like cobalt stones. She sat back, leaned into the couch, and crossed her arms. Then she recounted the facts. "Tom's mother used to drop him off at Bayside Plaza to watch movies. Genius Talon decided to use Tom as a runner at that mall because of course the police would never suspect him. He got Del to ask because he knew Tom would do anything for her.

"The next thing we knew, Tom was found dead in an alley behind the mall covered in blood and soaked in piss." Katie twisted around and stretched her legs out on the couch. "Some guys who were there said that it was Sid who beat Tom. They said Sid just went crazy, started hitting Tom out of nowhere. Sid swore that he was not even at the mall when this thing went down. He told the police he was with Del at her house. Del denied it. After Del denied that Sid was with her, Sid took a plea."

Katie looked squarely at me. "Del let Sid go to prison for life, Jenna. She *helped* Talon frame her little brother for murder."

"That's not all," Gail said. "Ida works at a massage parlor. Rumor is she's a prostitute. And Nicole has been in and out of prison and psych wards over the past several years. She had her first break about five years ago." Gail thought for a moment. "All we're saying, Jen Jen, is they're not the same people they were when you knew them."

Del was dead, Sid was disappeared, Ida and Nicole likely faced similar fates. What upset me most was that Katie and Gail had described exactly what I would have expected to come of these lives, had I allowed myself to think about it. I *had* known all along, in fact, as I kept my distance and demonstrated to myself—with a steady stream of accomplishments, affiliations, and acquisitions—that those things were not happening to me.

I say this not to belittle the friendships my present life is buoyed by, nor to trivialize the successes that, unlike many people, I will never have to doubt I have earned, nor to call into question the sincerity of my love for Madison, with whom, almost always for better rather than worse, I have been smitten since the day we met. No one takes a step without crushing bone. I am merely avowing the remains that have afforded me the traction without which one cannot dwell upon the earth.

"I'm going to see Pascale," I said flatly.

CHAPTER SEVEN

We were expecting a crowd, but there was none. It was five thirty when we approached, the house quiet—uninhabited, I would have thought, based on its state of disrepair. An old, gray Dodge with all four tires removed rested on cinder blocks implanted into the pebble driveway. Rust, like acid, seeped through the driver's side door and beyond. Black Sabbath screamed murder from the house next door, causing its walls to shake and the ground to vibrate.

Del's body was at the medical examiner's office. Pascale had let it be known that the family would hold an open house that night for people to stop by. When I decided to make the trip I had imagined a big funeral—an event at which I could have gone unnoticed, a church somewhere with a lot of people milling around. I envisioned myself with time to get a feel for things, to see Pascale, Ida, Nicole, Sid, maybe even Del's father, Andre, before they saw me, and to make contact only if it seemed right or even possible. Now I was walking straight for the front door of the tiny, near-vacant living room and felt conspicuous already.

Gail, about to knock, asked, "Are we the only ones here?" She looked at me. "It's not too late, we can still…"

The door opened.

A tall woman with short reddish-brown hair and square-framed glasses large for her face peered out at us. A smile formed as she acknowledged first Gail and then Katie. Reaching me, her eyes lingered with confusion, and then an almost imperceptible lift in her forehead suggested something else. Suspicion? I stood quietly and watched Pascale as she grew increasingly certain she recognized me. She should have recognized me. I was a little taller, maybe a little thinner, and definitely paler. But my hair was the same—light brown, shoulder length, curly. I had the same green eyes and round face, the same smile.

And I had been close to her once, found my place within these thin walls, tiny rooms, and one bathroom for six—including me, seven—people. I had nestled my way inside this home, in which the crowdedness, the deprivation, the chaos, even the violence converged into a thick mélange of fraught but passionate attachments and fierce loyalties. Pascale had considered me one of her own, insisted I call her Mom. She had come to rely on my cooperative spirit, good grades, and supposed moral certitude as examples to the others. She expected me in the afternoons, cooked the dinners she knew I liked, enjoyed having me around there. I had felt more loved in this house than I did in my own—more seen and appreciated.

Now she crossed her arms, shook her head from side to side, and said, "How do you like that? Look what death dragged in." Her accent was as heavy as it had ever been.

Gail was eyeing the car. She backed up a few steps to secure herself an unobstructed escape route.

"We mean you no disrespect," Katie started to say. "Jenna has come all the way from California…"

But I remembered her, knew her comment to me was an invitation, that she was actually glad to see me. "Hello, Pascale," I said matter-of-factly.

"So you're a lawyer, I hear." I nodded. She continued, "Del's little girl, my grandbaby, belongs with us."

At first, I didn't understand the comment. Then I realized the reason Pascale was glad to see me was because she had a plan and she needed me to help make it happen: she wanted custody of Khila. My confusion became awe as I began to wonder if I was there because Pascale wanted me to be. Had she orchestrated this reunion? It had struck me as odd when Gail was among the first people Nicole notified after Del died. But it made sense if Pascale had told Nicole to call Gail, because Gail was her most direct link to me. This family did not ask for help easily, but they needed it now. And the only way Pascale could let me be involved was if she thought I thought it was my idea.

"The law is on her father's side, but I can try." Accepting the challenge and hearing it as the invitation back into the fold I'd given up on a long time ago, I boldly stepped past Pascale into the tiny living room and left Gail and Katie, mouths agape, in the doorway. Now inside a space small and cluttered, the immediacy of the walls and the drop of the ceiling left me jarred and disoriented. The room was shrinking around me. No, I'd remembered this house as much larger than it was.

Pascale came as close to pleading as I imagine she ever could. "I was raising her, Jenna. When Khila wasn't with Del, she was with me. He can't just take her away."

Nicole appeared from the hallway. Blondish-brown hair lightly brushed her shoulders, and slight features and light eyes gave her an appearance of innocence and serenity that contrasted with the message the rest of her sent. Multiple silver studs outlined the rim of her right ear, a silver chain choked her lean neck, and she wore blue jeans and a tight-fitting zip-down black leather vest with nothing underneath. A leather purse hung at her hip from a thin strap across her chest.

Focused as I was on her attire, I didn't see Nicole's fist until it struck the bone under my right eye. My head lunged backward, and pain ricocheted through my ears and eyes and down my neck. My hands were fists, even before I felt overtaken with rage. White noise buzzed in my ears; I saw double as I forced myself to my senses quickly enough to protect myself from an anticipated second blow.

But as she came into focus, I saw Nicole standing calmly, arms folded neatly, waiting for me to join her. Then I noticed her fingers twitching and her mouth tightening and releasing. She twisted her neck slightly, jutted her chin, then dropped it to her chest. Neurological symptoms. I recalled what Gail had said earlier about Nicole having been in and out of psych wards, and I recognized the movements as side effects of antipsychotics, telltale signs of her life since I'd last seen her. My rage dissipated as quickly as it had flashed, replaced by a sadness so heavy it made a canyon of my heart.

"Where the hell have you been?" she demanded.

Calmer now, I knew the slug was Nicole's way of saying how desperately she had needed me these past years and how much I had let her down by disappearing.

"I missed you, too," I said, feeling the side of my face, slowly sliding my jaw from side to side. "Still the wild child, I see."

Katie, barely in the door, looked stunned. She ran her fingers through her fine white hair, blew out a breath. Gail, by the dining room table, glared at me, conveying an "I told you so."

Shaking her head with disgust, Pascale said, "I told you not to do that, Nicole." Then, while looking at me, she added, "How can we ask Jen to help us now? I told you, I can't afford a fucking lawyer." She turned the bottle of beer she was holding upside down and sucked from it. Her comment was not exactly comforting, but it did confirm my suspicion that I had been summoned.

Nicole ignored Pascale. She tightened her lips, squinted and shook her head. "Talon is *not* gonna get away with this. He killed her. I know he did. He did it for some fucking insurance money."

Katie walked over and nervously offered me a cigarette, which I considered and then declined. She put one in her own mouth and lit it with a shaky hand. "Okay," she stammered, "let's just everyone calm down."

Still cloudy from the punch, I wasn't sure I'd heard Nicole right. "What are you talking about?"

"He *killed* her. And now he's taking her kid to butt-fuck Texas."

Nicole's fists clenched, then released, and she shuffled from foot to foot, irritably. Her head jerked and her eyes rolled up in her head, then back. Muscle spasms and facial tics marked the ways she'd aged more than time did.

Gail's disbelieving expression said these were the rantings of a lunatic. Gail had rested her hand on the dining room table. Now her face was bent with disgust, and she was frantically trying to remove from that hand some substance it had come into contact with. It looked to me like chicken shit, but I didn't dare say.

"Well"—wiping her hand against her shorts—"*is* there insurance money?" She checked, wiped, checked, wiped. With Gail's germ phobia, I was just glad the chickens were outside, or we'd have been dealing with a catastrophic health crisis for the next week. Katie sat down on the forest-green couch, the cigarette tilted between her fingers. She too was watching Gail and trying not to laugh.

"Two hundred thousand dollars," Nicole blurted out.

"How do you know?" I asked.

"Del told Ida about it."

Pascale nodded along emphatically from where she was perched on the arm of the couch near Katie. Her body framed by the large picture window behind her, she gestured unenthusiastically toward an open envelope sitting on the table. "Says she had a heart attack and drowned." Pascale muttered on about how impossible it was for Del to have died the way the medical examiner said she did. Her anger exaggerating her accent. "They don't know what they're doing. I told those kike doctors I don't understand half of what is written there. No one will explain anything." She got more and more worked up until she was yelling and hurling insults in different languages at no one in particular.

I removed the document from the envelope and studied it.

"This is a preliminary autopsy report."

Pascale nodded.

"Already?"

Gail stepped in closer and read over my shoulder. "I've heard that drowning deaths in Miami get some kind of priority. It has something to do with encouraging tourism—or maybe not discouraging tourism. Something about tourism."

I laughed. "Reassurance Miami style—guaranteed a quick autopsy if you or a loved one drowns?"

Now Gail was staring at me.

"What?"

Smugly, she said, "Your cheek's a little swollen."

I could feel the tenderness in my cheekbone. I glared at Nicole as I left Pascale with her escalating and increasingly nonsensical ranting to go to the bathroom to see the damage for myself. On the way, I noticed the door to what had once been Del's bedroom was ajar. I pushed it open, half expecting to find Del there. When I didn't, it was crushing, like abruptly awakening from a dream in which I'm holding her, only to realize I'm hugging air.

I entered and looked around. The furniture was different. The room smelled of cigarette smoke and stale beer. It was smaller even than I'd remembered it, crowded further by an unmade double bed with stained sheets. The tired antique-white paint was peeling; the faded linoleum floor was torn in places and curling upward around the edges. Curtains yellowed from humidity, dust, and sun covered the jalousie windows from which one or two slats were missing. An insect screen provided a false impression of security. A small dresser held a framed photograph of Del from more recent years. She was holding a little girl—the near likeness of her—securely on her lap, smiling, her eyes looking to something beyond the camera.

From the window behind me, I heard Spanish music and kids talking and laughing. I looked out to the lawn across the street where a group of adolescent boys and girls faced each other in two lines, boys in one, girls in the other. A woman was instructing them in a dance routine. The kids were silly but mostly paying attention, some of the girls much taller than the boys. I heard someone say the word *cumpleaños*, so I assumed this was a rehearsal for a *quinceañera*. Del had been planning hers when I met her, but by the time she did turn fifteen, her parents' marriage had deteriorated and Pascale's drinking had become a daily event. Del's father Andre gave Del a silver-link necklace for her birthday, and Pascale did bake a cake on the day itself, which we had with dinner. But it was Norma, at that time still immensely fond of Del, who decided to throw her a party.

❖

We celebrated Del's fifteenth birthday at the Sand Dollar Motel. Norma and Mel provided all the food and drinks and a big cake, and we invited a bunch of friends to a night party on the pool deck. It was January 1983, and *Thriller* was hitting the top of the charts. Michael Jackson's voice amplified from a bulky portable cassette player while a bunch of people did the moonwalk off the diving board into the heated pool. Katie was off on the beach with Jason Schwartz, a football player she was dating. Andrew Torie and John Mason sat on opposite sides of Del vying for her attention. I watched Del flirting in two directions at once. Upset and jealous, I left to take a walk on the beach with Gail and our other soccer friends, Edie and Susan. We put rum in our Cokes and drank as we walked.

"Brent was hilarious." Susan was laughing and talking at the same time. "Did you see him on his hands on the diving board?"

"I saw you seeing him," Edie teased.

They had been best friends since kindergarten.

"Yeah, and? Maybe I think he's cute," Susan said.

"You're being quiet, Jen Jen." Gail tilted her cup to her mouth and took a swig.

Mostly, I didn't like getting high or drunk, because even back then

I worried about feeling out of control, but I was quiet about all that. I'd developed strategies for looking the part—holding a drink in my hand, passing a joint nonchalantly without ever really having hit on it. As was typical, I had taken a sip of the drink I was holding and then surreptitiously tossed the rest some distance back. Now, with images of Del squeezed between John and Andrew making my gut twist, I regretted it.

"Pour me some of yours."

"You finished that whole cup?" Gail shook her head and poured. "Be careful or your parents'll catch you."

The air was cold, but mild. The sand was soft and almost white, reflecting the moonlight. I noticed couples we knew disappearing into or emerging out of the sea grape caves that outlined the beach—shirts being rebuttoned, zippers being zipped. Katie and Jason were one such couple, and I watched them giggle and cling as they made their way into the dense, leafy caverns. It would never be like that for Del and me, I thought. We would never be that public or that unself-conscious about our feelings for each other. We would never be admired and envied for how cute we were together. We made out, fondled each other in her room at night, but it didn't seem to register as anything. Del, I was convinced, would cut me off physically the minute a guy got her attention. In fact, Del hadn't been on a date since our first kiss that past November. She hadn't had a boyfriend since the summer when we started spending all our time together. Recently she had told me she didn't want to date anyone, she felt better about herself now than she ever had. In that moment, with Del on the pool deck flanked by Andrew and John, these details seemed purely coincidental to how close she and I had become.

On our way back to the motel, we ran into Del walking with John on the beach. She had his jacket on for warmth. He had his hand on the lower part of her back, and she was leaning into him and laughing at something he had said. When I heard her laughter, I shrank inwardly, felt myself fragment into tiny pieces. The conversation started in my head. I began preparing to let her go, began telling myself it was bound to happen. A moment later I was angry that she would do this to me—just trash us like that.

When she saw us, Del stiffened and pulled away from John. "Hey," she said, mostly looking at me.

I jutted my chin at her, uttered an effortful *hey*. Bombs were exploding all around us, but no one else could hear them.

"We're just going for a walk," Del said. To me, "Do you wanna come?"

I continued past her, just her eyes following me. "We just got back." Someone announced from the pool deck that Norma wanted to cut the cake.

Del shrugged at John and said, "Oh well."

Norma lit the candles and Del stood over the cake, surrounded by my parents and maybe twenty of her high school friends who now sang "Happy Birthday" to her. John was next to her, holding her drink. I stood quietly off to the side watching her face in the candlelight, the slope of her nose, the fullness of her lips, the soft angles of her cheekbones. I was wearing a sweater she had loaned me and it had her scent. I tucked my nose inside the collar and breathed in a mixture of her detergent, her faded cologne, her soap, her bed sheets. When the song ended, someone said to make a wish. Del waited and seemed momentarily disoriented and dismayed, her eyes searching the crowd. When she found me her face softened. I smiled at her. She pulled her hair out of the way and blew out the candles.

It was after midnight when the last people left. Norma had arranged for a room for us to have a sleepover after the party. She and Mel took the room next to ours. Katie and Gail shared one double bed; Del and I shared the other. Katie was already crashed out on booze and pot. Gail, also drunk, was facedown next to her. Del and I lay awake staring at the ceiling, not saying anything.

Del sat up and whispered, "Come outside with me. I need to talk to you."

I was scared of what she was going to tell me, thought for sure she was going to confide in me about her feelings for John. My role as a placeholder was about to become obsolete. I pulled on sweats and reluctantly followed her out. We walked to the edge of the deck and stood side by side, leaning on the banister and looking at the ocean. The waves crashed on the shore; the air was soaked with salt and mild fish scents. The moon was a perfect crescent, a hint at something brighter to come.

"So, whad'ya wanna talk about?"

"This was the best birthday party." Del lifted her face and it brightened in the squinting moonlight. "Nobody's ever done anything like this for me before." She gingerly fingered the silver-link necklace her father had given her. "I thought it was gonna be such a sad birthday. But it wasn't. It was the best birthday, and I feel really happy." She waited for me to respond.

"Is that what you wanted to talk about?"

"Yeah, why?"

She was *thanking* me. Hadn't she known I'd been twisted in knots for hours, traveled all over the map? I'd gone from rage at her and wanting to be rid of her, to frightened of losing her, to missing her so desperately I couldn't breathe right. I had planned a breakup speech and a reconciliation speech simultaneously. I had lived through apocalyptic visions of my life without her in it. And there she was, not angry, not leaving, not talking about someone else she could conspicuously disappear into the sea grapes with. Just thanking me.

"John," I said.

"What about him?" Then Del realized why I was asking. "He doesn't matter."

"What does matter?"

Del dropped her chin and raised her eyes at me, a slight smile tilting the edges of her lips upward. "You know what matters." She squeezed my hand.

I felt her touch in every nerve ending, my stomach in tumbles. There had been that night a few weeks before when I had been horrible, tried to suck her after she'd been beaten up. We didn't talk about it again after it happened, but since then I had been leaving it up to Del to initiate anything physical between us. She seemed to know and to feel reassured by it. Now I stared at her lit by the moon, her shiny hair falling against her soft cheeks, her pupils large and encircled in gold. I couldn't resist.

"Come with me."

I led her to the stairs down to the beach. When our feet touched the sand I kissed her. Del pulled her head back slightly and stared at me; her breath was quick and audible. She seemed flustered by the kiss, and I wasn't sure at first if she had liked it. But then she cast a tender glance at me, and I knew she'd been moved in a way that surprised and pleased her. A wave crashed against the shoreline, reaching halfway to the motel seawall. The foam stretched out even farther and drenched our bare feet. The ocean was icy in the winter, and we did a little dance and leaped back to the motel seawall, where we landed on soft, dry sand and stood looking at each other and laughing.

Suddenly serious, I said, "Happy birthday, Del." I felt shy about what I was about to do, offered hesitantly, "I have a present for you." I took a deep breath. "A poem. I wrote you a poem." Her face opened with anticipation. My heart pounded and my hands shook. I blew out one quick breath. "Okay," I said more to myself. "Here goes." I lowered my eyes and steadied my voice:

I watched you sleeping on sun-warmed sand,
I wanted to be the towel upon which you lay,
I wanted to be the sunlight that your skin soaks in.

With you there and me here, I yearned
To mold our bodies like soft clay into one shape
With rounded edges and hollow spaces
In which small things—small treasures
Could safely, easily be concealed.

Like fog rolling in over hilltops in distant lands,
Sea foam covers our tumbled sandcastle,
And you breathe away the minutes,
As if we have forever.

I brought my eyes to hers. She was listening intently, her lips slightly parted, her brows raised with wonder. I said more slowly and confidently now:

When I look at you,
When I really look at you,
I know we do.

Del seemed stunned. There was silence but for the waves. I waited for her to say something—the longer it took, the more foolish I felt. Finally, I just asked, "Do you like it?"

Now Del had a delicate, almost pained expression; her breath was rapid. She nodded while blurting out, "I think I love you."

It was something neither of us had said before. She kissed me. I could feel the force of her whole body behind it, the intensity and decisiveness of her desire in the strength of her hands on my neck and the eager draw of her lips and press of her tongue against mine. My knees folded; we fell to the sand with her on top of me. She slid her hand down the front of my sweats and watched my face as she stroked my clit, entered me, stroked, entered, stroked, until I was chasing my breath and shaking under her.

"I love you," she whispered, her finger sliding on me, our gazes affixed as I came.

Afterward we sat with our backs pressed against the seawall. I was holding her hand, studying her gnawed fingernails.

"There's something I've been meaning to tell you." I glanced at her and then away. "I still feel bad about what I did. You know, that night a few weeks ago. I'm not apologizing," I added quickly. We both laughed a little. "I just want you to know I won't do anything like that again."

"It sucks that you had to see that the other night."

"It sucks that you have to go through that. Have you ever told anyone, a teacher or anybody?"

She shook her head. "I just have to keep the family together until my father comes back. My mom's really different when he's around. I think she's just so hurt right now because she still loves him." Del pressed my fingers. "You can't tell anyone. Okay?"

I nodded. "What you said before, that you love me. As a friend?"

She laughed. "Yeah, I finger-fuck all my friends." Then she said, "It's more than that. You get to me." Del touched my hair and then rested her hand on my shoulder. I was looking away now but could feel her watching me, my heart pulsing blood like a jellyfish jetting in a tide, my stomach undulating. Then she said, "Your poem…It's beautiful, Jen." She recited slowly, "One shape with rounded edges and hollow spaces in which small things, small treasures could safely, easily be concealed." I looked at her amazed. She'd heard it *once*. Then she said sweetly, "Like a baby."

Not what I was thinking when I wrote it, but it seemed right. I brought her hand to my cheek, kissed it, said playfully, "I *wish* I could have a baby with you."

She laughed lovingly, leaned into me. "Maybe it'll be possible someday."

❖

I was staring at the photo of Del and Khila when a face hooked around the door frame. "There you are," Ida said. She entered the room, her red hair brightening the gloomy space. I startled, quickly recognizing the reaction as one I'd had many times in response to such barging in by the other kids, when Del and I wanted privacy in a house and a family that afforded none. I recalled then how Andre and Pascale allowed Del to lock her bedroom door because it was the only way to keep her sisters out. It worked well for us, not only to keep Nicole and Ida from bugging us during the day, but also to allow us to have sex at night without having to worry about getting caught. If either Andre or Pascale found Del's door locked, they would think nothing of it, and we would have time to get our clothes on.

Recovering from the intrusion, I handed Ida the picture.

"When was this taken?"

"Maybe a year ago, I think." She shrugged, looked at me thoughtfully, and then handed it back.

She was taller than me now, her stick figure clad in tight blue jeans, three-inch heels, and a red tube top. Ida twisted back her thick, red hair and brought her dark eyes level with mine. Soft, well-defined features, a long neck, and bony shoulders all contributed to an appearance of fragility that in a different class frame might easily have been taken for exquisiteness.

"That's Khila?" Ida nodded. "Pascale wants me to help her get custody."

Ida laughed a little. "Yeah, well, hope that works out better for Khila than it did for me."

I had forgotten Ida was Del's cousin; she had come to live with Pascale when she was seven, after her mother died in a car accident. Pascale and Andre had intended to adopt Ida, but their marriage ended before they completed the process, so Ida grew up with Pascale as her legal guardian. It made no difference to Del. She insisted Ida was her sister and refused to refer to her in any other way. We would talk about it at night sometimes, how sad Ida had been when she came to live there, and how Del, who was only eleven years old, had tried to console Ida by saying she had a new family.

Ida slept with Del for the first year before she finally moved into her own bed in a room she shared with Nicole and, later, Sid. But it remained complicated with Ida, her wish to be what she believed was a legitimate part of the family constantly frustrated and undermined by increasing financial pressures and then Pascale and Andre's divorce. In fact, it was Ida who Pascale resolved to put into foster care after Andre left and she could no longer afford to take care of all four kids. Although she never told me this, I know part of the reason Del moved out at sixteen and began working for Ben Reed was so Ida wouldn't have to go.

"Del still bites her fingernails, huh?" I was noticing her hands in the picture.

"Hella short," Ida said. "Just last week when I was hanging out with her, I was thinking that it hurts just to look at them." Sadly, she offered, "I'm glad you're here. It's comforting. I don't know why."

I hugged her as if she belonged to me. She leaned her head into me; I kissed the top of it. "I'm sorry that I've been out of touch for so long."

"I understand," she said firmly. "You did what you had to do. Things sure have come undone around here, huh?"

Nicole popped in and pushed a cold bottle of beer at me. "Here, my mom said you can put this on your face to stop the bruising. Be glad it's not 'duck' tape." I put the bottle to my cheek and laughed, remembering how Pascale fixed everything with duct tape: cars, windows, sports equipment, furniture—injuries. To Ida, Nicole said, "You'll never believe who just called. Tar Baby."

Ida said, for my benefit, "He's an old friend of Sid's."

"He wants to talk to us." Nicole looked first at Ida and then at me. I had the feeling that as far as Nicole was concerned, any us now included me. "He wants to meet us at the tunnel."

"Seems kind of out-of-the-way," I said.

Nicole was moving toward the door. "Tar Baby works the concession stand at the pier. He's off in an hour. He said he has news about Del."

Ida shrugged at me. "Wanna come?"

"Might as well. I'm here anyway." My tone was casual, but privately I was overjoyed to be invited into their clan again. Also, I was curious about what news this person had about Del.

❖

Before we left to meet this Tar person, I read the autopsy report, again expressing surprise over how quickly it had been completed. Ida said reports were routinely produced within twenty-four hours on the less complicated cases. The idea that Del's death was being considered uncomplicated caused Nicole to be agitated all over again, but I focused on the findings.

Del's death had been attributed to a cardiac arrest. In general the findings were unremarkable. There were no bruises, no indications of sexual assault, and no drugs in her system with the exception of tobacco. Her skin was a bright pinkish color, and she had elevated levels of carbon monoxide in her blood. Her heart failure had been attributed to a carbon monoxide effect considered notable at around 20 percent, which the medical examiner speculated might have been brought about by heavy smoking in a closed cabin prior to diving, compounded by anemia, the result of a low-grade apparently chronic condition of anorexia nervosa.

Her bent hands had clawed the water. Debris in her mouth and throat suggested gasping while submerged, and the presence of foam in her throat and nostrils together with a watery substance exuding from her lungs upon sectioning all pointed to nonpassive water entry. The medical examiner was certain, on the basis of these details, Del had been alive when she went into the water. Based on the crime-scene analysis, she had been under only about twenty minutes before she died. The air in her tank was free of any contamination.

The report concluded Del had been in insufficient health to dive, and the air compression had stressed her already oxygen-and-otherwise-depleted system to the point of lethality. The medical examiner was satisfied that Del had died of natural causes. Her remains were scheduled to be released to the cemetery of her family's choosing within the routine forty-eight hours. I completed the report, stared at the page, the words written on it a momentary blur. One detail jumped out at me: the weight belt. When Del was found, the report said, she was still wearing a weight belt. Del was an experienced diver. If she had gotten into trouble, the belt would have been the first thing she dropped.

Still, the report was conclusive and, to my eye, convincing. Del had died of natural causes.

"It's bullshit," Nicole said. "Who dies of a heart attack at thirty-one?"

"Someone with anemia and anorexia who smokes before they dive, I guess."

Nicole moved from foot to foot, shifted her eyes rapidly, grimaced angrily. "It was murder."

I knew from the small amount of criminal law I had done that family members always suspect wrongdoing around an unexpected death. The way I understood it, rage was easier to stand than grief. Still, the weight belt bothered me, as did the news Del had been planning to leave Talon. Leaving or trying to is when most women get killed. Also, there were the disturbing things Katie had said about Del's behavior these past months. And then there was this other troubling detail about Talon, if true. He had arranged for a kid's brutal murder and framed Sid.

With all this in mind, I decided I would fax the report to my friend, Doug Andrews, for his opinion. Doug was senior forensic biologist at the FBI's crime lab in Northern California. The first time I met him, he was testifying as an expert witness in a criminal case. I was in my second year of law school and an intern with the public defender's office, and this was the first major trial I had been involved in. Most professionals in the criminal law world ran the other way when they saw an intern coming. Doug, this tall, roundish man in his mid-forties, with a conservative haircut belied by a discreet few-strand-braided tail, was warm, welcoming, helpful, and we became good friends.

Standing in Del's living room, surrounded by the people I grew up with, I drew comfort from my connection with Doug. Like Madison, Doug was part of the life I'd made for myself since leaving Florida. That I could speed-dial him on my cell phone, a person of his stature and influence, allowed me to feel the distance I'd traveled and to experience myself as the capable person I'd become. Back then, there were no adults in our lives who could help us. Now there was someone who could take action. Me.

CHAPTER EIGHT

It was close to seven p.m. when the five of us stood in the gravel drive outside Pascale's house debating who among us should go meet Tar Baby. Both Ida and Nicole wanted to go. And I wanted to go. I wanted to see Haulover Beach again and, in particular, the Sand Dollar Motel. Katie and Gail began to beg off going and then remembered Norma's charge to look out for me; they ultimately opted to come along as well.

Other people were starting to arrive to offer their condolences. They were Del's Cuban relatives from her father's side. The women wore fancy black dresses and hats with veils; the men wore suits and ties. They fussed over Ida and Nicole, their voices quivering. The women wiped their noses and dabbed at their eyes. The men stood behind them, hands in their pockets, eyes toward the ground.

Katie, Gail, and I waited in the car. Katie was in the front passenger seat tuning the radio to her favorite classics station. Gail was in the driver's seat, smelling first her hands and then under her arms, her face pinched like a prune. She had detected an odor and couldn't figure out where it was coming from. Between sniffs, "So you think Pascale manipulated us to get you here?"

"I wondered when you called me how you had found out so quickly that Del had died. Hadn't they just found her body? Definitely, she told Nicole to call you, knowing you would call me."

"So why not just call you herself," Katie said, as she landed on "Gypsy" by Stevie Nicks.

The song cracked my heart open like a dropped melon. I pushed aside my sadness to say, "Because, then coming wouldn't have been my idea. And you know how this family is about asking for help." I stared at the autopsy report I was holding in my hand, noticed again the words "bent hands" and "gasping while submerged." I tried to take a deep breath but found I couldn't. Ida and Nicole were standing on the lawn, nodding and commiserating. Nicole stepped from foot to foot, grimacing. She had her hand on the strap of her leather purse, rolling it between her thumb and her index finger—an action I'd heard psychiatrists refer to as pill rolling. Ida's heels kept getting stuck in the grass. It looked like she was balancing on a high wire even though she was just standing still. The air in the car was stifling. As we waited for the air-conditioning to win the battle, Stevie sang of dreams and memories and chances lost.

Now Gail had her nose in every vent, and Katie was staring at her curiously, sliding her eyes toward me, trying not to laugh. Katie lit a cigarette; the smoke filled the car before either Gail or I could act quickly enough to lower our windows.

I sank into the seat, pressed the now-warm beer bottle against my cheek, and said several times to myself, "Breathe. Just breathe."

❖

We stopped at Kinko's on the way to meet Tar Baby, and I faxed a copy of the medical examiner's report to Doug. I also made a copy of the original, which I rolled up and put in my back pocket. Then, roof down, we headed over the Seventy-Ninth Street Causeway in the direction of the beach.

Collins Avenue: four lanes dividing the ocean to the east from the bay to the west. On one side, the beach side, were small two- and three-story motels with neon signs that held out promise of "Deluxe" side by side with "Vacancy." On the other side were multistory condos set back behind high concrete walls. Spaced between them were fast-food restaurants, tourist shops, and seedy bars. When I was growing up in the seventies and eighties, Haulover Beach, where we headed now, was the most popular public beach for local teens. The bay side had parking, boat ramps, berths, picnic areas, restaurants, and the like. The "tunnel," a cement walkway running underneath Collins Avenue, connected the ocean side to the bay side. These days, wealthier white locals frequented beaches to the north in Hollywood or Fort Lauderdale or to the south in South Beach or the Keys.

As a favor to me, we parked at the Sand Dollar Motel and planned to walk to the pier. The Sand Dollar was the last motel on the strip, bordering the edge of the public beach. For many years my parents had managed the place for my mother's wealthy aunt, who lived in New York. She had purchased the motel so she and her friends would have a place to stay in the winters. When my great-aunt died and unexpectedly left the motel to my parents, it was a shocking windfall, delivering them overnight from being working poor to being defiantly middle class. As happy as they were about the inheritance and the hope it gave them for their future, it was also stressful for them, and it was confusing for my brothers and me. My parents now owned a valuable piece of property that they couldn't afford to maintain. Eventually it would become the gift to her favorite niece that my great aunt had intended, but initially and for many years after—our entire childhoods—my parents did nothing but work hard and worry about money.

My brothers and I grew up going to the motel with our parents. We entertained ourselves from sunup to sundown by playing on the pool deck or swimming in the ocean. Our mother ran the office. Our father did the maintenance and ran the pool concession, which included a small dive shop. An expert scuba diver, our father Mel encouraged my brothers to follow along. He taught them to dive, certified them, and then took them with him on ever deeper and farther-away diving adventures. When I—the girl—asked Mel to teach me, he was far less enthusiastic. In fact, he refused. In my early childhood, I learned running around without a shirt on and scuba diving were things my brothers could do that I could not. In my adolescence, the list was expanded to include enjoying food and loving a girl.

The prohibition against loving another girl lasted until the moment I laid eyes on Del; the diving prohibition lasted just a little longer. As we were becoming more adventurous sexually, Del and I were also sneaking off and teaching ourselves to dive, throwing together whatever gear happened to be around the shop and hoping it worked. While home on spring break from college, my brother Brian discovered Del and me experimenting with tanks and regulators in the ocean on our own and decided if we were going to do it anyway, he ought to show us how to do it correctly. Lemon Reef, located a hundred yards off the shore of the Sand Dollar, was our training site.

❖

Lemon Reef had been created in the early seventies, when the Miami Coast Guard began experimenting with artificial reef construction by submerging a bright-yellow 1967 Volkswagen bus in twenty feet of water on Miami Beach. The idea was to sink something substantial enough to allow for various sea animals and vegetation to adhere, forming a man-made reef to revive and sustain indigenous sea life. It was the beginning phase of the now ever-more-common artificial reef projects, and the enlightened municipality sank just about anything, including cars that would rust. Rusted metal, it turned out, was not conducive to generating plant growth. Thus the nickname, Lemon Reef: a large, roundish, bright-yellow vehicle that rusted under water. The project was abandoned in '78, a few years after it had been initiated, but the bus was never removed from the water.

Calling it a reef was a little controversial; the site wasn't exactly a point of Miami pride. In fact, some people referred to Lemon Reef as a junkyard because after it was determined to be defective as a reef, a major construction company used the site as a dumping ground. The company had to pay a fine, but the cleaning-up part was forgotten and the ocean left to fend for itself. Authorities discouraged diving on "the project," as city officials referred to it, because the rusty metal and sharp edges were considered unsafe. But the spot was accessible from the beach, so it had become a favorite—an attractive nuisance, so to speak—for local kids who were without access to a boat. For Del and me, explorations of Lemon Reef were a conquest, the reef itself our ironic playground, with squeaky swings and rusty climbing structures, graffitied walls and sandboxes filled with broken glass, syringes, and used rubbers. But we didn't care. To us, the reef was beautiful, some days in spite of its defective status and some days because of it.

By the time we began diving on the reef, in April of 1983, tiny elkhorn and staghorn coral had begun to grow in places where the sand met the cement. The concrete pieces lay in piles without logic, some still connected by rusty iron rods protruding from their exposed centers like broken flower stems in cracked pots. Anemones and other mollusk-like creatures covered exposed surfaces, giving soft movement and iridescent color to gray stone and rusty metal. Crabs pretended to be stones, eels found the cracks and crevices, urchins guarded the bus's exits and entrances, an octopus holed up in a heating vent.

A baby nurse shark making a brief appearance scared us out of our wits once. All we noticed at first was a several-foot-long shadow, which swiveled in sync with what we presumed it was attached to. From where we were inside the VW bus, we couldn't actually see. One of us had to go out there. Del poked her head up. When she saw the wide nose, the silly mustache-like feelers, and the three-foot-long physique, her cheeks rounded into a deep smile and she giggled into her regulator. With a kick of her legs, swing of her arms, and twist of her torso, she nimbly maneuvered in her bulky gear and swam up to see if she could play with it—if it would play with her.

The placid ocean glowed in the sunset; a pelican plunged and then surfaced, its beak pregnant with fresh prey. From where I was standing on the motel deck, I could see the place in the ocean where Del had died, stared at it, as if in looking harder, I'd find some clue to explain my increasing disquiet. Not that death ever makes sense. But I just couldn't reconcile Del, nimble and strong—as she chased baby nurse sharks, searched for sea turtles, traced every new life-form and nuance—with the image of her drowned body floating lifeless in that same place. A sharp pain moved across my chest, then settled into a leaden throb at my center. I recalled how Del's and my passion for the reef grew as our love for each other had deepened. Explorations of the reef the summer before our tenth grade year happened with explorations of each other's bodies, our emerging sexual feelings as delicate and at the same time determined as the baby coral taking hold on strewn cement.

Nicole decided not to bother with the stairs to the beach and led Ida and then Katie in a shortcut over the banister. As I waited for my turn,

I looked to Haulover Pier, a mile south. There was nothing between the motel and the pier but ocean, sand, sprawling sea grapes, and a lone abandoned lifeguard stand. This place, I thought, as I climbed from the deck to the sand, had been my other home for the first fifteen years of my life. I remembered us—the same people I was with now—as kids on that same beach, girls in bikinis holding still in hot sand for photographs or indulging in fearless sunbathing and shameless expenditures of time. It was amazing to think of it now, knowing how rapidly life had closed in on us all.

"So, *where* are we going?" Gail was the last one to climb over the railing. Katie, Nicole, and Ida were already starting to walk. "*Who* are we meeting?" She coordinated climbing, twisting, wiggling over, and talking at the same time, exaggerating the physical difficulty in an effort to appear more stereotypically feminine. In fact, Gail had girth and strength, and she moved with athletic command and confidence. "Tar…*who*?" As she stepped down, she grumbled about getting sand in her shoes.

"Take them off," I said.

"No. I just got a pedicure." She stepped gingerly between the cactus and the fern fronds that lined the motel railing. She was wearing baggy yellow-and-white shorts and a sleeveless yellow shirt. Her brown hair was thick from the humidity, curly in some places, frizzy in some places, zigzag in between. The sun found the lighter strands among the darker ones, creating natural highlights. She moved her wide shoulders, large breasts, and full hips as if they resisted her.

When we caught up to the others, Gail said irritably to Nicole, "Phone? Have any of your friends ever heard of a telephone?" Then she said to me, "Don't drug dealers usually have cell phones? What, we have to *walk* to talk to this drug dealer? He's the only drug dealer in Miami who doesn't have a cell phone?"

Nicole looked back over her shoulder and said, "He doesn't want to talk on the phone. He's scared he's being watched. He thinks his phone is bugged."

Gail came to an abrupt halt. Her eyes large with alarm, she said, "Okay." She was nodding, taking it all in now and giving it a true appraisal. "And we are going to *rely* on Mr. Tar 'my phone is bugged' for *information*?"

Katie and I looked at each other, studiously keeping our faces from cracking. “She does have a point,” Katie said matter-of-factly, her white-blond hair moving with the breeze. She slipped seamlessly into this atmosphere with her jeans rolled to her calves and bare feet.

Nicole’s face twisted and her eyes grew more severe. She was getting frustrated. Ida put a hand on Nicole’s shoulder to calm her.

“Come on.” I tapped Gail on the shoulder, tenderly. “I haven’t been to Haulover in a really long time.” I smiled at her and shrugged. “It doesn’t matter if this goes anywhere,” I said quietly and just to her. “It’s nice to be here again with you guys. It’s special. I really just wanted to go for the walk.” Gail looked at me, irritation pinching her features. She shook her head in protest, and then she continued on in the direction of the pier.

The five of us made our way along the ocean shoreline that evening in the day’s afterglow, warm water lapping rhythmically over bare feet, the receding waves leaving behind moist mountain ranges etched in the sand. The August breeze pulled gently at my shirt and jeans, as if trying to remind me of something—persisting, pestering even. And the salty air carried sharp scents: beached sea creatures left stranded at low tide, now in varying stages of decomposition, and sun-dried seaweed braided into lumpy strands entrapping trash, lone flip-flops, and broken bottles.

From where I walked, I could see edges of recessed sea-grape-thicketed landscape providing what was now a thin, trim barrier between the beach and Collins Avenue. At one time, the sea grapes extended far out onto the beach. In some places—like near the motel—the thick, twisting branches spread to near the shoreline. The bent trunks and knobby branches covered over by thick, round leaves looked like solid bushes from the outside, creating large recessed caverns and leafy caves. When we were younger, my friends and I explored the sand dunes and sea grape thickets, followed sandy paths winding through knotted and twined bramble covering the beach for half a mile, providing a common dwelling for squatters and horny beachgoers alike. In fact, many of us had, either intentionally or by happenstance, had our first full sexual encounters in the “Hobbit holes,” as we affectionately referred to the leafy caves peppering the dunes.

❖

The first time Del and I decided to get completely naked together, we sought privacy in one of those very burrows. It was after Del's fifteenth birthday party, and going there with me was her idea; it was her way of saying the hetero couples I'd watched on the beach that night had nothing on us. The conversation began when I had slept over the weekend before.

Del went first. "I'm *in love* with you. This feels right to me, Jenna. It just does." She was arguing with the countless voices we anticipated or believed we were already hearing all the time now. The voices of parents, siblings, teachers, friends who we knew would consider our having sex strange if not gross. Del's fingertips hooked around the elastic of my panties, daringly tugging at them. "I'm excited," she said. We'd gotten all worked up from kissing and fingering each other. She lifted my T-shirt and made her way down my body slowly, a trail of soft, dry, pleasurably ticklish kisses marking her path.

"I *know* you're excited," I teased. I watched her ease down my panty line, the edge of my pubic hair now revealed.

Caught, she giggled, slid her face down, kissed me once tenderly just above my exposed hairline. Then she looked up again. "I meant about us," she said, her eyes square with mine, "how I feel about you." Her chin now wedged on my belly button, Del tried to distract me by talking as her hands sneakily inched my panties farther down my hips. When her mouth touched me, I shook my head, playfully mouthing no to her. She said, "But I want to see what you taste like." Puckishly, "I want to *be* with you."

I was aching for her, but I still stopped us from going further. I said it was because it was almost morning—Pascale would be getting home from her bartending job any minute—and I didn't want to risk getting caught. The real reason: I had my period and felt self-conscious about how I might smell or taste. Del had shown me how to use tampons, put the first one in for me, but for some reason, I couldn't bring myself to just tell her what was worrying me. I felt more vulnerable with her than I had before. We were departing from our nondescript way of fooling around as girlfriends. We were deciding for the first time what kind of sex we wanted to have as lovers and talking about it.

Del gave up, crawled onto me, and cradled my face in her hands. Her lips close to mine, she said, "You're precious to me. I can't imagine ever loving anyone more." Her eyes were like ocean-green pools with swirls of gold in them; her voice was soft and confident.

I kissed her, nuzzled her nose, pressed my forehead to hers. "Marry me."

She laughed. "You're fourteen, I'm fifteen." I stared at her. "Are you serious?" When I didn't respond she shook her head. "How can you be so sure about everything, Jen? You're always so sure."

"I'm not sure about everything." I swept her hair off her face. "Just you. I'm sure about you. I want to be with you forever."

She smiled, then she kissed me. I kissed her back. Unable to sleep, we lay facing each other with our fingers intertwined and planned every detail for taking what we considered would be our next step.

❖

The following Saturday, we arrived at the beach early, having caught a ride with Norma on her way to work. We left my mother at the motel office, told her we were meeting Gail and Katie at the pier, that we'd find our own way home. We had arranged for time—a whole day, and privacy—a remote cave, and various comforts—blanket, radio, cooler. The sandy path to the cave wound through sea grapes dashed with the yellow of newly blooming acacia. I mindlessly pulled one of the flowers as we walked and searched it for its scent, shared the fresh, muted sweetness with Del. It was a crisp March morning. The sky was clear and blue and the Miami air had a subtle chill to it, a last vestige of winter. We entered—crawled under and into—the sea grape cave, two body lengths around and tall enough at the center to stand. I had accidentally discovered this particular spot years earlier, while chasing a wild Angora kitten deep into the bramble. I was cut and torn all over, but it was worth it when I did finally catch her and get to keep her as a pet.

In the cool shade of the cave, I spread the blanket and then turned the radio on low and focused on tuning in to our favorite station. "Gypsy" was playing.

I turned around to find Del dancing, her lithe body tracing the rhythm the way wheat traces a soft breeze. Her yellow bikini glowed against her tanned skin, her eyes were closed, and her movements were seamless and graceful.

Del reached up behind her head and removed the band securing her ponytail. Her hair fell out around her face, as she rocked her head first to one side, then the other, and sang along with Stevie. She opened her eyes, seemed pleasantly surprised to find me watching her, shrugged, smiled in a way that showed the slight misalignment of her bright teeth. Then she put her hand out to me. My stomach in flutters, my heart pounding, I stood on uncertain legs and faced her. Our hands came together first, palm to palm, our fingers intertwining.

"She's coming in the fall," Del said, referring to a Stevie Nicks concert. "Do you want to go with me?" She asked it with all the tenderness and uncertainty of a would-be first date. "I could take you for your birthday." I was turning fifteen in October.

My hands were trembling. "Definitely," I said, trying to swallow away my inexplicable nervousness. We had, after all, been making each other come for months.

"I'm nervous, too," she offered.

"You don't seem nervous."

Del guided my hand to the back of her neck, slipped her bikini string into my fingers. I caught the scent of her shampoo as I swept her hair out of the way with one hand and then pulled the string with the other, watched the loops of the bow shrink and then disappear. My hands went around her torso to undo the hook at her back. She smiled at me; I studied her.

Del reached around to the back of my neck, found my bikini string, and ran her fingers down it until she found the end. She held it up for me to see, smiled as she gently tugged at it, her expression and the gesture daring permission to pull it for real. I nodded. She slipped the string out slowly until the bow came undone, and my bikini top dropped by half, my pink nipples springing out from small, white mounds. Del lifted her hair off her face and cast a delicate glance at me. We were standing face-to-face with our breasts bare, any shyness or uncertainty in the past giving way now to excitement and pride.

I reached behind my back and pulled the remaining string. She kissed me and slipped my bikini bottom off. I lay down on the blanket tossed over a bed of fallen sea grape leaves and soft sand. Del removed her bottom and then slid in on her side next to me. She propped her head up on her elbow and smiled down at me. We kissed more, her breath tasting of recently chewed watermelon-flavored Bubble Yum, her hand moving down my belly to my clitoris. I felt her fingers enter and then rest inside me. Del's fine hair, almost red in the dappled sunlight, fell to one side; her green-gold eyes were firm and clear; her face was powerful and lovely against the canopy of foliage and filtered sky. In the future I would happen upon actual photographs of this same face and realize the sadness in its delicate contours and the wryness in this not-quite smile.

On my back, one knee bent upward toward the sky, I lightly touched Del's breast and watched her. Behind her in a patch of breakthrough sunlight I noticed the unlikely presence of weeping lantana making its way through and across branches and thick, round sea grape leaves—a splash of bright color against an otherwise austere landscape. My eyes moved from the budding yellow-and-white sand-born flowers to Del's face, and I sensed in her a similar contradiction, a similar ironic relationship to her own beauty. I ran my finger down the straight, narrow bridge of her nose set against her round face, traced the slight slope of her nostril, followed the outline of her slightly parted lips, as thick as the finger sketching them.

"They're too big," she said of her lips. She drew her fingers out of me and rested her hand on my inner thigh.

"Are you kidding? You're *gorgeous*."

"Everyone can see their own flaws," she said. "The flaws that other people can't see, I mean."

"I wish you could see yourself through my eyes." She kissed my hand. I lowered my finger to her pointed chin, then down her neck. I gently played with the silver-link necklace she was wearing. "I love this." She hadn't taken it off since her father put it on her neck. Now she reached around her own neck, undid the clasp, and leaned over to put the necklace on me. "No, Del." I tried to stop her. She pushed past my hand and put her arms around my neck, maneuvering the clasp until it caught and closed. Then she pulled on the chain a little, as if making sure it was secure, gave me the feeling she was claiming me. "It's a loan, okay?" I said, desperately wanting this from her but knowing she was heartbroken over how little she was seeing of her father now.

"I don't know." She was propped up on her elbow again, looking down at me. "I can't imagine wanting it back from you." She used the fingers she'd just had inside me to brush some sand from her face. "I love looking at you," Del said. "You have the greenest eyes. When you're in the sun, they're like malachite. And a perfect nose." She ran her finger down the bridge of my nose and over its round tip. "And a really sexy mouth. So sexy. Like Cupid's bow." I laughed. "I'm serious." She traced the upward angle of my top lip with her finger. "This is the bow, and"—moving to my bottom lip—"this is the string. And the way your lips cut high into your cheeks when you smile. I love your face. I like your hair, too. I know you don't," she said in response to my facial scrunch. She used the tips of her fingers to wisp curls from my face. "I like it long, the way it is now. Don't cut it, okay?" I nodded. She cupped my breast. "And you have the sweetest tits."

I put my palm to her cheek. "I *love* you."

Her eyes glistened. My hand went to her breast. I rolled us over so I was on top of her, her hair spread out behind her. We started kissing, I slid my hips over hers, and our clits touched for the first time, exciting me in a whole new way.

Del let out a high-pitched breath. I felt her tremble. "Wait." Her voice was soft but firm.

"What is it?" I lay on top of her, my torso arched upward, her hands up behind her head, my hands on hers.

She folded her fingers over mine. "I think," she said searchingly, "I wasn't expecting it to feel…" She had a deliberate expression tinged with fear. "It feels so…" She looked at me. "Private."

We were used to fooling around in her room, always worried about getting barged in on by nosey Nicole or upset-yet-again Ida. Out here, there was little chance of getting caught, and all we had to focus on was each other.

"Do you want to stop?"

"No," she blurted out and laughed at the same time. "Do you?" I shook my head.

She rolled us over so that now she was on top. She bit my lip, then my chin. She kissed my breast, then my belly, continuing lower, until her mouth and fingers were working their way through my pubic hair, pulling me apart. I pushed past the shyness, and I opened my legs wider for her. Del looked at my clit, then she glanced at my face, her expression tender and grateful. Her eyes closed and her mouth and nose melted into me.

It was hard to relax. I was preoccupied with the exposure, the moist leaf stuck to the back of my hand, the blanket not being big enough, the towel falling short as a pillow, Del's legs being in the sand. Del didn't seem particularly concerned with any of those things or even with whether I was responding. She just kept massaging me with her mouth, edging into different parts of me with her fingers, exploring me.

After a while of hanging out like that, Del sucking me and me watching her, she raised her face, rested her chin against my thigh, and said, "The sand is kind of irritating."

She got a better idea. She brushed the sand and leaves off, brought her legs around and straddled my breasts with her knees. She looked back and checked on me, then moved her clitoris toward my not-quite-yet-ready mouth. I shifted my position, and first my tongue and then my lips engaged. I tasted her for the first time. Del tipped upward a little and sucked the air. I breathed in deeply, the scent of soap mixed with something distinctly more her. She turned her face down, pulled her hair to one side, and placed her mouth and tongue on me.

I don't know if it was the lack of time pressure, the feeling of privacy, the clarity, finally, of our feelings for each other, but what we were doing felt easy. Once in it, we went surprisingly slowly, given how long we had waited. Del set the pace, overwhelming me with the experience of being touched and kissed so thoroughly. What I remember most about how she was with me was her earnestness. I studied the parts of her body I hadn't seen before, thrilled that I could, eased her cheeks apart, touched her pinkish-brown asshole with my finger. She adjusted to open up more, brought herself closer to my mouth. I entered her a little, lightly edged against the rim with the tip of my tongue—the taste sour and sharp.

My tongue found her clit again, and I moved my fingers in and out of her slit. She breathed in, then released her breath in muffled groans as she continued sucking me. My stomach swooped and stilled to distraction, and I had to close my eyes and grab hold of her for a moment to steady myself, the tension edging into hurt.

"Are you okay?" she asked, looking back at me.

"Yes," I said. "Keep going." Her clit came back to me, an exposed, vulnerable crimson protrusion.

I felt serious and focused and surprisingly confident. I slowly traced the outer edges of her pubic hair—the color of ginger—noticed the quarter-sized dark-brown birthmark on her inner thigh. Tan lines and shave lines demarked private from public, and I took immense pleasure in knowing my eyes could cross over them easily now. She had just finished her period, and I could see and taste the remaining traces of blood in her come, the reddish-brown hue coating my fingers after I fucked her.

I don't know specifically what she was doing with her mouth or her hands, but I wanted her to keep going. She seemed to know this intuitively, because she did. She kept at me, while whatever the feeling was took hold, with an intensity that caught me by surprise. I was along for a ride. I was fucking her with my fingers harder and faster without intending to, my mouth held on to her, my tongue held steady on her clit. I heard her sounds as my own breath got away from me, squeezing out in gasps. My abdomen, now with a life of its own, my entire body trembling reflexively in rapid succession, a lull, she kept going, another swell followed by ripples to my thighs, and then another. And she was coming at the same time, her whole body shaking, her come suddenly thicker and tangier in my mouth. And then we were both lying still, breathing hard, holding on to each other.

A little dazed from the intensity, I said, "That felt so good! That felt *so good*." She kissed my clit. I kissed her inner thigh, moist from her secretions and my spit.

I was still holding Del when she suddenly flipped off of me and reached for the radio. "I love this song," she said, as she turned up the volume. She sat up, her legs spread out in front of her, her arms supporting her weight, her confident nakedness a mere fact between us now. "Come Sail Away" by Styx played on the radio. "Wanna go for a swim?"

I shook my head. "No, not yet." I rolled onto my side, leaned on my elbow, and played with her small feet and stubby toes.

"What's wrong?" She wiggled the toe I was playing with to get my attention. "Why do you like this song so much?" She looked at me questioningly.

I shrugged my shoulders and said, "It's a great song. I just think it's a really sad song." I pulled her big toe apart from the smaller one adjacent to it and tried to crack the joint.

"So?" Then, "Ouch!" She yanked her foot to get me to stop.

"It might sound corny," I started to say.

"You?" she teased, Styx in the background.

I flashed a sarcastic smile. Then, refusing to be deterred, I said,

"You're that captain, Del," referring to the song. Her mouth tightened; she glared at me. She was already anticipating where I was going and was trying to ward me off. "You are," I persisted. "And you're trying to get your sisters and brother on board with you. You're trying to carry on for all of you." No movement, no indication she'd even heard me. "Del, maybe we should tell someone about your mom's drinking, that she hits you guys. Maybe we should ask for help." Del bit her bottom lip, her expression impassive. I was sure I was pissing her off, but I didn't care. Then Del's chin dropped to her chest. Her soft hair fell forward, hiding her face, and it took me a moment to realize she was crying.

I sat up, kissed the top of her head, leaned my forehead against hers, stroked her hair. She leaned into me, and I put my hand on the back of her neck. "Is it what I said?" Styx was jamming in the background.

Del climbed into my lap and wrapped her legs around me. "All I know," she said, "is you make me feel really good." She kissed me, nuzzled my nose and lips with her nose, kissed me more. She pressed her forehead to mine, followed by more kisses, more nuzzles. She watched me, her eyes still red from crying. "Is this what you expected," she asked, "being with someone for the first time?"

Her question confused me. I looked at her, trying to understand what she was asking me, and in a flash of overwhelming excitement and pleasure I figured it out. Mildly teasing, I said, "Are you losing your virginity today?" Sadly, it hadn't occurred to me what we were doing would mean that to her.

She nodded, and with some uncertainty and maybe a hint of hurt, she said, "Aren't you?"

"Yes." I said. "It's amazing being with you." I stared at her. "You're *amazing*." I tucked her hair behind her ear, kissed her breast, nearly level with my mouth. "Nothing could beat this." I pushed my fingers into her, watched her face change, thought she was shockingly beautiful. She moved in rhythm with my fingers for a long while until I felt her insides contracting, was aware of her breath on my face tinged with saliva. It covered me like mist, the scent a mixture of her insides and mine. I was watching her face pinch and relax as she came, pushing whatever was going to come out of her mouth back down inside her so she could feel it longer. Listening to her gasp, feeling her tremble, I came again under her.

We sat there in silence, both of us breathing hard, my hand still in her. I noticed the slim shape of her moist inner thigh hugging my hip. She kissed my forehead. "Damn," she said, returning now to her previous state of lightheartedness. "I was rockin' and rollin'." I squared our bodies and put my arms around her waist. Del wrapped her arms and legs around me and hugged me tighter. "Oh my God, Jenna." She turned her face away, as if protecting herself from feeling it too much. "I'm so close to you." Then she said, "I think they were multiples." I was focused on the residuals, my melted cunt and tingling body surfaces, the feel of Del's bare, moist skin against my own. She put her face into my neck. I pulled her hair back and kissed her cheek. "Do you?" she persisted, "think they were multiples?" I didn't answer, just wondered what she'd been reading lately. She smiled shyly. "You're beautiful, Jenna." It was not how I saw myself, which she knew. "You are." She fondled the necklace she'd given me earlier. "I'm in love with you."

Exhausted, I fell back onto the blanket. I looked up at her sitting on me. "I'm in love with you, too. Madly."

As we left the sea grapes behind, I caught myself believing we were on our way now to meet up with Del, and I felt desperately excited to see her again. My heart leaped, my hands yearned for her skin. Then I felt Del's autopsy report rolled up in my back pocket, a stark reminder that she was dead, that I would never see her again. A man-of-war lay just beneath the surface of the sand, its tentacles splayed out behind it like dripping vein-blue paint.

CHAPTER NINE

Tar Baby was waiting for us at the tunnel entrance. There was hardly an acknowledgment. He gestured to us and we followed him in silence through the tunnel to the bay side. Haulover Bay lay before us, the last of the sunlight sinking behind the trees in the far surround. We found an out-of-the-way picnic table near the water's edge. From where we were standing, we could see sundry critters scampering on and around the slippery rocks.

Tar Baby relit a half-smoked cigarette, pulled his shirt on over his lanky, tanned torso, pushed his wiry hair back from his face. "I can't believe she's dead," Tar Baby said to Ida, nervously. Ida nodded. "Man, she was so beautiful. What about her kid, Khila, how's she gonna take this? I mean, Del had problems, but she was a real good mother."

He was speedy, talkative. His still pupils and thick-brown-mucus-lined nostrils answered for his nickname. We stood there quietly, waiting for him to tell what he could. His eyes landed vigilantly on me.

"This is Jenna," Nicole said. "She's an old family friend." Gesturing to Katie and Gail, she added, "They're fine, too. Don't worry, it's safe." Nicole's eyes shifted, she stepped from foot to foot like the ground was hot. Her hands flexed and relaxed apparently outside of her awareness.

In response to Tar Baby's suspicion about us, Gail leaned her weight largely on one leg, crossed her arms, and shot me a just-give-me-an-excuse-to-leave glare. Katie stood beside Gail, calm, curious, quietly amused.

"Here's what I know." He blew smoke, flicked his ashes. "Tal owed some money on a gambling debt, and they did the drop so he could pay it back. They were using Lemon Reef as the meeting point to make the trade." He laughed, proudly announced his brown teeth. "Pretty ingenious, really, they just swim"—wiggling his fingers, he did a little performance improvisation—"right under the Coast Guard radars."

As I tried to understand it, I said, "It was a drug deal?" He nodded. "So, underwater?" I clarified, "An underwater drug deal?" Tar shot Ida a questioning look, as if he was confused by my confusion. "I don't get it," I said.

Ida said, "Well, it's not obvious, and anyway, I thought they quit that shit after the Thomas kid got killed." She was sitting on the picnic table, feet planted on the bench. Poised as she was, her long, narrow body and delicate profile had a mannequin-like quality. Her soft red hair glowed against the fading orange sky.

Nicole moved foot to foot, stepped back then forward, pulled both arms in close like a boxer, then pushed out like a push-up against the air. "Just explain it to her," she said impatiently. She took hold of the purse strap, and I realized rolling it between her fingers was her way of calming down when she was upset.

Tar Baby threw his hair back, patted his board-like stomach, and said, "You decide on a dive spot, set a time, and exchange money for drugs underwater."

"And then you just carry the drugs out of the water onto the beach?" Gail asked.

Hands out, palms up, he said, "People have their ways." Tar Baby laughed at his own thought, which he then shared. "We used to carry it out in a bag, put a few pieces of coral in there or a lobster or two. No big deal really."

I said under my breath, "Ass backward!" Then a little louder so only Katie and Gail could hear, "That's like counting to a thousand to get to a hundred." They laughed. Tar Baby's eyes fixed on us, the laughter making him nervous. "I'm just saying," I said louder, addressing Tar Baby directly, "seems like a lot of work for a lot of risk." He pressed his lips together, narrowed his eyes, and studied me momentarily, as if it hadn't occurred to him that doing drug trades underwater might be stupid. "So," I asked, "why did they use a boat if the whole point was to swim in?"

Tar Baby shrugged. "Don't ask me." He wiped his nose. "All I know is I used to go with Tal on these runs, and we *always* swam in. You know, didn't want to call any attention to ourselves. I told Nicole the boat was weird."

"Maybe Del wasn't healthy enough to do a beach dive," I said, remembering her physical condition. I pulled the copy of the report from my back pocket and began studying it. "The boat they used belonged to this guy, Sam Kramer. Do you know him?"

Tar Baby nodded. "He's the owner of a bunch of sleazy properties. Tal's his manager—The Collector, they call Tal."

"His boat is berthed at the Skyline Marina in Coconut Grove," I said. *The Collector?* It pounded in my head.

"Why go to the trouble of getting a boat to do this dive?" Gail asked me as if the question hadn't already been asked. "If Del wasn't feeling well, just do it with someone else." She suddenly remembered her supposed disinterest, looked caught, twisted her lips.

"Maybe the boat had the drugs on it." Tar was feeling around for another cigarette. "Could be it was a lot. A lot of heroin would require a boat." Katie gave him one of hers, even lit it for him. I watched him watching her.

My cell phone rang. Now Tar Baby was watching me.

The caller said, "How's the heat?"

"Doug!" I was glad to hear his voice.

"She was your first love, huh?" Without waiting for a response, he continued, "Geez, that's too sad. I don't know anything for certain yet. This isn't my area of expertise. But the connection between smoking and diving complications is more tenuous than is stated here."

I moved away from the group, turned my back to face the ocean.

"Funny," Doug continued, "you know, carbon monoxide poisoning is getting a lot of attention right now because of the terrorism hype. We just investigated a case of carbon monoxide poisoning in a suspected terrorist incident in Boston. That's why I know the amount of COHb—carboxyhemoglobin, that is—in your friend's blood, twenty percent, is low to be the cause of death. Again, I'm not sure yet, but I think something else contributed to the death. I'll give the report to our toxicology guy in the morning. He'll be able to tell us more."

The call ended. I dropped my phone to my side and stared at the horizon for a moment to think. I decided I wouldn't mention Doug's comments yet because I didn't want to agitate Nicole with further doubts until we had more information.

Tar Baby said to Nicole, "You think he murdered her?" I took a breath and moved closer. "He killed her on the boat and threw her over?" Tar shot Ida and Nicole a knowing look, said, "What an asshole."

"No." I knew from the report. "Del was alive when she went into the water."

Shaking his head from side to side, he said more to himself, "Sid went to prison and Tal killed her anyway." Tar Baby laughed oddly. "Who woulda thought?"

"*What?* What do you mean by that?" I knew as I asked it I'd sounded too eager. With paranoid people one must be painstakingly matter-of-fact, or they dash. He dashed by ignoring me. I dropped it, telling myself I'd find another chance to return to this.

A black Jeep had pulled up to the entrance to the parking lot. Tar Baby's eyes pegged Nicole. "Were you followed?"

Gail's face twisted; she clamped her palm to her forehead in a gesture of both disbelief and ridicule. The lot was closed, and when the driver of the car realized he couldn't enter, he backed up, turned around, and left.

"Well," Tar Baby said to Nicole and Ida, "the thing I came here to tell you. The guys Tal was making the trade with, they say they didn't see no boat anchored on the reef. And Tal was alone."

Nicole took it in for a moment, then turned to me and said, "So where was my sister?" Her vigilant eyes turned downward, as if they were suddenly the heaviest part of her. "Did she just stay on the boat?" Her pace from foot to foot increased, her face reddened, and I had the impression she was starting to rage.

I put my hand on her shoulder, which seemed to calm her, and repeated to Tar Baby, "We know Del went in the water alive." Privately I was trying to assess how credible this Tar Baby and his sources were, since the two bits of information, if true—that they hadn't seen a boat and that Talon had been alone—raised a critical question: Did Del die on Lemon Reef? Talon had told the police he and Del were diving on the reef when Del had a heart attack. If she'd died somewhere else, Talon's whole story was blown; he'd lose all credibility. More importantly, he'd look implicated.

Tar Baby nodded, shot smoke through his lips like they were a straw. “Tal was alone when he made the trade. They risked a lot to tell me that.” He paused. “They’re not lying.”

“Why are they doing this?” I asked. “Why are they *helping*?”

Ida chimed in, “Jenna, a lot of people hate Talon. He’s got his foot on a lot of people’s necks and if they could hurt him they would. Putting him in prison would be like killing the wicked witch.”

Nicole blurted out, “Blow fucking Toto. Can we just get back to Del?”

“If the boat wasn’t on the reef at the time of the drug exchange,” I said toward Katie and Gail, “then where was it?”

Tar Baby said, “Don’t know.”

I was searching the crime report. Phone call to police at 11:05, body submerged approximately seven hours. She had been taken from the water at 5:30 p.m. That put her entry into the water at around 10:30 a.m. “Time,” I said, “we need the exact time the trade took place.” He eyed me head to foot once and nodded—maybe he’d get the information for me, and maybe he wouldn’t.

We dropped Ida and Nicole off at Pascale’s. On the way back to Gail’s that night, both she and Katie suggested we go by Mel and Norma’s house to say hello. I didn’t want to. I wanted to go over the autopsy and crime-scene reports more closely. And I wanted to call Madison. And I was tired. I hadn’t slept or eaten since this thing had begun. Those were the reasons I offered for why I didn’t want to stop by Mel and Norma’s. The reason I didn’t offer: Del’s body pressed against mine, which this beach had encrypted in its granules. The feeling that being here for her funeral had everything to do with what had gone so terribly wrong between my parents and me fifteen years earlier.

❖

On the last night I spent with Del—Christmas Eve in 1983—we roasted marshmallows, played games, and then watched *It’s a Wonderful Life* on TV. Once Del’s sisters and brother were asleep, Del and I made our way into Del’s room. At some point, we made love and then fell asleep. I woke up a few hours later in a panic. I turned and looked for the time, drew instant comfort from realizing it was still dark. I delicately worked my hand away from Del's, disentangled our naked bodies, and covered her with the blanket.

I picked up the gold crinkly paper in which I had wrapped Kalki and his horse, folded it, and placed it neatly on her dresser next to her statutes. Then I wrote a note to her on it in velvety blue ink that bled a little at the edges. On her dresser, too, I noticed the ticket stubs from the Stevie Nicks concert Del had taken me to for my fifteenth birthday. I quietly got dressed. She had her face to the wall. She was crying, but I pretended not to notice. I did not cry that last night with her. I think I was still simply refusing to believe it was my last night with her. And I was scared and adrenaline-rushed, and getting dressed and home before my parents woke up and found me missing felt urgent and at the same time tedious to me. Trying to beat the sunrise, I jumped on my bike and headed back to my parents' house.

I was in my window, undressed, and in my own bed before I realized my dresser drawer was open. Its contents—Del's letters to me, our photographs, all the poems and stories I'd written—were gone. My heart pounding, I pulled on sweats and opened my bedroom door to see the light from the living room on. I could hear my parents whispering. I made my way down the dark hallway to find my mother and father at the kitchen table. Their bodies were a triangle, their heads the point. My photos, love letters from Del, and other writings were widely exposed.

"Those are mine," I said, mortified but unwilling to let them know that. They ignored me. "Those are mine," I said again.

"This whole thing has gone much too far," my mother said. "Your friendship with Del is too serious, it isn't healthy."

She was holding—had just been reading—a card Del had given me after our day at the beach.

"You've read the letters. Obviously, we're more than friends," I said.

"You *were* more than friends," my father threatened. He tossed a photo on the table.

I watched it slide a few inches. It was a photo my brother Lance had taken in the summer, of Del and me on the beach just after a dive on Lemon Reef. We had our masks perched on our heads, and we were hauling our tanks in one hand and our flippers in the other. I loved that photo. We were looking up at Lance and smiling, our bikini tops a little askew, our faces tan, our legs long and muscular.

"As long as you live in this house," Mel said, "you'll act like a lady."

A lady? Shocked and instantly, deeply contemptuous toward him, I shot back, "You mean like one of those *ladies* that stars in the porno flicks you have lining your bookshelves?" For as long as I could remember, we had as a family gingerly navigated around this topic. I mostly ignored the magazines, books, and tapes stacked waist high in Mel's bedroom that bore such titles as *Liberties with Little Girls* and *Beauty Does Beast*. On a few occasions in middle school, Gail and I had sneaked in and watched the tapes on Mel's Betamax machine. Some of them were dramatic and violent, some of them were mundane. All of them had women with freakishly huge tits and fire-engine-red lips, deformed, I realize now, from early experimentations with Botox.

Mel was out of his seat and back in it again, having slapped me hard in the face by the time my mother went on, ignoring both of our outbursts. "We've been nothing but good to you," Norma said. "Would you rather we were bums and drunks or if we beat you like Del's parents? Would that make you happy?" Now she was crying.

My hand on my cheek, I looked at my mother. *He just hit me in the face, did you not see that? Was that not a beating*? It was not worth saying out loud. She would never understand. In fact, I already knew from previous encounters like this one that in the morning she would be in my room to extend Mel's apologies, encouraging me to go and give him a kiss.

My cheek was pulsating. I felt my own breath enter and leave my body, and caught the swivel of the ceiling when I tried to land my gaze on something other than them.

Now strangely resolute, I asked, "What is the big deal, even if I am gay?"

"It's sick," Norma said.

"No it's not." I repeated what Elaine Fernandez, our tenth-grade English teacher, had said. "Even Sigmund Freud said being gay isn't a mental illness."

Norma's chin dropped, and her brows nearly closed in over her eyes with suspicion. "Was that man a homosexual?"

"Freud?"

"You are not homosexual, Jenna," Norma insisted. "If you are, God as my witness, I'll tear my clothes."

"Mom, you would rather your kid was dead than gay?" She didn't answer.

"Okay," my father said. "I'm gonna tell you what happens next. You don't have anything to do with Del or her family until we decide you can. If you do, we'll talk to her parents about these letters and what's been going on with you."

"Dad," I said, starting to cry and hating myself for it. "You know how they are. You know what they would do to her. You can't involve them."

"I can and I will. You're my first priority, so if you don't want Del's parents involved, then stay away from her, and I mean it."

"Dad," I pleaded. "Dad, wait." Just his eyes moved. I felt divided in two, half of me filled with disgust and hatred for this man, the other half strangely hopeful. I begged. "Please give me those back. They're my short stories. I wrote them."

"We'll give them back when we're good and ready. Now, go to your room. Del," he said, "is *personon grahtor*."

I looked to my mother for support, but I knew this whole thing had been her orchestration in the first place. Sometimes it seemed like Mel couldn't have a thought concerning me that Norma hadn't given him permission to have. It was as if I—the other girl in the family—could not exist for him except in the very precise and limited way Norma could tolerate. Any attempt at an independent relationship was a betrayal.

As I turned to leave, I heard her say quietly, "*Persona non grata*, Mel."

I went to my room, leaving behind our photographs, all of the stories I had written and all of the letters Del had written to me. They were photos and writings I would never see again. The only concrete evidence of a crime my parents felt desperate to have go away, they unilaterally chose to discard the photos, writings, and letters, and they informed me of this several days after it had been done.

❖

I resisted them, I did. It was the last night I spent with her; it was also in many ways the last night I spent with them. Everything changed after that. I never forgot her, and I never forgave them. But we did go on, if only on the surface. In the end, it is my parents who I drop in on, pick up at airports, call on holidays, and with whom I continue to share the day-to-day details of life. We go on as if there was never a night like that night, never a rupture that swallowed us whole and spat us out again in some hollow, mutilated version of our former selves, diminished by our willingness to carry on. And it is Del who, no matter how long I live, I will never see or speak to again. There will be no by-chance meetings, unexpected phone calls, spottings from afar.

I try not to see this in so simple terms as they won and we lost. And after many years, I confess, I am more able to get beyond feeling every loving exchange with my parents as a capitulation, to see things from their point of view, and to be with them in pleasant and appreciative ways again. But on that night, driving back from the beach with Gail and Katie, all I wanted was to preserve for a little longer the sand from the dunes still in my shoes, the sound of Del's voice carrying "Gypsy" in the nagging breeze, the memory of her face backlit by dappled sunlight. I wanted to know again, if only briefly, the exhaustion from sex and swimming and too much sun, to mold my body with hers, nuzzle into her hair, fall asleep with her in a secret cave on a bed of sand and sea grape leaves. I wanted to feel the day grow old and the weather change with the feeling of being with her undispelled.

CHAPTER TEN

Wednesday

I'd been lying awake for hours, suffering the intermittent trickle of cold air streaming from the vent over the bed. Central air-conditioning: I was ten or eleven when my parents finally could afford to install it in our house, replacing the bulky metal boxes that sat in the windows of each room. The unit in my bedroom ran so cold, ice would form on the blades. The ice eventually did damage to the cooling grid, causing a clanking sound—metal against metal—with each blade rotation. It was loud but rhythmic and, somehow, I got so used to it, that when we did put in central air-conditioning, I couldn't sleep for weeks because of the quiet. Habituation is an amazing human capacity.

Relieved by daylight, I flipped open my cell phone to see the time, six a.m., and then I retrieved two voicemail messages. The first was from the local Kinko's—I had received a fax. Very few people knew I was in Miami, so I assumed the fax was work related, probably from Bea McVee or my clerk, and had something to do with Flint and Baxter and Margaret Todd's challenge of my findings.

The second message was from Pascale. She'd called to let me know the medical examiner was releasing Del's body today, Wednesday. Talon, she said, was planning on cremating Del as quickly as possible, and then leaving for Texas with Khila.

I left a message for the medical examiner, asking to speak with him. I wasn't sure yet what I would say, but I'd been awake most of the night thinking about it. There were too many questions: the weight belt; the timing, coinciding with Del's decision to leave the marriage; Del's bruises and hygiene; Talon's other crimes and exploits; Tar Baby's information, which called into question where Del died; and Doug's doubts about the cause of death.

A drizzle tapped rhythmically on the sliding glass doors leading out to the patio of Gail's ground-floor condo. Outside, the drenched ground was carpeted with wilted leaves. In the corner of the patio there was a lemon tree spotted with lemons varied in shape and shade—small dark green to large bright yellow. A few lemons, those that had overstayed their welcome, lay strewn on the ground around the tree, turning pulpy. A colony of ants had appropriated one lemon, the yellow-to-brown skin practically liquid, cracked open or simply eroded in places. I sipped my coffee and stared at it, watched the ants make their way in and around the oozing, sun-yellow craters, cliffs, and canyons.

Gail's phone rang. It was Norma who had called early in the day in hopes of catching me. Gail, despite my protests, handed me the phone.

"So, are we going to see you?" Norma asked.

I noticed the one lemon sunk into the soft ground, wondered how much lemons weigh. "Yes," I said. "Can I call you later and make a plan?"

"What's wrong with making a plan right now? How about dinner?"

"Mom, it's eight in the morning, and you're already thinking about dinner?"

"I know you like my lemon lentils," she said, her tone softening, nearly pleading. "I could make you that for dinner."

My eyes had moved to the lemon ant farm. "Okay."

"When's the funeral?"

"I don't know." I braced myself for one of her digs.

"Sad." Norma said. I stood still, waiting for some expression of sarcasm to follow this unequivocally sympathetic remark. But all she said was, "I've often thought about Del."

"It is sad." I watched the water slowly forming into a drip off a hanging lemon's inverted pinnacle; it looked like a teardrop. It would be a bitter teardrop, I thought.

"Bitter," Norma exclaimed.

"What?" I was starting to feel a little strange, wondered momentarily if I had said that thought out loud.

"Bitter like a lemon is bitter—that was her life. You think I don't know that, but I do. I remember picking you up from that house when you were in tears. I remember when she had bruises and you rode your bike to her house in the morning to help her try to cover them up so she could go to school. We never told you this, but your father and I talked about adopting her."

I believed she'd had that impulse. I also believed it was one of many competing and conflicting impulses, and it lost big to the impulse to go to DEFCON 1 and batten down the hatches because her child was in a same-sex relationship.

"Good thing you didn't. Then we would have been violating two taboos."

She ignored me. "Do you have a ride to the funeral? You can use my car if you want to."

"I think Gail is gonna take me."

"Oy! You're going in that lemon?" She heard herself this time and paused. "I don't know why I keep talking about lemons."

I laughed in a way intended to comfort her. I decided to spare Norma from having to know she was reading my mind impressionistically. Maybe she was responding unconsciously to my acerbic tone, or the shortness of my replies. According to a psychologist friend of mine, people who are tuned in to one another—Freud referred to a radio frequency signal and receiver in describing this—can communicate thoughts and feelings without speaking. The hallmark of this idea, my friend said, is the human infant communicating to its parent all kinds of needs and experiences in ways other than through words. A critical aspect of good parenting, then, is one's ability to interpret accurately and respond sufficiently to nonverbal signals.

This channeling of lemon imagery was one of many examples of Norma's highly developed sensitivity in this regard. What confused me most about my mother was how a person capable of this kind of emotional resonance could simultaneously be so harsh. And how I could feel so close to the same person by whom I felt so consistently and brutally rejected.

Norma confused me, and I had long ago stopped believing in what I was feeling in relation to her in any given moment as the whole truth of us. I believed her when she said she thought about adopting Del, and I believed her when she said it didn't matter if Del was dead because "she was trash anyway." I believed her when she sent my friends to look out for me with Del's family, and I believed her when she made it clear that she would rather I was dead than gay. I believed her when she said she was sorry for throwing away my short stories, and I believed her when she denied throwing away my short stories.

It was all true and it was none of it quite true and it didn't matter anyway. What one could hope for with Norma was a moment—such as the one I was having with her now on the phone. So I preserved it by not calling attention to it, carefully keeping the conversation simple in a way calculated to prevent her from feeling revealed, and let myself feel close to her for as long as it would last.

My phone call with Norma was interrupted by my cell phone ringing. When I answered, a woman's voice said, "This is Dirk Beasley returning your call."

"Thanks." Her voice surprised me. Dirk seemed like a man's name, so I had assumed the medical examiner was a man. "You're the medical examiner working on the Adeline Soto case?"

"That's correct. Who are you?" Beasley's voice was deep, slightly raspy, with an attenuated Southern drawl.

"I'm a friend of Del's—of Adeline's, I mean. We want to meet with you before you release her body."

"Why?"

"I'd rather not discuss it on the phone. Can we come to your office?"

"I have a very busy schedule today." She paused, and then she said, "What's your question?"

Again, I said, "I'd rather discuss it with you in person." I had worked with dozens of forensic experts over the years. I knew if there was something more to Del's death, my relationship with this person mattered. I wanted to meet her.

Her reply was prickly. "You know, I have such a busy schedule. I can't do it today."

The firmness in Beasley's tone made me rethink my approach. I wasn't going to be able to talk her into an in-person meeting, and persisting was only going to irritate her. So I thanked her for returning my call and hung up. After I did, I felt frustrated, and I—well, I'm not good at taking no for an answer. I'm just not. I was going to see her anyway, I decided, as I realized Gail had asked me a question and was waiting for a response.

"What?"

Gail was sitting at her dining room table, coffee mug in hand, newspaper open and spread. "Do you think Bush could actually win?"

"Yes." I went back to the Beasley problem. Even if I could convince her to talk to me, then what? What did I want from her? Either they had the evidence to implicate him or they didn't.

"But why would we go to war with Iraq?"

"To oust Hussein. Can I borrow your car? I wanna go talk to the medical examiner."

❖

Beasley was far more likely to meet with me if I was with a family member, so I decided to go by Pascale's and get Nicole. On my way there, I stopped at the Kinko's—the one we had been to the night before—to pick up the fax that had arrived for me.

There was a different clerk behind the counter, a young Cuban guy wearing a pro-Castro T-shirt, who spoke halting English.

"Can I help you?"

"I think there's a fax for me."

He went off to find it.

As I waited, I noticed the sheer size of this space. Kinko's was a strange new creature emerging around the planet like the invasion of baobabs in the Little Prince's abandoned world, its huge roots careening through the center, threatening to crack open the earth. Copy machines cranked out pages in the background, emphasizing with each complete rotation the Clintonian shine placed on global production and efficiency. There was a second level to the store, dedicated to individual computers I assumed were available for people to rent. It was eight thirty in the morning, and there were already several computer stations occupied. One man, shoulders rounded over, head jutting, coffee in hand, met eyes only with his screen.

"Here you go."

The fax cover sheet said my name, phone number, and indicated there were ten pages altogether. Sender: UNKNOWN. Included in the fax was the criminal history for a Larry Keller. The crimes had been committed in the state of Texas. The record had been sealed when this Larry Keller turned eighteen. Keller was Talon's last name. The birth date on the record was 1968, making Larry Keller thirty-one, which seemed about the age I assumed Talon to be. If Larry was the name given to Talon at his birth, then I was holding in my hand Talon Keller's juvenile criminal record.

I searched the cover sheet for some clue as to who had sent the fax to me—a return phone number, some fax machine identification information. There was nothing. I began to scan the pages. He had a conviction for car theft at age thirteen. There were some drug-related crimes between ages fourteen and sixteen. There was also a sexual offense committed against a twelve-year-old girl, involving oral copulation, when he was fifteen, which apparently had been reduced to misdemeanor assault. Finally, there was a felony conviction—age sixteen—for animal cruelty. The last page of the fax was a copy of the district attorney's Complaint:

"Larry Keller ('Keller')—age sixteen—illegally entered the local SPCA at night, broke both of the back legs of six puppies, and then videotaped them as they writhed around on the floor in agony." According to the district attorney's account, while the increasingly crazed mother tried to gather and comfort her crying four-week-old pups, Keller could be heard laughing on the recording. I read the Complaint more than once, unable at first to believe it. I was stunned, first by the cruelty of the act I'd just read about and then by its implications for Del and Khila. I took a few breaths, reminded myself not to jump to conclusions. Doing even this horrific a thing at sixteen certainly didn't mean Talon had murdered Del now. But, honestly, this information made the question of whether Talon had killed Del inconsequential to me, compared with what I was imagining it must have been like for her living day in and day out with someone who was capable of doing such a thing.

"How do we find out who sent this?" I asked the clerk.

There were very few people who had access to a juvenile record. My first thought was a family member of Talon's who was worried about Khila had sent it, and if so, I wanted to know who.

The clerk nodded and began looking at the cover sheet with me. After a moment he said, "I'll be right back." He returned shaking his head. In a heavy Spanish accent he said, "There's no fax machine to link it to. It was sent by the Internet, but without an identifiable IP. I'm not sure how they did it."

It had to be Doug. I'd faxed him the night before, so he had the number to this Kinko's store. Also, he had access to confidential information and the means and know-how to send it in a way that would be impossible to trace. And he wouldn't want it to be traceable, because it was illegal for law enforcement to access criminal information for personal matters. So if he was going to get such information to me, this is how he would do it. Or, I thought, maybe Bea had sent it. She was also in a position to deliver such information anonymously. Regardless of who'd sent it, if it was true, the thought of Khila going off to Texas alone with Talon made me queasier than ever. In fact, I didn't want her left alone with him at all.

As I pulled up in front of Pascale's house, the mostly gray sky threatened more rain, but there were also some breakthrough rays. Whereas the night before, it had seemed depressed and broken-down, in the morning light, Pascale's house, with its neatly clipped bushes and freshly mowed lawn, appeared peaceful, orderly, inviting.

I remembered watching with Nicole and Ida from the living room, as Del—fifteen years old—mowed that lawn. It was her least favorite chore. She was dirty and sweaty and swearing as she pushed the mower along in her halter top and shorts, her lopsided ponytail swinging dramatically with each oppositional head shake. Pascale was taskmastering from a chair in the shade on the porch. Beer in hand, she pointed out the places on the lawn Del had missed, unconcerned with Del's indignation.

I knocked once, then again. When nobody answered, I tried the door, remembering the Sotos never locked it. With people coming in and out at all hours of the night, or falling asleep in front of the television and not getting around to it, the usual closing up rituals that many families practiced weren't really on their radar. True to form, the door did open, and I entered. From the television, which I assumed had been on all night, emanated the voice of a talking head, pontificating about the impact of the Lewinsky scandal on Gore's campaign chances. Sunlight came in through the window over the television and through a crack in the drawn curtains.

Then I saw Pascale. She lifted her head from where she was sleeping on the couch.

"Hi," I said. It was still hard to believe this was Del's house, and I was just walking in. I felt a rush of pleasure and reassurance—relief—

that comes from having fixed something broken. Except Del was dead. That thought vanquished any sense of having repaired this rift, leaving me then with only missed opportunity and bottomless regret.

Pascale pulled herself up on one elbow and stared at me for a few moments with a confused look on her face, as if she didn't recognize me. The television remote appeared in her hand from under the blanket, and she pointed and clicked. The light emanating from the television vanished, like a genie disappearing into her bottle, and then the room was silent. Open beer cans lined the coffee table within her arm's reach. I was thinking she'd had a lot to drink and didn't remember we'd seen each other the night before. I was about to remind her when I saw her face wrinkle and then tears start to slip from her eyes.

She wrestled herself to sitting, wiped at the tears, and then reached immediately for a cigarette. I watched her light it with a shaky hand. After drawing on it, she said, "When I woke up and saw you coming in, I thought you must be looking for Del." Her eyes were on a framed photo of Del—her high school photo—sitting on an end table beside the couch. Pascale pushed her skinny body back into the couch and pulled the blanket up around her waist. "Then I remembered."

When I realized what she was saying, I had to blink back my own tears. I sat down beside her, glad to be near her.

"For just a second," she said, "you were kids again."

"I'm really sorry about Del."

She used the blanket to clean her glasses and then put them on. "She was a good girl. She just got with a bad situation."

"I believe that," I said.

I wondered if I should tell Pascale what I had just read about Talon. I wanted to know if Del had known about this history, or if it was something Talon had kept a secret. Clearly he had moved out of Texas as soon as he could and changed his name.

"You want some eggs? I could make you some eggs." I shook my head. "You got my message about the medical examiner?"

I nodded and again noticed the cans of beer. "I want to ask you a question."

Pascale drew from her cigarette.

Gently, I asked, "Are you up for raising Khila now? Can you do it?"

Pascale saw me eyeing the beer cans and laughed a little, in a way that suggested she understood what prompted the question. "Khila's been with me most days since she was born. Del brought her here to keep her away from the fighting—and God knows whatever else was going on there." She looked at her cigarette-free hand, ran her thumb against the cuticle of her pointer finger.

Again I thought of asking her if they knew about the puppies. I decided not to. If Doug or Bea had sent the fax, they could get in trouble. I had to keep the information to myself until I knew who had sent it and why. What I asked instead was, "What was Talon's real name?"

Pascale hesitated for a moment, searched around the way one does when trying to recall. She shook her head. "I don't know. I maybe knew once, but I don't know."

"Do you know if he has a criminal history?"

Another head shake. "I don't think so. But that's only because he's good at putting the blame to other people."

"Like Sid?"

She nodded.

The front door opened, startling us both. A man entered in the flood of light. He was large necked and thick through his middle with muscles. His jet hair was crewed close to his head, and he had small black eyes. His nose was a perfect triangle out from his tight face. He was tan and clean shaven, and he had bright white teeth. A blue-green falcon's claw—one to two inches in length—was tattooed over his left eye.

"Ma," he called into the room. Then he saw Pascale. "Oh, hi." He swung his head around in the direction of the picture window. "It's dark in here," he said, as he pulled open the shades.

A young girl came in behind him. She was stick thin, with shiny golden hair. She had eyes the color of straw and lips to grow into. As I realized who she was, I felt a pain in my chest so sharp I skipped a breath.

Khila beelined across the room to be near Pascale. She sat down on the arm of the couch that Pascale was leaning back against, tucked her hair behind her ear, and put her hand on Pascale's shoulder. Pascale placed her hand over Khila's.

Following Khila into the house was a tall woman with dark hair and bright lipstick who looked to be in her early twenties. The five-inch strap heels she was balancing in forced each foot into the shape of a waterfall. She moved so she was shoulder to shoulder with Talon and took hold of his arm. Her muguet cologne made my eyes water.

"Sorry to barge in," Talon said loudly. His broad body diminished the small living room, made it feel suddenly crowded. "Khila said she left a shirt and pajamas here when she slept over on Sunday. We need them because we're packing."

I leaped up and moved to other side of the room, compelled to put more space between him and me. Also, I think I didn't want to be sitting while he was standing. Near the kitchen now, I backed up until I bumped into the dining room table and rested my hand on it for additional support.

Pascale stood up, too, and with Khila's hand in hers, they walked into the kitchen to get Khila a glass of milk. Passing me, Pascale said, "This is Jenna, Khila. She's an old friend of your mom's."

Khila stared at me, her face expressionless.

I noticed the sheer glow of Khila's tanned skin and her sunlight hair. Her little fingernails sported the remains of peeling polish, which I imagined she and her mother had put on together, and she wore small gold earrings that caught the light when she tucked her hair behind her ear the way Del used to. I pushed through my sadness and smiled at her. "It's nice to meet you." She didn't respond.

"Oh," Talon said. "You knew Del?" He sat on the couch in the place where I had been sitting. The dark-haired woman sat down next to him.

I didn't answer him. I was watching Pascale and Khila in the kitchen, standing side by side. Pascale was filling a glass for Khila, who, unless I was imagining things, had not taken her eyes off me. Out of the corner of my eye, I saw Talon reach over and put the picture of Del, which was sitting on the end table, facedown.

I watched Del's high school image disappear at his hand.

Realizing I'd seen him, Talon shrugged and said, "Don't want to upset Khila."

When Pascale and Khila came out of the kitchen, Talon patted the space on the couch between the woman and himself and said, "Khila, come sit down."

Khila froze.

"Khila," Talon said again, this time more firmly, "come sit down."

Khila glanced at Pascale.

Pascale smiled and said to Talon, "Who is your friend?"

Talon mimicked Pascale's accent, saying "My friend ees Marcella. Marcella, this is Pascale." He laughed a little, a combination of a blurt and a giggle, raised his brows at me in a gesture of imagined solidarity.

Just when I thought Pascale had successfully turned the attention away from Khila, Marcella said in a high-pitched baby voice, "Khila," patting the couch next to her, "come sit with me."

Khila shook her head, took hold of Pascale's hand, and pushed her body up against Pascale's. She looked sideways at me, her forehead wrinkled with worry, her lip trembling, losing the battle against her tears. For a moment, I wondered if she knew about me. I decided she was just casting a wide net, seeking support from any possible quarter. She did not want to go near that woman.

"Khila!" Talon warned.

Marcella placed her hand on Talon's thigh, as if holding him back. She turned to Khila, smiled, and said, "Khila, I know you miss your mommy, but we're together now. It's very exciting. We're going to Texas." Khila was unmoved and Marcella's tone grew more desperate. "I'm going to be your new mommy."

Talon looked evenly at Khila.

New mommy? Had I heard her right? Did she just say that to this child whose mother had died only a few days before? Out loud? Without the least bit of self-consciousness? I saw this all the time in my line of work, this annihilation of a child's history after the dissolution of a marriage or, even, a death, the supplanting of one parent with another, making a child accommodate a parent's new life, as though she had never had one of her own, and taking her compliance as evidence that she's in agreement with what's happening to her. But it was usually done with more subtlety. And most people wait a little longer than two days to introduce a new parent, but not this guy. It was obvious by how blatant he was being that Talon knew Del's family was powerless to do anything to stop him. And worse yet—bringing this woman to Del's mother's house, putting Del's picture facedown in Pascale's living room, and mocking Pascale's accent—he clearly took pleasure in forcing them to watch as he got away with murdering Del and now sought to destroy any memory of Del and her family for her daughter.

I thought of the writhing puppies, eyed the photo of Del facedown, pictured Del wearing shirts buttoned to her neck and sunglasses to hide bruises, watched Marcella insistently patting that space next to her on the couch, and I had not a doubt left that Talon had killed Del.

I asked Khila where her shirt and pajamas were. She shrugged.

Pascale took my lead and said, "Come with me, and we'll find them." It bought me a little time to think about whether there was anything I could do to keep Khila from leaving now with Talon. What Talon had done to the puppies was pretty bad, would give any child-protective-service worker pause, and he had hit Del recently and left bruises. Her friends had already testified to that. The current violence against Del suggested Talon's psychological problems were not limited to his adolescent years. Still, it wasn't enough for me to feel certain authorities would place Khila with her grandmother, even temporarily. The worst thing I could do was act too quickly and without convincing evidence, because then I would lose credibility and put Talon on the alert. If I wanted to help Khila longer-term, I had to suffer her obvious distress for now.

Pascale returned with the pajamas and shirt in hand. "Khila is wondering," Pascale said, "if she can stay with me while you pack." Khila was behind Pascale, again with her eyes on me.

Talon said, "No."

Khila started to cry.

Talon quickly took the clothes, stood up, and began toward the door, expecting Khila to follow him. When she didn't, he stopped and turned around slowly, looking at her questioningly. She crossed the room to him. "That's more like it," he said to her, guiding her out the door in front of him. He looked back at Pascale and said, "I'm not gonna let her see you if you're gonna make her cry." Khila walked with her head down and shoulders hunched.

Marcella looked first at me, then at Pascale, and then she rushed out of the house, as if afraid to be alone with us even for a second.

Through the picture window, Pascale and I watched Talon head-tuck Khila into the backseat of the car and slam the door behind her.

"I didn't want to let her go with him," I said.

“I’ve been doing it for ten years,” Pascale replied.

Ida pulled up. Upon sight of her, Talon’s demeanor shifted instantly from irritated and forceful—as he had just been with Khila—to warm and relaxed. His eyes widened with innocence, his mouth softened into a gentle smile, his shoulders dropped, his arms came in closer to his body. The transformation was startling. One would never have guessed he had been ruffled in any way only moments before. Talon and Ida appeared to exchange niceties. Ida hugged him and shook Marcella’s hand. Then she knocked on Khila’s window and waved to her inside the car. She did look twice at Khila, I think registering Khila’s upset.

Nicole’s voice carried from the hallway. “Was that Talon?” Pascale nodded. “What the fuck was he doing here?” Nicole stopped just inside the living room and took measure. “What is that smell?” she said, as if it were a personal affront. “It’s like gardenias over death.”

Pascale disappeared into her room.

Nicole rolled open some windows, and then she swept up all the beer cans at once and headed for the garbage. “Pascale’s drinking again like she did when we were kids.”

The comment surprised me. “Why, did she stop for a while?”

“Hell yeah. Years. Del didn’t want her to drink around Khila. And Khila was always here…so.” Nicole fell into the couch and lit a cigarette. “I’m no shrink,” she said, “but I think Pascale feels really bad about what she did to Del. You remember?” I nodded. “Sometimes I think helping Del with Khila was her way of making up for all that, because she’s really different with her than she was with any of us.”

Ida walked in. To me, she said, “Tell me he did not just bring his new girlfriend over here.”

“New? She’s moving to Texas with him.” In response to my comment, Ida’s face twisted in a mixture of disgust and bewilderment—and pain. I had the oddest feeling she was *jealous*. I told myself it couldn’t be.

“He is just out of control,” she said. I waited for her to ask about Khila’s upset, but she didn’t.

As I righted Del’s photo, all I could think about was getting to Beasley as fast as possible. I now knew I had to convince her to hold on to Del’s body. I was afraid that once Talon took Khila to Texas, we would never get her back. If there was reason—advances in the investigation, late-surfacing evidence, something in the final toxicology report—to bring Talon back, Khila could be placed with Talon's parents in Texas. I didn't know anything about Talon's parents, except that they had raised him—*The Collector*. Well, that, along with not wanting Khila to have to be alone with Talon and Marcella for even a day, was enough for me. Pascale did have her shortcomings, but "best interests" is a relative beast. And I was now prepared to do everything I could to help Khila stay with Pascale if she wanted to.

My goal, desperate as it sounded, was to convince the medical examiner to hold on to Del's body long enough to find proof Talon had killed her. If I could produce enough evidence to have Talon become the focus of a murder investigation, then Khila—who was ten years old—could request to stay with the grandmother who had raised her.

CHAPTER ELEVEN

Now on a mission, my first stop was Dirk Beasley's office. The Miami morgue was a huge complex, first occupied by the current chief medical examiner sometime in the 1980s. Frequented by students and experts from around the world, it was a fully operative forensic training facility, with crime-lab services in forensic pathology, toxicology, serology, entomology, and botany. They did fingerprints, DNA testing, firearms examination, and a host of other forensic-science services on the premises. When I realized this, I understood how they had produced Del's preliminary autopsy report so quickly. In San Francisco, it usually took weeks to months. However, it also suggested the people conducting the examination and producing the report may have been students overseen by one of the more experienced medical examiners. Maybe they'd missed something.

The building we entered had an open, relaxed feel to it, more like a college campus than a death-processing factory. The morgue itself was on the first floor, accessible through glass doors that led to a waiting room decorated in pastels and furnished with soft chairs and wall art. I checked the directory of names and found Beasely's office number. The area where the examination rooms were located was highly secure, nearly impossible to access without authority, but the administrative offices were on a separate wing. One lone receptionist's desk stood between us and them. I was about to approach the receptionist and ask for Beasley, hoping Beasley would agree to see us, when the receptionist took a call and then disappeared.

We quickly passed her desk and made our way down a long corridor until we came upon Beasley's door. Just then, the door opened and a tall, square woman in a white lab coat came out. She had short salt-and-pepper hair, was maybe in her mid-fifties, and wore thick-framed glasses and no makeup except for a touch of lipstick. I knew immediately she was gay.

"Dr. Beasley?" She stopped, nodded. "I'm Jenna Ross. I'm here with Adeline Soto's sisters. We were hoping we could talk to you."

Shaking her head, she said, "I already told you that it wouldn't be possible today."

"Well, I know, but I need to talk to you. I thought if we just came over you could give us a few minutes."

Walking quickly in the other direction, she tossed over her shoulder, "I don't have a few minutes right now. I'm already running behind. The preliminary report is done—I've made my findings. If you'd like me to explain them to you further, you'll have to make an appointment." She strutted off in brown saddle shoes with toe and heel playing the terrazzo floor like a queer incarnation of clog dancing.

"Dr. Beasley." It just came out. "She was my first love. In high school. We were lovers in high school."

Beasley stopped, turned, and fixed her sight on me.

Her clenched brow and tight lips suggested she was grappling with the implications of what I had just revealed. She nodded her head slightly, and her expression softened to sadness. Out of the corner of my eye I could see Ida and Nicole looked shocked. I realized they were hearing me say this for the very first time. I had never actually told them Del and I had been lovers. No doubt they assumed it. Nicole had seen us kiss once, made Del do her chores for a week under threat of telling. But I had never talked with Del's sisters about us.

Beasley ushered us into her office, which was small for four people. There was a bookshelf on one wall, a large desk, and a couple of chairs. Beasley went behind her desk. I stood across from her. Nicole and Ida were shoulder to shoulder behind me.

She began, "I'm sorry for your loss." I looked at Ida and Nicole before I realized she was talking to me. "I'm not sure what else I can tell you."

"We have reason to believe that there's more to this death, that it might not have been by natural causes."

Nicole seemed surprised and relieved to hear me say I thought Talon might have killed Del. She stepped in closer to my side and rested her hands on her hips, emphasizing her chiseled biceps. Ida stepped back to the wall, her expression impassive. Lipstick redder than her hair and dark, bowed eyebrows made her appear both silly and sad—like a Pierrot clown.

Beasley was immediately unimpressed, maybe even irritated. "Based on what?"

"Based on what we know about the marriage Del was in, about the man she was married to."

Nicole said, "He beat her. We saw bruises. He has an insurance policy on her. That should tell you everything you need to know right there." She was stepping side to side, grimacing, and clenching her fists. As she talked, she became increasingly amped. "And he's got a girlfriend. He brought her over today. She smelled like gardenias over death."

I planted my hand firmly on Nicole's shoulder and left it there, hoping it would help her to be quiet. Every time she started to speak, I squeezed and she halted. If I knew her symptoms were from antipsychotic medications, Beasley would definitely know. We needed Beasley to believe us, and we had no margin for error. My primary goal was to convince Beasley to hold the body and stop Talon from going to Texas with Khila for as long as possible. But something else took hold that surprised me about myself in that moment. I placed such a high premium on being rational, yet I wanted this person and the institution she represented to care about Del and about what had happened to her. It was the friggin' *Miami morgue*. They processed 2,500 bodies a year, 50 bodies a week, 7 bodies a day. But suddenly, I couldn't help it. I wanted Beasley to give a damn about Del. I wanted anyone who touched Del's body to care about her.

"Del called the police on Talon four times in the last year alone for domestic violence," I said.

"I'm aware of those reports. The police reports were part of why we expedited the autopsy. Not only was this a drowning," she said, "there was a disturbing history." Beasley avoided eye contact, giving me the feeling she was saying only a little bit of what she knew. I wondered if she was thinking then about his juvenile history. She gently added, "A lot of men beat their wives. It doesn't mean he killed her. Del had no new injuries that could be associated with her death."

New? The word floated like a zeppelin between us. "She was thirty-one years old, and she had a heart attack? You're satisfied with that?"

"You should listen to her," Nicole said, swinging a thumb in my direction. "She's a—"

Extra hard squeeze and a threatening glare on top of it. I didn't want Beasley to know I was a commissioner because it would make her far less likely to relate informally with me. And it would make it much harder for me to interact with her without it seeming like I was using my position to influence the outcome of the investigation.

Nicole took hold of the strap of her leather purse and began pinching and rolling it between her thumb and index finger, which helped to pacify her.

More patiently than perhaps I deserved, Beasley said, "Your friend did not die in a struggle. She had no bruises to suggest there had been any kind of assault connected with her death. Not conclusive until the final toxicology report is in, but basic blood analysis suggests no drugs except for tobacco—and laxatives. She weighed ninety-eight pounds—I'm guessing the laxatives she was consuming in large doses had something to do with that. And by the condition of her lungs and the percentage of COHb in her blood at the time of her death, I'm guessing she was a heavy smoker and had smoked probably a pack or more before she dove that morning. Not a good combination—smoking and diving. We try to tell people that, but we still get these kinds of deaths more often than you'd believe."

I felt appreciative of Beasley, because it was evident that, busy as she was, she had Del's details clearly in mind. I stopped myself from repeating what Doug had explained to me about the tenuous connection between smoking and diving; I didn't want her to feel second-guessed by another expert. I couldn't say anything about whether Del had died on the reef, since our only point of contact for that information at the moment was a heroin addict.

"The weight belt." I landed on it like a stone I had leaped to in crossing some great gap. "Del was an experienced diver. If she was drowning, she would have dropped the weight belt."

She pressed her lips together and raised her brows acknowledging I was right. Then she said, "We considered that." Palms up, Beasley added, "She probably panicked. There is enough here to easily explain this death. I'm sorry for your loss, but…"

"Please give us a little more time," I said. "Another day or two before you close the investigation and release the body to be buried." I was in the strange position for the first time in a while of making a plea rather than receiving one.

"I'm not going to hold the body longer than the usual forty-eight hours without a very good reason and," Beasley said with some care, "I haven't heard one yet. The autopsy is done, the preliminary report is written. It's been released to the family. Her husband wants her body released. He has control in these matters." She held the door open for us to leave.

"Just give me until Saturday." I walked backward; Beasley was walking at a quick pace toward me on her way down the hall. She passed me and I followed her. "Friday," I bargained to her back. "Give me two days. Friday."

From behind me someone yelled, "Look!" It was Nicole. "My sister never got a single break in her entire life. Can she just have a few more days in the fucking morgue?"

Beasley stopped and turned, her expression one of annoyance. "She was scheduled to go this afternoon."

"I know. Please." I held her gaze, forced her to tell me no again to my face.

She shook her head and looked at me curiously, as if to ask why this mattered so much.

"If you release Del's body, he'll cremate her and then leave with their daughter for Texas. Once Khila goes, I'm afraid we won't be able to get her back. If we're right about him…If he murdered this child's mother…" I stared at her, overwhelmed by the implications and unable to complete the thought. "Give us a few more days."

"To do what? What are you going to do that the police and the crime-scene team haven't already done?"

"I don't know."

She breathed in and out. "Your first love, huh?" I nodded. She stared at me, and I could see a kind of recognition in her eyes as she began to nod her head along with mine. "I'll give you until Friday morning—Friday eight a.m.—to do whatever it is you think you're gonna do. In the meantime, I've got other work to do." She walked away, calling behind her, "You girls be careful, now."

❖

Our next stop was Pascale's house. Pascale was shut away in her room with the lights off and the shades drawn. She did emerge, likely having heard us come in. She seemed frail, her complexion waxen, and she moved and spoke slowly. "Any news about Khila?" She held on to the wall for balance.

We shook our heads.

Pascale went back into her room.

Ida was standing at the picture window. She shrugged and matter-of-factly informed Nicole and me, "There's a black car out there that's been following us since we left this morning."

That got Nicole's attention. She went to the window. "Which one is it?" Ida started to point. Nicole caught her hand. "Just describe it, Ida. If someone is following us, we don't want them to know we know that."

"That black thing across the street."

"The Jeep?" Nicole's eyes narrowed. "Wasn't there a black Jeep at bay side last night?"

"There's a million of those cars," I said.

"I'm just saying," Ida was turning away from the window, "It's out there now, and it's been following us."

"I'll see if I can get the license-plate number." Nicole left out the back door.

Ida disappeared down the hallway without saying anything. I knew she'd been upset since Beasley's office, and I had some idea why, but I didn't feel like talking to her about it. Instead, I turned my attention to the question of where Del had died.

Talon told the police Del went into the water with him around 10:30 that morning for a quick dive on the reef before breakfast. Her heart failed about twenty minutes in. He told the police he tried to do CPR in the water. When that didn't work, he dumped the air from her buoy compensator, took her tank off, and then pulled her onto the swimming ramp and tried again. Then he swam to shore to get help. In response to why he'd left her, as opposed to calling in over the radio, he said, and it was confirmed, the radio was broken. His first contact with the police from shore was reported to be 11:05 a.m.

Maybe the boat had been anchored on Lemon Reef and the divers just hadn't seen it. But why would anyone anchor a boat at a site where a drug trade was taking place if the whole point of choosing an underwater-dive exchange had been to avoid Coast Guard scrutiny? Boats were stopped and searched routinely in those waters. Talon knew that.

What Talon likely did not know: it was possible to trace the trajectory of a human body in an ocean current. In the eighties and nineties, controlling the influx of "illegals" had become a national obsession, and the navy had been given a huge amount of money to monitor the more vulnerable national coastlines, including Miami's. The Naval Oceanographic Office, using the science of geophysical fluid dynamics, could now trace the path of a dead body in an ocean current.

And I was familiar with this brand-new science because, last year, Jake Mansfield—a scientist working for NAVO testifying as an expert in a murder trial—had applied it to track the trajectory of a boy's body in the bay; his testimony led to the father's acquittal. When I subsequently represented the father in family court, I used Jake's testimony to confirm the father's story that the boy had fallen into the water from the dock near their home and not from a boat some distance away, as Margaret Todd, who was representing the mother, had theorized. In the process of figuring all that out, I had spent a lot of time talking with Jake, and I had his private cell-phone number. I called it now to ask him for help.

"I hear congratulations are in order, Commissioner."

"I've missed you." I was picturing his receding hairline and hazel eyes, and the way his eyebrows lifted when he tried to keep a straight face. "How have you been?" As I asked this, I found myself looking out the window to see if the black Jeep was still there. It wasn't.

"I've been fine." Jake's voice was soft and inviting. "I've missed you, too. I got used to talking to you every day, then the case ended and...occupational hazard, I guess. So, what's up?"

"I need a favor."

"What is it?"

"I'm in Miami," I said, and then I told him why.

"Well." Jake sounded as if he was just settling in. "First of all, I'm sorry about your friend." The following silence was brief but thoughtful and vital. "I'll make her part of my study. I need real-life applications to consider." He hesitated for a moment and then added, "You do know that this is experimental. We're getting more reliable with replications and a larger sample size, but it is very new. The navy is letting me testify, but only California civil courts as of yet."

Nicole came in through the front door and announced, "The Jeep took off before I could see the license plate." She plopped down on the couch.

I cleared my throat, swallowed some water from the cup beside me, and then gave Jake what information I had.

Jake said he would run the calculations and call me back when he knew more. In the meantime, I prepared to move on to the next item on my mental list: Sid. What Tar Baby had said—*Sid went to prison and Talon killed her anyway*—meant he thought Sid had gone to prison to protect Del. I had to talk to Sid. I wasn't sure he'd remember me, so I wanted Nicole or Ida to come along, and because of Nicole's criminal history and navigating prison security, Ida seemed like a better choice. I found her asleep in Del's old room.

Ida lifted her heavy head, her voice groggy and then pissy. "He's in the friggin' Everglades. We can't just go and see him." Her eyes began to close again; her head drifted downward as if caught in the pillow's gravitational force.

"I've interviewed people in prisons a hundred times. We can so go and talk to him. He might have information about Del." My voice caused her to jolt. I continued, "I need you to come with me because he's not gonna remember me, and he'll be more likely to talk to me if you're there."

She lifted her head again and rubbed her eyes. "Yeah, well, I don't know about that. We didn't have such a cozy visit the last time I went to see him. Let's just say"—she thought about it—"he doesn't approve of my occupation." She laughed to herself and shook her head. "He's dealing drugs and doing time for murder, and he's judging me because I give massages for money." She pushed her hair back with both hands and then fell back into the pillow. "Go fuckin' figure."

I hadn't been able to sleep well since my alcohol-induced one-hour nap on the plane, and I could feel my patience running out. "Will you come or not? I can go with Nicole, but it's easier to get into the prison with you. You're not a felon."

"Jenna." Ida sat up. "What are you doing here? Why are you here?" The blanket fell out in ripples around her, covering the bottom half of her body and giving her the appearance of being in water up to her waist.

"Why are you asking me this now?"

She waited for an answer to her question.

"To tell you the truth, I really don't know. At this point, I'm just trying to make this turn out the way everyone thinks Del would have wanted it to." Sharply, I said, "Satisfied?"

"No." Ida laughed harshly. "Why do you care now more than last week, or the week before that?" Her eyes fell flatly upon me. "You messed her up when she was alive. Now you want to make it up to her, after she's dead?"

My heart hit a speed bump.

"You were the best friend Del ever had. She loved you with all her heart. After you turned on her, she was never the same. Like a part of her just quit."

"I *never* turned on Del." A drumbeat started in the hollow of my chest, and my stomach began to twist. I felt immense sadness being in this room with Ida instead of Del, remembering us there. I knew where this conversation was going, and it was Del who I wanted to be having it with. I clamped down my jaw to stop myself from crying.

"Fine." She fell back against the headboard. "Keep telling yourself that." Her face was firm, her eyes narrow, her tone pointed. "But you know what I think? I think you hurt her more than anyone else ever has."

"That sure says a lot, considering you think Talon killed her."

"Nicole thinks that. I don't. They had problems but not like that. Tal loved Del. He hit her, but you might have hit her, too." Smiling to herself, Ida said, "She sure knew how to push people's buttons."

"So where I'm concerned you're defending her, and where he's concerned you're…what? Blaming her?"

"No, I'm saying that hitting her doesn't mean he killed her." Ida shook her head at the nuttiness of it all. "They've been at it a long time. Del was pregnant the first time Talon hit her. There were a lot of ups and downs with them. The truth is, Del was *crazy* about him. And he was crazy about her, threatened to kill himself if she left him." I suppressed an eye roll. Ida *would* be reassured by that. "That's how much he needed her. I know that's not what you want to hear, but it's true." She smiled in a way that seemed cruel and intended to hurt me.

What was I going to do, browbeat her with facts? Suicide and homicide, flip sides of the same coin for batterers; first assault during pregnancy, a clear indicator of severe violence later in the relationship; everything she was saying to convince me otherwise further confirmed my belief that Talon had killed Del.

"Ida," I said, "how do you explain what he did today? How do you understand him showing up here with this new woman—insisting Khila think of her as her new mother. You call that love?"

"I call that grief."

I shook my head.

The liner under Ida's eyes, still thick from the night before, was running a little. She sat holding her legs close to her chest like a little girl. "What you told Beasley today, that you and Del were each other's first loves, you were just making that up, right? You know that's not true."

"So is that what this is all about? You're just mad at me because I told Beasley Del and I were lovers." I blew out a loud sigh. "Ida, you didn't *know* about me and Del?"

"You and Del?" She paused, and then she said, "I know about you." Shrugging her shoulders, she added, "I mean, you know, to each her own."

"To each her own?" I was biting back rage now as well as tears. "You mean, as long as it's not your sister we're talking about."

"It's *not* my sister we're talking about. Del wasn't gay."

I breathed in, trying to stay in the conversation, to see it through to a better place. Ida had this side to her, a kind of pathological naïveté that could be just vicious. "Then what are we talking about, Ida? What do you think happened between Del and me? You obviously feel like you know."

"Because Del talked to me about it."

The beat in my chest went from whole to quarter count.

Ida's red hair was pushed back from her face, and her skin looked drawn and bland. She seemed tired and old. I noticed in a way I hadn't earlier the heavy makeup, the big jewelry, the exhaustion, the jadedness. She'd clearly worked the night before.

Ida said, "Del told me you were gay, and that you wanted a relationship with her, but she didn't want that. She just wanted to be friends. You punished her by refusing to be friends with her."

"Del and I were lovers. We were together for over a year."

"She let you fuck her. I know that."

"She wasn't just letting me fuck her. She was in it, too," I said, less confident than I sounded.

"She wasn't comfortable with it, Jen. She wasn't comfortable with what she did with you. She had a right to feel that way. But you got pissed at her because she just wanted to be friends, and to get back at her you told other people about what you guys did together."

Ida's words were causing shock waves, unearthing buried memories, the last fights we'd had, actions I'd regretted, pain I'd caused her—and Del's face when she turned away from me in disgust at the end and thereafter.

My first impulse was to defend myself. Parts of this were true, sort of, but… "It wasn't like that," was all I could say. I breathed in a sob. "I mean"—I put my hand over my mouth, thought for a moment—"I can see now that maybe I told Gail as a way of distancing myself from Del. But it wasn't out of spite."

My voice sounded hollow. What I had been most aware of always was *my* pain, how Del had hurt *me*. My eyes went to the urine-yellow stains in the linoleum floor. Realizing the spirit of what Ida was saying was what mattered most, I stopped arguing and forced myself to listen to the ways in which I had hurt Del—something I had never done before.

"It's just that Del felt so exposed and humiliated. She said you bragged about the sex you guys had like a stupid guy. I mean, *you went into detail*. She couldn't understand why you had done that to her. You were her best friend. She trusted you. To her it felt like you torched the friendship, which was what she cared about the most. People were always saying shit about her—what a whore she was, superficial, slut. You know." I nodded. "I think when you started talking, when *you* did it too, that was it. She gave up. It was like she just stopped caring, like she became the thing people said she was." Sadly, Ida said, "Del wasn't those things. She was private and loyal."

"And loving," I said, as tears streamed down my cheeks. I'd given up on trying to hold them back.

"She was so hurt, Jenna. I don't think she could even tell you how hurt. I don't think she ever got over it."

The rain had stopped, and a stream of light filtered in through the window above us, speckled with dust particles and illuminated with colors, like a tiny rainbow—yellows, reds, blues, pinks. The colors changed depending on the angle from which I viewed them, and I thought to myself that the end of a relationship is no different.

I don't know how long we sat in silence before Ida asked, "Why do you want to see Sid?"

I wiped my face with my shirt, resisted explaining myself further. I knew my reasons for telling Gail didn't matter. In my world, consequences outweighed intentions. Not an easy transition to make, but I had to get back on track. I had to talk to Sid and see what he knew. Visiting hours were from noon to six p.m., so if we were going, we had to leave.

I stood up and began toward the door. "Remember when Tar Baby said Sid went to prison and Tal killed Del anyway?" Ida was looking at me with a glazed-over expression. "You remember, or not?" Finally, she nodded. "So what did he mean by that? Did Sid know Del was in danger? Did he go to prison to protect her?"

"To tell you the truth, it doesn't matter to me. I don't think Del was murdered." Ida got up and began walking out the door with me. "I think it's better if Nicole goes with you to see Sid. I doubt Sid would even see me right now." In response to my look of confusion, she confessed, "He thinks Tal and I had a thing." I didn't respond. Then Ida said, as an afterthought, "He's been trying to reach us."

"Who?"

"Sid. He has something from Del that he wants us to see. Wouldn't say what it is over the phone."

I stared at her, not knowing which of the last two comments to respond to first or how to respond to either. "How long has he been trying to reach you?"

"How should I know? I've gotten two—well, maybe three—messages from him. He's probably called other people more."

"Maybe you could've mentioned he was calling, just in case he hadn't called anybody else. I mean, Nicole's phone's disconnected,

Del's dead, your mom's not doing too well at the moment, and your dad is somewhere else on the planet. So maybe you're the one he'd try to contact."

Ida had no idea I was being sarcastic. She just nodded, smiled, and said, "Good point."

As we walked down the hall toward the living room, the phone rang, and I heard Nicole answer it in her urgent way.

Now she was holding the phone in her hand, looking at the receiver. "That was Tar Baby." Her brow furrowed into a question mark. "He said, 'Ten fifteen,' and hung up."

"That must be the time the trade had taken place." I glanced out the window, semi-aware I was checking to see if the black Jeep had returned. Maybe it was exhaustion, or maybe it was the image of the mama dog nuzzling her maimed puppies, or maybe it was seeing Khila in distress and feeling helpless to do anything about it, or maybe it was image of Del trying to claw her way to the surface, but at that point, I believed Talon to be capable of anything. As absurd as the idea of our being followed might have seemed to me the day before, I could no longer just dismiss it.

"Let's go see Sid, Nicole."

CHAPTER TWELVE

I parked outside the prison. As I watched to see if we'd been followed, I couldn't help but notice Nicole removing knives from her pockets and razor blades from her shoes, apparently in preparation for passage through a metal detector. Then she removed the leather pouch she always had hanging from a string across her chest and put it in the glove compartment.

"What is that?"

Her head bobbed to some internal beat. "My survival kit."

Her answer left no room for follow-up, and I realized I probably didn't want to know what was in it anyway.

We made the hundred-yard trek up the newly paved walkway to the prison entrance. It was an imposing building, a city block in size and several stories high. The walls were cinderblock, with small windows that had bars over them. There was a gate approximately twelve feet high around the perimeter and guard towers in key locations manned by uniformed people with guns.

Because of Nicole's criminal history and my out-of-state "special visitor" status, it took forever to get past security and into the visitors' area. Nicole had to be searched, and I had to clear my visit with the watch commander, who had taken a long lunch that day. Now, waiting for Sid, Nicole and I sat like mirror images in parallel universes. Both of us silent, my head propped by my right elbow, her head propped by her left elbow, we gazed warily at the beige wall before us. Neither one of us knew how to understand Ida.

"I don't know," I said, my breath feeling as stale as the air in the room. "Either Ida is really stupid, or she is trying to protect Talon."

"She's trying to protect herself." Nicole dropped her head back, her soft, light hair falling back with it. "Ida has fucked every one of Del's lovers." She looked at me. "Except you. Right?"

I snorted.

"Can you imagine," Nicole said, her mouth twitching, "if Ida did sleep with Talon behind Del's back, and then he killed Del? Oh God." More twitches and jerky leg movements. "Ida can't think that. She'd never forgive herself."

"Do you think we can trust her?"

"I don't know. Ida's always been jealous of Del, ever since she came to live with us. She's done a lot of fucked up things to Del, but she loved her, too. So which side wins in this depends on which way Ida's psycho winds are blowing. Anyway, I have to trust her. She's all I have left."

"He was so horrible today," I said. "The kid's mother has been dead two days and not only is he bringing his girlfriend around, he's letting this woman refer to herself as Khila's mother. And the woman is *doing* it. I don't know who between them is sicker, him or her."

Tables with connected benches lined the length of the long, narrow room, bookended by two solid metal doors. One door—the door we had entered through—led in the direction of the outside world. The other door, the door Sid was escorted through, led deeper into the prison maze. We were meeting in the visitation area located just on the periphery of the prison grounds, inside the walls, but outside of the prison building proper.

Sid was dressed in a jean shirt, jean pants, and black boots, all slightly too big for him. Ankle and wrist shackles attached to a waist chain rattled as he walked. He sat across from Nicole and me, seemingly unaffected by his circumstances or surroundings.

An envelope lay between us on the table, most conspicuous for its having created huge delays in our visit as the prison guards read its contents and searched it for contraband. I had recognized the writing on the envelope immediately as Del's, delicate and even.

"They searched it coming and going," Sid said, flicking the envelope a couple of centimeters toward us. "Just the same shit. It takes an hour to move ten feet in this place. I'm guessing this is what you're here for." Now he pushed it across the table. "Sorry to bring you all the way out here, but I don't say squat on these phones."

"We came here to see you," I said. He ignored me.

Nicole eyed the envelope hesitantly. "What's in it?"

He stared at her, his black eyes tearing up. I reached to pull it closer in order to look inside. Sid slammed his hand down on the letter, making a loud pounding and rippled rattling noise that startled Nicole and me and drew the guard's attention.

"Who the hell are you?"

"Relax." Nicole spoke softly. "This is Jenna. She's an old friend of Del's and she's a judge. She's helping us figure out what happened." Nicole nodded reassuringly at him. "She's already helped us a lot, Sid." Sid released the letter.

I scanned the beige linoleum floor to its periphery, framed by beige plastic wallboards dashed with roach traps. The traps were filled with dead roaches and roach body parts—antennae, legs, wings—roaches who, in the interest of escaping their deaths, had sacrificed an appendage or two. In leaving parts of oneself behind, at what point, I wondered, is keeping on going no longer worth it? The garbage in one corner of the room was overflowing, remains of meals stale to both my nose and my eyes. I hadn't noticed any odor until I saw the exposed, aging, part-eaten scraps of food. The colors melded into one another, the beige floors into the beige walls, the beige walls into the beige ceiling, the beige surround encompassing the beige tables and benches, just a wash of beige. By the time I brought my eyes back to the table, even Sid and Nicole looked a tint of beige for a few moments.

Nicole opened the letter and began reading it. "It says that if anything happens to her, there's a box on the top shelf of her closet in her bedroom that she wants us to get."

"What's in it?" I asked.

"Don't know, but I think that her being dead probably counts for something happening to her."

"Why'd she send this to you?" I asked.

Sid sighed, shrugged his shoulders, shifted in his chair. "Not sure. I'm the one she could be sure'd be home to get it, maybe."

"She knew he was gonna kill her?" Nicole asked.

He tilted back in his chair. "Talon made it really clear to Del that she never gets out. If she tried, he told her he'd kill her or Khila, or both. That's his way. If she did something he didn't want her to do or didn't do something he did want her to do, he'd go after what she loved the most." Sid paused and took a breath. "But the last couple months, something's been up. I don't know why, maybe because Del met someone. He could cheat on her but not the other way around." Sid rolled his head, as if to relieve a strain in his neck. "I know what he's capable of, so I've been getting ready for bad news." He directed his next comment to Nicole. "You know that Thomas kid? You know I never went anywhere near him. Tal tried to get me to go to the mall that day because he was trying to set me up. When I didn't go to the mall, Del called me and asked me to come over."

"I've always believed you," Nicole said. "I know you're innocent."

He laughed once. "I'm not gonna go hit some retarded kid. Talon got other guys to kill him and say it was me. Sick motherfucker forced Del to put the final nail in my coffin." Sid kicked at the floor angrily, the ankle chains clanging against the wooden legs of the table. "Well, now Del's dead."

"You plead?" I asked.

Sid breathed out a laugh. "That or face a capital trial for killing a retarded kid. Figured I'd stay alive, try to get myself out of this mess." He added, "I know how crazy this sounds." He was talking to Nicole, but did glance momentarily in my direction for the first time. "But I'm telling you, Talon set me up. He made sure I was at the house with Del when the murder went down. Then he told Del that she wasn't allowed to give me an alibi. It was one of the times when he was trippin', thinking she was cheating on him. He was proving his power over her to all his buddies. I heard he took bets that she'd do what he wanted her to do. He had her doing all kinds of sick shit to show her off. Well, and to make a few bucks, but she drew a line." He looked at us sideways, laughed at some silent joke. "I hate to say it, but that's probably what you're gonna find in that box, videos of her with other men. Be prepared."

"I don't understand." I scanned his face, absorbing what I was hearing. "You mean sex tapes?" He nodded. "Why? Why'd Talon do that?" *What is it with this guy and the videotaping?* "Why'd *she* do that?"

Sid shrugged a little. "Don't know." Then he considered what he was about to say next. With a slight smile and raised brows, he offered almost mischievously, "It is Del we're talking about."

The three of us, wide eyed and puckered lipped, nodded in sync.

Serious again, Sid said, "I know recently he threatened her with selling the tapes on the homegrown market if she didn't do what he wanted her to do. For some reason, he was getting more desperate. Maybe he knew she was really gonna leave his ass."

"Who were the guys in the tapes?" Nicole asked.

"Men they picked up at bars and shit. Guys looking for head who didn't mind being videoed."

I noticed again the roach traps, the linoleum floor, the walls, the doors, the garbage. Then I noticed Sid looking at me differently, felt him taking me in. He was a little boy when I stopped coming around, but some part of him now remembered me. His face changed, went from hard to soft, and his black eyes grew sad. He stared at me as if he were just now seeing me for the first time. And in his softness, he was newly familiar to me as well, with his black, baby-fine hair, thick eyelashes, and dark bowed brows. It was not hard for me to believe Sid had taken a plea to protect Del, because I knew he would have done anything for her. What was hard to believe—shocking—was that she'd let him.

❖

"Del," the little voice had said. "Del." I opened my eyes. Sid, then two and a half years old, was standing at the side of Del's bed, his eyes an even height with mine. He was holding his stuffed bear and his blanket. He said, "Del." When she didn't hear him, he said it again just as softly. "Del."

I roused myself. "Hey, what's the matter?"

Sid stared at me for a moment, his black eyes glassy, his soft black hair bed messed. "I no feel good." Del sprung up from behind me. "I no feel good," he said again.

"Jenna," she reprimanded, "why didn't you wake me up?" Del climbed over me from her place near the wall, landed on the edge of the bed, and picked Sid up onto her lap.

I sat up. "He just came in, I think." Rubbing my eyes, I said, "I just woke up, too."

Her hand on his forehead, Del looked at me. "He has a fever." She hugged him and stood up. "I think he needs aspirin. Go put water on for tea." I climbed out from under the covers and followed her out of the room. Del went to the bathroom with Sid. I went on to the kitchen. Moments later, Del appeared. "We don't have any aspirin. Can you go get some?"

It was two a.m., but I didn't hesitate. We searched our pockets. I had one dollar and Del had two, leftover from a movie we'd gone to earlier. I pulled on clothes, stuck my feet in loosely laced sneakers, and headed out the door. My plan was to ride my bike to a minimart a few blocks away that we knew to be open all night. It was the summer before our tenth-grade year. The warm night air was dense with moisture. Its thickness and stillness had trapped in it scents of engine oil, burned trash, fresh paint, mixed with something raw—cut grass, maybe. The houses were dark, the windows in them darker. Fences threw shadows. There were voices in the distance, but I couldn't tell from which direction they came.

As I approached the end of the block and turned the corner, I was surprised to run into a group of young men huddled in a circle. They had cigarettes and beers and were laughing loudly and talking in Spanish. They parted to clear the way for me, and I rode through them. One of the men called to me, then said Del's name. I stopped, took a better look, and realized he was a guy who often flirted with her. Another said something in Spanish I didn't understand. The guy standing next to him who spoke a little English interpreted. "Where are you going so late? He wants to know."

The man who had first called to me was behind me again saying Del's name. He apparently had recognized me as her friend. He was gesturing big tits, to identify her to the others, and laughing. The other guys nodded agreeably and laughed, too.

I said, "I'm getting baby aspirin."

The man who had asked where I was going now became more alert. "Baby aspirin?" he said with a heavy Spanish accent.

"For Sid." I pointed in the direction of Del's house. The man spoke in Spanish to a woman sitting on the porch. She disappeared into the house, returning a few moments later with a bottle of baby aspirin.

I took it from her and held out to her the dollars I had in my pocket.

She declined the money, smiled warmly. "*Mamita*, how old are you?" she asked in uneasy English.

I was backing up on my bike to turn it around. "Fourteen."

"Go straight home," she said. "You hear me?" I nodded, thanked her, and rode away.

Back at Del's, I let myself in and found Del in the bathroom with Sid. Sid was sitting in the tub; Del was helping him drink tea and honey from a cup.

I handed the bottle to her and told her where I'd gotten it. She fed Sid two aspirin.

"He had diarrhea," Del said, explaining the bath. "I called my mother."

"Is she coming home?"

Del shook her head. "She can't leave work. She told me to call my father." Del ran a washcloth over Sid's back, tousled his hair.

He watched her, smiled a little, played with a boat in the water, said her name—"Del"—to himself.

She gave him more tea. "I called the number I have for him."

I sat down beside her and tucked her hair behind her ear to get it out of her way. She turned her face to me but kept her eyes someplace else. "A woman answered."

"Did you ask for your dad?"

A slower, more deliberate head shake. "I hung up." Now she looked at me. "I can't believe he's gonna do this. He's just gonna leave her with four kids. She can't do it. He *knows* she can't do it."

Del released the plug to allow the tub to drain. "Stand up," she said to Sid. He did. Then he raised his arms over his head asking to be picked up. Del wrapped him in a towel and lifted him to her. She put him down on the floor and got a clean diaper. Sid lay down for her and allowed her to diaper him. "Come on," she said, lifting him again. As she headed for the door she called back to me, "Can you get Benny?"

I picked up Sid's bear.

The three of us lay down in her single bed together, me so close to the edge, I had to lie on my side and balance my weight inward. Our bathing suits hung in Del's window over her bed, drying in the night air and tracing the light breeze. Sid was between us, dressed in soft, clean pajamas and clutching Benny. He quickly fell asleep, his breaths low hums and occasional snores. Del whispered over his head, "I think the aspirin helped. He feels cooler." Her hand moved from his head to my hair, which she stroked, then wrapped around her fingers. I took her hand and kissed it. "What do you think is going to happen to us?" she asked.

❖

Sid had been a very pretty boy, and now he was a very pretty man. He was staring at me, his expression a mixture of sadness and curiosity. "What is it?" I asked, the love I was feeling for him now palpable.

"Del did whatever Talon told her to do. Except"—his eyes fixed on me—"she wouldn't fuck another woman." He laughed as if he'd just said the most absurd thing. His head slightly tilted, his eyes narrowed, his tone questioning. "I mean, of all the places to draw a line, right? Not even when she was tooting. She wouldn't fuck another woman, not for money, not for nothin'." To me, his voice daring, "Why do *you* think that is?"

"How should I know?" I said, unsure of what he wanted from me and feeling strange and confused by this information. "Maybe it grossed her out." I meant, *maybe I had.*

"Right." His tone was resigned, his owl eyes drifting away hopelessly.

My heart sank as I began to understand what he was struggling with, what seeing me had brought up for him. The idea that Del couldn't help it was all he had left. What if Del had kept some things sacred, and he just hadn't been one of them? He'd gone to prison for her, when maybe she had had the wherewithal to act protectively.

Sid shifted in his chair, wiggled his wrist a little to release some pressure from the wrist cuff, and then he turned his attention back to his own story. "Del told the police I wasn't with her that day, even though I was. After that I pleaded because, you know, my alibi went south and I looked like a total liar every which way."

"You said Del met someone," I said. "Did you ever meet him, or do you have any idea where we might find him?"

"Shit no!" Sid dropped his head back and closed his eyes. "I wish I did, because whoever he is, he knows the whole story, and maybe he could help me out now that Del's dead. Talon did this to her. I know it, and he's gonna get away with it the way he gets away with everything." In order to run his right hand over his brow he had to lower his left hand to the waist chain. "I should have known better. Del begged me to take the plea for her sake and for Khila's. If I refused, then I think in the end, she would have said what was true. But she was so desperate, and I knew what else he did to her, I knew she was right to be scared. She said she needed time to work this out. She swore she would find a way to get me out." Staring at me, he said, "Now what am I gonna do?"

Sid impatiently waved his head at the guard, signaling he was ready to go. The guard approached. As Sid stood up, I looked at him, aware I might never see him again. I wanted to say something encouraging, but what?

Over his shoulder he said to Nicole, "Tell Mom I said hi."

❖

As we left the prison grounds, Nicole said, "So what now, Sherlock? We break into asshole's house to get that box, get caught, he goes to butt-fuck Texas, and we live next door to Sid. Isn't that what you legal people call poetic justice, or some shit like that?"

I laughed a little. "No." I tried to roll down my window, eager to let the air wash the stale prison scent off me, only to be reminded the window was stuck and the handle broken.

Nicole put a cigarette in her mouth and hit the lighter. "You're a judge, goddamn it. Can't you just tell the police this was a murder? Can't you just tell them to go get the box from Talon's house?" It took her several tries to line the lighter up to the tip of the cigarette. "Or what about my brother, don't you know anyone who could help him, you know, get out of prison?"

I tried to respond to her questions, but all I could think about was the nausea I felt and trying to keep from vomiting. Nicole was swerving in and out of the lane on the road, the car was filled with cigarette smoke, my window was broken, and when I shut my eyes I saw roach traps and writhing puppies. My phone rang, and had it not been Jake Mansfield, I would never have risked answering in that state.

"I'm not finished yet, but I thought I'd let you know she's a half mile away from the range of endpoints that are possible, given the place she reportedly started from."

I undid my seat belt, climbed over the front seat into the back, and cranked down the first window I could reach. The air rushed in, dense and humid, and I felt the nausea subside by degree. Now sober, I asked, "What are you saying?" We were driving on Route 41, banked on one side by slash pines and on the other by snarls of prickly leaf vegetation.

"I ran the numerical, controlled for shallow water, surface drift, and gravitational force, and even with allowing for a significant margin of error, she ended up in the *opposite* direction. To end up where she was, from where he says she started out, she would have had to drift *against* the current. Either she swam there or she was put there, but she did not drift to that spot from the reef coordinates you gave me."

Heat seeped out in waves from the blacktop, warping the air. Other cars were way ahead or way behind. I grabbed my pad and pen from the front seat and wrote everything he said down. Then I got off the phone and told Nicole to pull over. When she did, I jumped out of the car and stood still for a moment, trying to get my bearings.

With the nausea subsided and the smoke cleared, I saw the terrain of the Everglades surrounding us and realized I must have slept through this stretch on the way there. I walked down the road in the stifling heat. Without asking why I was walking or where I was going, Nicole just followed me slowly in the car. Florida as I knew it: miles of flat, dusty, brown ground and tall, mostly leafless sticks for trees. And then, with no prior warning, no gentle transformation of terrain, one arrives at the edge of a slow-moving river or a bed of tall grass, teeming with plant life and animal flurry. It's not that these shockingly beautiful places are hiding so much as just peacefully, quietly coexisting with the banal and the hideously ugly. We were upon one of the many Everglades sloughs known best and most illustratively as liquid ground. This particular river, which I thought might be the Shark River Slough, connected the fresh water of Lake Okeechobee to the Gulf of Mexico and the Keys. It was all continuous and interdependent—and delicate. If one stood in this spot long enough, one could sense the earth breathing.

The sunlight bent through cypress trees and cast white light over the water and saw-grass surface. The current moved at a snail's pace, up to and around an isolated mahogany "island." The islands are mounds in the slough created centuries ago by coral cliffs abandoned by receding seawater, now calcified into limestone beds that provide havens for mighty oaks and majestic mahoganies. Many of the trees, like the one before us, were young, the more mature ones having been logged a long time ago for furniture. The contradictions—at once hard and soft, wet and dry, salt and fresh, still and moving—were overwhelming.

Nicole and I found a dry spot under a tree by the water, where a slight breeze swept over the grass. Nicole was worried about alligators and couldn't relax. I, on the other hand, was having more trouble with the mosquitoes, which—I have always been convinced—prefer Jewish blood. A blue heron posed serenely in the distance.

"Talon is lying, Nicole. What my friend just explained to me is that there is no way Del's body drifted from Lemon Reef to where she was found."

"How? How does he know that?" Nicole crossed her arms defiantly. She crossed her legs, then uncrossed them, then reversed the process. She flicked her finger as if she were holding a cigarette. I noticed her facial tic, and the jerky hand and leg movements she worked hard to conceal by staying in perpetual motion.

"This guy that I asked to help me is an expert in that exact question. He has this method for studying bodies floating in currents."

"How come the police don't know what he knows?" She was listening to me and watching at the same time for alligators. She shook her head and said to herself, "They're fucking fast, those suckers."

"I think because the science is so new. It's still experimental." I swatted my neck, which made Nicole eye the car longingly.

"So she didn't drift to where they found her. I doubt she swam there. He wouldn't drag her there all the way from the reef, would he?"

Then it occurred to me. "She was already at the spot where they found her. That's where she died."

Nicole looked a little uneasy, her eyes shifting back and forth, grappling, always grappling with some invisible constraint or intrusion. "So what you're thinking," she said, "is that Tal killed her, and then he swam to the reef and made the trade?"

Nicole hit my arm to get my attention. I looked up and she gestured behind me with a lift of her chin. Standing off in the knee-high brush, the color of wheat, was a smooth-coated panther with liquid brown eyes and ready, sprung ears. She matched her background almost perfectly, making it hard to find her twice.

"Something like that. It seems risky, killing her and then doing the trade. He didn't want her floating out there with other divers around."

"Well, that's why he hooked her to that chain."

"Maybe." I brought my knees to my chest and hugged them. "I think he made the trade and then went back and killed her. My only problem is timing. We know he made the trade at ten fifteen. Assuming it took fifteen minutes to swim from the reef back to the boat, he was back around ten thirty, which is when he said Del went into the water. He called the police from a landline at eleven oh five. That means he only had thirty-five minutes to kill Del, move the boat to Lemon Reef, swim to shore, and then get to the phone." I was thinking out loud. "So the death had to be quick. She had no marks, and there were no drugs. There was no sign of a struggle. She wasn't hit or strangled or even held underwater, that we can tell. She was alive when she went into the water and dead from a heart attack, with Talon having moved the boat and gotten himself to a shoreline phone, thirty-five minutes later. How *is* that possible?" Thinking further, I said, "We don't have the full toxicology, so maybe it was a drug they haven't detected yet."

"How long was Del underwater?"

"No way to know exactly. They estimate between six and seven hours."

Nicole raised her chin and grimaced slightly. Then she lit a cigarette, a ritual I now recognized as part of the perpetual-motion phenomenon. "Well, isn't it over anyway, on the fact that she didn't die where Talon said she did? Can't we just tell the police Talon is lying, now that we can prove it?"

I watched the smoke from the cigarette rise, felt it trying to write something on the air. "It's more than we had before," I said gently. "But we don't know if Jake's findings will be admissible here, and I want to figure out how Talon killed her before I leave it to the state of Florida to make a case against him." I looked for the panther, the heron, one of Nicole's alligators, and found none of them. "Get me back to town," I said. "I promised my mother I'd come over for dinner."

CHAPTER THIRTEEN

Thursday

I woke up thinking about the box Del had described in the letter she sent to Sid and wondered what was in it. The thought was residue from a dream about Del, but I couldn't remember now what the dream had been about. I rose slowly. Dinner at my parents' had been uneventful, and I did feel better for having seen them. Norma showed me pictures from her last trip with Brian. Mel managed to look like he was participating in the conversation, his eyes on me while his ears labored in the direction of the television. He was a news junkie.

I was planning to go for a run with Katie, so I got dressed, then went to the closet and searched through my bag for my running sneakers. Then I tossed the bag back into the closet messily, on purpose, not closing the closet door. Gail's guest room had pale peach and aquamarine walls, and wall-to-wall cream-colored carpet. The furniture around me—slick, black-and-chrome, modern—was accented with pastel pillows, ceramic fixtures, and a large mirror in a gold frame. I sat down on the bed adorned with a cream-colored satin duvet and panicked momentarily as I felt its softness grab hold of me. The low ceiling pressed down on me, the shiny objects stood firm like miniature soldiers keeping guard, as the structure and decor of this square space conspired, I was suddenly convinced, to trap me in a *Golden Girls* rerun. I chafed at the aesthetic and fought an irrational wave of anger at Gail.

Then I talked myself down, reminded myself I should be happy for Gail. This condo was a triumph for her, the appliances and central air-conditioning and dedicated parking space and gardeners paid out of association dues, her daily proof she hadn't let life outwit or overlook her. She kept a guest room, and she was now proudly and generously letting me stay in it. I returned to the bag, shook it into place on the closet floor, and shut the door. Still, I did hate the Georgia O'Keeffes; I wished there were just one Stevie Nicks poster here, not framed, but taped to the wall.

❖

As I waited for Katie to arrive, I allowed myself to remember the October '83 Stevie Nicks concert. We had seats on the lawn in the periphery of the stadium. Katie, Gail, Edie, and Susan passed a soccer ball around in one direction and a joint in the other. I was on a secret date with Del for my fifteenth birthday. We sat next to each other on a blanket in the grass, our legs extended, outer thighs touching. We were watching Stevie Nicks dance, her black gauze wrappings a flowing silhouette against the backlit stage, like a crow, wide winged against a full moon, the stark image intermittently rendered opaque by a floor of dry ice melting upward.

It was the first and only time we made a public claim, high on pot and emboldened by the smoke and mirrors of a flamboyant stage queen and the music and lyrics of "Landslide." Edie, Susan, Katie, and Gail knocked the soccer ball around on the lawn behind us, too stoned to notice us, or us too stoned to care. Jason Schwartz was with them, trying to keep Katie interested in him beyond her thirty-second limit. I was loving Del, loving the moment, and allowing sex to be the nearby and ever-more-poignant promise it always was for me when I was with her in public. The night heat was so intense it made the loose tank tops we wore feel thick. I watched a single bead of sweat form under Del's arm, then trail down and disappear into the indent at the edge of her rib cage where the upward slope of her breasts began. My eyes traced the lift of her shirt to the point—her nipple—peaked like a cliff at the edge of a steep incline.

It started when Del, not trusting I would let myself get high, took hits from the joint we were sharing, covered my mouth with hers, and injected me with smoke. We ended up kissing without fully intending to, and then caught ourselves. But the feeling of fooling around in front of other people had gotten us both pretty roused. Now, eyes fixed on

Stevie, Del tossed her hair so it fell loosely and evenly around her face and said, "Which panties are you wearing?" It was more a demand than a question, as if she had a right to know.

I whispered in her ear, said each word slowly. "Blue. Silky." A daring smile. "Bikini." I'd worn her favorite pair for our date. Del breathed in through clamped teeth. I was surprised and thrilled when she casually placed her thigh over mine. I watched her maneuver her short skirt to do it. Staring at her upper thigh, I glanced around to see if anyone we knew was watching, then slid my hand up her skirt, worked my fingers under her panties, and touched her. She was swollen and soaked. My mouth near her ear, I more breathed than said, "Damn!" I thought we were just teasing each other. It was something we did more and more in public—cop feels, steal glances, pass love notes in class to see who could make the other blush first and then most. I couldn't believe it that night when Del pushed my hand in farther and kissed me in the way I knew her to mean it.

Because Del wanted to keep us a secret, I had resisted for nearly a year the overwhelming urge to tell everyone I knew I was fucking her. This public display of us was something I wanted desperately, but I hesitated nonetheless. I thought it was the drugs bringing her out that night. I feared she would regret our having done this when their effect wore off—that her shame would cause her to withdraw from me or to punish us in some way.

"Are you sure?" I asked, my gaze dropping from her eyes to her mouth. We had gotten good at sex by then, and the halting felt unnatural, but I was offering Del a chance to catch herself, snap to reason, remember our status, abandon her Rubiconic impulse. Del smiled a little, nodded, and pulling her side of the blanket with her for cover, slid onto me. Two bodies, one motion, hidden only by nighttime shadows and the blanket we had been sitting on. My fingers cramming into her; Del moving onto me, her mouth on my mouth, her palms pressing on my tits, her fingers seizing my nipples. Hair loose, tongues tangled, the rhythm and force of her coming on me, the smell, taste, feel, and sound of her everywhere—like breathing underwater.

❖

I don't know why some of us made it and some of us didn't. She shouldn't have not. Del—sun-soaked, water soluble, as graceful traversing warring clans in school or working the register at the motel dive-shop as she was abandoning a volleyball game for a plunge in the ocean—Del knew bubbles travel upward. Brian, being his big-brotherly self, made certain of it when he taught Del and me to scuba dive. When diving, Brian said repeatedly, should you lose your way, become disoriented and confused about which direction is up and which direction is down, just follow the bubbles. Bubbles always travel upward. This one fact was supposed to bring us both home safely.

❖

"Still feel like coming here was the right thing to do?" Katie asked. We had been jogging side by side in silence for a long distance.

"I don't know."

I drank the hot Miami air, realizing that, no true San Franciscan after all, I thrived on it. I thought about Sid. As my body welcomed the wet heat, my mind flashed suddenly on images of Thomas, a baffled boy long acquainted with the limits of bodily control, being beaten incontinent and then out of existence. And of a mother being brought to this scene or left to imagine it. And the rest: the scheming and manipulation, wheeling and dealing that must have taken place behind the scenes to end up with one stupid, seemingly innocent, nineteen-year-old boy of color taking the fall.

"Seeing Sid in prison was so hard. I could still see the little boy in him." We ran on, the repetitive, rhythmic sound of sneakers against sidewalk and synchronized breath-filled strides following us or anticipating us.

I revealed this next bit of information reluctantly, unsure as to whether it was just more of the same sex-hype lies that had plagued Del throughout her entire adolescence. "Sid says Talon was into watching Del, videotaping her having sex with other guys. It was a control thing. He thinks that's probably what we're gonna find in that box. Why she would want us to find that, I have no idea."

Katie laughed a little. "I wouldn't mind watching those."

Whoa! Not the response I was expecting from Katie. For one thing, it was blatantly homoerotic—unconscious, perhaps, but nonetheless blatant. And it stung because I knew what she meant. I understood too well the pleasure we all could take in Del's humiliation.

"Don't get mad at me for saying this, but guys were always talking about how, you know, *good* she was." Katie smiled slyly. "I'm just curious. That's all."

I nodded, trying to fashion a quick response that would somehow redeem us both. "You mean you want to study her *technique*?"

Katie laughed. "Well, when you put it that way…"

I shook my head. "I can't believe we're having this conversation."

She looked at me sideways and with suspicion. "You're not even a little bit curious, Jenna? You're not a little bit tempted to watch them, just to see her like that?"

❖

When it came time to leave the Stevie Nicks concert, we checked in with each other and realized no one had made a plan for us to get home.

Gail said, "Don't leave it to Katie." The rest of us laughed.

Katie rolled her eyes with annoyance over the amount of attention her recent solution of giving blow jobs for rides was getting. "I only did that twice."

Andrew Torie, one of the rich kids at our school, appeared out of nowhere, his timing, as always, impeccable. He stared unabashedly at Del, her long hair catching the moonlight like silk, her tank top askew, hanging loosely from her thin neck and shoulders. She was revved, sweaty, a little disarrayed from having just been fucked. He knew Del was stoned, could smell sex on her, and—true to his vulturesque ways—circled in wait.

"Andrew will give us a ride home," Del announced.

I shook my head. "My brother will come and get us." I looked at Del firmly, hoping to sway her in my direction.

"It's fine, Jenna. Andrew's right here." She leaned in and whispered, "I don't want Brian to see us stoned."

Andrew dangled gold keys from his fingers, flashed the Mercedes symbol to which they were connected like it was a backstage pass to life. "Got my dad's car." Then he shrugged at his sidekick, Donald

Magowsky, and they both began to walk away. He was playing chicken with Del. She fell in behind him.

Katie looked at me and said sarcastically, "His *dad's* car." She watched Del leaving, shrugged her shoulders as if to persuade us to just go along with the plan. The rest of us followed Katie following Del following Andrew toward the exit. Somehow Donald ended up in the driver's seat of Andrew's father's Mercedes. Katie grabbed the front passenger seat. Gail climbed into the backseat by the window. Andrew pushed Del into the middle of the backseat and slid himself in next to her, closing the door behind him. That left the rear floor of the station wagon for the rest of us.

As we drove along, I watched Andrew creep in on Del, putting his arm over the back of the seat behind her like a bad junior high school movie date. I began to eye the tire iron on the floor beside me. Del glanced back at me and smiled reassuringly. Edie and Susan watched me watching Andrew, both of them slightly stiff and suddenly dead sober. Andrew hooked his elbow around Del's neck and let his hand fall to where I could no longer see it. I watched Andrew intently, my hand moving slowly until it butted against the cold metal.

Del leaned forward, shifting out from under Andrew's arm, ostensibly to ask Katie something. When he moved his arm, she sat back. He waited until she relaxed again and then put his hand back where it had been, this time sliding his whole body in closer to her and smiling at her. I was stiffening with rage, envisioned smashing Andrew in the back of the head with the iron rod. I kept telling myself Del would not want me to make a scene. If I did hit him in the head, she'd probably be pissed off at me for calling attention to us. These thoughts were only barely working. If I killed him, however, I would have to go somewhere and that would mean being separated from Del. He touched her hair. I postured to slam him, one thinning thought remaining between the iron rod now firmly in my grasp and the back of Andrew Torie's oval head: *forced separation*.

Gail who, like Susan and Edie, had been tracking me, blurted out, "I'm getting carsick."

"Gail says she's carsick," Edie repeated, only louder, her eyes dashing back and forth from my hand to Andrew's head. She looked at Andrew, her tone urgent, "Gail says she's carsick, I'd pull over if I were you."

Susan chimed in. "Unless you want to bring your dad's car back with throw up all over it."

Katie, who was busy finding radio stations, tapped Donald on the shoulder. "Gail feels sick. Pull over." Donald kept going. Katie turned around and looked at Andrew.

"*Whatever*. Pull over." Andrew sounded irritated.

When we stopped, Gail got out, and in the same motion, Del scooted away from Andrew toward the other door. I relaxed and leaned back against Edie, who put her arms around me. Gail walked around for a minute. Then she came back to the car and said to Del, "Will you switch seats with me? I need to be in the middle." Del agreed.

Obviously bummed, Andrew said, "I thought carsick people need the window seat."

Gail, who seemed proud of her intervention, climbed in beside him. "Nope, not for me. I have to be able to look straight out. If I'm stuck looking at the back of someone's head, that doesn't go too well."

As we drove off, Andrew said to Gail, "Why don't you lose weight? If you weren't so fat, then you probably wouldn't get carsick."

When it was about Gail, I could fight, but all I could think to say was, "Why don't you eat poison and die? You spoiled-rotten piece of shit."

Andrew was startled but tried not to show it—like trying not to blink when someone nearly flicks you in the face. "Huh." He was stalling, trying to think of a comeback.

Katie, having somehow figured out the ruckus had something to do with Del and me—or just wanting to get rid of Del, because she had a crush on Andrew—turned around and said to Andrew, "If we get off here, we can drop Del and Jenna off first."

Andrew grinned. "I'm gonna take Del home last."

Del was quietly staring out the car window. She was upset, and by the feeling cast by her last glance in my direction, I knew it was with me. Maybe because I had let my jealousy show; maybe because she had wanted something to happen with Andrew and felt thwarted; maybe because I was not a real boy, and I could not restore her to honor in the way a real boy could, or protect her in the way a real boy could. A real boy, I thought, could have claimed her, given her an alibi that made her rejection of Andrew make sense, fucked her on the field trying to be noticed. Del's response to Andrew's invitation to be the last one dropped off came slowly, her words written from her mouth one letter at a time. It felt to me like hours before her thought had been completed. Without moving her face from the window she said, "Jenna is sleeping over. And I've really gotta get home." I told myself it was the pot, that it really hadn't taken her so long to set the record straight.

Pascale was out cold on the couch. The younger kids were asleep. We crept in, the permutations of light from the television hurling our stretched, oddly angular shadows onto the wall and ceiling of the square room. We went down the hall toward Del's bedroom. Del turned off at the bathroom without giving me any indication of what her plans were or whether I should follow her. I sensed her rage at me and sheepishly went to her room to wait for her. I took off my clothes, found the T-shirt I planned to sleep in, and pulled it on over my head. Then I looked around in my bag for my toothbrush.

A few moments later, Del appeared, face moist and scarlet from washing, her hair pulled back in a neat ponytail, a toothbrush hanging from her mouth, toothpaste bubbling from her lips and down her chin. What she had to say to me couldn't wait a moment longer.

Hoping to prevent a fight, I said, upon her entering, "I'm sorry I acted jealous."

Her eyes burning, tears forming, "Fuck you, Jenna," Del yelled-whispered. "I can't believe you stuck up for Gail and not for me." All at once, she fought to speak, to hold back tears, to brush her teeth, and to keep toothpaste in her mouth. "He was putting his hands all over me. Why didn't you say something about *that*?"

How, I thought, taken aback by the idea of what she had actually been hoping for from me. Expecting. I felt confused by her suggestion; where I thought my inadequacy was a given, she felt it was a matter of choice. I was distracted and disarmed by this glimpse of myself through her eyes. Not used to being undone in a fight, I groped for a more familiar mode and landed on accusation. "You were flirting with him. Gail was threatening to throw up on him. She was easier to stick up for."

Del's face cracked indiscernibly; she walked out to lose the toothbrush. Reentering moments later, "Okay," Del said, "that's really funny. Don't make me laugh, Jenna. I'm really mad at you." Her eyes filled again. "I wasn't flirting with him. *We* had just been together. Did that mean anything to you?"

Mean anything to *me*? "Why'd we have to go with him?"

"I was thinking about getting us home. That was it."

I looked at her. "Del, you do flirt a lot." Gently, "Sometimes, I think you do it without even knowing it."

She pushed me back onto the bed and then fell in beside me. We were on our sides facing each other.

"It's hard to say no to Andrew. I don't know"—she hesitated, then she admitted—"I think it's because he's rich."

I was surprised. "So?"

"That's easy for you to say."

I stared at the wall behind her, pained and enraged that she felt small compared to Andrew Torie. Nothing could have been further from true, but I believed she didn't know that. I laced my fingers with hers.

"Del, we're going to college." I thought about how powerful she had seemed to me at the concert that night, how beautiful and self-possessed. And here now, with her sweet face and sad eyes and tender touches, she made my heart hurt. "We have two more years, five semesters, and then we'll be out of here. We can go someplace far away, and we'll only come home if we want to."

Del deserved for it to go that way. She covered bruises to go to classes and took care of her sisters and brother and she never got a B. Honors Algebra, AP English. And it wasn't just that Del was doing so much with so little. It was that she was doing so much, with the little she did have constantly being stripped away.

"And who's going to pay for it?"

"I don't know. Scholarships. We'll take out loans. We'll work. We'll do whatever we have to do."

Del smiled a little, but her tone was sad. "Are we going to college together, now?"

"I hope so." She looked away. "What is it, Del? Why are you against that idea?"

"I'm not against it. I just don't think it's gonna happen." She paused to collect her thoughts. "I think you're gonna get into a really good college, Jen. And I don't want to hold you back."

I didn't respond. When we talked about the future, we fought. Any school that accepted me would also have accepted Del. And even if I had gotten in someplace she didn't, she knew I cared more about her than going to some stupid Ivy League. She knew I'd be perfectly happy at a state school if it meant we could go together. She knew I wanted to be with her—out in the open and forever. But for Del, no matter how close we felt or how in love we were, there was always this sense that what we had together was different than, outside of, what our real lives were and would be.

She took my face in her hands and said, before we fell asleep, that I was the air she breathed; she loved me more than anything; she couldn't stand the thought of her life without me in it. She said being with me was all she wanted, all she cared about, but she denied us any fidelity or future. I let it go at that because I was scared. I had already begun in some small way to realize it wasn't her desire for me she was calling into question—it was her desire to live at all.

"Andrew scares me," Del said, changing the subject away from the future she wouldn't commit to. "He comes on so strong. I don't know what to do when he's like that. I just go along with it, until I can figure out something else." My hardened expression told her I wasn't buying it. "I like the attention, Jenna, I admit that." This statement seemed at the time like the greater truth. I've since come to realize that what rage is to me, sexual feelings were to Del: a circuit breaker for terror.

❖

"I am glad I came," I said resolutely.

Katie nodded acceptingly, her breathing becoming more audible. Some distance later, Katie began to pick up speed. I increased my speed as well. She was running harder and breathing harder than I was; sweat soaked her shirt and streamed down her face.

"Damn cigarettes," she said, without a hint of slowing down. Her strong arms pumped, her long legs carried her along in powerful, graceful strides. We kept it up for about forty minutes, running in a five-mile loop.

Toward the end, approaching the block Gail lived on, Katie stopped running.

"Shit, you're in good shape." She fell out onto the grass and began to stretch. I joined her, falling on the side of the road into a small patch of prickly crabgrass and shoots of volunteer milkweed. Exhaust fumes from passing cars left an oily residue in the air. "You've changed a lot," Katie said. "You're happier. What's she like?" She paused, then, "Madison?"

I noticed the tiny orangish-yellow flowers, reached out and touched one. "She's smart and beautiful. I feel lucky." I noticed Katie's age then, the lines near her eyes when she squinted, the early specks of gray floating in her blond hair. She was looking at me, too. "What about you, are you with anyone?" I began to sift through the patch of clover beside me, looking for one with four leaves.

"He's married," she said. "I know it's really masochistic, but I can't help it. I keep going back."

"Probably you go back a little less every time." I could tell the comment surprised her; she was trying to decide if it was true. "Patterns are deceptive."

Clouds moved in to block the sun, and a pigeon hopped along the sidewalk in front of us. I didn't notice it had only one leg until it had passed. After a long silence I asked, "Do you remember the day we beat Key Biscayne for the state championship?"

Emphatically, as if she'd been anticipating it, Katie said, "I don't want to reminisce about the soccer team." The force of her rejection startled me. I felt quickly and deeply ashamed of my own need to talk about something that had happened over fifteen years before. Katie looked away. "It makes me feel pathetic, like there's been nothing to speak of since. You've done things with your life, Jen. You have a lover and a good job. Me"—she dropped her chin—"I peaked in the tenth grade."

I understood then that we both felt ashamed of the extent to which those things we had gone through so many years ago continued to plague and please us. "Just let me say this, okay?" I was staring at the patch of clover, running my hand through it. "It's been on my mind for a long time." She permitted it with her silence. "That day, that game, it was the three of us together who scored the winning point. Gail floated the ball half a field, I trapped it, dribbled, pushed it through, and you were there, right where I knew you would be. You faked and shot—what, fifteen yards, maybe?—to the high corner and scored. It was truly magnificent."

"I do remember that."

A scout from Florida State University who was present at the game had expressed an interest in recruiting her, made reference to the likelihood of a full scholarship—something that was just starting to be possible for girls in soccer. Katie had been only a sophomore.

"I remember feeling, that day, like the three of us together could do anything." I kicked the ground, toed the dirt, looked away. "Right after that, my parents found out about my relationship with Del. Gail's mother sent her to live with her father in New York, and you"—she knew where I was going, began crying before I got there—"Jason Schwartz raped you." Heat from rage permeated my arms and the back of my legs, and rose from my neck to my face. I bit down to contain it, and in my well-practiced way, quieted my voice to appear calm. "Life just crushed us, Katie."

"Not *you.*" She wiped at her tears defiantly. "How did you know about that?"

"I could tell. I knew something bad happened to you beyond what you were saying. I put that together with the timing of the abortion and—"

"How? What was it about me that made you think that?"

"You were vacant." I left out the part about how she couldn't walk right for a week.

Quietly, and with just a hint of suspicion, she asked, "You knew when it happened?"

"Pretty much. I think I figured it out when I went with you to the clinic. We were on the bus going home and you were holding my hand really tight, and you just seemed so sad."

Her face was drenched. "I never told anyone. I mean, I didn't even…You know, for the longest time, I just thought we were fooling around and I told him I didn't want it to go any further but he did, so he took it further. I didn't think about it as rape until I was in my twenties. It was rape." She nodded. "I tried to get away but he held me down."

She didn't say it, but after it happened, soccer never held the same interest for her. Nothing did. She just became more and more promiscuous, as though she could disappear the non-choice under a mountain of bad choices.

Back to thinking about Del, I said, "That story about the Thomas kid is pretty bad. All of it—the videotapes, framing Sid, being an accomplice in a murder. Del got in way over her head with this guy."

"The part about Sid bothers me more than anything else," Katie said. "It wasn't like Del. She was so protective of her family."

"I think," recalling what Sid had said, "it may be that both Del and Sid were protecting Khila."

Now Katie laughed a little. "Del used to bug me, you know?" She drew her knees to her chest and wrapped her arms around them. "I hated what happened to you. I don't think I ever told you this, but I thought she was cruel to you. And, to be honest," Katie said, "there was the sex thing. I was always hearing how good she was at it from the guys who dated me next. And Del and me competed for Andrew Torie and she won."

"Andrew Torie?" I cut her off, bitterness silting my voice. "Did you *thank* her?" Katie seemed thrown by my instant rage. "Such a creep," I said, shaking my head in disbelief of his outrageousness. "Where is he now?" I didn't give her a chance to answer. "Probably a gynecologist at some preppy Ivy League college campus health center, where he has a captive caseload."

With a look of disgust, Katie laughed. "Why do you hate him so much? Oh"—her head tilted in my direction—"isn't he the one who told everyone Del fucked him in the back of his daddy's Mercedes station wagon?"

I shrugged as if I didn't know, but I did—and he was, and she had.

"Some first time that must have been. Almost as bad as mine."

It was a kick in the stomach.

"Katie." My chin fell to my chest. My voice was slow and stern, and I was desperately trying to hold on to the idea that it's not malicious, this relentless disavowal of same-sex love. "When Del fucked Andrew in the back of his father's station wagon, it was not her first time." I took a breath, saw her eyes search and her face fall. I knew she was struggling now with the realization of how she had injured me. "I know he told everyone it was, and I know she didn't correct him. But it wasn't."

"Oh my God," Katie said. "I'm sorry. I'm sorry."

"It's okay," I looked at my watch. It was already ten a.m. "I want to go and get that box from Del's house."

Katie nodded. "I figured you would."

"Look, you don't have to go with me. I'll understand if it's too weird, or too dangerous, or too whatever. Gail kept me up half the night lecturing me on how I should let the police handle it from here." I imitated Gail. "'I called you because you're a judge and I figured Child Protective Services would listen to you. I didn't think you'd turn this into your own private murder investigation.'"

Katie laughed at my mimicry. "She knew *exactly* what you would do."

Just then, I noticed a black Jeep with tinted windows, and my heart jumped. It slowed down a little, then sped up and turned a corner quickly in the direction of Gail's house. I was able to make out two letters—S and E—on the license plate before it was fully out of sight.

Katie tossed the clover she was twirling between her fingers and moved to stand. "So you think he killed her?"

I nodded, watching for the Jeep to return. "I just don't know how." I wondered if I was starting to lose my mind, reminded myself there must be a million of those cars.

"Take Nicole," Katie said. "She's good at break-ins."

CHAPTER FOURTEEN

Back at Gail's, I left a message for Nicole on Pascale's answering machine. Then I returned Bea's call.

"Things are settling down in Baxter and Flint," Bea said. "It's helped a lot that Carlos Robles is the minor's attorney. He supports your decision, and he's managed to calm Margaret Todd down a bit. Apparently the baby is doing fine, and the mother is seeing her every day. So it was a good call. It took a lot of guts." I was relieved. I had been expecting to return to a battle and was glad not to. "How's it going there? Are you okay?"

"Fine," I said, consciously omitting any mention of the box and my intention to go and get it. I thought about asking Bea if she'd sent the fax, but I knew she wouldn't be able to tell me if she had. I doubted it was Bea who'd sent it anyway, since the last thing she would have wanted to do was get me more worked up.

Bea didn't believe I was fine, but it was not her nature to pry. She just asked if there was anything she could do. I said there wasn't, that I would see her in a few days. Then we warmly ended the call.

❖

I poured myself a glass of water and went to sit on the lounge chair on the patio. The sun on my skin made me sleepy, and I lay back and closed my eyes. I thought about the Jeep and whether Talon knew we were looking into Del's death. I didn't want to believe Ida had told him, but how else would he know? Ida's love-hate relationship with Del made it hard to know how to be with her. She'd given me important information, but I wasn't sure I could trust it. Still, the conversation I'd had with her the day before had stayed with me, left me wondering how to measure how much damage I'd done. Especially when so much else contributed to the harm at the same time. The law has formulas for apportioning blame; the human psyche doesn't.

Before I told Gail about Del and me, before things really spun out of control, I knew we were in trouble, and I wanted to get help. It's no excuse, but it seemed to me at the time like the worse things got, the more adamant Del became about not asking for help and the more worried I became about both of us. In the end, by the time I talked to Gail about what was happening, it was as if Del and I had been in a bad accident. On impact, I was hurled from the car, and although it would be a very long time—years—before I hit the ground, my landing would be far softer than the crash itself had been for Del.

There was one time I came close to asking a teacher to help us. It was early November, just after the Stevie Nicks concert. I was sitting alone in Elaine Fernandez's classroom, upset about having just learned our tenth-grade class was doing *How the Grinch Stole Christmas* for the Christmas play. Del breezed in. I hadn't seen her yet that day, and she surprised me with how beautiful she looked. Her hair was tied back in a ponytail. She was wearing a sleeveless button-down linen blouse, a short beige denim skirt, and sandals. Her cheeks were rouged and her lips lightly glossed, making her seem older than her fifteen years.

"What's wrong?" She stopped a few feet away. "Gail told me you're upset." I told Del about *Grinch*. She stared at me blankly. "Yeah, so? Big deal." I glared at her for not understanding. Del widened her eyes and raised her brows. "Jenna." She spoke slowly as if trying to get through to me once and for all. "You can't expect the school to do *Metamorphosis* for the Christmas play." She was trying not to laugh.

"It's a gay adolescent coming-out story," I said.

"It's a man turning into a bug."

"That's the same thing, Del. Ever heard of *metaphor*?"

She shook her head at the futility of arguing with me about this and just moved closer to me. "Nobody understands what you mean by that." Del lifted herself up onto the table to sit beside me and crossed her legs.

"I don't understand what you mean by that, and you've explained it to me five times."

I didn't respond. I was looking down at the terrazzo floor, searching it, my eyes filling, tears starting to dribble out. I was thinking about Gregor's good intentions and how they didn't matter, how since he had become a bug, nobody could see how hard he was trying or recognize the same good-naturedness he still possessed, which they had loved in him when he was human. Overnight, his grotesqueness became the only filter through which he was apprehended, through which his motives were discerned.

Del looked at me, said with alarm, "Jenna, why are you crying?" I shrugged my shoulders and wiped at my eyes. She closed the classroom door, rested her hands on my thighs, and leaned in so our foreheads were almost touching. Then she waited.

I spoke and cried at the same time. "They hate me."

Softly, "Who hates you?"

"My parents," I said. "They hate me." I raised my eyes to hers, whispered, "Because I'm a girl." It was something I had felt for some time but had never said aloud.

Del's eyes were somber and still, her lips slightly drawn in. She was trying to figure me out. She sat next to me again, put her hand on my back.

"I'm that bug, Del."

She moved her gaze away and then back, and then as if it was the only thing she could think to do to comfort me, she wrapped her arms around me. "I love you."

The door opened and Fernandez, our tenth-grade English teacher, entered. She paused at first when she saw us, her expression unchanged. Then she closed the door behind her. I trusted Elaine Fernandez. She had introduced me to Kafka and was the first Freud enthusiast I'd ever met—talked openly to her tenth-grade class about bisexuality as the norm and Plato's mythic hermaphrodite as the precondition to heterosexuality. Black hair framed the black eyes now settling on us. Del slowly let go of me and then shrugged in Fernandez's direction, as if to say she didn't know how to help me. Fernandez lifted herself onto a nearby table and faced us.

Del sat beside me with her hand on mine. "She's upset about the play," Del said. "But I don't understand—"

Fernandez nodded and interrupted, "I thought your paper on *Metamorphosis* was excellent, Jenna."

"I'm Gregor," I said and started to cry all over again.

Fernandez watched me, her expression kind and open. She studied me momentarily and then said, "Because you might be gay?" I froze. Yes, I had said as much in my paper, but hearing her say it out loud was unsettling. Del jerked her hand away from mine. There was a lengthy silence, the three of us just looking off in different directions. Fernandez then looked squarely at Del and me and said with apparent concern, "Are you girls okay?" Her mouth drew into a straight line across her face. Her eyes were solid and stern. She expected an answer.

Del crossed her arms. "We're fine."

It wasn't true. Pascale was drinking more, the beatings were getting more frequent and extreme, the sex between Del and me was becoming bolder and more desperate, and I was becoming aware that it—the sex—meant something different to me than it did to Del. For all of it, I was terribly worried about us, and I wanted very much to talk to someone about it.

I touched Del's arm, said gently, "Del."

She answered with a threatening glare. I said nothing more.

The patio door slid open and Nicole stuck her head out. "Talon's at my mother's house with Khila. It's now or never for that box." I threw my legs off the lounge to stand. "Ida says she's gonna call us as soon as Talon leaves," Nicole said. We both froze for a moment, wondering the same thing. "She's not gonna call us." Nicole moved from foot to foot. "I know she's not gonna call us."

"It doesn't matter. Let's just go."

Talon and Del had bought a small house in Pembroke Pines, an area north of where we grew up. To get there, Nicole and I exited I-95 at Pembroke Road and headed west. After we turned off the freeway, I kept my eye on the mirror, looking out for the black Jeep. I didn't see it. With no sign of being followed, I lost interest in the Jeep and began to look around. Not long ago, the street we were on had been a narrow two-lane road, which crept along through open fields, one-level apartments, and run-down wooden shacks for stores with gravel lots for parking.

Miles of dirt, dry shrub, and straw grass accompanied one en route to the few pockets of modern development spread far apart. That was how I remembered Pembroke: dirt roads, white people, pickup trucks, and backwoods poverty. Now we drove on a newly paved four-lane roadway, edged with concrete strips of white storefronts that boasted big windows and tacky signs. Traffic lights with four-way signals dangled over corners where stop signs had once sufficed. Horns honked, voices carried, engines revved and spat, buses unapologetically sprayed soot into the faces of unsuspecting pedestrians.

I watched Nicole's face, her slight nose, full lips, distinct cheekbones and chin. Her hair fell casually to her shoulders, folded like a habit behind her small, stud-framed ear. She looked straight ahead, concentrating on the street, studying it, anticipating its next move.

Back to thinking about the fax, I asked, "Do you know what Talon's birth name is?"

"Larry." Nicole laughed. "It's funny when you think about how different the names are. He just wants to scare people. Gets off on it."

"Do you know if he has a criminal record?"

"Don't know. Can't you find out? You must have access to criminal records."

"Not without breaking the law," I said. She had a funny expression on her face, and I knew that it was because my concern for the law sounded ludicrous given what we were on our way to do at that very moment. It seemed different to me. Breaking into Talon's house felt like a personal risk, whereas accessing confidential records felt like an abuse of power. There was more silence, and then I asked, "Do you still like Elvis?"

Nicole seemed surprised and pleased. "I love Elvis. I can't believe you remember that."

"I do remember that about you. The first time I ate over at your house you watched *Love Me Tender* on television, and Del and Ida made fun of your Elvis crush." She smiled. I began to say something else, stopped, thought about it, decided to go ahead. "Remember the Christmas Eve that I hung out with you guys? The year your dad left." She nodded distantly. "I remember he got you that neon poster of Elvis in a metal frame, and you hung it over your bed."

"That was the saddest night," Nicole said, with the obvious intention of bringing the conversation to a close.

❖

Nearly a week had passed since the Christmas Eve when I had left Del crying in her bed and had come home to find my parents at the dining room table with my stories and letters and photos. The fight with my parents had ended with me being grounded for the remaining week of Christmas vacation.

During that week, I had hardly left my room, could do little more than sleep and cry. Then on the Saturday before school was starting, I awoke with a strange symptom. My top lip was swollen, as if I had been stung by a bee or bitten by a spider. It was neither of those things, as it turned out to be a stress symptom that recurred somewhat frequently over the next few years. I had my period and had bled through my sweats, but I was not particularly motivated to clean up or change my sheets. That morning, when I did finally get up to pee, I realized the grotesque image I breezed past in the mirror—menstrual bloating, fat lip, frizzy and clumped hair, eyes and face swollen from crying—was me.

I opened the medicine cabinet in the bathroom to look for aspirin. Beside the aspirin was a bottle of Valium, which I opened instead. I stood by the sink and stared at the small pills, dumped some into my hand. I had never thought about killing myself before. What led me to consider it then was a future without Del in it. It was an unbearable thought. I missed her. Every breath was a reminder of life without her; every inch of my skin ached for her. I sobbed uncontrollably, felt pain I could never have imagined coming in waves from wake to sleep, following me into dreams, worse than ever upon awakening. I would emerge from a dream about her, eager to tell her about it, and face my empty room and the dead phone beside my bed. I would lie there doubled over, trembling and waiting for the stabbing in my chest to pass. My heart was singed and there was no relief in sight. I put the pills back in the bottle and left it on the shelf, marking the bottle in my mind like a dog-ear on a page to which one intends to return.

My volume of Kafka's stories lay open on the bed beside me. I turned to *Metamorphosis* and began to read yet again of Gregor Samsa's transformation into a giant bug. Some people believe the bug was a cockroach, some a dung beetle, others say Kafka never intended it as any particular kind of insect. Great debates have taken place: Roaches are flatter with longer legs; dung beetles go through a quick metamorphosis like the one in the story. In fact, it only took Gregor one night to undergo a transformation from a human into an insect. What changes in the human condition might a week bring?

The disconnected phone lay silent beside my bed, the sun came and went, marked only by a pinstripe of light landing on the wall by which it announced its arrival and departure each day. Was this the lesson my mother intended for me to learn, that my desire in and of itself was a betrayal? Was that what she'd learned a long time ago—that sexuality, rather than a tender inclination toward expression, is something to be refused? What frailties and fears reside in the strata, rhythms, and recesses of our minds has everything to do with the ways our hearts were broken as children. One learns to know and not know, inquire and then precipitously withdraw, look on and then away, listen for and then categorically reject—to pray rather than to think.

Katie tapped on my bedroom window the Sunday night before school was starting. I climbed out to meet her.

"I've been calling and calling," she said.

"I'm on punishment."

She crunched her brows and dipped her chin. "You? Why?"

I shrugged. "What's up?"

"Please don't tell anyone, okay?" I nodded. She started sobbing. "I need an abortion, can you go with me to the clinic? I have an appointment tomorrow. We need to leave at lunch break."

I reflexively agreed. This was one of those things you just do for a friend.

"Please don't tell anyone," she pleaded again. "Not even Jason knows."

"I won't. I promise. If Jason doesn't know," I said, "then how is he gonna help you pay for it?"

She didn't answer.

❖

Nicole and I continued driving north onto a narrow cul-de-sac of small stucco tract houses. We stopped in front of the one I presumed was Del's, its fresh white paint speckled with particles of silver reflecting the sunlight, momentarily reminding me of the white light emanating from the heat of a sparkler on the Fourth of July.

"Maybe they left a window unlocked," I said, the thought of breaking in suddenly more real and unsettling. It was a meaningless distinction, legally. Unauthorized entry is unauthorized entry. I began to reconsider, realizing I was about to risk my career, my marriage, and possibly my freedom. I heard Bea McVee's cautionary *Do I need to worry about you?* I thought about Madison, my house, my life in San Francisco. Weighing against these: the wrongs I couldn't right for Del and myself when I was a kid; the image of her hooked to a chain thirty feet under the water; Khila's pleading eyes; and the thought of Talon having murdered Del and now trotting off to Texas with Del's daughter and some bizarre woman who referred to herself as Khila's new mommy. I couldn't let that happen without a fight. I told myself we'd be in and out, as I climbed into the backseat to let myself out.

Nicole said, "I know where there's a key."

Stepping out of my side of the car, I felt reluctant to put my foot down on the notably white sidewalk for fear of soiling it. It took me a moment to realize the glistening cement in front of Del's house had been bleached. The lawn was thick and green and manicured, the bushes clipped and shaped.

"She was such a neat freak," I said, remembering her clean room and ironed clothes.

Across the street, a face peered out from behind a curtain in the window. A man's face, Caucasian, with a thick jaw and dark hair. Those were the only details I could make out from where I was standing. He was clearly watching us. My heartbeat quickened at the possibility that he was Talon's friend and he would call him. But even from a distance, and with so little of him visible, something about the way he was hiding and watching made me reconsider.

"We have to go quickly," Nicole said.

Nicole agreed with me about Del having been a neat freak as she led the way around to the back of the house. She ran her fingers across the frame over the back door, announced the key proudly, as if she'd just made it appear from behind some unsuspecting child's ear. "I told her a thousand times that's the first place a thief's gonna look." Putting the key in the door, she said, "And I should know, two felonies for B and E."

The shallow walls were upon us quickly, with looming low ceilings and little light. We entered through a room with a couch and a television. The room was filled with empty boxes, which we assumed were there because Talon was packing. We passed the small U-shaped kitchen and entered the living room/dining room. The wood shone, the metal sparkled, the carpet stood at attention. Chairs were tucked beneath the dining-room table, pillows were intentionally placed. I thought of the state of my own laundry, the toss my own house incurred on a normal day—puppy toys, stacks of books, clothes left on the bathroom floor, dishes in the sink, discarded pages from Madison's drafts hurled in the direction of the wastebasket. On a bookshelf among many framed photos was an eight-by-ten photo of Talon and Khila.

"There is not a single picture of Del."

Nicole whispered, "It's like a museum in here."

I was thinking sort of the same thing—how Del's house had the feeling of something that used to be alive, something exhibited as a stand-in for itself.

"And they have a kid?" I noticed the near-perfect image of a filled candy bowl reflected in the coffee table on which it sat, and the CDs and tapes alphabetized by performer and stacked in perfect succession.

"I know," Nicole said. "What does Khila do in here, stand still?" Nicole started toward the kitchen and then froze. She reached back for my arm. "Jenna, what is that?" She was pointing at a camera bracket affixed to the ceiling above the dining-room table.

I moved closer. On the table was a five-gallon plastic water bottle half-filled with pennies. What must have been the same number of pennies were stacked in piles on the table. Also on the table was a video camera, the one that apparently fit into the bracket.

"I haven't been here in years." Nicole was looking around, clearly spooked. "I told the idiot to leave him after the first time he hit her. You might say I wasn't exactly a welcome guest after that." She entered the kitchen and began opening drawers. "I told her he was gonna kill her."

"When?"

"When? Every time I saw her, that's when." She was searching through a cupboard.

I studied the pennies for a moment, looked again at the camera. There were two connectors coming out of the ceiling next to the bracket. I guessed one was for power and the other fed what the camera was recording to a recording device of some sort. The house, it was now becoming clear to me, was hardwired for surveillance and taping devices.

I breathed one deep breath, as if preparing to swim a long distance underwater, and began down the dark hallway toward the bedroom. Immediately to the right was the bathroom. I stuck my head in and checked the ceiling. There was a bracket in the corner clearly intended for a video camera. My arms went numb to my fingertips as if the blood had drained from them, and a shiver went down my spine. I'd seen it all before—or at least read about it—in the cases we'd reviewed on the domestic-violence-death autopsy team, the worst of which often involved video- and audiotaping devices.

I continued down a short hallway. To the left was what appeared to be Khila's room. Her things were stacked neatly and had already begun to go in boxes. To the right was the master bedroom. A double bed, sheets and blanket folded army style, occupied most of the space. There was a capped camera affixed to the ceiling in that room as well, directed at the bed. I hesitated, wondering now how many cameras we couldn't see and whether all of those were capped.

I wandered slowly around to a wooden dresser beneath a window against the far wall. Afternoon sun came in through a crack in the drawn shades, casting light on the few personal effects—a jewelry box, a brush, a few hair ties—all neatly placed. I inched open the shades and saw the shape of the man's face across the street. I could make out his form enough to know he was still watching the house.

The closet door was slightly ajar. I made my way to it to find the box we were there to retrieve. Hanging on the inside of the door was a white T-shirt, wrinkled and worn. I felt it, could swear it was still warm, still thrown in the cast of her body as I remembered her.

❖

From the isolation of my Christmas-vacation punishment into the crowded high school hallways, I was carried along in a state of suspension. I waited for Del at the hall locker we shared until well after the bell had rung, but I didn't see her. First period, we talked about *Lord of the Flies*, our reading assignment over the break.

"Jenna, you like Freud," Ms. Fernandez said. "Tell us about the struggle between the superego and id in this story."

I hadn't read it. AP English, and I hadn't done the assignment. Del was supposed to be in that class but she hadn't shown up. I was writing her a letter, telling her how much I loved and missed her. Fifteen minutes into class and it was already a page-and-a-half long.

Shrinking from the request, I said, "I'm not sure." I discreetly moved the letter closer to me, hoping Ms. Fernandez would just move on to someone else.

"Go ahead," she said encouragingly. "I'm asking you to try to apply the Freudian scheme we've been studying to what happens in this novel." Moving closer to me, she added, "I would think it would be a fun question for you."

I felt upset that I couldn't answer.

She looked down at my desk. "Are you writing a note?" She snatched it from me, held it out to the class like a white hanky. "You all know what I do with notes, share them with the class and ask for a critique of your content and style. Shall we?" A few people laughed.

I was paralyzed for a moment. Then I stood up, walked over to her, looked her in the eye, and pleaded. "Please don't. Please."

My heart was pounding fiercely; I could not believe I had been so stupid, put us in such jeopardy. She saw my desperation and hesitated. I had already decided I would not let her read it, even if it meant physically stopping her. I was surprised to find Edie and Susan quickly standing behind me. Edie gently tugged at my sleeve. Susan respectfully asked Ms. Fernandez not to read the note, suggested she just give it back. Ms. Fernandez, not quite sure what to make of any of this, handed the note back to me. I grabbed my things and exited the classroom. I could hear the blood pulsing in my head, felt pressure in my temples and ears, and my legs gave way. I fell against a wall and slid down it until I was firmly on the ground where I sat until the bell rang. The bell: it signaled both the end of that period and the starting gun for our cattle run to the next. By third period, rumors about Del were spreading like some airborne disease. People asked if I'd seen her and said she'd been in a car accident.

❖

Nicole barged into the bedroom. "Man, Jenna, you should see the kitchen cabinets." She was shaking her head and blowing out air. "The Tupperware is color coordinated. This seems like a bit much, even for Del. I really want to get that box and get the fuck out of this creep hole."

I was with her.

She passed me and climbed upward into the small space, using a lower shelf for leverage. She stuck her head far into the closet. Moments later she backed her way out with a brown box in hand.

I felt Del's T-shirt one more time, put it to my face and breathed it in—detergent mixed with faint cologne. But beneath that I found something more familiar, an essence of her that I remembered in her pillow, her bedsheets, her skin on a hot day. I placed the T-shirt back on the hook.

Once outside, I put the box in the car and then headed straight for the house across the street.

Nicole raced after me. "Where are you going? What are you doing?"

I saw the face disappear from behind the windowpane. I stopped at the sidewalk, waiting to see if he would come back to the window, trying to decide if I should knock on his door. I reminded myself it was Thursday, and I only had until Friday morning to get enough evidence to Beasley to warrant opening up a murder investigation. I rang the doorbell. Nobody answered. I rang again. No answer.

"Jenna," Nicole said, "what are you doing?"

I don't know how I knew it, I just did. "I think this is the guy Del has been seeing. He's been watching us the whole time."

"How do you know he's not watching the house for Talon? He might be Talon's friend."

"He would have called him by now. Talon would be on his way here. Ida would have warned us."

A moment's pause to consider the possibility that Ida would not have called us, and then Nicole said, "Move," and pushed me out of her way. "He might be able to help Sid." She began banging on the door. She stepped back and yelled, "Open up, fuckhead, we need to talk to you." I went back to the car for a pen and paper. Nicole continued banging. "I know you're in there. I saw your ugly ass. Del was my sister, did you know my sister?" Nicole spun on her heels, grabbed her head in frustration, and screamed, "She picked the biggest fucking losers."

As she banged harder, I wrote a quick note, telling the man who we were and leaving my cell-phone number. I slipped it under the door. The next thing I knew, Nicole was at the window banging and yelling. I shouted for her to stop and ran toward her, but I was too late. Her fist hit the glass, and it broke. Blood began to trickle down her arm. I ran over and grabbed her to stop her from doing any more damage. She was banging on a different window with the other fist, clutching her injured arm to her chest like it was a wounded wing. I pulled her away from the house and stood looking at her cut hand, which was not as bad as I had first imagined, while I tried to think of what to do next.

"We should go," I said, pushing her in the direction of the car. "Right now." I had put my name and phone number under his door. If he wanted to find us, he could.

❖

Still unnerved by the broken window and the blood, I stared at the box at my feet. I didn't feel ready to open it; I was afraid of what was in it. We drove in silence, my stomach twisting tighter, as I pictured the cameras throughout Del's house and what I imagined them to be for. My mind went to the puppies, to the description of Talon laughing as he videotaped the mother trying to comfort them.

Nicole was unfazed by the window incident, the rage evaporating off her instantly, like sweaty skin coming into contact with air conditioning. Her knuckle was cut but had already stopped bleeding. In the calm person in the car, there was no trace of the crazy person who had broken the window.

After some time, Nicole said, "Marshmallows." Then she smiled.

"What?"

"The Christmas we hung out all night, we roasted marshmallows in the backyard."

I nodded, staring out at the road.

"I saw you guys that night."

"What do you mean?"

"I spied on you through Del's bedroom window. I *saw* you. It was…you guys were…"

"Don't," I managed to say, realizing now what she was about to tell me. I remembered us making love and how it had felt to be with Del like that and then to leave her. "It's private."

"I know. It's just, you know, you sucked each other for such a long time."

Now I was shocked. "What is *wrong* with you?"

"I've just always wondered," she persisted, "didn't your jaw get tired?"

I stared at her.

"I've always wondered that because"—she paused, smiled a little at me—"well, mine does."

I went back over the exchange, unsure as to what I'd just heard. "Nicole," I was finally able to say, "did you just come out to me?"

She smiled hugely. "Well, yes, but I really do want to know how you went for so long, because my girlfriend needs it for a really long time before she can come."

After a few moments of processing this, I said, "Did Del know?"

"What, that I like girls? Yeah, she knew."

"That you saw us?"

"Oh, hell yeah." Nicole laughed. "She denied it, though."

I raised my brows and nodded, as if to say *Of course she did.* I reached for the box to open it. As I did, I noticed a black Jeep in the rearview mirror. The license plate included the letters S and E.

CHAPTER FIFTEEN

Nicole hit the gas, and I felt the tires grab the road. I was trying to keep my eye on the Jeep as Nicole wove in and out of traffic. Her idea was to lose him; my idea was to keep track of him. In the end we decided to do both. The storefronts bordering the street had parking in front of them, and once far enough ahead of the Jeep, Nicole jagged to the right and slipped into a spot. Then we waited. Not a minute later, the black Jeep passed us. We nestled in and followed it from a few cars behind. The Jeep continued on route and then got back on the freeway heading south. We kept after it. It was a little hard to feel inconspicuous in this ancient puke-green station wagon that coughed up more smoke than Pascale, but that didn't stop us.

"Write down the license-plate number," Nicole said. "Get someone to run it for you."

"Just don't lose him," I said.

"It looks like he's going back to Miami Shores, maybe to our house."

It seemed like that to me, too, until the Jeep exited at Miami Gardens Drive in North Miami Beach and headed east. As we approached Biscayne Boulevard, the Jeep seemed to vanish. I scanned in different directions, trying to figure out where he could've disappeared to, and then I noticed the small street mall on the corner.

We found the Jeep in the mall parking area, the driver gone. I suggested we sit on a nearby bench and wait for him to return.

"Then what?" Nicole asked.

I stared at her. "I haven't figured that out yet."

While we waited, Ida called to tell us Talon had left Pascale's. Then Gail called to see where we were.

Madison called to say hi. She was doing a reading in New Haven, the setting of her novel.

"How's it going?" I asked.

"It's a little stressful. You know, the people who are in it feel exposed, the people who aren't in it feel left out. How's your day going?"

"Fine." I decided not to mention the break-in or that we were now following someone who had been following us. I knew she'd be upset with me for taking such risks, and I didn't see the point in worrying her. Madison talked about her reading, her visit with old friends, and then about our mutual friend, Anita, who lived near us in San Francisco. She'd just learned that Anita and her girlfriend, Claire, were having a commitment ceremony, and we hadn't been invited.

"And this upsets you, why?"

"Well, I know we haven't spoken to Anita in a long time, but we did fix them up."

"Can't think of a better way to get rid of a high-maintenance friend than to fix her up."

Madison laughed appreciatively. "What makes you think Anita is high maintenance?"

"Well," I said playfully, "there was the time she was stood up by a blind date and called the police to report the person missing."

"Right." More laughter.

We continued chatting happily until Madison had to go.

An hour passed, still no sign of the driver of the Jeep. Nicole sat with her eyes closed, a cigarette burning between her fingers. I watched the people walking by, many of them elderly. I had forgotten this about Miami Beach, the huge elderly Jewish population that I had been surrounded by when I was growing up, many of whom had numbers on their arms. In my home, the Jewish Holocaust was dinner conversation. That is, when climbing out of working-class status wasn't.

The sun had moved and was now shining directly on us. My face rose to meet it, sweat trickling down my back. The mild burning sensation on my cheeks felt familiar and comforting. I closed my eyes and breathed it, absorbing it in my lungs as well as my skin. When I closed my eyes, the warm, moist air swathed my body, reminding me of the humid Everglades. I had visions of first the road we'd been on the day before and then the slow-moving current that gently divided around the mahogany islands. Now the cars passing on Biscayne Boulevard sounded like a river, and I pictured the current gaining speed, rising, swelling into waves that crashed against the trees and erased the mounds. The sound of the crashing waves turned into a cacophony of voices, many talking at once, urgently. One person after another asking if I knew what had happened to Del, to her face.

❖

By third period, rumors of Del and a car accident were circulating, and scores of students and teachers had asked me if I'd seen her. I finally found her in the girls' locker room with Katie and Edie and other soccer friends. Sitting on the bench by her gym locker, Del watched me approach. One moment the gym teacher and others were there looking on, the next moment they were gone, and we were alone—or thought we were.

"Del, your face." I stopped some feet away, suddenly nauseous and light-headed. I took deep breaths and swallowed to keep from retching. Her eye was puffy and purple, her bottom lip was split. I could see it hurt her to talk. I steadied myself by putting my hand on the wall of lockers near me. "Why didn't you just stay home?"

"I wanted to see you." She stared at the floor, her cut lip twitching. "She went berserk on me last night." It sounded like "burshurk" because of her lip. "'Cause you haven't been around. She thinks I dropped you to do drugs or have sex or…*whatever*. She gets these ideas in her head and…She's fucking crazy. I don't know how much more I can take." Del's voice cracked as she said, "I miss you *so* much." Her face stretched into a grotesque clown-like grimace, her head fell forward, and she began sobbing.

I moved toward her. She met my hand with hers, slipped her fingers between mine. I went down on my knees in front of her, my face near hers. My other hand went reflexively under the side of her shirt to find her skin. When her shirt lifted, I noticed her side was the color of a storm—blacks and blues and reds and purples and tints of yellow. Starting up, I said, "That's it. I'm telling Fernandez. She can't keep doing this."

Del tightened her grip on my hand. "You can't. Foster care. We'll get separated. Who's gonna take four kids, Jenna? Who's gonna take Nicole?" Her breath was an overnight stale mixed with something mediciney.

I sighed, settled back down in front of her. "I'm really sorry, Del." Not knowing what else to say, I added, "I love you."

Del tenderly kissed my face. I felt the rough edges of her bottom lip, where a scab had begun to form, tasted traces of blood when I kissed her back. Then we were both sobbing, wisps of her hair sticking to her skin and mine, our spit and snot intermingling, drawing lines between our faces.

I was the first to let go. I sat back against the wall of lockers and groped for something to say to keep us afloat. What came out was, "It's gonna be okay."

"What is, Jenna?" She shifted her position, her physical discomfort apparent. "What about this is going to be okay?"

Right. I changed the subject, said playfully, "I saw Nicole today. All the kids were heading into school, and she was heading in the other direction. I yelled at her to go to class."

Impassively, Del said, "Sometimes I wish someone would just give those girls a shot and put them to sleep."

It took a moment for the words to sink in. When they did, I felt my spine tremor and my hands draw cold. I knew by her remark that this one week had been more time than was necessary for Del to realize just how little control she really had, or that her wanting mattered none, or that her attachments were a liability. I'd prefer, even now, to dignify her wish to put Ida and Nicole to sleep. I'd prefer to understand it as an impulse to spare her sisters, as a moment of profound empathy of which I knew Del to be capable. Whether it was that or something else, whatever had happened inside of her that week, whatever extremes she had visited, desperate states she had encountered, Del was letting me know—warning me—she had changed.

I put my hand on her knee.

Her face softened, and her tone became loving and precariously hopeful. "Can we go somewhere private and talk? I want to be alone with you."

I started to say yes, and then remembered I couldn't. When I told Del I had plans with Katie, her brows crunched suspiciously.

"I haven't seen you in a week, Jenna. Where are you going with her?"

Reluctantly, I said, "I can't tell you."

"You can't *tell* me?" She laughed. "Why not? We tell each other everything."

The locker-room door, which we couldn't see from where we were sitting, opened. Some girl, I think it was Edie, called out, "Social worker is here, looking for Del. Some agency that protects kids."

"We should go."

Del glared at me.

"I promised Katie. I can go with you tomorrow, Del."

Del's face was still and sad and cold—lifeless as steel. She turned away from me for a moment, as if responding to a distant voice or receiving counsel. "I'm going home." She stood up and walked out, the heavy metal door slamming closed behind her.

Del was in and out of school the rest of the week, dodging the social worker. Annie Sloan had spied on us, seen us kiss in the locker room, and now people were talking about us, low-grade rumblings running the gamut from confusion to concern to perverse interest. The interest made any attempt at contact between us conspicuous, so when Del was in school, we avoided each other, passed in the halls with hardly a glance.

On Friday of that week, I invited myself to have a sleepover at Gail's. Around midnight, I borrowed Gail's bike and rode to Del's house, desperate to see her. I was relieved to find Pascale's car gone and Del's bedroom light on. I left Gail's bike on the porch, made my way to underneath Del's bedroom window, and lightly tapped on the glass. It felt like hours, searching for her face. In fact, it may have been only moments before she came into view, a look of surprise. I smiled and started to wave. From behind her another face emerged and came into focus—Andrew Torie's. Sharp pain shot across my chest. As if his moving toward me pushed me away, I lost my balance and stumbled backward, repeating, "I'm sorry."

My hands shaking, heart racing, I returned to the porch to retrieve Gail's bike.

"Jen, wait," Del said, as she came out, pulling sweats on over a pair of shorts.

"Andrew, Del? *Seriously?* Andrew Torie?"

"We're just hanging out. I promise." I shrugged as if it didn't matter what they were doing, but it did. "Do you want to come in? Andrew has coke. You want to try it?"

"No. Tell *him* to leave." We were suspended in a stare. "He doesn't care about you. He's gonna use you."

"I'm just getting to know him." She put her hand on my arm. Her touch reverberated. "I'm cold," she said. "Are you gonna come in or not?" She tugged at me playfully. "Come on, just give him a chance."

"I miss you." I pressed my forehead to hers. The intensity of the contact seemed to take her by surprise. Her eyes closed, her lips trembled. Tears came on contact. I touched her hair, squeezed her hand. "Please, can't we just talk now?" Her lips were instinctually edging toward mine and mine toward hers, infants rooting. Our tongues touched slightly. "I can hang all night."

"I can't." Slowly, she said, "If you want, we can try to be friends. Come inside, hang with me and Andrew. I…" She stumbled over the words. "I can't be alone with you." Her hand on my face, her mouth near my mouth. "Do you understand?" She whispered, "I need you. You're my best friend, Jenna. Isn't that enough?"

"*Friends?* And what are we going to talk about, Del, having sex with other people?"

Angry herself now, she said, "What is so wrong with that? I want to have sex with other people. It's having sex with you that's a problem. I don't want to do that anymore. I'm not gay."

"Having sex with me is a problem?"

"See, you're doing it right now." She backed away. "Either I have sex with you or we're not friends, right? Is that what you're saying? I'm cold. I'm going in. You can come if you want to."

"Del." Confused and desperate, I grabbed her arm. "Stop walking away from me." She stopped. "I didn't know you wanted to sleep with other people. Is this because Annie saw us?"

She yanked her arm away. "It's not gonna work for us—that's all I know."

Her solution that night, to just be friends, felt like the "sleep" shot she had wished for her sisters. It was a way to be rid of us, but without having to watch me suffer—to have us fade into nothingness. I felt my insides heaving as I returned to the bike. I wanted her to call me back, hoped she'd relent, get rid of Andrew, be with me. She didn't. I turned back to look for her, and she was already in the house going to Andrew, the door quietly closing behind her.

My heart felt like a rag having the life wrung out of it. I flashed on the pills in the medicine closet in my parents' house. I didn't have a shot to put myself to sleep, but I did have those pills. Had I been going to my parents' house, I might have taken them. I don't know. The pull to do so was very strong; I resisted it with everything in me, like riding into a strong wind, the whole way back to Gail's.

It was upon returning to her house in this devastated state that I told Gail about Del and me. Once I started talking, I couldn't stop, and in answering the many questions Gail asked about how it started, how far we'd gone, what it was like to have oral sex, I opened up about my feelings for Del, my fears about being gay, and my sadness over the breakup. Gail's response—accepting, curious, impressed—made my feelings for Del seem more normal and legitimate and eased my fear of having to now face this loss alone. It was also true that Gail's interest and acceptance pulled for more and more detail, and before long what had begun as a wrenching outpouring turned into boisterous bragging.

I woke up the next morning, my stomach in knots, my head throbbing, my memory hazy. I knew there had been a betrayal the night before. With heart-stopping angst, I remembered telling Gail about Del and me. I hadn't just told her about us, I had gone into great detail about very intimate things. I can say I was drunk on grief. I can say I was saving myself. I can say I was hurt and angry because Del had chosen Andrew over me. I can say all those things, and they might be true. But I had to tell Del what I'd done, and now, in the light of day, anything I thought had justified my actions the night before seemed indefensible. I knew she would never forgive me. For Del, it was not so much the secrecy, but rather that the privacy of our relationship had been an invisible membrane protecting us from the abuses and exploitations that all other realms of her life had been subject to. Now that I had exposed us and her feelings for me, like everything else precious to her, we could be used against her.

❖

As I waited for the driver of the Jeep and watched the people passing by, I thought for the first time that the ways in which Del and I kept missing and hurting each other in those last days were not so much mistakes or misunderstandings as decisions that each of us was making to let the other go.

It was five p.m. when a woman exited from the apartment building across the street, made her way toward us in the crosswalk, and then headed in the direction of the Jeep. Nicole was fast asleep on the bench. She was snoring, a string of drool dribbling from her open mouth. I thought about waking her up and then decided I was better off doing this alone. I stood up and walked quickly to catch the woman, reached her as she was opening the car door.

She posed, sandal on the cabin threshold. One hand rested on the top of the open door. Her expression inscrutable, her accent subtle and of Latin origin, she said, "Can I help you?"

I was taken aback by how beautiful she was: late twenties, tall and lithe. She was wearing a straw-colored fedora and dark sunglasses. Her light-brown hair was woven into a french braid that fell past her shoulders. She was tan with red lipstick and rouged cheeks. And she wore a floral pattern tie-neck halter top and matching wraparound skirt, with her slight midriff left bare.

"Why are you following us?"

Now she recognized me and her face softened a bit. "I thought I lost you at the intersection."

"Apparently not."

Nicole came running up, panicked and out of breath, wiping the drool from her face. To me, she said, "Where did you go? What are you doing?" When she saw the woman together with the car, she said, "Who the fuck are you and why are you following us?" As Nicole spoke, I noticed the woman's wrist, which bore the unmistakable years-old scars of vertical razor cuts. I also noticed she was driving a rental.

"You're Del's sister?" the woman said. "You look just like her."

Nicole's face opened and her tone changed. I think she was realizing the woman was attractive. "Uh, who are you?"

"I'm looking for Adeline Soto."

Nicole and I exchanged a curious look. "You don't know, do you?" The woman glanced at me. "You're from out of town?" She neither confirmed nor denied it. "Del's dead," I said. "With all of the election news, her death hasn't gotten much publicity, I guess."

The cool veneer cracked momentarily. Her legs swayed and her jaw tightened. She gripped the door more firmly in an effort to conceal her sudden shakiness. "When?" Her expression impassive, her tone sullen, she said, "When did she die?"

"Your turn," I said. "Why are you following us?"

"I was trying to find Del." To Nicole, she said, "I thought if I followed you, I'd find her."

"Why are you looking for her?" Nicole asked.

The woman climbed into the Jeep. "I have to go now."

Nicole grabbed the door. "Tell us who you are."

The woman yanked the door shut, started her engine, and pulled out. Her actions were so determined I was certain if we had been in her way, she would have run us over.

"What the fuck?" Nicole said, backing up a few feet. "This just gets weirder and weirder. Those fucking cameras in her house. And now this. Who *was* that?"

"I think I know."

Back in the car, I called the one person I knew could tell me more about this woman and what she was doing here. The administrative assistant answered.

"Margaret Todd, please." I told her who I was.

Moments later, a different voice said, "This is Margaret Todd."

"Jenna Ross, do you have a minute?"

"Depends on what for."

"A favor. A personal favor." There was a lengthy, uncomfortable silence. "Margaret, I need to know if a friend of mine was trying to use the underground. I wonder if you could help me find out."

"I don't have any connections with any underground. That's illegal." I didn't respond. After more silence, she said, "Why?" Her question confused me. "Why do you want to know?" When I didn't answer, she added, "I just need to make sure you're not using me to get some skank off the hook for hurting his wife."

"Would you give me a *fucking* break?" I blew out a breath, tried to get my heart rate down. "I'm in Miami trying to figure out if my first love was murdered by her husband. I think she contacted some folks to get away, and if so, they probably know her story. Can you help me or not?"

Slightly kinder, she said, "I don't know. Miami?" Then she said,

"Give me her information, I'll call around. If I find out anything, I'll call you back."

❖

Pulling into Pascale's, I eyed the box. "What do you think is in it?"

"Whatever it is," Nicole said, "it can't be good."

"Well, if it is videos of her having sex"—I tapped the box with my toe—"I don't care if it is evidence. I'm burning them."

Chapter Sixteen

Now in Pascale's living room, Nicole, Ida, and I sat around the lacquered coffee table, our eyes dodging back and forth between the contents of the box and each other's faces. A fly buzzed around and between us, occasionally slamming itself into a window, refusing to believe in the glass.

"Okay?" Ida said. She held up a wooden figure, examined it.

I immediately recognized it as Matsya, the fish.

"Hey, let me see that."

Nicole raked through the box recklessly, unwrapping the apparently carefully wrapped objects and tossing them about. "Fucking Del's toys. She wanted us to risk our lives to get her old toys?"

Gail and Katie, having just arrived, threw open the door, and the last remains of light from the day filled the room, momentarily brightening the interior.

"What did you find?" Gail looked into the box, then at the statue Ida was holding, and her expression went from eagerness to befuddlement. Then she laughed hard and loud. The laugh began someplace deep in her throat, built momentum like a wave swell as it gathered at the roof of her mouth, and then it burst out of her. "Mystery solved." She laughed harder still. "You just risked your entire career for those."

I wondered if part of Gail's glee was payback for the fifteen-mile bike ride I'd made her go on with me to get Kalki for Del.

Katie was still trying to catch up. "Uh, what are these?" She glanced at Gail and then shook with noiseless laughter, her eyes beginning to water.

I was the only one excited by the contents. "They're Avatars. Del collected them." I fumbled through the box. "I was wondering where these were. I thought she might have thrown them out."

My hand hit the paper before I realized what it was: gold, crinkly. There were objects wrapped inside it. I opened the paper to find Kalki and his white horse. On the inside was the note I had written to Del before I left her on the last night we spent together. *I love you*, it said. *No matter what happens, I promise, I will never let go of you.* I studied the pieces, turned them over in my hand, felt an energy emanating from them that made my palm hot and my skin tingle. These objects had outlived their context but maintained their poignancy. I rewrapped them and placed them back in the box.

"Great," Nicole said, calmer now. "I risked a third strike for"—she was holding up one of the pieces and studying it—"a turtle."

I smiled. "That's Kurma."

Pascale entered from the hallway, cigarette dangling from her lips. She was looking for a match. She had joined us when we had first arrived, eager to see what was in the box, and then when she realized what it was, she'd returned to her room disgusted. Now her usually strict posture compromised, her complexion ashen, Pascale staggered a little, mumbling as she passed us, "Fucking Omri. That old woman was always telling those Indian stories. I couldn't get Del to do shit when she was around." Her accented words were slurred from trying to talk with a cigarette in her mouth and also from alcohol. She used the stove to light her cigarette and then disappeared into her bedroom.

Ida and Nicole exchanged a worried look.

Ida asked Nicole, "Is she returning messages?"

Nicole shrugged.

"The funeral is Saturday, and all these people are calling, family and friends, and we have no idea if Pascale is even letting people know." Ida rubbed her hand along the arm of the couch. "She's just refusing to see anyone."

"Put the date, time, and location of the funeral on the answering machine message," Gail suggested.

I continued to study the wooden sea turtle, the size of my palm. I noticed the lines sketched on its shell, its beak-like nose, its deep-set eyes. Nicole sat beside me, smiling now as if proud of what we had just done for Del, even if it hadn't led to much. Katie and Gail plopped down on opposite sides of the couch and stared off in different directions. Gail pushed her hair back off her face and let go a long sigh. I looked at my watch: seven thirty p.m. Beasley would be releasing Del's body in the morning. I was out of ideas.

My phone rang. When I heard Margaret's voice on the line, I went out to the porch for privacy. "The first contact was last week. The woman you met today expected to meet Del Tuesday afternoon, but Del didn't show."

"So Del was trying to escape? Did you get any information from them about what was happening to her?"

"They wouldn't give me any specific information about her."

I made the decision now to share with Margaret what I had learned about Talon from the anonymous fax.

"Jesus," she said. "Puppies? Who could do something like that? The underground people must have known about that incident, because they were really worried about Del, and you know, they see a lot. No idea who sent it?"

"No."

"And he videotaped it? He videotaped the puppies after he'd maimed them? Huh, as interesting as it is horrific." I told her about the cameras in Del's house, and about the sex tapes. Margaret took a deep breath. "You know those surveillance cases are usually the worst."

"I do know." There had been a knot the size of a fist in my gut ever since I'd entered Del's house, a twisting feeling that left me on edge, as if anticipating danger, but having no idea from which direction it would come.

Margaret said, "The domestic-violence-death autopsy team reviewed one case where the guy videotaped beating his wife, including the beating that killed her. The psychologist who testified for the defense in the murder trial said this man taped the beatings because he dissociated during them—like a blackout. It was too hard for him, when he came out of these things, to find his wife battered and have no idea how it had happened. Then there was another guy who taped beatings because he liked to masturbate to them later. Talon seems more like the second guy, I think. Or maybe a combination."

She continued. "What happened to your friend seems especially tragic. The current laws are trapping women, forcing them to stay with men who are violent or lose custody of their kids to those men. Imagine that for a choice. Postfeminist fathers' rights discourse." Sarcastically, she added, "You know all about it." Then, "Call me cynical, but it used to be that a lot of loser fathers didn't give a shit about their kids after divorce. After the laws changed—deadbeat dad laws beefed up, child-support payments getting calculated according to the amount of time each parent had—all of a sudden, men are going to the mat for their fifty-percent timeshare. Not *sixty* percent, mind you. They don't want more work. They don't want to actually be responsible for doctors and back-to-school night, they just don't want to *pay* anything. When it means they might have to open their wallets, they're as precious about their parenting rights as they are about their penises. They're hiring lawyers, lobbying legislatures, getting gender-neutral language written into codes." She laughed grimly. "If women had been as effective at getting equal pay as men have been at getting equal parenting rights—well, imagine what the world would be then. As it is now, because of these laws, women are doing all the work in half the time and with none of the financial support."

She stopped. "Anyway, I'm sorry to go on like this. I'm not telling you anything new. It's just…" Margaret sighed. "Del must have been pretty desperate, Jenna, and she must have felt like she didn't stand much of a chance in court."

I usually resisted and resented Margaret's diatribes, but in that moment, all I could feel was a sense of solidarity and gratitude. "Thank you for your help, Margaret."

"Safe travels." She hung up.

I closed my phone and stood in the warm air. Voices carried from the living room. I leaned against the porch rail, my gaze drifting to the melancholy houses around me.

❖

"This can't be what Del meant," Ida said about the statues. She was folded into the couch between Gail and Katie, staring at the letter we had retrieved from Sid. "It doesn't make any sense." Her red hair was almost orange in this light, her tone somewhat restrained. "There was no other box, Nicole?"

"For the fourth time, *no*." To me, Nicole said, "That guy you told me about. He can prove Talon lied about where Del died."

Katie added, "And there are police reports."

I sat on the floor next to Nicole, tugged at the shag carpet beneath me. "I don't know whether Jake's report will make any difference here."

"Jenna," Nicole said in frustration, "Del was hooked to a chain thirty feet under the water. How could that be an accident?" She shifted her weight, put her face in her hands.

"I'll give Beasley the information from Jake. Maybe it'll make a difference to Beasley, maybe it won't. I don't know. Beasley already knows about the police reports."

Katie lit two cigarettes and, without asking, handed one to Nicole. Nicole took it with less than a nod of acknowledgment. I breathed in the scent of sulfur from the match against freshly lit tobacco, and longed.

Ida was still staring at the letter Del had sent to Sid. She shook her head, reading aloud, *"If anything happens to me, there is a box on the top shelf of the closet in my bedroom."* She put the letter down. "It's weird." Ida seemed more awake all of a sudden than she had since I'd arrived. "Del wouldn't have hidden anything in that house. Mr. Bleach-the-Sidewalk was too on top of her every move. And those fucking cameras were enough to…" Ida's mouth dropped open. "Oh my God." She leaped to her feet. "Del's bedroom," she near shouted, "Del's *old* bedroom."

Heads turned. My eyes met Gail's—now fully engaged—as we lunged forward, falling over ourselves and each other to follow Ida down the hallway. Ida threw open the closet door and stepped on a suitcase to access the shelf. She scrambled around, moving objects, making shuffling noises, until we heard, "A box!" The suitcase she was standing on was indenting beneath her weight and beginning to tip as she balanced and reached. "There's a box up here." Ida pulled the box out, gracefully teetering as the suitcase began to cave and topple. She rode it to the ground, stepping off just in time to achieve a soft landing. Then she grinned hugely, as if she'd just saved the day, and presented the box to me.

"Good job," I said.

❖

The box contained three close-up photographs of Del, like mug shots, her cheeks swollen and bruised, her lip cut, her nose bloody. Del was staring into the camera defiantly, daring it to lie. The photos of her like this were familiar to me, yet not. With the passing of the years my memories of Del had assumed more of dreamlike quality. I trusted less and less the image of her bruised face as I remembered it. Now, as an adult, I looked again at this bruised face and felt at once the unmediated horror and odd reassurance of confirmation.

There were copies of police reports, seven different instances in the last two years. Also in the box was a miniature tape for a microtape recorder. There was a log with dates and brief entries describing incidents of beatings and threats. There were both Del and Khila's passports, along with some cash. Finally, there was an envelope full of Post-its.

Each Post-it was dated and had an instruction on it. For example, one Post-it said the date and then directed Del to sort through boxes of nails in the garage and put them in separate containers by size. Another instructed Del to complete a list of household chores—bleaching the sidewalk, scouring the sink, scrubbing the toilet, sorting the sock drawers. Many of the Post-its gave the same instruction. Sorting the jar of pennies by date appeared to be a favorite. Each note was closed with "I love you" and Talon's signature.

We sat around the table in silence, Nicole, Katie, Ida, and me, staring at the contents of the box now spread out on the dining room table. Gail left to buy a microtape recorder so we could listen to the cassette. I stared at the photos of Del, wondering who took them. I thought of the spying man who had seemed so poised to witness earlier.

Nicole was the first to speak. "I don't get it. What's with the pennies?" She was holding a Post-it in her hand that said:

7/27/99
Hi honey,
Hope you slept well.

The pennies need to be sorted today. It would be great if you could put them in order by date and stack them in groups of fifty. I'll be home by five and expect them to be done by then.

Love you so much,
Tal

By the look on Nicole's face, I knew we were both recalling the five-gallon jar of pennies we'd seen at Del's house.

Ida said in a tone that sounded more like a confession, "They collected them."

She swallowed hard, looked around the room, and shifted in her seat uncomfortably. I could see in Nicole's narrowing eyes that her patience with Ida was thinning. Ida must have sensed it as well, because she became more forthright with her information.

"Tal would leave Del these notes in the morning when he went to work. He'd tell her to polish and sort all the pennies in that jar and then stack them in piles of fifty. When he came home, he'd check to make sure she'd done it. Then he'd put all the sorted pennies back in the jar and make her start all over the next day. The exact same thing all over again."

It was an excruciating image, Del, day after day, sitting at a table for eight hours putting pennies in piles of fifty by date. "Del told you this?" I asked.

Ida played mindlessly with one of the notes, turned it in her fingers, looked past me when she spoke. "I went by sometimes when Tal was at work, and I'd sit with her while she sorted—or whatever she was doing, cleaning the windows, organizing the kitchen cabinets. One week he had her sorting this huge mess of nuts and bolts every day, over and over again, the same rusty bolts. She'd sort them, and then he'd come home, spill them out, and have her do it again the next day."

"This seemed normal to you?" Nicole blasted in Ida's direction. She slammed her hand on the table and kicked her chair back. "I don't know whose side you're on." She looked as if she was about to pounce.

Ida kept talking. "It started about six months ago." Beginning to cry, she said, "I wish I had told someone, or at least tried to get her to leave him. She was my sister—I loved her." Her spine firmed with conviction, her chin lifted slightly in my direction. "Jenna, you know I loved Del. Del didn't talk to me very much about Talon. For one thing, if I said anything to her about him and he found out, he wouldn't have let her see me anymore." She added, "And she didn't trust me with him." Ida snuck a glance in Nicole's direction. Nicole shifted her face away in condemnation. "I knew they were fucked up, but I couldn't do anything about it." Now Ida was sobbing. "Del said the chores were important to Talon. She knew it was weird, but she said she didn't mind. She didn't mind him watching her on the toilet, she didn't mind him telling her what she could and couldn't eat. I tried." She wiped her nose on her sleeve.

"Nicole," she continued, "I told Del she was getting thin. She said she wasn't eating because Tal thought she was fat, and she wanted to look good for him. What was I supposed to do? She loved the guy." We sat in silence, each of us aware that Del weighed ninety-eight pounds when she died. Ida moved her finger along the surface of the table drawing circles, the way a Buddhist might rake sand. "It got really freaky really fast in the end. Tal put cameras in all the rooms. I mean, he videotaped everything anyway. Don't know why. He was just weird like that. He cut off all her money and her credit cards. He controlled what clothes she wore, who she saw, when she got up, when she went to bed, when she took a shower or a shit. He controlled everything. But she never complained. She just did what he told her to do. I thought like a scene. You know, an S-and-M thing."

"How do you control when someone takes a shit?" Katie asked.

"Maybe that's what the laxatives were for," Ida replied.

I watched Ida's face for a moment. I could see it changing as she said these things out loud to us now. She was realizing she had been duped, wondering how it was possible that she had stood idly by while something hideous had gone down. I understood—I really did—how one could go along with something like this, thinking it's not a big deal or not understanding it is a big deal because the person it's happening to seems so okay with it. It's the nature of perversion to make something horrific seem perfectly normal, acceptable, natural—in Ida's case, enviable.

Nicole's neck twitched, her eyes rolled, her hands clasped the air then released it. The spasms were clearly more pronounced when she was angry. "And the tapes. Why was she making sex tapes?"

Ida was surprised, her brows raised, lips slightly parted. Then she scrunched her forehead and said, "She wasn't making sex tapes. Are you talking about…" She hesitated. "They weren't sex tapes. Not like bad sex tapes, I mean. Talon would get some guy from a bar or something, and videotape Del blowing him. Then they'd watch it together, and it would get them off. I mean, Del was into it, too. She told me she was glad he was so into watching her and not other women." Ida shook her head. "Look, I loved her, but you guys have this idea of Del like she's some innocent, misunderstood angel or something." She breathed out a laugh. "Jenna, you're going on some idea that you know her sexually because she experimented with you a couple of times in fucking high school. You don't know anything about her. She was *tooting* when Talon *met* her."

Nicole looked at me. "That's Ida code for 'I fucked him and she deserved it.'"

I ignored both of them. I was doing what I tended to do when flooded with too much painful information at once, focusing on one detail—the Post-its. I stared at one instructing Del to sort pennies, my mind filtering through everything I'd heard, trying to make sense of it.

I said, "He was keeping her busy." Everyone turned from Ida to me. "Talon thought Del was having an affair. So when he went to work, he gave her these assignments, so she couldn't go anywhere or do anything. He was keeping her busy."

Katie sat with her legs neatly crossed, Del's journal split open on her lap. Her fine white-blond hair caught the light and glistened. She raised her chin and pressed her lips together. Then she said, "Listen to this." She read aloud the journal entries documenting one assault after another. They were matter-of-fact, more reports than accounts.

The first incident had been entered in 1992 when Khila was three years old: *I got home late from work last night. Talon immediately accused me of being with someone else. I asked him to lower his voice because I didn't want Khila to hear us fighting. Talon called Khila into the room and hit me in front of her.*

The entries went on this way, one after another, year after year. The police seemed to be the intended audience. In fact, when a police report had been filed, its number was referenced. The fact that Del had been so divided in this way—living out her life and documenting it—was chilling.

The entries also documented dates and times when Talon videotaped Del doing sex acts with other men. These incidents, too, were entered without much emotion or detail. What the descriptions did convey was a downward progression from more or less consensual on Del's part. At first, the sex acts were something Del did because it pleased Talon. Then the taping became something she did because he insisted on it. By the end, he was bringing these guys home to punish her. He was forcing her, threatening to expose the tapes if she didn't do what he told her to do.

Del also mentioned another tape she believed existed: the tape of Thomas's murder, the one piece of evidence that could exonerate Sid. Talon, she wrote, videotaped all his crimes, and there was no way he would have passed up on that one. The cameras made it hard for her to search the house, which was another reason she thought Talon had installed them. But she'd still managed to get into most of the places she thought the tapes might be hidden. If they weren't in the house, there was only one other place he would leave them.

Del described in the last pages of the journal her fear that Talon was going to kill her, and she wanted to find the tape that proved Sid was innocent and destroy the sex tapes so Khila would never see them. The tapes, she believed, were on Kramer's boat.

"*That's* why she went with him." It hadn't made sense to me until then. I kept wondering why, if she was leaving Talon or she was afraid of him, she had gone with him on this last trip. Now I understood. "She was looking for the videotapes." As I said it, Gail returned with a microtape recorder.

❖

The tape Del had left in the box, dated July 27, 1999, began with her asking Talon in a strained but calm voice if they could talk. When he agreed, she said, "I don't think this is working."

Her voice was deeper than I remembered, but so familiar, and hearing it instantly made my heart billow—and then shrink, as I remembered where I was and what had happened.

Del's tone was even. "I feel like we've tried for a long time. I don't think it's working," she repeated. A lengthy pause followed. Nervousness creeping in, her tone edging from reasoning into pleading, Del said, "Tal, you can keep everything. Keep the house, the car, the bank account, whatever you want, you can have it. I don't want child support. I don't want anything. Just let me take Khila and leave. We'll go to my mom's. You'll see her whenever you want." More silence. Del's voice trembled now, but she kept on. "You know you haven't been happy with me, either. I know you're sleeping with other women."

Her tone, although sad, had a tender, open quality that I remembered and loved about her.

Talon was calm and matter-of-fact as he said, "I've told you before, I'll tell you again, you're not leaving with Khila." One could imagine him smiling coldly as he said, "You're very sick, Del. You have serious mental problems and everyone knows it." As if speaking to a child, "Do you get what I'm saying? You will never get Khila."

Del said, "How do you know what the court would do? She's with me all the time. You've never taken care of her. You hardly know her."

Talon let go a deep, gargling laugh. "With your history of drugs and tooting, you think you're gonna get custody of *my* kid?"

"That was a long time ago," Del said.

More laughter, louder, harder. "What've you been smokin'?" Then Talon said, "Those cocks you've been sucking. Remember those? Who says you didn't get paid for that? What would the judge say about those videos? Nice motherly behavior, don't you think? Real ladylike."

"Those tapes," Del said, her voice cracking a little, "say as much about you as they do about me. I did those things in the privacy of our marriage. You made those tapes."

"Prove it," he said sharply. "I'm not in them." He laughed once. "Who's gonna believe a word you say? You're lying white trash."

"Maybe I am. But there—" Del started then stopped. Her voice became more forceful with the second attempt. "There *is* someone who would believe me." She paused. "And she would help me keep my daughter."

Silence. I was looking around at the others now, trying to get a sense of whether they had any idea who Del was talking about. They didn't. I thought it must be the underground folks.

"Who?" Talon shouted. "Who would believe you? The other guy you're fucking?" Either he had disregarded or hadn't heard when she'd referred to the person as a *she*. "Tell me who you've been talking to." His voice was louder and clearer, perhaps because he was moving closer to the tape recorder. "Do you have an attorney? Did you get an attorney? Who would believe you? Who have you talked to about me, Del?" There was a slam and some shuffling.

"Get your finger out of my face," Del said.

His voice deep and creamy smooth, Talon said, "I'll put my fingers where I want to put them."

Del let out a cry of pain and he laughed over her. There was silence except for more muted, ruffling sounds and a single sharp inhale.

"Do it then," Del said. "Choke me. If you have the guts. Usually you send somebody else to do it for you. Or set people up, like you did my brother."

Del's composure somehow returned, and her voice steadied. As with the journal, it was clear now that she was addressing an outside listener. This was all for the tape recorder, and she was artful at incitement, the way she had been when she was a kid and she was provoking her mother.

"You threaten to kill yourself. When that doesn't work, you threaten to kill me. You fuck me whether I want you to or not. You make me suck dicks just to prove your power over me. If I don't do what you want, you threaten to take Khila away from me." First sign of tears. "You made me frame my own brother. I fucking *hate* you." A loud thump followed.

Talon screamed, "You trying to hit *me*? You fucking stupid bitch. You try to hit *me*? Now," he taunted, "you could have *really* hurt me." There was scuffling, struggling, muffled cries, Del resisting.

"Get off, get your knee off my ba—" A loud cry before her voice was stifled for a moment. She screamed, "Get the fuck off me. I'm sick of you hurting me."

I stared at a spot on the wall darkened from mold, believing momentarily it was a bruise. My body stiffened to stone, the slightest muscle movement threatening to crack me in half.

Nicole was on her feet, walking in a circle and rocking her head back and forth, like a robot whose circuits were overloading. "He's hurting her. He's hurting her."

Ida hit the stop and the rewind. "Shut up, Nicole, I can't hear the tape." She pushed play.

"You hit me first," Talon said, sounding like a four-year-old. Then he yelled, "You're no victim, you cunt."

Talon's voice strained oddly, and I realized that at the same time as he was yelling, he was also crying, or trying not to. Beneath his rage was a desperate plea.

"You think I don't know you're fucking somebody else? You bring it on yourself. I go to work every day to support you and Khila, and you wait until I leave to fuck some other man. Do you honestly believe I would let another man raise my daughter?" He cried and screamed, "You leave me, you *fuck* with me, and you will be sorry."

"It's none of your business who I sleep with. I want a divorce."

We all winced and braced ourselves, hearing her say it.

"None of my business? None of my business?"

There were struggling sounds, blows and crying, incomprehensible words. Del began pleading for him to stop, to get off her. She was crying. He was cursing. Something crashed.

Talon yelled, "You'll never get Khila." More slams. "You hear me? You'll never get her. You're nothing but a cunt whore, and I know you're fucking someone else."

There was silence except for Del's crying. Talon said in a chillingly calm way, "You know what, forget about it. You want to go, go. Get out, but you're not taking Khila. You're a worthless piece of shit." Del cried harder. "You're nothing but a parasite, just sucking the life out of me." A few moments passed with Del sobbing, and then Talon said, "Khila's not gonna grow up like you. I'll be remarried in a year, and Khila will have a different mother. So you're doing us all a favor. Get the fuck out."

There were more words that were hard to understand—Del screaming something about Talon taking Khila from her—cut off by a slamming door. Then there was sobbing and the jolting sound of the recorder clicking off. She was gone.

Katie uncrossed and then recrossed her legs, shifted in her chair. Gail lay motionless on the couch. Nicole stared hatefully at Ida.

Ida cried. "I didn't know, Nicole. I swear. I didn't know it was this bad."

Del's pleas still ringing in my ears, my breathing felt shallow and incomplete. The recorder clicking off had submerged her yet again. I moved away from the others, found my way to Del's old room, closed the door, and fell back against it. I folded in half, gasping and sobbing. My limbs shook and I felt sick, my stomach turning in on itself again and again. My abdomen cramped. I slid down the door to the floor and buried my head in my arms, waiting for the cramp to pass. I twisted to my feet, stood in the middle of this room in which I had spent so much time, in which such intimate parts of myself had taken form and expression. I felt her there, saw her face, heard her voice, caught the scent of her hair as it brushed over my face. *What happened? What happened? How'd I miss this? Why didn't I know how much trouble she was in?*

I did the only thing I could imagine doing in that moment. I lay down on the bed and called Madison. She was at the airport in New Haven waiting for her plane back to California. She listened to the whole story, which I might have told her twice. She just kept saying how sorry she was. Comforted by her voice, I longed to crawl through the phone and into her lap. I longed for my house in San Francisco, the scent of lemon blossoms, the sight of the Bay Bridge in the sparkling light.

Now I looked at the photograph of Del and Khila sitting on the dresser. I picked it up and touched Del's face. It made me start to cry again.

"She went on that boat to get those videotapes, knowing he might kill her. Why did she agree to do those things in the first place? To frame her own brother?"

Madison's tone was matter-of-fact but poignant. "She agreed to sort pennies, didn't she?" There was a moment of silence, and then Madison added, "Del had a baby with somebody who was a lot sicker than she realized." She paused. "She's spent the last ten years running interference and navigating around Talon to keep her kid safe. And maybe she loved him, too."

"He thinks he's so clever, this guy. He thinks he's so clever because he keeps getting away with brutalizing people who can't defend themselves."

"Jenna," Madison said. "Do you want me to come there? I can take the next plane to Miami right now."

"No." I missed Madison and I did want her with me, but I was afraid to expose my life with her to this horror. "I'm fine. Really. I'll call you later."

"Don't do anything, Jen…" I heard as I closed my phone.

CHAPTER SEVENTEEN

I lay in Del's old bedroom, staring at shadows on the ceiling, trying to assess whether with the tape there was enough evidence to open an investigation. The sheets reeked of cigarette smoke, which had attached to my skin and clothes and remained with me after I sat up. Without giving it much thought, I headed into the tiny bathroom, closed the door, and stripped. The bathroom was the same as I'd remembered it, except for the sink, which had been replaced after Nicole yanked the last one out of the wall during one of her fits. The medication she was on must be working, I thought.

Water sprayed from the showerhead. It was too hot, but I didn't adjust it. I sat naked on the shower floor embracing my legs, resting my chin on my knees. I tried to think of what to do next. The steam rose around me, left me momentarily confused about the law of gravity. My mind a sift of images: the yellow Post-its, the stacked pennies, the bleached sidewalk, the manicured lawn, the organized Tupperware, the roach appendages, Sid's eyes, Talon's falcon tattoo, Del's face, Del's face, Del's *face*.

It is uncanny, I thought, the extent to which only the names and faces change. Over and over, women who have never met, have never had cause or occasion to cross paths, stand in court telling the same harrowing story. There are some variations. I'd recently heard from a woman whose husband had taken to hitting her in the back of the head because it was more difficult to detect bruises there. Nevertheless, woman after woman describes a life of increasing isolation from friends and family, no control of finances, diminishing work options, more restrictive clothing requirements, increasingly outrageous allegations of promiscuity, forced religious practices, fewer and fewer degrees of freedom of movement in the outside world, surveillance. Before long, diet, hygiene, and toileting practices are being orchestrated.

I thought again about the videotapes, about Del sacrificing Sid, and I wondered when Del had become so confused. It was before Talon. It was before Ben Reed. I recalled the night that Del had sex with Andrew Torie in the back of his father's station wagon.

❖

For six weeks since the night we had talked outside her house, Del had been showing up with Andrew everywhere and avoiding me. Now she came to my window and woke me up. She felt mortified about having had sex with Andrew earlier that night, kept saying she didn't know why she had done it. She dreaded going back to school and facing the gossip. With no place to go, we walked the streets together, our hands tucked into our jacket pockets trying to keep warm.

Underlying her disgust over having slept with Andrew was her rage at me for telling Gail about us and her sadness over our coming apart. Her father was engaged to someone else, and Pascale was on a rampage. Del said she felt like dying. I tried to hold her, and finally when she did let me, she molded to me and collapsed into sonorous, wrenching sobs. Then she rested quietly, allowed me to comfort her, stroke her hair.

We began walking again and finally ended up back at her house as the sun was rising. She kissed me on the lips when we said good-bye, her hand falling from my cheek to fondle the necklace she had given me.

"Do you want it back?" I asked, dreading her answer. I wanted to keep it.

She shook her head indicating that she didn't.

I watched her go inside.

When I called to check on her the next morning, she was more distant than ever; I had to say my name twice before she recognized me. I was left to wonder if the entire encounter had been a dream. The mascara stains on my jacket from having held her while she sobbed were the only evidence I had of being with her the night before.

❖

After that night, Del was hardly at school. I heard from Ida she'd failed all of her classes that semester. There were rumors about her having sex with different guys. I never knew if they were true. Katie thought they were because apparently she dated the same guys next. None of us tried out for the soccer team the summer before eleventh grade. Gail's mother had decided she needed private time with her new husband, and she sent Gail kicking and screaming to New York to live with her father for her last two years of high school. Katie was too involved in dating and drugs. I didn't see her at all that summer.

I did manage to maintain my grades the last semester of tenth grade, but by the summer I was crying constantly and refusing to leave my room. My parents took me to a psychiatrist, an elderly guy with bushy, gray hair and round spectacles. He was nice enough. He advised my parents to forget about the gay thing, said it was a phase and it would pass, and he prescribed me Elavil for depression. It was one of those old-fashioned antidepressants with a side effect of weight gain. By the time eleventh grade started, I was thirty pounds heavier.

On the first day of eleventh grade, I ran into Del. I was walking into the building and she was walking out with Ben Reed. He had graduated a few years before and had a business selling flowers from street carts.

Ben saw me first and said, "Holy shit, Jenna, lay off the cake!"

Del noticed me and in what seemed to be a reflexively protective impulse glared at Ben. Ben quickly apologized and slithered by, leaving Del and me alone face-to-face for the first time in six months, the first time since we'd walked all night.

"What are you doing with him?" I asked. "He's a scumbag."

"I need a job. He's hiring." She looked away then back, as if thinking twice. Then she asked matter-of-factly, "What is up with your weight?"

"I don't know." I felt hideous and ashamed to my core. The weight hadn't bothered me that much until that moment, until I was standing next to Del, loving her, missing her, remembering myself when I had been with her. "I'm taking some medicine."

"What kind of medicine?"

"For depression."

"How's gaining weight supposed to make you less depressed?" Without waiting for an answer, she started past me.

"Del."

She stopped, turned, her expression implacable. She swept her hair away from her face, exposing large, gold hoop earrings and heavy makeup. She stood firmly on serious heels, the inverted V of her tight jeans cutting high into her crotch. Skinnier now even than before, her breasts looked larger, pushed up and in for a cleavage effect. There was no sign of her silliness or vulnerability. I thought of the honey-haired girl who pinned me to the bed and gave me my first real kiss, giggled when I came undone; the serious girl who fretted over her younger siblings and preferred reading to socializing; the earnest lover, whose mouth had touched me *everywhere*; the sweet friend with toothpaste-tinged breath and her face near mine as we talked all night. I thought of us on the first day of tenth grade—just one year before—when we'd believed we'd have each other forever. We were tanned and strong and confident and ready. Now she was jaded, impermeable, unforgiving, and I was desolate and bereft. *I miss you*. "Nothing." I clamped my teeth in an effort not to cry.

Del noticed the silver necklace. "You still wear it?"

"Always."

She smiled.

"Do you want it back?"

"No. You keep it."

"I'll keep it for you. Okay?"

She nodded and then walked away.

Del lasted a month into the eleventh-grade year before she formally dropped out and moved in with Ben Reed. I quit soon after her. Our paths rarely crossed after that.

❖

When I think back on the phone call the morning after we'd walked all night—how eerily unfamiliar I was to Del just hours after we'd had such an intimate talk—I can see Del was fragmenting. I might see familiar pieces of her from time to time, like on the night we talked, or in the way she glared at Ben for saying something hurtful to me, but I would never again know her whole. Nobody would. Because minds do blow and hearts do break. Those are not just sayings. And wolves and roaches are not the only creatures that chew off their legs to get out of traps—human beings do that, too.

The steam in the shower absorbed me, heat rising, carrying my anger upward with it. My rage looking down at me, a naked body, curled in a ball, skin red from hot rain. What to do now? We knew Talon had lied about where Del went into the water, and we could provide evidence of that. Maybe Beasley would consider it, and maybe she wouldn't. We now knew there was a long and extreme history of domestic violence evidenced by police reports, photos, and a log of abuses. In addition, we had the tape of her telling Talon she wanted to leave him and of him threatening her life. It was likely all admissible in this post-OJ era. So maybe we did have enough to at least get the prosecutor involved in an inquiry, to hold up Talon's move to Texas, keep Khila here for a while. Maybe with a thorough investigation they would find more—the more they needed to prove murder. Or maybe Child Protective Services would listen to the tape and decide Talon wasn't the best person to place Khila with.

I got out of the shower to answer my cell phone. It was Doug Andrews, and he dove right in. "My guy from the lab said something's not right. Twenty percent carboxyhemoglobin in her blood is low for a carbon monoxide fatality and it's high for a smoker. Maybe we're seeing numbers that are well past her peak, so it may have been much higher at some point. Anemia might affect it, certainly, but again, twenty percent is low to bring on a heart attack. It's possible. Anything is possible with diving, you know, it's like flying, we're not meant to do it." There was a momentary pause, and then he said, "I guess what the ME's office is saying is between the COHb and the anemia, the compressed air just put too much stress on her heart. But we think they're wrong. We're guessing cyanide. You don't see it very often."

"*Cyanide?* But the autopsy, I mean, wouldn't they know, wouldn't it be apparent in a basic blood analysis?"

"No, it won't even show up in the comprehensive toxicology report, unless they're testing for it specifically. It's not a common form of murder. And he's smart for putting it together with diving. It's just commonly believed that divers increase their risk of heart attack when they smoke before they dive. Carbon monoxide poisoning, cyanide poisoning—easily mistaken."

He continued, "No indication of an almond smell, or at least none detected. That's not conclusive—some people can smell it and some people can't." Thinking aloud, "Well, and that may explain why he sank her rather than just pull her to shore. He was hoping the body would disappear and there would be no evidence of poisoning, or she would be submerged and her body saturated for several hours, and any smell would be diluted." I heard him shuffling papers.

I took a deep breath, my first one in nearly an hour. "So, what now? It's one thing to know this, it's another thing to prove it. What's the half-life? Do I tell the lab to run special tests?" I imagined the journal and the tapes would be enough to get Beasley to agree to further testing.

"Cyanide is tricky," Doug said. "Tell them to test for cyanide specifically. They'll know what to do. And keep in mind, once they embalm, any signs of cyanide may be destroyed. There's always urine. It's not a great way to test for cyanide, but it could work, although there may not have been any in her body."

I said jokingly, "Porta-Potty on the boat?" He laughed.

Porta-Potty. As I put my still stale-smelling clothes back on, I realized I had already decided I was going to the boat for the videotapes. I couldn't fix the ways I'd let Del down fifteen years ago, but I could do my best now to retrieve the evidence that could exonerate Sid and, in the process, destroy the sex tapes for her.

❖

The way the heat held constant in Miami, even at night, was something I'd forgotten. As we left Pascale's house to go to the boat, I braced myself for a chill. But the air I stepped out into was warm and heavy and moist—disarming. Smells lingered from the day: roof tar, gasoline from a neighbor's lawn mower. And kids' voices carried from the corner, where a group of them had gathered to fight or flirt, it was hard to tell.

Now heading east in Gail's car, Jed Bush dominated the radio stations with endorsements for his brother. A police car appeared behind us. A siren blipped, and then stripes of red and blue began spinning inside the car like a frenetic American flag. Gail startled, glanced in her rearview mirror, and began to pull over. But the police car suddenly shifted lanes and targeted the car next to us. There was palpable relief as we slipped by. We were like minnows, grateful the shark had eaten someone else.

Katie was in the front passenger seat. She persisted in searching out music, relaxed only after she found an old Billy Joel song—"Only the Good Die Young." Ida reached over Katie's shoulder and turned it up, and for a moment the mood lifted, all of us recklessly belting out the words along with Billy, accompanied by hand and head gestures. It felt insane. It felt, in our quick harmonizing, memorized lyrics, mutual gestures, and ready abandonment, familiar.

When it was over, Katie lowered the volume on the next song, and no one said what we all must have been thinking—that it was Del we'd been singing to.

Nicole lit a cigarette and announced, "Pascale said Talon's planning on taking Khila to Texas on Saturday, right after the funeral." Her anger increasing, she looked to me. "Jenna, did you hear me?"

I didn't answer her. I was worried about Talon taking Khila to Texas, too.

Annoyed by the smoke from Nicole's just-lit cigarette, Gail pulled over and put the roof down. I expected relief from the heat as the top lifted and folded, but the air outside the car was exactly the same temperature as the air inside the car.

We drove the strip of Coconut Grove with its shop-lined streets, crowds of pedestrians, neon lights, and loud cars. I spotted the Hindu Market where Gail and I bought the wooden Kalki figure for Del.

"That's it," Ida said, pointing to an entrance into the boatyard. "Lot number thirty-two."

I sighed. *How did she know that?*

Gail parked and we tumbled out.

"Okay, so now what?" Katie asked.

I began to look around. It was quickly apparent that boarding Kramer's boat meant getting wet. The berths were lined side by side in a U-shape, and they were secured behind razor-wire-topped ten-foot gates that required keys or combinations to open.

"I'm going aboard," I said. Nicole was beside me instantly.

Gail and Ida remained with the car parked near one entrance, facing the berth. Katie took a flashlight and went to the only other entrance. Each understood to turn the headlights or flashlight on if anyone entered from either side.

Nicole and I found our way to the edge of the pier and onto the steep layers of rocks—an unintended stairway into the bay. Without saying anything, I stripped down to my sports bra, briefs, and sneakers. When I looked over, Nicole was naked but for her sneakers and the leather pouch she always wore.

To my questioning expression she replied, "What? I don't wear underwear."

I shook my head at her appreciatively.

The greenish moon was close in and full, drawing in the tide and disquieting the surface of the bay. I placed a small flashlight between my teeth and waded into the murky, algae-thick film brimming the water's edge. The bay was chilled but nothing in comparison to what they call a beach in Northern California. I pushed gently off the rocks, slicing the muck and slipping along the petulant surface. Nicole put her survival kit in her mouth to keep it dry, and then she followed with determination. She wasn't a strong swimmer, but she had insisted on going with me, not trusting me to be able to successfully commit a felony on my own. We made our way across the liquid courtyard. I watched Nicole struggle to hold her head out of the water and move her arms and legs at the same time, denying or, in any event, refusing to let show her considerable vulnerability.

Kramer's boat was easily distinguished by the web of yellow crime tape streaming from and around it. I climbed the partially submerged stepping ladder leading to the swimming platform off the back of the boat and sat down, waiting for Nicole. She came up next and sat beside me, greatly relieved, it seemed, to be out of the water. She was breathing hard; I could practically hear her heart pound.

As she caught her breath, Nicole said, "This is the first time in ten years I feel like I'm doing something to help my sister. It's because of you. If you weren't here, Talon would have gotten away with this for sure."

"He still might."

"At least we're trying. At least we're doing something."

I noticed her clear eyes and the way her wet hair cut across her cheekbone. She seemed sober and present in a way I'd never experienced her before, and I wondered if the *doing something* about the injustice in her life was the real medicine Nicole had needed all along.

We crawled onto the rear deck through the port entry; I turned on the flashlight; and from where we were huddled at the back of the boat, I began to survey the layout. The boat looked to be about forty feet long. It had a large bow for sunbathing, a smaller rear deck, and between them a cockpit that housed the main control center. The bridge was perched above the cockpit; the cabin apparently ran below. The cabin door was in front of us, between the captain's chair and a passenger seat, inside the cockpit. Flashlight in my mouth, I crawled on my hands and knees to the door and began to reach for the release, hoping it wasn't locked.

Nicole tugged at my ankle urgently. She crawled beside me and whispered, "Check for an alarm before you do that."

I could feel the boat gently rocking. I shined the light along the door seam and did notice a clear wire embedded in the lining of the frame.

Nicole wiggled closer to the captain's chair and searched around under the console. Then she ran her hand along the walls and across the floor under the chair. Feeling for and finding a compartment concealed beneath the snap-in carpet, she retrieved a multipurpose pocketknife from her survival kit and then used the screwdriver to remove the cover. I watched her feel around with agility and speed, locate the correct fuse, and disable it.

Now back at the cabin door, Nicole went once again into her bag of tricks to retrieve, of all things, a lock-picking kit. She giggled at my shocked expression. "I never leave home without it." She proceeded to tease at the lock on the cabin door while I checked to make sure Gail and Katie's signal lights were still off. After some time passed, Nicole said, "It's not working. I don't know this kind of lock." She became resigned to the idea that we might have to break it. Seeing as tampering with a crime scene is a felony, my preference was to get in and out without a trace.

"I have an idea."

I wedged the tip of a screwdriver between each pin and hinge, leveraging the pins against the hinges to lift them out a bit. Then—the heel of my hand a hammer, the screwdriver a chisel—I nudged the pins the rest of the way out. With the hinges off, the door was free to pivot on its lock, gaping like a tipsy doorman. We were in.

The cabin was darker than the night. My flashlight beam leading the way, I stepped in. We were in the salon area. There was a galley to our left. The bay was lifting and churning, rocking the boat to the rhythm of the waves pounding her sides, a low, constant drumbeat. The cabin smelled of salt air, dank carpet, and what reminded me of a sun-dried wet suit. I moved the flashlight around, noticed there was not a thing out of place. No strewn clothing, no dirty dishes, no tossed-about gear, no unmade beds.

"He cleaned up," I said.

"You mean covered up."

I pointed the flashlight down, remembering something Doug had taught me. When concealing a crime, people almost always forget about the floor. According to Doug, more crimes are solved by what is inadvertently left behind on floors than probably anything else. In this instance there was nothing of note. In fact, the only thing out of place in the entire cabin was the vacuum, postured casually but prominently against the cabin wall, as if intended to taunt us. It told me, loudly and clearly, yes, he had killed her, but he had covered his tracks so thoroughly we would never prove it.

There was one bathroom, and I headed right for it to see what kind of head the boat had. I was expecting a flush marine head on a boat this size, but fortunately, Kramer had been in the process of upgrading the bathroom at the time that Talon and Del had used the boat and was relying temporarily on a Porta-Potty.

"What are you doing, Jen? You think the tapes are in the head?" Nicole spoke and laughed at the same time.

With my light concentrated on the Porta-Potty, I said slowly, "I think I know how Talon killed Del. Well, at least what he used to kill her. I need to find something to prove it." I breathed out, turned, and faced her. "I think I need a sample from the Porta-Potty."

Clearly knocked off balance by this, Nicole let out a nervous giggle. "Jenna, that's insane. For one thing, I'm sure she wasn't the only one using that thing."

"I need to get samples of the contents of the Porta-Potty to take to the lab. I think he used cyanide to kill her."

"They have her body. What's a little more piss gonna do?"

"The contents of the Porta-Potty are from *before* she was submerged for seven hours." I was looking for something to put the samples in. Kramer was a dealer, so baggies came to mind. I went through the kitchen drawers until I found the stash: sandwich, snack, and—sure enough—single-grape size. "I know this seems desperate," I said, "but it's all I can think of at this point." I began searching for a spoon.

Nicole shook her head, put her palms up as if stopping traffic, and said, "All I can say is you must have *really* loved her."

I shook my head at her with appreciation as she stood buck naked but for her sneakers and her survival kit. "You look for the tapes."

"Right." She scanned the cabin, checked the spaces inside the built-in benches, and searched haphazardly in the drawers and cabinets. "I'm sure the police have searched the whole boat already." Pointing up, as if at some invisible other, she said, "The police don't know it's a drug boat, do they?" Then she mumbled to herself, "Where would they put the drugs?" She studied the floor. Down on it now, Nicole began lifting the snap-in carpet and peeling it back from the wall in different places. "They have to be in the floor."

Armed with a sandwich-sized plastic bag and a soup spoon, I made my way to the head, took a deep breath, unscrewed the lid from the Porta-Potty's storage tank, and lifted—empty. It had been not just dumped, but cleaned and sanitized. I immediately told myself it didn't matter, it was a long shot anyway, we were really there for the tapes; still, I felt devastated. And as I secured the lid, I felt my weight in my hands and wrists and realized I was using the toilet to hold myself up. *When did he clean it?*

He emptied the toilet, went through my mind again and again. It was a maddening thought that looped like a tuck stitch around and back again, knitting the pieces and parts of Del's life into a macabre tale before my eyes. The final proof for me that Del was murdered came not from what was in that tank, but from what was not in it. Had the police not noticed a clean head on a boat that had been occupied overnight? It struck me as a blatant confirmation of Talon's guilt and revealed his apparently correct reliance on the police to do a cursory investigation and then close the case.

"It's empty, wiped clean," I told Nicole. "He beat us to it."

"Yeah, well," she was still working the edges of the carpet, her face close to the floor, as if she were using her nose to guide her. "No one knows hell like the devil." She glanced up at me. "Maybe what we have is enough, Jenna."

"It's going to have to be. We're out of time."

I went to the cabin door, lifted my head into the night, checked Gail and Katie for lights; there were none. The waves drummed softly on the side of the boat, and from where I was standing I could see the bay was choppier than it had been just minutes before, and I could feel the breeze ever-so-slightly quickening.

"Bingo!"

I turned back and directed my flashlight at the ground near Nicole's hands. Under where the vacuum had been sitting, Nicole had lifted the rug to reveal a square hatch in the floor, approximately three feet by three feet. The compartment was locked, and the hinges were sunken into the floor, so my trick with the pins wouldn't work here. Nicole took out her tools and once again went to work.

I stood and watched her, remembering how, when we were kids, she repeatedly broke into Del's room using a paper clip. Del finally got tired of it and broke off a piece of wood inside the hole in the doorknob.

Nicole approached the lock from upside down, sliding the slim silver device with the pin-thin head into the keyhole. "I know this type of lock," she said. She was talking to herself, saying things like, "Three pins, find the right torque. Shit." There was a click or two. "Almost," she said. "It's three pins."

I nodded as if that mattered to me, when in fact I had no idea what she was talking about and little faith this would work. The boat rocked more emphatically and my heart started to race. I listened for sounds then went to the cabin door and put my head out to check the signals: darkness. Still, I glanced around the vacant docks before going back inside.

Nicole had started over yet again, gently inserting the silver wire into the hole of the lock, which was followed by more fumbling and cursing. Her hair fell forward; she repeatedly used her free hand to push it from her face. There was a crackling sound and then nothing. "Fucking bitch," Nicole said and then dove back in.

"We're pressing our luck," I said. "We should go." Nicole ignored me and kept at the lock. I wandered with my light, allowing the beam to fall in corners and at angles. I studied the blue any-weather carpet, the walnut paneling, the compact, self-sufficient details. The salon had a couch and a television. The galley had a small sink built-in to a wood countertop, and a tiny stove. More clicks and curses. I was starting to feel nervous. We'd stayed too long. "Nicole."

Nicole answered, "One, two"—*click*—"got it!" With what looked to me like a quick twitch of her hand, the keyhole rotated. Nicole turned the knob, the hatch in the floor sprang, and my hope we'd retrieve the tapes sprang with it.

The space, a three-by-three-foot square, was I guess about two feet deep. It, too, was empty. I let my flashlight linger on the empty space for a moment trying to regroup from what was now my second major disappointment.

Nicole stared into the compartment. "You know," she said, "it's really small for cargo." Her forehead lifted. "It's a decoy." She reached into the compartment and began running her hands along the sides, feeling the edges and the corners. It seemed desperate to me, but I got down beside her and began to do the same on the other side. I ran my hand along the walls made of pine, my fingertips tracing the seams in the corners, then along the floor. I stopped when I felt an irregularity in the wood on the side closest to me—a little ridge.

"Shine your light here."

The wood looked uniform to the eye but felt slightly raised. With the light directly on it, I could see beneath my finger a round hole about two inches in diameter that looked as if it had been plugged with matching wood. I picked at the plug with my fingernail and it popped out. Inside the hole was a metal latch. I lifted; there was a loud clicking sound; and the floor of the box, which I could now see was on tracks, slid away, revealing a deeper, larger compartment below.

Nicole grinned hugely. "Now that's what you call a cargo compartment." She stuck her head down and in and swung her flashlight around. "There's a duffel bag." She lowered herself in and then moments later reappeared, tossing the duffel bag out ahead of her.

I unzipped the bag. "VHS tapes!" For a moment I felt almost giddy.

Nicole closed the hatch and put the carpet back in place.

I started out of the cabin with the duffel bag, leaving Nicole to put the vacuum cleaner where she had found it.

"Careless," she said to me.

Almost to the cabin door, I turned to see she was referring to the plastic bag I had been carrying, which I'd left on the floor when I had gotten involved in helping her with the compartment.

"I'll do better next ti—"

Thump! Over us? Behind us? No way to know from which direction it had come or in which direction it was heading. The boat pulled and rocked, feet pounded so loud I thought the ceiling would give way. It was like being trapped inside a shaking can. My only thought was to get out of the cabin. I didn't want to get caught below, where there was less chance of other people hearing or seeing a confrontation. I ran for the exit. As I reached it, a figure leaped at me from the dark. Clutching the bag, I breathed in a cry. Fright took hold like a seizure: heart pounding, throat closing, legs giving. I fell backward into Nicole. She caught me and then pushed me aside, ready to fight. There was a silver light reflecting from her hand. In my panic I wondered, *Why is she carrying a mirror?* Then I realized it was a blade.

"He's coming."

Scrambling to recover, it took me a moment to hear the voice and recognize the face as Gail's. She was fully dressed down to her sneakers, soaking wet, breathless, and she had muck in her hair and hanging from her nose.

"I knew you wouldn't see the damn signal, I knew it. He's coming. Talon's coming!"

My hand went to Nicole's arm, to the hand holding the blade. "Put that away."

Nicole passed me and went to the fuse box. I began reconnecting the cabin door. I was still shaking, my knees still wobbly, as I used the flashlight to find the pins I had placed on the deck nearby.

"Forget it," Gail said. "We've got to go. We've *got to go*."

We were huddled in the cockpit as voices carried from some yards away. Nicole whispered that one of the voices was Talon's, and then I noticed the blade again. I could feel the front of the boat shift from his weight. They were stepping from the dock onto the bow.

"Put that away," I again whispered to Nicole. I began pulling on her to leave.

Then a woman's voice carried. "Excuse me." The boat stilled momentarily. "Do you guys have a light?"

There was more shifting of weight, the boat tilted and then equalized, a man's voice sounding farther away, said, "Sure."

"How you doin'?" the woman said, her tone suggestive.

"Fine," the man answered. It was Talon. "How *you* doin', sweetheart?"

Gail looked at me, her hand planted firmly on her head, where it had been for a good minute now. She whispered, "That's *Katie*."

Nicole quickly, calmly moved toward the fuse box, as I slipped the first pin into the hinge, then the second. I couldn't find the third pin. The boat was shifting, another man's voice said, "Tal, let's go."

"I'm fine," Katie said, projecting her voice, it seemed, in order to let us know she was there.

"Do you know where lot twenty-nine is? I'm meeting up with some friends there." Again, the boat stilled.

"Oh, are you new around here?"

"Just visiting with my friend. He owns that boat over there. I'm staying with him."

I swept my flashlight across the nearby space until I spotted the third pin, and while reaching for it, my flashlight caught the reflection of a glass object tucked in a lifejacket underneath a built-in bench—an ashtray. I flashed on Pascale two mornings before; the first thing she'd done when she'd woken up was reach for her cigarettes. I knew then how Talon had killed Del. It was the one thing he could count on. First thing she'd do when she got up: smoke a cigarette. She might not eat, she might not drink, but she would definitely smoke. Maybe Talon had overlooked the ashtray in his clean sweep. Maybe it still contained cigarette butts, and they would be the proof I needed.

"If you head that way, you'll get there," Talon said. "I've got to go, but if you give me your number, I'll call you."

I slipped the last pin in as Nicole reconnected the alarm.

"Her *real* phone number." Gail grabbed a fistful of her own hair and whispered, "The idiot just gave that psychopath her real phone number."

"I guess some things never change," I said, pushing a still-in-shock Gail toward the back of the boat. Following her, I looked into the ashtray hoping to find a cigarette butt. The ashtray was empty, eat-off-of clean. *No one knows hell like the devil.*

The boat was shifting. Talon and his friend were taking the steps that went from the bow to the bridge over the cockpit to get to the rear deck. They reached the molded stairs leading from the bridge to the rear deck just as we scooted out of the port entry and onto the swimming platform. There was no time to think about what to do with the tapes. For now, I left them on the platform off the hull of the boat.

❖

As I lowered myself into the water, I caught a glimpse of Talon. He looked momentarily and waywardly in our direction, as if he could smell us. I heard him say, "Hurry," to the man he was with. We waited, silently treading water at the back of the boat, Nicole with her pouch in her mouth, me bobbing up and down, trying to watch them, to figure out what they were there for.

After a few moments, we heard something like a growl and then the sound of feet running toward the back of the boat. If this had gone differently, if Talon had not appeared that night, I would have carried the tapes back to the car, found the one that exonerated Sid, and destroyed the rest. Unfortunately, that's not what happened. And now Talon was running to the back of the boat, the duffel bag was on the swimming platform in plain view, and I had to decide between him retrieving the tapes and me sinking them.

It wasn't really a choice at all. I wasn't going to let the tapes of Del fall back into Talon's hands, and as for the videotape of Thomas's murder, if Talon retrieved it, it would be gone, and we couldn't use it for evidence anyway. So I pulled the duffel bag into the water and joined Nicole and Gail on the shadowy side of the boat, out of view. The bag became saturated and grew heavy until it was completely submerged. I let it go, pictured it and its contents sinking to the bottom of the bay.

Talon said, "Motherfucker. When? Who? Where could they be?" The boat shifted as he frantically went to one side then the other or walked in a circle, I couldn't tell.

The other voice said, "Well, who else knew about them?"

"Everyone who was fucking in them knew about them. But the only one who knew they were on the boat was Kramer."

The other voice, "Man, it has to be him. He has the key to the locker."

"Fucking Kramer," Talon said. "I'm gonna kill him. I'm outta here Saturday right after the funeral. I gotta find those tapes, *pronto*."

I felt the weight of the boat shifting again as Talon and the person he was with disappeared into the cabin. A few moments later, they left, Talon still cursing and saying something about Kramer being a pervert. We pushed off and swam back to shore.

Back in the car, we heard that lights had gone on, cold water and thick muck had been braved, and ten-foot fences had been scaled. I asked Katie, "How did you get over the razor wire at the top of the fence?"

Brows furrowed, she said, "What razor wire?"

I left it at that.

CHAPTER EIGHTEEN

Friday

It was eight a.m. when Dirk Beasley pulled into the parking lot. I was waiting to have what I knew would be a disappointing conversation with her. I had the box Del had left; I had Jake Mansfield's findings; I could try to explain what Doug had said about cyanide. But I knew all of it together wasn't enough for Beasley to determine that Del had been murdered. The best I could hope for at this point was getting Beasley to agree to run more tests to see whether Del did have cyanide in her system.

"I have something for you." I was holding the box.

"Come inside," Beasley said. We walked down the corridor to her office without talking. Once inside, she asked, "Who are you?" The question surprised me. I hesitated, uncertain as to how to respond. "I received a report yesterday from a Jake Mansfield from NAVO. Do you know him?"

"I do. He's a friend and a colleague. I worked with him on a case last year."

"You're an attorney?"

"I'm a newly appointed commissioner in California, but I was an attorney when I worked with Jake."

"I've been interested in his research for a while now," Beasley said. She held out her hand, directing me to have a seat across from her at her desk, and offered me coffee, which I gladly accepted. We sat among framed certificates not yet hung, books in piles, and documents with diagrams of bodies on them. Her salt-and-pepper hair framed her face, giving her a soft, boyish look. She had a pair of horn-rimmed glasses hanging around her neck, which she took off and put on as needed.

Suddenly, as if it had just computed, she said, "Commissioner?" Beasley stared at me for a moment. Playfully, she asked, "What are you, nineteen?"

I laughed. "After this week, I'm not sure anymore. I'm thirty."

Until that very moment, the fact that the room we were in had no windows had not bothered me. Now I was sure the smooth-walled, halogen-lit space was shrinking to the size of her stare. She was taking measure, trying to decide what to make of me.

"Impressive," she said. "And Adeline, how did she end up here?"

"Well *there's* a question. How much time do you have?"

Beasley conceded with a tilt and a nod, and let the question go. She opened and began sifting through the contents of the box I'd placed between us on the desk. When she got to the Post-its, she held one up and studied it. "What are these?"

I explained about the tasks and Talon's belief that Del was having an affair. I told her about the house and the cameras. "Do you know about his juvenile history?"

Beasley raised her brows, pressed her lips together, and nodded. "Of course I know about his juvenile history." She paused, and then she said, "He took a poly, you know?"

The comment surprised me. It was information she probably shouldn't have shared. Maybe it was my professional position that encouraged a feeling of inclusion; or maybe it was our connection in a cosmic sense around being gay; or maybe it was her read of me as someone sincere, but I knew now she trusted me.

"He passed," Beasley said. "They questioned him for several hours. He didn't lawyer up, and he agreed to do a polygraph, practically begged for one. Cried like a baby through the whole interview. By the end, the police felt sorry for him." She continued, "Look, Jenna, Dr. Mansfield's information together with some of this stuff gives us enough to question Mr. Keller again, but…Mansfield's results are not admissible here, and…"

I knew where she was going. Without a murder weapon or physical evidence linking him to the death, this was a long shot.

"I can't prove it," I said, "but I think Talon used cyanide to kill Del. I think he put cyanide in her cigarettes."

"No way. I did this autopsy. I can smell cyanide, and I didn't detect any."

"She was submerged for hours. Maybe that diluted the smell."

"Venous blood was not the right color for cyanide."

"She was anemic." I knew from Doug it could explain this.

Beasley was quiet but her eyes were busy; she appeared to be running through a mental list, considering different possibilities. She put her glasses on and looked again at the box, in particular at the photos of Del's bruised face. "The truth is, the level of COHb has bothered me this whole time. I kept thinking she must have been off her peak. And her throat was a mess, but we just attributed that to swallowing saltwater. And"—she pointed to her own mouth, made small circles around it with her pointer finger—"some other things. Bacteria in her throat. Crabs got her lips, and…" She stopped speaking.

Crabs? Her lips? The words coiled around my heart like a boa and began to squeeze. I heard Del say, *I'm a really good kisser. Do you wanna see?* My head fell forward to balance the sudden tilt in the room, and I took a few deep breaths, trying to ease the striking pain in my chest enough to continue the conversation. Hers were the first lips I'd ever kissed. Her lips had formed the smile that launched my heart into outer space, spoken the I love yous that brought purpose into my life, made the most private parts of me feel known and loved, mixed our insides, leaving us intertwined forever.

The expression on my face must have matched the horror I was feeling, because Beasley lowered her glance apologetically and seemed mildly embarrassed for having gotten carried away. "Suffice it to say, your explanation may be better." She appeared again to be tossing ideas around in her mind. "I'll run more tests on the body."

It was the best I could hope for.

"So, how do you think this actually worked? What's your theory?" She asked the question as if we were colleagues.

With the image of Del's scavenged lips stark in my mind, I began, "I think Del died where she was found. That's where Talon had anchored the boat, not on Lemon Reef as he claimed. The boat trip," I said, "was part of a drug deal that Talon had arranged, with the exchange to occur underwater, on Lemon Reef. He went alone that morning to make the trade and left Del with a pack of cigarettes laced with cyanide. He knew the first thing Del would do when she woke up was smoke. When he got back from the reef, Del was unconscious. I think he believed she was dead. He dressed her in her bathing suit. Then he put a mask around her neck, some flippers on her feet, and a weight belt around her waist, to make it look like they had been diving, and he threw her overboard. But she wasn't dead. She woke up and struggled to get to the surface. That was when she took in water, had a heart attack, and died."

I hesitated. "I'm not sure why he dragged her to the chain, though. Why not just let her sink and drift?"

"He was storing her there." Matter-of-factly, Beasley added, "If you're correct, *if* this was murder, maybe he was planning to go back later and dump her body farther out at sea."

Storing her. I found myself nodding along with her, as if all of this made perfect sense. I knew I was in an altered state, present and not, believing it all and disbelieving it at the same time. I blew out my cheeks to gather my strength and finished us off. "Then he cleaned up, sanitized the head, moved the boat to Lemon Reef, set the tanks up to match his attempted rescue story, and swam for help."

She leaned back in her chair, looked at me across her piled-high desk, and said, "We'll check her out. When are you heading back?"

"Sunday." I met her eyes and felt myself begin to smile just a little. Relief, maybe, at having succeeded in getting Beasley to take seriously the possibility that Del had been murdered.

She smiled, too.

❖

I was not quite out of the building when my cell phone rang.

"Jenna? Is this Jenna Ross?" The voice was reluctant, anxious. "I'm Steve. Steve McCulick. I, uh, I got your note about Del…You know, the window."

"You're the guy Del's been seeing."

"Seeing?"

He was like a frightened critter. One got the image of a trembling rabbit or some such thing. I was standing perfectly still in the threshold with the phone to my ear. The clerk at the front desk was sending me the evil eye for letting the air-conditioning out. He kept waving and pointing at the air vents, but I was not drawing breath in fear I might scare this jittery Steve McCulick away. I said in the gentlest tone I could muster, "I'm glad you called."

"Yeah, well, uh, I know Talon killed her, and I want to help if I can. Even though"—a lengthy pause to take a few deep breaths—"he might kill me, too."

I let the door close behind me, finally, and began walking toward Gail's car. "I understand. How do you want to do this?" Now I stood in the parking area, surrounded by rolling greens scattered with flowering pigeon plum trees and swamp dogwoods no longer in bloom. Cars buzzed by on Tenth Avenue. The air was perfumed with fresh-baked doughnuts from a bakery across the street.

"There's a café on Miramar Parkway and South University Drive, near where I work, called First Round. I could meet you there," Steve said.

❖

Pascale was on the couch, cigarette burning in the ashtray next to her, her eyes fixed on what appeared to be a high school report card. She was showered, made-up, dressed. I hadn't seen her so put together since, well, I couldn't remember when. The house had an airy, open feel. It reminded me of Saturday mornings when everybody was doing chores or had just done them.

She looked up when I walked in, let the paper she was holding sit open on her lap. "I heard what you did last night for Del."

I shrugged, one of those single-shoulder, didn't-much-matter shrugs. "I was hoping we'd find some evidence to prove he killed her, but we didn't. You heard what we did find? What was in the box?"

She closed her eyes and nodded.

I went and sat beside her. "What are you looking at?" I asked, leaning over to see. It *was* a report card, Del's report card from the first semester of tenth grade. "Wow." I reached into her lap and tilted the page a little to see it better. "She was smart, huh?"

Pascale put her hand on mine and squeezed it. "That poor child. What a life she had." She removed her glasses to wipe tears. "I did it to her." She paused, stared at the report card. "She was such a good girl. I chased her out." She looked to me then, not for forgiveness or reassurance. She wanted me to accept this from her, to be a witness to her acknowledgment.

"Nicole told me you've done a lot to make it up to Del in recent years. She said you really took care of Khila for her."

Pascale's face lifted a bit.

Ida came out from the hallway and greeted me warmly. "How'd it go with Beasley?"

"It went okay," I said. "As best could be expected." I made my way into the kitchen for another cup of coffee, and then I sat down at the dining-room table. "She did say she'd test for cyanide, so if there is any in Del's body, then we might still be able to prove that Talon killed her. It's a special test, though, so I don't know how long it's gonna take to get the results. There's nothing stopping him from leaving tomorrow."

"The floater guy. What about him?"

I said I didn't know whether Jake's finding would matter or not. "Is Nicole still sleeping?" I was hoping to take her with me to see Steve.

Pascale said, "Nicole left early this morning. I have no idea where she went."

"We've really got to get that girl's cell phone fixed," Ida said. "Force her to join the human race."

❖

Ida went with me to meet Steve. On the way, she said she'd never actually been introduced to him but did know of him. Steve lived in the house across the street from Del and Talon. He became friends with Talon first. Over the past two years, he and Del had grown a lot closer, and Del had come to rely on him. In fact, these days, Steve knew Del better than anyone, because Talon trusted Steve, and Steve and Del could come and go from each other's houses without too much scrutiny or suspicion. Ida wasn't sure whether Del had ever slept with him; she suspected she had, but that they stopped because they were both too afraid of Talon finding out. I should have come to expect this from her by then, but as Ida explained all of this to me, I kept squelching the impulse to yell at her for not having bothered to mention these things sooner.

Ida dropped her chin and drummed with her hand on her thigh, as if giving herself encouragement. Then the conversation took a surprising turn.

"I'm sorry about the other day, in Del's room." She blew out a breath, pushed her hair from her face to reveal her steep cheekbones. "I think I was hard on you. I thought it was fucked up how you dropped information about you and Del to Beasley. And I've been feeling like you just showed up and took over, acting like you're more important to Del than you really were. It's not like Del's here to set the record straight. And if she was here, I don't think you're the one she'd be calling for help."

"Clearly not. Clearly, she'd die before she'd call me." Now I took a breath. "Del always refused to let how we felt about each other make any difference."

Ida seemed surprised by my agreeing with her.

"But what if she was important to *me*, Ida? Isn't that reason enough for me to be here, trying to help if I can?"

Softly, she said, "That's why I'm apologizing." She faced the passenger window and tilted her head, revealing the long line of her neck. "I've been off about a lot of things, Jenna. I've got to make some changes. After I heard the tape last night, I decided I'm done. I'm *so* done. My job is easy money—sort of. But it's not worth it. I've gotta go back to school and figure it out for real."

I felt like I had to ask. "Ida," my voice was calm but a little wary, "how did you know which lot Kramer's boat was docked in?" There was an awkward silence. "Had you been on it before?"

"How else would I know? I fucked Tal on it." Her stare was fixed on her window. "I know how bad that sounds, but Del wreaked plenty of havoc on my life, too. And Talon is complicated. You don't know him."

I didn't know him, and I was sure she was right about him being complicated because people are. But still…this man, who had done these things?

As if in response to my thought, she said slowly and thoughtfully, "Talon's intense. He focuses on you with those black eyes and he grins, and you just feel like the most important person in the world. All is instantly forgiven when he pays attention to you. And he's strong and funny. He has a kind of boyish appeal that a lot of men lose, this giggle that is really so cute and contagious. It's hard not to feel swept away by him. One minute, you're just having an innocent conversation, and the next, you're mesmerized and you've slipped into something else. It's like you find yourself flirting, hoping something happens that you didn't even know you wanted." Plainly, she concluded, "I got seduced."

I noticed she was crying, and my heart went out to her. Ida had felt invisible for most of her life, wedged between a beguiling, endangered older sister and an insane, dangerous younger sister, both of whom had right of biology over her. Her own devastating loss had been eclipsed by the gratitude she'd been immediately expected to show for being taken in—but not really. Ida's provocations, I knew—and I knew Del knew—were a way of reassuring herself that she existed, had some effect on others.

"What was it about Del," Ida asked, "that brought out the absolute best and worst in people?"

❖

The small café had just a few tables and a bar with stools, but the high ceilings made it feel cavernous upon entering. Linoleum squares zigzagged in a pattern that gave the floor a high-stakes feel. Three walls were glass, looking out onto the intersecting avenues. It was empty but for a table near the back, at which sat a tall man with broad shoulders. He had dark hair and a clean-shaven square jaw. His hairline receded some, giving the impression of a larger forehead, and he wore reading glasses, which he immediately took off when he noticed us. He waited to see if I was looking for someone, too, and then he nervously smiled and waved to me.

We sat on wooden benches across from one another, ketchup- and mustard-crusted dispensers and other condiments aligning the wall to which our table was adjacent. There was a sticky substance in the exact spot my elbow naturally fell, and I finally gave up trying to wipe it and put my hands in my lap.

"I'm Steve," he said. Ida and I introduced ourselves. "I take it I met Nicole yesterday?"

I nodded. "Sorry about your window."

He laughed a little. "I've been hearing about her for a long time." Then he said, "And you're Jenna, huh? I've been hearing about you, too." I was desperate to know what he had heard, but I waited for him to tell me. He took a sip of his coffee, asked if we wanted any. I said no; Ida said yes. He called the waiter over and ordered her a cup. Then he stirred some sugar into his cup and tested it. "You were Del's first love," he said. "She told me she lost her virginity with you on a beach." He chuckled and shrugged as if he was not quite sure how it would be possible, but he was open to the idea.

I could see out of the corner of my eye Ida looking at Steve with disbelief. I smiled, feeling shocked and thrilled to know Del had represented us that way.

"What about you?" I asked. "Were you and Del lovers?"

"No," he said, "not exactly. I wanted to be. But Del was totally focused on Khila and on trying to get out." Steve looked around a bit aimlessly. "And to be honest, she really just needed me to be her friend now because she was in a bad situation and it was getting worse. I don't know what you already know." He glanced at me but didn't wait for a response. "Del's been wanting to leave Talon for a long time, but she couldn't figure out how to do it. She was convinced he had enough bad on her to take Khila away. Then she heard you were a judge, and she thought maybe you would know how to help her."

I was taken aback. Was I was the woman she was referring to on the audiotape?

"She was trying to figure out how to get back in touch with you," Steve said.

"All she had to do was call. She didn't know that?"

"She was getting ready to call you. She got your number from your friend that she worked with."

Which friend? Gail and Katie would have told me—better have told me—if Del had asked either of them for my number.

He added, I assume in response to my confused expression, "Well, actually, she stole it off your friend's cell phone." He shrugged as he said, "I guess she didn't want to ask for it. She thought your friend wouldn't give it to her without asking you first, and she wasn't ready to talk to you yet."

"What was she waiting for?"

He twisted in his seat, tilted his head to loosen his neck. "Del heard that Talon made a video of that thing that went down"—he looked to Ida—"when the Thomas kid was killed. Del thought it could get Sid off." To me, he said, "She wanted to get the video before she called you.

I told her not to wait…But she…" He dropped his head in a gesture of defeat.

Ida was staring at me, and I thought she was trying to figure out if we should tell Steve about the video from the boat. But what she said then was, "Sid is really innocent?"

Steve seemed surprised by the question. "Yes. You didn't know that?"

Ida shrugged.

I started to speak and then stopped myself from asking her if she'd been sleepwalking for the last twelve hours. Had she just missed the whole part about why we had gone to the boat? Then I remembered what she'd revealed to me in the car, about how she'd slept with Talon, and I knew there was just so much information that Ida could bear to take in about him and about what he had done to Del and to Sid. As Nicole had told me earlier, if Ida slept with Talon and Talon killed Del, Ida would never forgive herself.

"Sid's innocent," Steve said. "I know because I saw Sid at Del's house at the same time that the Thomas kid was killed. I was with Del when Sid showed up. Del started acting really strange. She pushed me out the back door so that me and Sid wouldn't see each other. I watched from my own house until Sid left, which was several hours later."

I exhaled, allowed myself to take minor comfort from the knowledge that the tape I might have destroyed wasn't the only evidence of Sid's innocence. Steve could testify. We were silent for a few moments. He stirred his coffee; I watched the light reflecting on the back wall.

Ida said, "We thought Del went on the boat to get sex tapes back."

"Oh, I think she did. She wanted to get those tapes, too." Steve hesitated. With scrunched brows that conveyed bemusement, he said, "Talon videotaped all his crimes." Tone shifting from confusion to challenge, he added, "He's a fucking freak. I think the tapes were like trophies or something. Or"—he shook his head slightly, twisted his mouth—"Del thought Talon taped that shit because he couldn't remember it after he did it."

"Yeah, but the sex tapes weren't a crime," Ida said. "Del agreed to do those."

Steve's otherwise gentle and kind demeanor gave way to a flash of anger. "She didn't *agree*." His face squared with Ida's. "Who said she agreed?"

Ida's hand jerked and hit her coffee cup, knocking it over. The coffee spilled onto the table and over the edge into Steve's lap. Ida sputtered apologies. Steve scooted out of the booth as Ida and I threw napkins at the caramel liquid expanding to and around every border like mud in a slide. The waiter came quickly with towels and cleaned up the spill. Steve held a napkin against his shirt, trying to absorb what he could to prevent a stain.

When he sat down again, he continued without missing a beat. "Look, I know it's hard to understand, but I've spent a lot of time with Talon, and I'm telling you he's a really sick guy. The sex stuff was his way of punishing Del. If she did something he didn't like, he'd bring some strange guy home and put her through it. He'd make her prove she loved him by doing things she didn't want to do." He sighed, looked around, ran his hand through his hair. "She made the best of it, especially at the beginning. Maybe she even got into it sometimes, I don't really know. There were some good times—I don't mean to say it was all bad—long periods when they got along okay, I guess, and she felt hopeful about the marriage." There was a weighty pause. Steve drew a breath. "Then, about eight or nine months ago, Del got a job waitressing at the deli. It was work to her. But he got convinced"—underscored by a karate chop to the air—"she was having an affair, and that's when things got really twisted." Steve's voice dropped on the word *really*.

"Talon got insanely jealous, but he wouldn't admit it. He was beating her, trying to get her to admit that she was doing something wrong. There was all this sex stuff. She was constantly having to calm him down and reassure him. Then he started choosing her clothes, telling her when she could take a shower. He started controlling *everything*. She couldn't take a shit without him watching. It was *horrible*," Steve continued, "and she was suffering." He looked at Ida now. "That's when we started trying to collect evidence—the photos, the tape."

Ida's cheeks were flushed and her breathing was heavier than usual. Her dark eyes shifted back and forth nervously. She looked like she was about to vomit. I put my hand on her shoulder to calm her.

"About a week ago," Steve said, "Talon hit Khila. Del wasn't home when she was supposed to be. He didn't know where she was. He decided to teach her a lesson by hurting the kid." Steve sighed, glanced at me, then at Ida, then back at his cup and said, "I thought I'd seen Del as upset as she could get, but I was wrong. I think the only thing that stopped Del from killing Talon that night was the idea that you could help her get custody."

A week ago had been around the time Del contacted the underground people. Tears welling, I looked at a spot on the table between us. I imagined how desperate she must have been feeling to have made that call.

"That's when the trip came up. She'd thought for a while that Talon kept the videotapes on Kramer's boat, so she agreed to go." I could see Steve tremble, his face drifting to the window. "I know I should've come forward a lot sooner about the Sid stuff—about everything that was going on. But Del was terrified, and she was right to be, 'cause, well, here we are. Now it doesn't matter about her. And anyway, I think she would've wanted me to help Sid now. She never got right about what she'd done to him."

His look was equal parts agony and anger. "I can't believe she went on the boat instead of leaving that sick motherfucker. She was so close to getting out. Del couldn't live with what she did to Sid, and she didn't feel like she would ever be able to fix it. The closer she got to freeing herself, the worse she felt about what happened. It was the bind Talon put her in—she couldn't free herself without leaving Sid in prison for life. She couldn't free Sid without running the risk of going to prison herself." He fidgeted with his napkin and then said, "The tape was the only way she could think of to help both of them."

The conversation with Steve—his confession, really—was interrupted by a frantic call from Pascale. Khila was missing.

CHAPTER NINETEEN

The drive back to Pascale's was a blur of gray rooftops and green highway signs. We serpentined through stop-and-go freeway traffic; my heart raced the speedometer. On the main roads, I rolled past stop signs and darted through yellow lights, all that rushing to land at Pascale's house with little additional information and nothing to do now but wait.

Khila had snuck out sometime in the night, and Talon had discovered her missing when he had gone to wake her that morning. He was out now with the police looking for her. Pascale and I paced the boxlike living room, taking turns peering out the window every few minutes in hope of seeing the kid coming up the driveway. I had to keep my mind from going to the most frightening places, imagining Khila out there alone at night, getting picked up, somebody hurting her, still hurting her. Or was she dead? Was that the news we would get this day?

As concerned as I was about Khila, I couldn't help noticing Ida was acting oddly. She stood staring off, not saying anything for long periods of time, the blink of her long lashes the only sign of life. Then she would ratchet her body or clench her fists, cringing, it seemed, at some intolerable thought or idea.

Talon called several times over the next hour to check in, not trusting Pascale to notify him if Khila showed up at Pascale's house. Pascale smoked and paced.

With bridled impatience, Ida asked, "Where *is* Nicole?"

Only then did it occur to me that Nicole had to be with Khila. Khila knew Nicole was the one person in the world who would have done anything for her and not given a care about getting in trouble for it. If she was trying to run away, Nicole was the person she would have gone to. When I told Pascale I thought Nicole was with Khila, it was clear she hadn't yet considered that herself. Realizing I probably was right, she sighed, her face softened, and she sat down for the first time in over an hour. She lit a cigarette and took an extra-long draw, and then she let the smoke seep from her lips. I sat down on the couch next to Pascale, noticed the raised veins in her bony hand. "So where would Nicole take her? To a friend's house, maybe?"

"Nicole doesn't have any friends," Ida said. "They're probably just driving around. Nicole'll bring her back."

More time passed. I filled it by retrieving messages from work, returning a few calls. I called Madison to tell her what was happening but could only reach her voicemail. Ida had a deck of cards out. She was playing solitaire. She seemed in a kind of private agony, her jaw tightening to a bulge, her face a twist of grimaces and squints that seemed to be getting more extreme. I suspected whatever was going through her mind had to do with the things Steve had told us about how Talon had treated both Sid and Del. I talked Ida into playing spit with me, hoping to distract her from whatever was plaguing her and to help her feel less alone.

The back door was open. A warm breeze ruffled loose papers and relieved the otherwise stifling heat. The house smelled of coffee, still brewing, menthol cigarettes, and something like wet leather, from the moisture and heat that blew in with the breeze. Ida and I had pushed the coffee table aside to make room and were now on the living floor engaged in a fierce spit battle, hands flying, cards slapping, when my cell phone rang. I grabbed the phone and answered it as I slammed down my last card.

"Jenna, it's Margaret Todd. I thought you might want to know Del sent you the fax. I mean she arranged for it to be sent to you."

"What?" I went out to the porch for privacy.

"Let me explain. Del told the underground folks about Talon's juvenile record. They accessed it with the intention of giving it to her to bring with her to California on Wednesday morning."

Had I heard her correctly? "Del was coming to California?"

"Yes." Margaret continued, "It was information she thought you should have to help her explain why the situation was so urgent. When Del didn't show for the meeting on Tuesday, they thought that maybe she'd met up with you on her own. So they faxed it to you."

"How did they find me?"

"Your cell phone. They located the nearest tower and sent the fax to the Kinko's closest to it." Then Margaret said, "It's so sad, Jenna. Del was a day away from your doorstep."

Margaret's comment lingered before it landed, the harshness of it at first unthinkable to me. I tugged at my hair and stared at the ground. For a moment I was outside my body, watching myself. In suspension, the sorrow I was feeling and everything I now knew had happened to Del seemed alien and unreal, a movie about strangers from strange lands who videotape their loved ones in forced sex acts and hit their kids to teach each other lessons.

My upset was interrupted by Nicole pulling in to the driveway. Before she'd come to a complete stop, Khila leaped from the car. She stomped by without acknowledging me and entered the house with an air that at once conveyed resistance and capitulation. I ended the call with Margaret and followed Khila in. Khila landed on the couch, face in a scowl. Angry as she appeared, she did look rather adorable in her Miami garb: aqua-blue shorts, yellow tank, and sandals. Her gold hair was pulled back from her face in a ponytail, her reedy arms and legs crossed and braided. She dropped her chin and lifted her severe eyes to communicate her displeasure.

Nicole entered sheepishly behind us, saying, "She's mad at me for making her come back." She explained that somehow Khila had found her way to Pascale's in the middle of the night.

"It's not mysterious," Khila said sarcastically. "I walked."

Khila had woken Nicole by tapping on the window of Del's old room; they'd been driving around ever since.

"She doesn't want to go with Talon," Nicole said.

Pascale returned from the kitchen with a glass of milk for Khila. Khila shook her head. Pascale rested the glass on the coffee table and sat down beside Khila on the couch. "You don't want to go with your father?"

Vigorous head shake.

"You're sure?" I asked.

"I'm sure." She examined me for a moment, her expression solemn. Then she said, "They're making me call Marcella mom." Her eyes welled up. "You don't believe me?" she said, even though there was no indication of disbelief. "Look." She pulled a silver chain from her pocket and held it up to reveal a dangling charm, expecting me to take it, which I did. "My father makes me wear this." It was a medallion, intentionally broken in half. The half Khila had was inscribed with the word *daughter*. Glaring up at me, Khila said, "Guess what the other side says."

"Mother?"

"Yes. And guess who's wearing it." Facial scrunch, as if she'd just been assaulted by a bad smell. "Marcella. I'm not going with my father. I know he's gonna hit me again if my mother's not there to stop him. And I don't want to call Marcella mom."

Not only was Khila the splitting image of Del, but I saw a determination in her eyes and a tightness in her mouth that reminded me of Del when she was being stubborn. And for Del, stubbornness was often connected with loyalty, as it was for Khila in this moment. I was moved by how similar they were, how spirited Khila was, how unapologetic about her devotion to her mother. She was doing everything in her ten-year-old power to stay close to Del, and I was going to help her in any way I could.

I began by telling Ida to call the police and to let them know Khila was at Pascale's and that we needed their help.

"I don't know if this is going to work," I said, "but I'll try to help you stay here if that's what you want."

She watched me, her face slightly more open.

The police, I knew, had the authority to let Khila stay with Pascale on an emergency basis, while Child Protective Services investigated any concerns. CPS could place Khila temporarily with Pascale if the concerns were substantiated. Pascale could then file for permanent guardianship in probate court. It was a long shot, especially since Talon had never abused Khila directly, at least not to the extent that CPS would get involved. But there was the law that made domestic violence in front of a child child abuse. And we had a few more things going for us. Khila was ten and articulate and definite; we had a tape recording and other evidence of Talon physically abusing Del; Child Protective

Services had access to his juvenile history; and Khila's mother had just died. Presumably, that would garner some sympathy from CPS and the court, and give Khila's request more weight.

Had I thought it through better, I would have realized that when we called the police, they would notify Talon, and he would no doubt get to the house before them, which is what happened. It seemed like only seconds before Talon blew open the living room door. He was red faced, bloated with rage, and he immediately began screaming at Pascale.

"You were behind this. I'll take you apart, do you hear me? You fucking drunk. You mess with my family again and I'll take you apart." He shifted his pointer finger from Pascale to Khila. "Let's go. You have any idea how worried I've been? You're in *so* much trouble."

Khila started to cry and shake her head.

Nicole was standing by the living room window, a few feet from Talon. She discreetly slipped her hand into her leather pouch, and I wondered if she was going for her blade. From where I was standing, my back to the wall separating the kitchen from the living room, I could see out past Nicole to the street through the picture window. I began scanning for the police. Pascale lifted off the couch and placed her frail body squarely between Talon and Khila.

Talon began reaching around Pascale to grab Khila; Pascale shifted to block him. Nicole stepped in to stand beside Pascale and squared her face with Talon's in a standoff. She had her hand deep in her bag, and I knew she was ready with the switchblade. I opened my cell phone to call the police again. Talon started to break through Pascale and Nicole and put his arm out to grab Khila. Khila moved to stay out of his reach. From behind came a scream—a war cry—followed by a bang-cracking sound: a chair flipping over, its back slamming against the linoleum.

Ida, a shape-shifter, morphed from sitting, to lunging, to wrapping both hands around Talon's throat. They looked momentarily merged, like a grotesque creature with two heads and four legs. She'd caught him by surprise and had managed to lock on before he had a chance to fend her off. Ida squeezed. Talon's eyes bulged, and he made a thwarted gargling sound.

"Liar," she screamed. "Monster."

Talon used one hand to try to pull Ida's hands off his throat and with the other pushed his palm into Ida's nose. Her nose began to bleed, but she held on.

I stood frozen, looking on in horror. Nicole rose to protect Ida, blade now firmly in hand. Pascale twisted, gripped Nicole's wrist, bent it back, and peeled the knife away from her. Given how infirm Pascale had seemed in the last week, I would never have believed she could move like that.

Talon hit Ida again, ripped her hands from his throat, lifted her off the ground, and slammed her into the wall behind him. Ida made a loud *oof* sound, air rushing out of her lungs. She slid down the wall to a sitting position, blood still trickling from her nose to her mouth and chin. I moved toward her from one side and Nicole from the other to see if she was okay. Ida used one hand to pinch the bridge of her nose to stop the bleeding and put the other hand up like a stop sign, signaling to us that she was fine. She had a remarkably nonchalant expression on her face.

Talon held his throat, spit flying from his mouth like sparks. "You fucking, sick bitch."

Ida glared at him over the fingers clipping her nose and said, "You have no idea what a sick bitch I am, and you better pray that you never find out."

Talon turned to Khila and said, "We're leaving. Now!" He reached to grab her. He kept one eye on Nicole. Pascale shifted again, keeping herself between Talon and Khila. Nicole stepped in farther, placing herself shoulder to shoulder with Pascale.

Khila said, "I'm not going with you." She was on the couch, knees pulled to her chest, arms wrapped around them, tears streaming. "I want to stay with my grandmother."

Ida pulled herself to standing and passed me on the way to the bathroom. She indicated again that she was okay, even smiled slightly. Strangling Talon had been satisfying for her.

I was still with my back to the wall, cell phone in hand.

Talon said, "Khila, get up." He was eyeing Pascale as he spoke, sizing her up, trying to figure out if he could just bulldoze through to Khila. Then he eyed Nicole, who did seem to pose the bigger problem for him. He knew that if given a reason, she would kill him and call it self-defense. But that wasn't enough to deter him. He shouldered through Pascale and Nicole and grabbed hold of Khila's arm.

Khila cried out and looked to me now, her face soaked, her gold eyes desperately sad and fearful.

My heart was racing; I felt as if I had abandoned all reason, but I couldn't stop myself. I jumped in and grabbed Talon's wrist. It was like a small tree trunk, thick and round, the edges of my fingers barely making it to the underside of his forearm. On shaking legs and consciously trying to keep my voice from quivering, I looked him in the eye and said, "Khila's not leaving with you until the police tell us she has to."

Ida came back from the bathroom and moved in next to me. Now four of us surrounded Talon, staring him down, providing a barrier for Khila. Talon twisted his wrist to get loose of my grip, which forced him to release Khila's arm. In the twist, I felt his immense strength, and I knew he could easily have broken through us and taken Khila if he'd wanted to. Instead, he stepped back and eyed me, aware, I think, that I was a witness he did not know, and he was uncertain what to make of me or how to behave in front of me. He remained, even in this moment, cautious and scheming.

To me, he said, "Who the fuck are you?"

As if it were the opportunity she'd been hoping for, Khila jumped from the couch to behind Pascale, hooked her neck around Pascale's waist so she was looking Talon in the eye but still had Pascale between them, and declared, "That's Jenna. She's Mama's first love."

Talon said, "What?" He took a few steps back and nervously grinned. He turned an eye to me, then to Khila, and then finally to Pascale. "What is she talking about?" To Khila, he said again, "What are you talking about?"

"Sounds pretty clear to me," Nicole said, the corners of her lips edging upward.

"Khila," I said, "how do you know that?"

Her momentum from having confronted her father carried over. She put her hands on her narrow hips, pushed her chin forward, and said, "My mama told me." Khila lifted her face, tears running down it. "She said if anything happened to her, I should ask my grandma to find you. She said you would help me." Khila glared at her father. "I'm not going with you and Marcella." To me, she said, "I'll run away."

Talon looked around with a stunned expression, his shoulders caving, his hugeness shrinking—air out of a beach ball. Maybe it was the emergent realization that Khila would not merely go along with his plan; maybe it was how the people in Del's life were finally fighting for her; maybe he was already beginning to understand killing Del wasn't going to save him from his powerlessness and despair, after all, but his face cracked in a way that hinted at surrender.

Talon watched Khila for a moment, his eyes growing larger and more porous—the way a sponge expands as it absorbs water. He fell back into the chair behind him and put his face in his hands. He looked like a little boy now who'd been held at arm's length, his punches repeatedly coming up short, until he'd punched himself to exhaustion. It had been like hitting air, trying to destroy aspects of Del's inner life he'd had no access to—her attachment to Khila, to her family, maybe even to the person she'd known herself to be when I knew her.

I stood staring at Khila, unable to speak. Then my eyes went to Pascale. Pascale had a slight smile on her face. She lifted a brow, nodded, and said, "How'd you think I knew you were a lawyer." Her smile stretched a bit wider, her gaze fell to the top of Khila's head, and she said, "You were her idea."

My throat tightened, tears began slipping out. "Khila, *you* sent for me?"

"I just told my grandma that my mom said she should call you." Khila tightened her ponytail and jutted her chin. "She wanted to take me to California. There were these people she talked to who were gonna help us get to you."

I felt an ache deep in my chest, unreachable by breath, my pulsing heart floating on rapids down a river of sorrow that was our history—and now our destiny. It was a strange combination of buoyancy and sadness, a mixture of pride for Del, for our devotion to each other over time, together with a sense of devastating regret over missed opportunities and moments of failed courage.

Through the living room window I noticed a police car pulling up—then another, and another. Men in uniforms were quickly at the already-open front door. I prepared to explain, got ready to give my argument as to why Khila should not have to go with her father if she didn't want to, when a white car pulled up with an official seal on the driver's side door. It was the medical examiner's vehicle.

An officer entered the house and asked for Talon Keller. Talon looked up with an innocent expression and nodded. His expression turned to shock as the officer began saying, "You're under ar—" He stopped when he noticed Khila.

Pascale gathered Khila up in her arms and whisked her from the room.

"You are under arrest for the murder of your wife, Adeline Soto." Now there were other police officers there, pulling Talon to stand, cuffs out, guiding his arms to behind his back. "You have the right…" The cuffs zipped tight.

Just then, Dirk Beasley stepped out of the ME's vehicle. I ran out to greet her, passing Talon on the way. His head was down, his shoulders rounded. He looked small and frightened. He met my eyes and I met his. He seemed confused, as if he felt misunderstood.

To the ground, he said, "She always does this, makes me look like the bad one. She always comes out smelling like a rose."

"Who?"

Eyes back to mine. "Del."

My stomach clamped. I don't know if it was his pathetic expression or his referring to Del in the present tense, but I was sure that in a bizarre way it was news to him when I said, "Del's dead, Talon."

He scrutinized me, his black, beady eyes scanning my face, taking in this information. He pinched his brows and pressed his lips together, concentrating, working to grasp it, deciphering it, as if communicating with someone who speaks a different language, sifting through the bits and pieces of common understanding to arrive at a shared idea: death. He knew not of it.

I left to see Beasley.

Crossing the grass, I asked, "Did Del's body test positive for cyanide?"

"I don't know yet." She closed her car door. "I came to talk to her family, because I'm recommending a criminal investigation. I got to thinking after you left and decided to have the crime team take one more look aboard the boat. I went with them this time."

We took a few steps in the direction of the house.

"I was struck," Beasley continued, "by how spotless the boat was. Someone had definitely cleaned up. So I asked the next question: Cleaned up how? And that's when I noticed the vacuum cleaner standing right there against the wall in the cabin. We checked the bag in our first go over, and it was empty. This time, we took the whole machine apart, and we found a half-smoked cigarette in the brush roll. There were traces of cyanide in the filter, and we've got a partial print match on the paper."

"Talon's?"

She nodded. "Adeline's DNA on the same cigarette gives us the murder weapon. With the stuff Adeline left in that box, Dr. Mansfield's analysis, and the cigarette, we're feeling pretty confident about talking to this gentleman."

CHAPTER TWENTY

Two Weeks Later

It was two weeks before Beasley officially released Del's body. I had gone back home and now returned to Miami with Madison to attend the funeral. Much had already changed. Beasley's tests had detected cyanide, Talon had been charged with murder and was being held without bail, and Khila had been placed with Pascale. The district attorney had agreed to talk with Steve McCulick about Sid. When news got out that the police had a videotape of the murder, the guys who'd actually killed Thomas had begun racing each other to offer State's evidence against one another and Talon.

Pascale had given me some of Del's ashes, and I wanted to take them to Lemon Reef before the public funeral planned for that afternoon. We arranged to meet up on the bay side in the morning. Gail and I had already rented a boat and some diving gear by the time Katie arrived. As she pulled up to the dock, we were surprised to hear the Red Hot Chili Peppers' "Scar Tissue" blaring from her open windows.

"I think we've moved into the nineties," I said.

Gail laughed.

Soon after, Ida and Nicole arrived with Khila shouldered between them. Madison and I had visited with Khila the day before when we'd gone by Pascale's to get the ashes. I'd shown Khila Del's wooden carvings and told her about each one. As was true for Del, Kurma was Khila's favorite. But this was the first time I was seeing Nicole or Ida since my last visit. Ida's bruises from her fight with Talon had healed. She seemed sober and solemn. She said hello to me and then averted her gaze quickly in apparent shame.

"Hey," Nicole said, joining me on the boat. Her marble-sized dimples magnified her smile. She hesitated, swayed, punched me in the arm. "How are ya?"

I laughed, happy to see her, too. "I'm fine." I lifted my chin at Khila. Her expression remained implacable, but she did return the gesture.

"Where's Madison?"

"At Gail's house. I thought it was just the five of us."

"Khila insisted on coming," Nicole said. "She wants to go to the reef with you."

"Do you know how to dive?" I called out to Khila.

She and Ida were playing cat's cradle with a piece of string they'd found. Khila turned her attention from the game and stationed her sober eyes on me. After a few seconds, she nodded. Ida and Nicole were nodding, too, and smiling like a pair of proud new parents. I did get the feeling Khila would be the most backed-up person on the planet with these two beside her.

"Oh yeah!" Nicole said. "I can vouch for that. Del taught her. She's good at it. Even has her own gear." Nicole gestured to the small tank and the mesh bag she and Ida had brought with them.

"How is she doing?" I asked more quietly.

"I'm not a shrink," Nicole said irritably. She handed me Khila's stuff to secure. Then, "I don't know," she conceded. "She doesn't talk very much. We're thinking maybe we'll get her a therapist or something. God knows, if we raise her, she's gonna need one."

"Good." My response, a mere nod, was nonchalant, but I knew what a huge concession that was for this family who never asked outsiders for help.

Then Nicole said quickly, as if to get it over with, "I'm going to one, too. A therapist." She faced away. "I started this rehabilitation program—for crazy felons. It helps us get jobs and mental-health services." Now she was looking at me again, seeking approval. I smiled, trying not to show too much enthusiasm in fear it would raise the stakes for her. "I was wondering"—Nicole moved foot to foot nervously—"if you'd write me a recommendation. I need a letter from someone who doesn't have a record for this training program. It's to be a welder."

Of course I will.

❖

We were off soon after, heading into the sun. The choppy water looked like icing on a cake, catching the light and giving the surface a silvery quality. Warm wind rushed against our faces, and sea spray covered us in a cool, misty cloud. I drove through the Haulover Bay Pass, opened up the engine, and headed for the ocean. The front of the boat rose and fell over the waves, pounding the water, making each landing louder and each lifting lighter than the last. There were sailboats marking the horizon. The sky still conveyed the tender, orange glow of morning; the air was salty-sweet and new.

Anchored on the reef, we sat in a circle along the edges of the small boat facing each other in silence, rocking with the waves. The plan had been simple and straightforward: place Del's ashes on the reef. But having Khila there made me want to do something more, to make it all last a little longer.

I said, "So, I think it would be good if each of us told one story about Del. Would that be okay?" To Khila, I said, "Would you like that?" Khila's eyes were filling with tears. Holding firmly to the side of the boat and looking down, she nodded. I turned to Gail and said, "You go first. What's your favorite story about Del?"

Gail addressed Khila, and in an uncharacteristically gentle and loving tone said, "We played soccer together—Jenna, Katie, your mom, and I."

Khila turned in Gail's direction, her face slightly more open.

"Well! It was the last game of the season, and we were playing North Miami Beach for the regional championship. If we won," Gail proclaimed, "we got to go to Tampa to play in the state tournament. We were ahead one to nothing, thirty seconds left in the game. The clock is ticking. All of a sudden," to me and Katie, "that blond girl, the one with the red headband who we always had to double cover, broke away with the ball and started heading for the goal. There were only two people between the blonde and our goal. Our goalie and—well—your mom."

Nicole clamped her hand to her head. When Khila looked at her, Nicole shrugged and said, "Del was good at a lot of things, but…"

"She sucked at soccer?" Khila asked.

Everyone nodded.

I was surprised to find myself laughing in that moment, my hand wrapped around the plastic container that held Del's ashes in it, which was hanging from my neck on a long string and resting against my chest.

Gail was running in place, the small boat rocking harder. "Our goalie runs out to intercept Blondie, and Del, not sure what to do, goes into the goal and just stands there. The goalie, Susan, twists her ankle and falls, and the blonde cuts around her." Gail cuts, cranks her leg back. "And then Blondie shoots at this wide-open space all the way on the other side of the net from where Del was standing. I swear, Del threw herself, literally flew—I'm telling you, she must have been four feet off the ground. She took the shot right in her stomach. We won the game because of her." Gail sat down, gave one reassuring nod in Khila's direction, and then stopped talking.

The waves cradled the boat, the air was still and warm, a seagull flew in close to us, let go a throaty *caw*, and then swooped upward.

Katie began, "My *favorite* story about your mom might be the time I saw her dancing at the Stevie Nicks concert."

Katie glanced at me. It was the first time she had ever given any indication she had seen Del and me fooling around on the lawn that night. Khila was waiting for her to continue.

"Del was wearing this light gauzy tank top and this short jean skirt. She was barefoot and her hair was loose and a little wild. And she was watching the stage and dancing—kind of like she was dancing with Stevie Nicks. You couldn't take your eyes off her, Khi. I mean, your mom was so graceful and beautiful."

Katie dropped her chin and shrugged to say she was done. Khila searched around, landed on Ida.

"I have so many stories about your mom," Ida said, "but my favorite might be when I first came to live with Pascale. Del made me so welcome. She just started calling me her sister, and she shared everything she had with me. She let me wear her clothes, play with her games. She even let me sleep with her."

"Yeah, for like the first year," Nicole teased.

Ida took a deep breath to keep from crying. "I remember being so scared and Del hugging me and telling me everything was going to be okay, that as long as she had a house, I had a house." She swiped at a tear, brought her arms in close to her body, and focused her sight on her own feet. "Nicole, you go."

Nicole began crying and talking at the same time. "I guess my favorite story about your mom was a few years ago. I had a bad car accident and I was in the hospital." Nicole paused, grimaced slightly, looked at Khila, and said, "I was with Angie. I don't think you ever met her." Khila shook her head to say she hadn't. "Anyway, Pascale was pissed as hell at me for having a girlfriend, and she wouldn't let her visit me in the hospital."

Ida said, "Angie was the one Pascale called the Refrigerator."

Nicole nodded. "Yep." Looking at Khila, she said, "She was a little thick around the middle." We all laughed. "*Anyway*, Del snuck Angie in to see me, and then she stood guard, so I wouldn't get caught." Nicole was sitting back on the edge of the boat, her hands holding on to the sides like she was on a wild ride. She shrugged, smiled a little, and said, "Del never talked to me about her and Jenna, even though she knew I saw them together. So that was the only time she made me feel like she understood what I was going through."

Khila watched me now.

"My turn?" *A favorite story about Del?* "Well," I said, "there was the time we went searching for Kurma."

❖

The currents had been unusually strong that day, visibility was poor. It was the last weekend of summer before tenth grade, and we had wanted to get in one more dive before school started. I wasn't sure about the plan, especially when I saw how choppy and dark—almost black—the ocean looked from the beach. Del was determined to make the dive. A guest at the motel had mentioned he spotted a sea turtle on the reef, and Del loved sea turtles.

"Let's go," Del said, "before Kurma figures out it's not a real reef." We were standing in waist-high water maneuvering to get our flippers on.

As we snorkeled out to the reef, I said a few times that the water felt rough. Del insisted it always felt rougher on the surface. We'd be fine, she said, once we went under. By the time we did reach the reef, I was already feeling the pull in my lungs and the burn in my legs. I had a cold, and on top of that, the tooth-grip in the regulator mouthpiece I was using was bitten through. I had taken it without really looking it over. Nevertheless, in search of Kurma we went.

Now I sat on the sandy bottom, cross-legged, communing with a yellow tang that seemed to find me interesting, while Del explored the submerged refuge. The tang came close to my face, turned a side to me, and watched me with its black marble eye. From where I was, I could vaguely make out Del by the bus, trying to get my attention with a wave. Then I realized she was signaling for me to follow her, I assumed because she wanted to show me some plant or animal she'd just discovered. Shaking off the ache in my temples and the pressure in my cheeks, I followed Del into the metal cavern. My mouthpiece swooshed around a bit, and I awkwardly used my lips to fix it in place, could feel the low-grade strain in my jaw.

I was moving toward the driver's door to exit, still in pursuit of Del, when I noticed a blue ribbon eel poking out from a hole behind the steering wheel, where the speedometer must have been at one time. I looped to get a better look, hit the regulator against the steering wheel and knocked it from my mouth. It should have been no big deal, but I panicked and chased after it—like a dog after its tail. When I twisted, I jammed the steering wheel between the tank valve and the tip of the tank harness. Then, hoping to free myself, I twisted further, and the steering wheel wedged under the valve. I couldn't move my upper body. Back then, tanks were held in place by bulky harnesses with shoulder and waist straps. So again, no big deal, pull the straps, take off the tank. But then there was the BC, which had its own set of straps, not easy to distinguish in a panic. I was confused, my heart was racing, my head was pounding, I couldn't breathe, and all I could think to do in the moment was try to grab around for my regulator, and when that didn't work, struggle to get unstuck.

I must have looked like a turtle on its back when Del arrived. She moved quickly and decisively, handing me her mouthpiece to give me air and unhooking my straps in one motion. In my haste to breathe, I forgot to purge Del's regulator, so when I breathed in, rather than air, my throat flooded with saltwater, and I started to choke. I dropped her regulator and shot out of the bus. I was craving the surface, thinking only about the cramping in my lungs, the dire airlessness seizing me. Del grabbed my ankle and yanked me back, then climbed my body and set her hands firmly on my shoulders. We twirled and rolled from facedown to belly-up while she pushed her regulator into my mouth, purged it herself, and then tightened her hold on me. I sucked in the air, felt her chest pressed against my back, her arms surrounding me. My lungs filled, the pounding in my chest softened. She hugged me from behind until I calmed down, and then she let me go.

At the surface, Del swam in close to me and removed the regulator from her mouth. "You okay?" she asked, as she inflated my BC for me.

"I am now."

She had retrieved my tank, which she now handed to me, and then she inflated her own BC, so we could float together on our backs like otters. But with the strong current, the trek to shore was still arduous, and by the time I was in water shallow enough to stand, my legs could barely support me. I used what strength I had left to pull myself out of the water, my tank and flippers towing behind me, and then collapsed in the sand at the shoreline. Del fell onto the sand beside me and we sat there, leaning back on our arms, looking out at the ocean.

"You know," Del's tone was both matter-of-fact and poignant, "you can't just race to the surface like that."

"I know. I panicked."

"Especially if you panic. You scared me, Jen." She said this in a way I took to mean that I had her to consider in any decisions I made now. She was reminding me we belonged to each other. What happened to one, happened to both—our fates inextricably intertwined.

"I should have told you I didn't feel good. I won't dive like that again. Okay?"

She brushed the sand from her fingers and then used those same fingers to sweep the hair from my forehead.

I stared out at the ocean and felt the sadness of the best summer I'd ever had ending. "Do you think that going through hard things really makes you stronger?"

Del laughed once. "I sure hope so."

❖

"It's funny," I said to Khila. "Everyone thought of me as the athlete. But Del was stronger than me. When she sat on me that day, I wasn't goin' nowhere."

Khila smiled, her first real smile of the morning, and I had the impression this idea of her mother as strong and competent deeply pleased her.

We were quiet for a few moments and then I asked Khila, "Do you want to tell a story about your mom?"

Khila shook her head to say that she didn't, but she took firm hold of the small gold cross she was wearing on her neck, and I knew it was something her mother had given her.

"I'm going to take your mom's ashes to the reef. Do you want to come?"

"Yes," she said. "I want to go with my mom."

Gail was already suited up and sitting on the side of the boat. She waved to me and then flipped backward into the water. I caught a glimpse of the edge of her flippers as they followed her overboard.

I went next.

Under and breathing, the water was clear and cool and carrying me. I let myself sink a little, listened to the sound of my mediated breath, as I waited for Khila to join me. My eyes followed streams of bubbles upward to the surface, where shards of white light marked the barrier between water and air. Khila entered legs first, shattering that light, sending its silvery refractions to the furthest mnemic reaches.

She was beside me now, and I waved for her to follow me. The bus and the surrounding debris lay out below like ancient ruins in a field of autumn. We descended slowly, moving backward in time and space, in defiance of much of what I know to be true about the physics of being human: breath cannot be drawn underwater; life moves toward light; time passes. It occurred to me, then, that none of this has ever held true for my friends or me. We were the lost girls. At fourteen and fifteen, standing at that precipice, overlooking the feminine fate awaiting us, we stepped back, joined hands, formed a circle, and danced.

❖

Lemon Reef was once broken concrete slabs and rusting carcasses. Now it presented itself as a sophisticated and nuanced orchestra of light, texture, color, movement, depth. Schools of silver darted and dangled. Lawns of sea grass sprawled, canvassing the ground like a blanket of translucent green. Khila noticed a stingray moving along the sea-grass bed. She tapped me and pointed to it. I showed her an octopus slithering along the coral hedge, its tentacles coordinated like fingers playing a piano. Iron rods jetted from porous coral banks formed around haphazardly strewn concrete masses. Living tubular branches reached hither and yon, directing traffic, breathing the water, filtering the light, tying sprawled concrete to rusting metal. Sponge beds of red, yellow, and blue lined the inner spaces of the broken windows and empty tire hulls of the VW bus toward which we slowly, deliberately made our way.

By 1999, 90 percent of Florida's reefs had lost their living coral cover, and the conditions that were killing the existing reefs made the success of artificially cultivated coral gardens, not yet firmly established, even more precarious. Lemon Reef had, against all odds, thrived. There were more varieties of fish and plants than I had remembered—life everywhere, color booming, danger lurking. It was no longer possible to swim through the VW bus covered with mollusks and urchins and anemones. The sharp-edged door frames had become nestling spots for dual-eyed cowards who crammed into corners at the first hint of invaders and watched from inside their shells. The windows and doors were masses of fiery coral, staghorn branches, and expansive elaborate fans. And within these, crabs scampered, starfish clung, and eels poked. A queen angel reigned majestic over smaller, simpler creatures. She fully expected admiration and deference.

With Khila and Gail beside me, I opened the container and placed Del's remains inside the yellow bus. It was then that I saw it hovering over us like a flying saucer. Its powerful flippers moved like wings as it swam to the surface for a quick breath then angled downward and shot through the water in our direction. It swam past us, close enough for me to feel its wake, then circled around and stilled a few feet away, level with our eyes. Its own were onyx bulbs, set deep in its head like headlights.

Overjoyed, I laughed into my regulator, signaled to Khila that everything was okay, that the turtle wasn't dangerous. She nodded as if to say she already knew that. I moved slowly toward it; it came toward me; we met somewhere in the middle. I was close enough to touch it.

Then it moved closer, its beak and eyes growing huge in my mask. I lifted my chest, maneuvered onto my back; it swam over me, our bellies nearly touching. I righted myself, swam over it. Its shell was the color of fall leaves, fading easily into the background of rust and sand and sea grass surrounding us.

We tangled around each other a few more times, front to back, back to front, crossing over and around each other like a Möbius strip. I noticed the cobblestone-shaped markings on its head and the scaly texture of its flippers. It was an odd creature: old and new; a snail, a bird, a snake, a fish; graceful, yet clumsy; extremely vulnerable despite its considerable armor; ill equipped, yet prepared for anything. I fell in love with it, wanted to stay and play with it forever. But it trailed off after a final loop, ribboned once around Khila, and then swam away.

We watched it until it was no longer in sight.

About the Author

Robin joined the Bold Strokes Books family this year with her debut novel *Lemon Reef*. As a psychologist who also has a law degree, Robin has worked with families experiencing domestic violence in both legal and clinical settings, and she has written numerous articles and chapters for professional books and journals on the subject. In Lemon Reef, Robin explores laws that may inadvertently force women to remain in violent relationships, lest they give up their children. *Lemon Reef* is also an exploration of childhood loves and losses, alternative sexualities, and the ways in which class, culture, and gender shape and sometimes limit who we are and what is possible for us.

Books Available From Bold Strokes Books

Oath of Honor by Radclyffe. A First Responders novel. First do no harm…First Physician of the United States Wes Masters discovers that being the president's doctor demands more than brains and personal sacrifice—especially when politics is the order of the day. (978-1-60282-671-7)

A Question of Ghosts by Cate Culpepper. Becca Healy hopes Dr. Joanne Call can help her learn if her mother really committed suicide—but she's not sure she can handle her mother's ghost, a decades-old mystery, and lusting after the difficult Dr. Call without some serious chocolate consumption. (978-1-60282-672-4)

The Night Off by Meghan O'Brien. When Emily Parker pays for a taboo role-playing fantasy encounter from the Xtreme Scenarios escort agency, she expects to surrender control—but never imagines losing her heart to dangerous butch Nat Swayne. (978-1-60282-673-1)

Sara by Greg Herren. A mysterious and beautiful new student at Southern Heights High School stirs things up when students start dying. (978-1-60282-674-8)

Fontana by Joshua Martino. Fame, obsession, and vengeance collide in a novel that asks: What if America's greatest hero was gay? (978-1-60282-675-5)

Lemon Reef by Robin Silverman. What would you risk for the memory of your first love? When Jenna Ross learns her high school love Del Soto died on Lemon Reef, she refuses to accept the medical examiner's report of a death from natural causes and risks everything to find the truth. (978-1-60282-676-2)

The Dirty Diner: Gay Erotica on the Menu, edited by Jerry L. Wheeler. Gay erotica set in restaurants, featuring food, sex, and men—could you really ask for anything more? (978-1-60282-677-9)

Sweat: Gay Jock Erotica by Todd Gregory. Sizzling tales of smoking-hot sex with the athletic studs everyone fantasizes about. (978-1-60282-669-4)

The Marrying Kind by Ken O'Neill. Just when successful wedding planner Adam More decides to protest inequality by quitting the business and boycotting marriage entirely, his only sibling announces her engagement. (978-1-60282-670-0)

Missing by P.J. Trebelhorn. FBI agent Olivia Andrews knows exactly what she wants out of life, but then she's forced to rethink everything when she meets fellow agent Sophie Kane while investigating a child abduction. (978-1-60282-668-7)

Touch Me Gently by D. Jackson Leigh. Secrets have always meant heartbreak and banishment to Salem Lacey—until she meets the beautiful and mysterious Knox Bolander and learns some secrets are necessary. (978-1-60282-667-0)

Slingshot by Carsen Taite. Bounty hunter Luca Bennett takes on a seemingly simple job for defense attorney Ronnie Moreno, but the job quickly turns complicated and dangerous, as does her attraction to the elusive Ronnie Moreno. (978-1-60282-666-3)

Dark Wings Descending by Lesley Davis. What if the demons you face in life are real? Chicago detective Rafe Douglas is about to find out. (978-1-60282-660-1)

sunfall by Nell Stark and Trinity Tam. The final installment of the everafter series. Valentine Darrow and Alexa Newland work to rebuild their relationship even as they find themselves at the heart of the struggle that will determine a new world order for vampires and wereshifters. (978-1-60282-661-8)

Mission of Desire by Terri Richards. Nicole Kennedy finds herself in Africa at the center of an international conspiracy and is rescued by the beautiful but arrogant government agent Kira Anthony—but can Nicole trust Kira, or is she blinded by desire? (978-1-60282-662-5)

Boys of Summer, edited by Steve Berman. Stories of young love and adventure, when the sky's ceiling is a bright blue marvel, when another boy's laughter at the beach can distract from dull summer jobs. (978-1-60282-663-2)

The Locket and the Flintlock by Rebecca S. Buck. When Regency gentlewoman Lucia Foxe is robbed on the highway, will the masked outlaw who stole Lucia's precious locket also claim her heart? (978-1-60282-664-9)

Calendar Boys by Logan Zachary. A man a month will keep you excited year-round. (978-1-60282-665-6)

Burgundy Betrayal by Sheri Lewis Wohl. Park Ranger Kara Lynch has no idea she's a witch until dead bodies begin to pile up in her park, forcing her to turn to beautiful and sexy shape-shifter Camille Black Wolf for help in stopping a rogue werewolf. (978-1-60282-654-0)

LoveLife by Rachel Spangler. When Joey Lang unintentionally becomes a client of life coach Elaine Raitt, the relationship becomes complicated as they develop feelings that make them question their purpose in love and life. (978-1-60282-655-7)

The Fling by Rebekah Weatherspoon. When the ultimate fantasy of a one-night stand with her trainer, Oksana Gorinkov, suddenly turns into more, reality show producer Annie Collins opens her life to a new type of love she's never imagined. (978-1-60282-656-4)

Ill Will by J.M. Redmann. New Orleans PI Micky Knight must untangle a twisted web of healthcare fraud that leads to murder—and puts those closest to her most at risk. (978-1-60282-657-1)

Buccaneer Island by J.P. Beausejour. In the rough world of Caribbean piracy, a man is what he makes of himself—or what a stronger man makes of him. (978-1-60282-658-8)

Twelve O'Clock Tales by Felice Picano. The fourth collection of short fiction by legendary novelist and memoirist Felice Picano. Thirteen dark tales that will thrill and disturb, discomfort and titillate, enthrall and leave you wondering. (978-1-60282-659-5)

Words to Die By by William Holden. Sixteen answers to the question: What causes a mind to curdle? (978-1-60282-653-3)